AETHER'S BLESSING

AETHER'S REVIVAL BOOK 1

DANIEL SCHINHOFEN

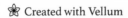 Created with Vellum

CHAPTER 1

G regory stretched as the morning sun slipped past the shutters, the light bathing his face. "Ugh, stupid ball of hate," he muttered as he sat up. Rubbing at his eyes, he wondered if today would go the way he had hoped for, for so long, or if the world was about to kick him in the nuts.

A heavy knock rattled his door and the deep voice of his father boomed, "Gregory Russel Pettit, get your ass out of bed. It's your age day, for Krog's sake."

"I'm up!" Gregory shouted back, before lowering his voice, "You old cranky bastard."

Mumbles and heavy footfalls going away from the door was the only response from Gregory's father.

"At least Mom would have been nice about it," Gregory said, feeling the ache in his chest.

The image of her standing across the room, chiding him gently, made the pain deepen. Gregory could almost see the strawberry blonde hair, green eyes, and smiling face that she wore when she had last done so. *Come on now, it's your age day. You've been waiting for this for the last ten years. I know you'll be a mage, so don't hang around in here.* Gregory supplied her voice to go with the image.

"You're right, Mom," Gregory sighed as he got out of bed, "even if the ceremony isn't until midday."

Getting dressed did not normally take long, but today, it took him almost twice as much time. Every mark he had left on the room made him pause— the gouge in the window when he had thrown a knife at a bat; the cracked floorboard that he had tried to pry up, thinking there was treasure underneath, when he was five; the notches on the doorframe as he had grown taller.

Finally dressed, he took another long look around the room. "Goodbye... after today, I'll be off to the academy, and I doubt I'll be back." Gregory was not sure if he was talking to himself. What he hoped was that his mother's spirit was watching over him, or even the room. Saying goodbye made him feel better.

With everything that was legally his packed in the bag slung over his shoulder, he was ready to go. Opening the door, he could hear his father's mumbled curses along with the clang of the soup cauldron. As he went down the hall, he braced himself for his father's normal rants. *Today I'll be civil, for Mom. She would want me to leave on a good note.*

Leaving the short hall, Gregory entered the main room. His father, a bear of a man, stood over the wood stove. Gregory pulled the two leather jacks off the wall and filled them with water from the barrel in the corner to put on the table.

"I'm glad we'll finally put this foolish nonsense to rest today," Carmichael grunted as he brought the small cauldron over to the table.

Gregory's jaw set, but he bit back his normal reply. Instead, he grabbed the wooden bowls and spoons that they always used and set one in front of his father.

Carmichael eyed him, "Not going to talk back today? Good. You're finally growing up and accepting the idea that you'll be joining the mine after all, then."

Gritting his teeth, Gregory did his best to do what his mother would have wanted him to. "If I test negative, then I'm sure I will, but I haven't given up on my dream, Father."

Snorting, Carmichael served himself a generous portion of the thin soup and broke off a chunk of stale bread. "That's your mother's doing. She never should have filled your head with those stories."

The pain and anger surged up in his chest. Gregory's teeth ground as he clamped his mouth shut, both hands gripping his thin knees painfully tight. *Don't react... don't rise to the bait. He's goading you,* Gregory told himself over and over again.

When he could open his hands, he served himself and saw that his father was almost done eating. "Mother did tell me the stories, Father, and she cautioned me, too, but she knew that dreams are worth having."

"Dreams!" Carmichael spat the word angrily. "Dreams!? Dreams are what took her from us!" His heavy hand thumped the table, making everything on it shake. "Her damned dreams... always ready to listen to them... leaving us..." His father shoved himself away from the table and stormed off.

Gregory sat there, stunned. In the years since her death, his father had never walked away like that. Anger and sadness would normally lead to his father fighting with him, leaving Gregory bloody and beaten, but still clinging to his dreams.

Alone at the table, Gregory stared at the puddle of soup spilled on the wooden surface without seeing it, then shook his head and began to eat. *I'll need my strength if the rumors are true. Mother, will you be proud of me?* Gregory wondered as he ate.

His father had not come back by the time he finished, so Gregory cleaned up the table and dishes, putting everything back in its place. His hand lingered next to his mother's bowl, which had a thin layer of dust on it. He dropped his hand and turned to face the empty room.

"I'm off to start my journey. Thank you for all you've done for me. I'll try to make you proud, Mother... you too, Father." With nothing more to say, he bowed his head for a few seconds before he walked out of the small home. Two paths led from there; one toward the mine, and one to the village.

Walking down the familiar road, Gregory thought back to all the times he had come this way over the years— every other day for school for most of his life; for supplies when needed, after mother died; and the few times he was free to go visit his friends.

Never did ask why we live so far from the village. I always assumed it was Father's doing, but maybe it was Mother's? When she was alive, Father always did as she asked. She was never wrong... the thought hung in his mind for a moment, but he looked down at the ground sadly. *Foolish, you just don't remember her being wrong anymore.*

He took his time getting into town, recalling more childhood moments. He remembered the tree that Gunnar fell out of a few years ago, which had knocked out two of his teeth, and the bush that he and Gunnar had hidden behind to scare the Delarosa twins eight years ago.

The sun was well up by the time he made it to the village. The festival pole was brightly decorated, and the sound of music drifted to him on the light breeze. Age day came on the same day every year, but that date was different depending on where in the Velum Empire you were. It was so the proctors could go from place to place testing the children who had become adults. In Alturis, it was two days short of midsummer.

The village bustled with activity, as the traveling merchants that always came with the proctors set up around the village square. Touching the nearly empty pouch on his hip, Gregory sighed, knowing he would not be buying anything today. Two steps past the first building, he was suddenly on his back in the dirt.

"Greg! Thought for sure your old man was going to lock you in today," Gunnar laughed from above him.

"Get off, you lumbering brute," Gregory laughed. "What if the twins see you?"

"Too late," came the laughing reply from Eloria. "We knew you two were close, but not *this* close."

"Well, it would explain a few things," Amoria added with a laugh.

"Fuck me," Gregory sighed.

"Sorry, I'm just not that kind of boy," Gunnar laughed as he got to his feet and offered a hand to Gregory.

"Thank the gods," Gregory grunted, dusting himself off.

"Ready to find out?" Amoria asked, stepping behind Gregory, and helping clean the dust off his upper back.

"Have been for years, even if no one from the village has been chosen for the last twenty. Today, I say goodbye to you all, though I'll come back as soon as I can."

"He's always been confident on that front, at least," Eloria sighed.

"It'll be good for him," Gunnar said. "Krog knows he'd never survive in the mine."

"I'm not like you, you brute," Gregory said, looking at his friend. Gunnar was the third largest man in the village, behind their fathers.

"He's not wrong," Eloria said. "You've never filled out like your father. You've always taken after your mother."

Gregory chuckled, "You mean I'm a kind, sensitive man, who cares for those around him, instead of a giant lumbering beast? Thank you."

"She means you're a beanpole," Amoria corrected him gently. "Frankly, it's idiotic for your father to push you to follow in his footsteps. You could apprentice to our father. The offer is still open."

"I appreciate it, but I'm leaving today. Your father was always kind enough to humor your attempts to get me on as his apprentice. We all know that you or your sister will be taking over the business."

Amoria's face went through a few emotions before she sighed, "Us, or one of our husbands."

"And they will be lucky men," Gregory said with all sincerity. "You two are the beauties of our humble village." He meant what he said: the brown haired, hazel eyed, olive-skinned women were the best-looking women in the village, taking after their mother.

Gunnar shook his head, "Past that, we have hours still until we're needed at the square. Shall we join the others, or go to my home instead? Ma was baking sweetbread when I left."

Eloria perked right up, brushing her long hair behind her ear, "I love your mother's sweetbread."

"If we don't let her go, she'll be impossible for the rest of the day," Amoria said.

"Hah, as if you don't love it, too."

"To Gunnar's it is," Gregory said, trying to defuse the impending argument.

"Onward," Gunnar laughed, pointing toward his house as he began to walk.

"Onward! To the sweets," Eloria laughed as she grabbed Gunnar's extended arm and hung from it briefly.

"Greg," Amoria said softly as she fell into step beside him, "I wanted to ask you something, but I don't want to upset you."

"What if I don't become a magi?" Gregory asked the question he knew was coming.

"Yes."

"I don't know, Ria. I don't believe that will happen... but, if it does, I'm going to be a wreck. You know that."

"We all do," Amoria said softly, reaching out to take his hand in hers. "I'll be here for you, like I was when..." She trailed off, not wanting to finish.

His hand tightened on hers. "I know. If I was going to stay here... maybe I'd have the courage to..." Gregory trailed off, knowing if he finished, it would ensure he stayed in the village.

Amoria's heart skipped a beat and she held his hand tightly. "First, we have to complete the coming of age ritual. The sweetbread should help. I know you don't eat well most days. I have some jerky in my pouch, too, if you'd like to share it."

Always taking care of me, Ria... You deserve so much more than this village will ever give you. More than I'm going to be able to give you, no matter what happens today. Gregory thought and smiled softly. "Maybe after the bread."

"Okay."

Walking behind Eloria and Gunnar, a moment of knowing came to him. Gunnar and Eloria would marry and have three children that they would dote on. Gregory stumbled, distracted by the certainty of the knowledge.

"Greg?" Amoria asked.

"My feet lost their way," Gregory chuckled. "Luckily, you had my hand."

Amoria blushed, "As long as you need me to."

She was the one who picked me up after Mother was found. Father was as broken as I was, and he didn't have anyone to help him. Maybe that's why he became so bitter and angry. Amoria's soft hand squeezing his broke him out of the thoughts.

"Oy, you two coming?" Gunnar laughed when he looked back and saw them trailing behind.

"As if we'd get lost on the way," Gregory called back.

"But if we take too long, El might have eaten all of the sweetbread before we get there."

"Who had the majority *last* time, hmm?" Eloria sniped back at her sister.

"And who was it the four times before that, I wonder?" Amoria returned the jibe.

"Easy," Gunnar said when Eloria opened her mouth to retort. "I'm sure Ma is making enough for everyone to have their fill."

Eloria snorted and pulled on his arm, "Let's go. If they want to stroll and miss it, let them."

"Go on, Gunnar. We'll be right there," Gregory said when his friend started to dig in his heels. "Always listen to the woman you'll marry."

Eloria went beet red, letting go of Gunnar's arm and walking faster. Gunnar rolled his eyes and frowned back at Gregory, silently chiding his friend. Amoria let go of Gregory's hand and took off after her sister.

"El, wait for me!" Amoria called after her sister.

Gregory slowed his pace more as the three left him behind. The sound of merriment coming from the square was at odds with the weight he felt on his shoulders. *Shouldn't have said that, but she's always been hanging on him... it's obvious they're going to marry. He'll work in the mine, probably be the next foreman. Maybe they'll have forgiven me by the time I get there.*

* * *

"Excuse me, I'm coming in," Gregory announced, pushing the front door of his friend's house open. Pausing to unbutton his boots and put them next to the others, it struck Gregory that he had stopped doing the same at home after his mother had passed. *A week after Mom died... so much changed with her gone.*

"Gregory, it's good to see you today," Mrs. Emery smiled as she came out of the main room. "The others have already started eating."

"Thank you, Mrs. Emery."

"What delayed you?" Mrs. Emery asked.

"Stray thoughts."

"I'm sure you're having a lot of those today," she said kindly. "I agreed with my boy; he was going to go get you if you weren't at the square in another hour. Happily, your father didn't try to keep you home."

"He wouldn't break the laws, not like that," Gregory replied. "He just expects me to fail and go crawling home to beg his forgiveness." His voice had taken on an angry edge that he tried to bite back.

"Things have been tough for you and your father since Marian's passing. I always hoped that the worst of it would pass, but I've come to accept that it won't. You have a place here tonight, if you need it." Her voice held equal parts sadness and warmth.

Gregory bowed his head to her, "I won't be needing it, but thank you."

"Of course, you are going to go on to greater things. Your mother always told me so— she would talk about little else when we had tea together. I've never known anyone who believed as strongly as she did, besides maybe you."

Throat tight, Gregory nodded his head. "Thank you, Mrs. Emery."

"Oh, here I am prattling on when you came here for the sweetbread. Come now, let's get you some food and maybe some of that juice you like so much, hmm?"

Gregory chuckled, "I liked it when I was a child, but I've grown out of that."

"Of course, of course," she smiled, leading him into the main room where the others sat around the table. "Gregory made it. I trust you've left him some."

Eloria pouted, but nodded, "We didn't eat it all... yet."

"Thank you, Elly," Mrs. Emery smiled at her. "I'll make another batch tomorrow. Why don't you come over and I can show you how to make it, okay?"

The others blinked at the offer, because Mrs. Emery's sweetbread recipe had always been a tightly guarded secret. Eloria spoke up when the silence started to stretch, "I'd be happy to learn, Mrs. Emery."

"Tsk, call me Yeva," she corrected Eloria. "After midday, you're an adult, after all. There's no harm in starting a little early."

"If that's what you want, Yeva."

"Good. Now Gregory, you sit over there and I'll go get that juice."

When she went into the kitchen, Gregory chuckled, "Sharing her recipe? I never thought I'd see that happen."

Gunnar grimaced and kicked Greg under the table. "She's always liked El."

Gregory kept the pain off his face, even though he could feel the bruise forming on his shin. "You're right, she has always taken a shine to her."

"Even more than me," Amoria said. "El's always been welcomed here a bit more readily."

Gunnar coughed, "Well, yeah, that's true... Krog's buttocks... Fine!" Taking a deep breath, Gunnar looked at Eloria seriously, "El... I was going to wait for this, but since Ma is already moving forward, I can't not. Would you consider me as a suitor?"

Eloria spluttered and started coughing, the glass she had been drinking from forgotten in her hand. Amoria patted her sister on the back, and Gregory did his best to not laugh at the panic on Gunnar's face.

"Now!? You ask me *now*?!" Eloria finally managed when she could speak again. "Gunnar, you stone headed moron!"

Gunnar's face fell, and Gregory no longer found it funny. He started to interject, but Amoria beat him to it.

"El, don't. He is trying, at least."

Eloria's face fell and she began to cry, "I've been waiting for years, years for today to come. I always hoped that you would give some hint, any suggestion, that you liked me as more than a friend, and you spring this on me, now? I wasn't ready for now... after the ceremony, I would have been."

"Son, why are you making her cry?" Yeva asked, bustling back into the room and thunking a cup of juice down in front of Gregory. "Go on, now. Take her to your room and talk with the poor girl."

Gunnar stammered, but quickly got to his feet and held out a hand to Eloria. Eloria was still sniffling when she took his hand and let him lead her from the room. Amoria watched them go with a bit of jealousy on her face, her eyes flickering briefly to Gregory and then away. Gregory missed her look as he watched two of his best friends start down the road that he had briefly glimpsed less than an hour before.

"Three kids, huh?" Gregory muttered as he watched them leave the room.

"Three would be good," Yeva said, taking a seat at the table. "I swear he's as awkward as his father was at that age. I'm glad he finally asked... he's been pining for her since the second time she came to visit. No offense to you, Amoria."

"Oh, none taken. She's been the same for him. When he hit his spurt and grew into the broad-chested man he is now, she couldn't stop gushing about him," Amoria replied, but a hint of sorrow entered her voice. "I guess that means I'll be taking over for Father, after all."

"You'll do well as the clothier," Yeva said, patting her hand. "Tomorrow can bring all kinds of changes."

"I know and I hope," Amoria said.

Gregory felt as if part of the conversation was going over his head, but he took a drink of juice instead of asking about it. Taking a chunk of the sweetbread, he absentmindedly chewed on it and wondered what other unexpected events the day would bring.

CHAPTER 2

"Remember when he tried to surprise her and she almost broke his nose?" Amoria was giggling when Gunnar and Eloria came back into the room.

"I remember that," Gunnar chuckled. "Only time my nose stung like that outside of physical training."

"I recall Gregory laughing about it," Eloria snickered, "right until Ria kicked his shin."

Gregory chuckled, "Well, I did deserve it. I had been going to surprise her, too, but it was so damned funny to watch him that I forgot to."

"Hey, where'd all the bread go?" Eloria asked, seeing the empty table.

"We ate it while talking about old times," Amoria smiled. "You'll be getting more tomorrow when you learn how to make it."

Eloria pouted, "Yeah, but I wanted more now."

"The other loaf just came out of the oven," Yeva said, coming into the room with a freshly sliced loaf on a platter. "You still have an hour, so eat up. I'll bring some more tea and juice."

The front door opening and closing made everyone turn to look.

Gunther Emery stepped into the room, looking grim. "Gregory, glad I found you. Come with me."

Getting to his feet, Gregory was puzzled. Gunther still had his boots on and looked serious instead of happy. "Sure, but—"

"Later. Come now," Gunther commanded, striding from the room with quick steps.

Gregory got his boots on in record time trying to keep up with the large man. "Mr. Emery, what is it? You're not like this."

"Your father has made a grievous error," Gunther said as they headed for the square. "You might be able to save him."

Brow furrowed, Gregory bit back his reply and instead seethed inside his head. *What in Aether's name, Father? This day is for those who have reached our age day. Stupid old fool, always causing trouble.*

As they got closer, Gregory realized the music had stopped and the sound of merriment had died off entirely. A shiver ran down his spine, and he knew his father was riding the line of life and death.

"I've brought his son as requested, Proctor," Gunther announced as the crowd parted for them.

"Have him come forward," the proctor's voice was pitched high, but full of confidence.

When Gregory made it past Gunther, he understood. Proctor Bishop was dressed in the regalia of the Velum Empire, looking imperious instead of friendly. Her hawkish nose and strong cheekbones spoke of noble heritage. Her gray eyes were cold and angry at the moment, making Gregory's muscles tighten. He had never seen her angry in all the years she had been coming to test those becoming adults.

"I'm here, Proctor."

"Is this *man* your father?" The proctor's foot was on Carmichael's back, driving the burly but struggling man into the dirt.

Gregory swallowed hard. His father was the second strongest man in the village, and the proctor, who looked as slight as Amoria, was holding him down with her foot as if he had the strength of a toddler. "That is my father, Proctor."

"His name?"

"Carmichael Pettit."

"Carmichael Pettit has committed the crime of interfering with the testing of youth and striking a proctor. I've been told that he has stood in the way of your dream of being a magi. Is this true?"

Gregory hesitated, but opted for honesty, "My father has not been supportive, but he has never done anything to stand in the way of my dream."

"Do you wish to add anything to sway my judgement for the crimes he has committed?"

Gregory hesitated. "My father was a good man. I admired him, looked up to him, and hoped to be as strong as he was. When my mother died, he changed. Her loss made him bitter— he grew angry, even violent, but I always hoped he would accept my dream. I would ask you to show him leniency, if not for my sake, then for my mother, who loved him with all her heart."

The proctor stared at him for a long moment before she lifted her foot fractionally and looked down at Carmichael. "Did you wish to say anything before you are sentenced?"

"Don't take him," Carmichael grunted. "He's all I have left of her. Tell him he's a failure and leave him here."

"You wish to keep him because he is all you have left?"

Face crumpling, Carmichael did something very few had ever seen him do: he began to cry. "Yes."

"You know that what you have done are crimes, one of them with the sentence of death, do you not?"

"Yes."

"Very well, Carmichael Pettit. I, Proctor Samantha Bishop, have stood in place of a magistrate for your crimes. You have been found guilty and I will pass judgement. Before I do, would anyone here like to speak on behalf of the defendant?"

Gunther stepped forward, "If it pleases the proctor, I would like to speak."

"State your name and what you wish to say."

"I'm Gunther Emery, and I wish to speak on Carmichael's goodness. Before Marian's death, he was the best man I've known in my entire life, always willing to help anyone at any time. It was thanks to his help that many of us got our roofs fixed when the blizzards came over a decade ago. When Marian died, he changed... he stopped being social, he drank more, and started to have violent outbursts. This year, as age day came closer, he stopped drinking. I hoped then that he was coming out of his darkness, and I still think he can. I will vouch for him and help him find his way again, if you grant him mercy."

Carmichael looked at the dirt, touched by his friend's words, but unable to reach out in kind. One by one, the other miners spoke up, offering similar sentiments. Each voice made Carmichael twist inside as he faced what he had become over the years since his wife's death. Tears continued to fall from his eyes as he listened to them all vouch for him.

"Well, it seems you are quite loved here, Pettit, even if you've pushed them all away from you. Do you wish to change?"

"I do," Carmichael managed to get out as he tried to control his emotions.

"Even if your son tests as a magi and leaves with me?"

A long moment of silence passed before Carmichael nodded weakly. "I will no longer try to deny my son's dream."

"Very well. After hearing all the testimony on your behalf, and as I have never heard of you having troubles before, I shall show mercy. Carmichael Pettit, you are sentenced to five years of hard labor as a servant of Alturis. Elder, you will make sure he can survive for the five years, but all the extra coin is to go to improving the village." Removing her foot, Bishop knelt next to Carmichael. "You are also banned from this event every year until you have served the five years. Go home and reflect on your crimes against me, the empire, and especially your family." Her hand flared blue as she touched his back, making him cry out in pain. When the flame died away, she stepped back.

Getting to his feet slowly, Carmichael bowed humbly to her, "As you decree, Proctor."

"I'll help you home," Gunther said, going to his friend's side.

As the two of them moved away from the proctor, Gregory looked at Carmichael. Seeing the once vibrant man broken, beaten, and humbled was hard for Gregory to take, even though he had wished for it often over the last few years.

"I'm going, Father. I'll make you proud of me, and I'll come home to visit when I can," Gregory said.

"I'm sorry," Carmichael whispered before he dropped his head and shuffled off with Gunther's help.

Once he was gone, the proctor spoke up loudly, "Now that the problem has been resolved, let us have merriment again. Today is a joyous day! Today is the day your children become adults. Some of them may join the magi, aiding the empire in keeping us safe."

The band began to play, one by one, until they were all in unison and playing a happy upbeat song. Gregory turned to leave, but a hand clamped down on his shoulder, stopping him dead.

"A word, Pettit," Bishop said softly, guiding him away from the square.

Gregory did not have a choice as Bishop moved him at her leisure, away from the square. Once they were out of sight of the crowds, she let him go. Gregory winced, a bruise already forming on his shoulder.

"Tell me what is it you seek, that the academy is your dream."

Gregory stared into Bishop's stormy gray eyes and swallowed hard. "My mother told me tales of magi who helped create the Empire, like Lionel Lighthand."

Bishop's lips twitched into a smile briefly. "Lighthand... yes, he was a great man. You think that if you are able to wield aether, you'll be like him?"

"No," Gregory replied. "I hope to live up to their legacy, but I doubt I'll be anywhere near him in terms of power or ability."

"Humble, but who isn't this far removed from the center?" Bishop sighed. "I wish you the best of luck. Being a magi isn't as easy as many think it is."

"I think it'll be the hardest thing I've ever done in my life."

Bishop looked around for a moment before snorting, "Yes, yes it will be. Beyond the mental and physical demands placed on you by your teachers, you'll face another challenge that will be even harder to defeat: dealing with your peers, some of whom come from wealthy and powerful families. The few magi who come from the fringe are never prepared for it, and most fail."

"I won't fail," Gregory said firmly, the anger inside of him flaring.

Bishop laughed darkly, "Hold to that anger and determination. You'll need it, if you can even touch the aether."

"I'll not just touch it... I'll grab it and make it see me," Gregory growled, forgetting who he was talking to.

"We shall see," Bishop laughed as she walked away from him. "I'll see you soon, Pettit. Don't disappoint me."

Watching her walk away, Gregory realized what he had said, and a cold sweat broke out across his body. Breathing fast and hard, he started away from the square, his steps unsteady as he considered what Bishop might have done if she had taken offense.

* * *

Gregory's friends came out of the house just before he made it back to Gunther's home. "There he is," Amoria said, rushing toward him. "What happened?"

"Father attacked the proctor," Gregory said blankly. "She gave him mercy. He has to work as a servant to the village for the next five years."

"He what!?" Gunnar shouted in shock and outrage.

Gregory took a few minutes to explain what happened. When he finished, Amoria reached out for him, but stopped just short of touching his shoulder. Gunnar was pale, and Eloria was holding his arm tightly.

"Are you going to be okay?" Amoria asked as she withdrew her hand.

"I don't know," Gregory admitted bleakly. "I think I made my path forward even tougher than it was going to be."

"We have some time before we need to be at the square. We could visit the merchants until then," Amoria suggested.

"We could," Eloria agreed.

"Greg?" Gunnar asked, concerned for his friend.

"We should," Gregory said, shaking his head to chase away the dark thoughts he was having. "Not that I can buy much, but who knows what we'll find?"

Touching Gregory's shoulder gently, Amoria gave him a tight smile, "We're here with you."

Feeling the warmth of her hand on his bruised shoulder, Greg took a deep breath. "Thanks, Ria. You always help me when I need it most."

"I'll always be here for you, Greg," Amoria said, taking her hand off his shoulder and taking his hand in hers.

CHAPTER 3

G regory was able to forget about his talk with Bishop until it was time to head for the middle of the square. Each step made his stomach churn and his heart clench. This was going to be the moment his dream was either realized or broken.

By the time they joined the others, they were last in line. Gunnar moved Gregory to the front of their small group. Bishop stood on a small stage, and the first new adult, Stan, knelt before her with his head bowed.

"Child, you come before me on the verge of adulthood," Bishop said. "Today is your age day, and you should rejoice. Today also marks the chance for you to join the ranks of the magi. Let us see if you have the spark of Aether inside of you."

Stan trembled as her hand touched his head, his breathing fast, hands clenched into fists. "I'm ready to become an adult, Proctor."

"Aether, have you blessed this child with your grace?" Bishop asked the sky, and blue flame covered the hand that gripped his skull.

Stan's screams of pain filled the still air as everyone watched with stony faces, having experienced the same on their age day, or wide-eyed as they saw what they would endure in the years to come.

After what seemed like forever, the blue flame retreated into Bishop's hand and she released Stan, who fell forward, crying. "You are now an adult, but no magi. May you find your place in the empire and grow strong."

Stan's father rushed up to help his son down off the stage and away. The moment he was gone, Chester stepped slowly onto the stage and hesitantly knelt before Bishop.

"Child, you come before me on the verge of adulthood," Bishop began the ritual phrasing again, her face blank of emotion as she did her duty.

One by one, the line before Gregory diminished until he was the next one. All of them had failed to receive Aether's blessing, and that ratcheted his anxiety to a level he had never known.

When Rebecca was escorted away by her mother, Gregory put his foot on the stage, his heart thundering in his chest. *It's now, now, that I become a magi. Are you watching, Mother?* The question echoed in his head as he advanced the few feet to kneel in front of Bishop.

Bishop watched Gregory with the same blank expression she had been wearing during the whole ritual. Her voice held an odd inflection to Gregory's ear as she spoke the words, "Child, you come before me on the verge of adulthood. Today is *your* age day, and *you* should rejoice. Today also marks the chance for *you* to join the ranks of the *magi*. Let us see if *you* have the spark of Aether inside of you."

Gregory felt the fear fall away as the moment gained a crystalline clarity. "I will be a magi, Proctor," his voice was firm, steady, and carried in the stillness of the moment.

"Aether, have you blessed this child with your grace?" Bishop asked the sky before the blue flame covered the hand that was gripping his head.

Gregory's jaw clenched as Bishop's grip seemed poised to crack his skull like an egg. That pain fled as blue flame crashed into his very being. Somewhere inside his pain-filled mind, Gregory knew it would last only moments, but it felt like time was stretching out before him, promising years of torment. Somewhere during the pain, blue flame ignited in his own body and a rush of energy filled him, infusing his very being with aether. The pain dimmed and receded, but the flames continued, now feeling as though they were embracing him like a lover.

Sound came back to Gregory as the moment passed, but instead of falling forward, he pushed himself to his feet. His eyes were burning blue, and his entire body was outlined in aether.

"Magi, the Velum Empire welcomes you. From today forward, your life belongs to the empire until you complete your duty. Say goodbye to your friends and family, for today, you are no longer who you were, but a novice."

Gregory turned to look at the crowd, who stared back at him with fear and wonder. Eyes going to the side, he found Gunnar's firm gaze and broad smile, Eloria's disbelief, and Amoria's broken smile and tear-filled gaze.

"Thank you, Alturis, for all you've done for me and my family," Gregory said. "If I can, I will come back and repay the kindness that is owed."

"Step behind me, Novice," Bishop said. "I still have children to welcome to adulthood."

Gregory did as she said, starting to come to terms with the fact he was Aether blessed and was going to the academy to train. *Mother, thank you. Father, I hope you will accept this in time.*

Gunnar was the next one to step onto the stage. He looked at Gregory, who had stopped glowing blue, before he knelt before Bishop. Bishop repeated the ritual words, carrying on as if nothing had happened.

Gunnar crashed forward in pain a few moments later, before pushing himself to his feet. Panting, he stared at Gregory, "Better make us proud, or I'll come find you."

Bishop stared at Gunnar hard, even when Gunther came and helped him off the stage. The two of them did not go far; Eloria was next, trembling as she stepped onto the stage.

Eloria's screams made Gunther grab his son when Gunnar tried to reach for her. A few seconds later, she fell to the stage unconscious. Breaking his father's grip, Gunnar jumped onto the stage and scooped Eloria into his arms. Leaving the stage, he kissed her forehead gently, which caused a small stir in the crowd.

"There is one child left. Please pay her the respect she deserves on this day," Bishop said, which silenced the crowd.

Amoria's hands shook, but her steps were steady as she advanced and knelt before Bishop. Bishop repeated the words she had said for every other person who had knelt before her. Amoria's screams were in a different octave from her twin's. She slumped to the stage a moment later, and Gregory started to move forward, but Bishop's arm barred his path.

Tony, Amoria's father, rushed forward and helped her from the stage. Amoria was crying as she looked back at Gregory. The pain and loss in her eyes made his heart tremble, but he stayed where he was.

"Alturis, today, you have been blessed. Aether has given one of your former children his grace. Say your prayers that he completes his tutelage and can serve the Velum Empire as a proud magi."

The assembled villagers bowed their heads and spoke the words that many had never uttered, "Aether, blessed be you, for this gift to our village. May the empire smile upon us for strengthening their might. Thank you, Proctor, for helping our children become adults. May Aether and the empire reward you for your duty and diligence."

"The ceremony of age has come to an end. Celebrate, people of Alturis, for today marks a day your village should be proud of," Bishop's voice was warm and full of cheer as she spoke. "Elder, let the drinks flow with the Emperor's blessing, for new magi should be celebrated with reverence and abandon."

The crowd cheered loudly, and many headed for the tavern. Bishop stepped back, turning to face the new magi, who was still coming to terms with the fact that he had achieved his dream.

"Gregory, you are to meet me here at sunrise. We have more villages to stop in before we make our way to Kendlin, and from there, the Magi Academy. Tonight is your night to celebrate, because after today, you are a magi of the empire."

"Yes, Proctor," Gregory said stiffly.

"Go enjoy yourself, but pay attention to your dreams tonight.

Tonight, you take the first step of being a magi." Without waiting for an answer, Bishop stepped off the small stage and walked toward the tavern, people parting for her as she went.

"You did it," Gunnar smiled as he came over to congratulate his friend. "I always wanted to believe, but..."

"I know," Gregory said, stepping off the stage and taking his friend's hand.

Eloria and Amoria were crying together off to the side. Tony Delarosa held Amoria and stared at Gregory. Gregory felt ashamed that he could not pay back the kindness that the Delarosas had shown him over the years.

"Your path is going to be tough," Gunther said, slapping Gregory on the back. "Don't worry about your father. I'll keep an eye on him for you. When you come back, he might have had time to accept this, so give him a chance."

"Thank you," Gregory said, unable to say more.

"You're an adult now, and a magi," Gunther said. "Come on, it's time for your first drink. Tony, we're taking him to the tavern," Gunther called over to Amoria's father.

"I'll be there in a moment," Tony replied.

Gregory let himself be hauled after Gunther, with Gunnar beside him. The flame he had felt inside himself earlier was now a banked coal, waiting to be called on again. The warmth of it in his chest made his steps seem lighter, but the coldness in his gut made him realize today was his last day with his friends.

CHAPTER 4

The tavern was packed with villagers celebrating the fact that one of their own was going off to be a magi. Gregory was escorted in by Gunnar and Gunther and everyone inside turned and cheered for him. Gregory was surprised— almost all of them had looked down on his dream of being a magi, telling him that belief alone was not enough. Twenty years between someone being blessed by Aether had made the villagers a little jaded, but now they acted as if they knew he was right all along. A path was made for him to the bar, with his friends following him.

Raymond, the bartender, smiled at him when Gregory made it to the bar. "There's the new magi. What will it be? An ale to start with, or are you going for something a bit more potent?"

Gregory had tried ale before when he and Gunnar had snuck some out of a small keg Gunther brought home. It left an unpleasant aftertaste in his mouth. "Maybe some mead?"

"Heh, going soft? That's fine. They say magi and alcohol don't mix well," Raymond laughed as he pulled a mug and set it in front of him.

"I'll have your shine," Gunnar laughed. "Always wanted to try it, and the first drink is on the Emperor, after all."

Raymond laughed back, "Now *that's* the spirit!"

"For me as well, Raymond," Gunther added.

"Father and son. Knew he'd take after you," Raymond grinned. Setting up the drinks, he shouted over the crowd. "Attention! Oy, shut your gobs! Thank you. A toast to our first magi in twenty years! To Pettit!"

The crowd hoisted their drinks when Raymond did, and all eyes went to Gregory. "I'll do the village proud," Gregory said, raising his own mug. "Alturis!"

"Alturis," the cry came back from everyone in the tavern.

Taking a big swallow of the mead, Gregory's lips twisted. *Too damned sweet*, Gregory thought as he put the mug down. The crowd parted to reveal the Delarosa family, heading up to the bar.

Gregory's eyes locked onto Amoria's hazel eyes, her tears making his heart twist. Amoria did her best to smile, but she could not manage to keep her sadness out of it. The coldness in his gut began to spread as he watched her.

"Berry wine for all of us," Tony told Raymond, ordering for his whole family.

While Raymond got their drinks together, Amoria came to a halt inches from Gregory. "I... Greg..." Her words failed her, and more tears fell.

Setting his cup down, Gregory pulled her into a hug. "Ria, I'm sorry, but I am a magi."

Clutching him, she sobbed, "I know. I'm happy for you, really. I just... I always hoped you'd stay here with me."

The coldness enveloped him entirely, except for his chest, which burned hotter. "I'm sorry, Ria. I'll always be grateful for you being my friend."

"A moment!" Gunther shouted, drowning out all the conversations in the bar. "Thank you. Since we are seeing our new magi off to serve the empire, it would be best if we revived the old tradition. Who will contribute to his journey?"

"I will," Tony said, swiftly emptying his belt pouch onto the bar and separating out all the coins inside from the odds and ends. Stuffing the items back into his pouch, he left the vela on the counter.

"Gregory, you will do our village proud. If you had not been a magi, I would have taken you in as an apprentice, but now, I will do my best to see you off with as much as I can."

Others lined up to do the same, while some slipped out of the tavern. Gregory watched the people leaving and bit back his comments. The pile of nickel-silver coins grew as people added what they could contribute. Most of the coins were on the low end of the vela, but it was still more than Gregory had ever seen in one place. When the tavern door reopened, it caught Gregory by surprise as some of the villagers who had left came back in, adding more to the growing pile.

Taking a long drink from the mead, Gregory winced at the taste. Amoria held his hand, her tears finally stopping. Eloria watched the two of them, then leaned over to whisper to Gunnar.

The line of people eventually stopped, and Gunther spoke up again, "Now that is the spirit of Alturis. Gregory, come collect the gift we bestow upon you."

Gregory cleared his throat, "Thank you. I know my dream of being a magi drove a lot of you up the wall, but this is humbling. I will never forget your support." He scooped the coins into his pouch, which was now close to full.

The loudest cheer yet erupted from the crowd. People began to file back out of the inn, as the other events of the day were going to be starting soon. A few came over to give him personal well wishes.

"Did you want a refill?" Raymond asked them. "On me."

"Pass," Gregory said. "Turns out I don't care for mead. Too sweet."

"You probably also need to collect your things," Raymond nodded.

"Have my things already," Gregory said with a touch of bitterness.

Raymond eyed Gregory for a long moment and shook his head. "I'll gift you something later tonight after I dig it out of the store room."

"Want to see the other contests?" Gunnar asked, cutting in on the conversation.

"Not really," Gregory admitted. "I don't know what I want. I mean... this is what I'd always dreamed about, but now I'm feeling lost."

"Gregory, can we talk for a moment?" Tony asked.

"You're staying at my house tonight," Gunther told Gregory. "Come by when you're ready. Gunnar, girls, come on. Let them talk."

"See you in a bit," Gunnar said when Gunther's hand grasped his shoulder.

"Soon," Gregory replied, his stomach tightening further.

Eloria walked out hand in hand with Gunnar, while Amoria kept looking back. Her mother kept her from staying, but each step seemed harder for her to take.

Tony stepped over to the side of the room with Gregory behind him as the tavern rapidly cleared out because the contests were about to begin. Taking a seat at a table, Tony waited for Gregory to do the same before he spoke.

"Gregory, I never thought today would happen like it did. I didn't really believe that you would become a magi. Do you know that Amoria was going to press you to court her after today?"

The tension in Gregory's stomach worsened. "I didn't, but I would have asked her myself if..."

Tony sighed, "Thank you. That would have been for the best, but now, it's a moot point. I knew today would bring changes, but I never envisioned it happening like this. I have just one favor to ask; don't take advantage of her today. I know you wouldn't, but... Amoria is distraught. Sleeping with you will only make it harder for her in the future."

Gregory blinked, surprised at the frankness. "I would *never* do anything to hurt her, sir. She has always been there for me. I owe her so much."

"Good. They already convinced their mother to let them stay at Gunnar's tonight, where I'm sure you'll also be staying, so I'll hold you to your word." Getting up abruptly, Tony left him at the table.

With Tony gone, he sat there alone, lost in thought until someone sat down across from him. Blinking as his train of thought came to a halt, he was surprised to see Bishop sitting across from him.

"Proctor?"

"It looks like your dream has a chance of coming true," Bishop said, though not unkindly. "Do you feel completed?"

"No," Gregory replied. "I feel like I'm losing everything I know. This is just the first step of a very long path to be a magi."

"Good," Bishop nodded. "Your friend, Delarosa, do you think she'll wait for you?"

Gregory frowned as he thought about it, "I wouldn't ask her to. I don't know what the academy will entail," Gregory added slowly. "I always thought it was just a place where we're taught how to control aether."

"Partially," Bishop admitted. "It is also the most miserable you'll ever be. The instructors won't care if you learn or not, the older students might pick on you, and your fellow novices will try to tear you down. Do you wish you had been a failure, after all?"

Gregory answered instantly and honestly, "No. This is my dream, Proctor."

"Good. It'll be a hard path, but those who want it enough can make it. The great thing about hard paths is that they forge the best magi... if they survive." Bishop stood abruptly, "I look forward to what you do in the future, Novice."

Gregory watched her walk away, the warmth of his aether slowly pushing back the uncertainty he had been feeling. Pushing himself to his feet, he headed for Gunnar's. It might be early, but he would have to be ready to go even earlier.

Gregory was lost in thought as he walked, thinking about what life would have been like if he had been a null. He was a few houses away from Gunnar's when a scream brought him to a dead stop. Head whipping toward the noise, Gregory saw a huge wolf stalking along the street. The massive wolf paused, turning its head to look at Gregory. Red eyes gleamed in the daylight as its lips drew back into a snarl.

"Bane wolf," Gregory whispered in fear. The spark of aether in his chest burst into flame.

The moment aether filled Gregory, the wolf seemed to smile. A deep howl erupted from it as it stared at Gregory. The air vibrated around him and he tried to move, only to discover the air itself holding him in place. Eyes widening, Gregory felt a surge of fear as the bane wolf charged at him.

Shouts filled the air, but Gregory knew no one would be there in time to help him. *Is this it? Do I get killed before I get to learn?* The question filled his mind, and the anger that he had harbored for years burned in his veins. Gregory growled back at the wolf when he suddenly realized that he could move. He darted at the creature, his arms glowing with blue flame.

The two of them collided, and Gregory moved on instinct, shoving his left forearm into the beast's gaping jaws. His right hand came crashing down on the bane wolf's snout just as its teeth clamped down on his arm. Gregory's scream of pain and the wolf's yip mingled as the pair hurt each other. Falling backward when the bane wolf bowled him over, Gregory kept hammering at its snout, even as it savagely shook its head and tore deep gouges into his arm.

"Greg!" Amoria's voice sent a surge of panic into Gregory.

"Stay back!" Gregory shouted, but the wolf had released his arm and bounded backward.

"Bane wolf!" Eloria screamed, and more people could be heard taking up the cry.

Gregory scrambled to his feet as the wolf spun and charged Amoria. Amoria stood frozen, fear written across her face as the bane wolf barreled toward her. Gregory knew he would never make it in time, but he rushed after the wolf, his heart in his throat as blood poured from his injured arm.

Gunnar appeared around the corner of a nearby building just in time to knock the wolf away, sending him and it tumbling. Gunnar's cry of pain rang out, along with Eloria's scream.

Gregory made it there a moment later. Wrapping his arms around the beast's neck, he pulled backward. The wolf's front feet left the ground as Gregory lifted it off his friend. "Gunnar, run!"

Gunnar scrambled back, his left hand bleeding profusely and two of his fingers missing. Amoria and Eloria were already there, pulling Gunnar away, their eyes wide as they stared at Gregory.

"Damned bane beasts," a voice growled. "Turn it toward me, Novice."

Gregory reacted to the commanding tone, yanking the few hundred pounds of savage beast completely off the ground and to the right. His eyes widened when he caught sight of a blue blur heading for his arms. The wind of something moving fast ruffled his hair and the weight of the beast vanished from his arms. The body of the bane wolf flopped to the ground, spraying blood, while the head of the beast tumbled away.

"Never thought a bane wolf would turn up here," Bishop said as she snapped her sword, sending a line of blood to the ground. The blue flame coating the blade vanished when she sheathed it. "Are you injured?"

Gregory blinked as her words finally penetrated his head. "Yes, but so is Gunnar."

"Let me see your arm," Bishop said, advancing on him, ignoring the bloody ruin that lay at his feet.

Gregory looked down at his injured arm. Deep bloody valleys marked where the bane wolf's teeth had bitten into his flesh. Pain suddenly flooded into his body, and he wobbled on his feet.

"Dismiss your aether," Bishop commanded sharply.

The blue flames on his arms winked out and she grabbed his ruined arm. His nostrils flared as new pain flooded his mind and he almost fell, but managed to keep his footing. Bishop's aether coated his arm an instant later, and the pain was snuffed out like a candle. Exhaling in relief, Gregory started to thank her, but his vision wavered and he felt himself falling.

"This is why novices shouldn't be in combat," Bishop's terse voice echoed in his ears as he collapsed into unconsciousness.

CHAPTER 5

Gregory blinked as a room swam into focus around him. When it settled down after a moment, he wondered why he was standing just inside an opulent bedroom. "Why am I here?"

A soft, sultry voice answered him from across the room, where darkness converged, "So we can meet, dear one."

"What? Who are you? Where am I?"

"We are inside of you. I am that which you always yearned for. I can be anything you want me to be... if you can tame me."

Shivers ran down his arms, and the words brought a hundred different images to his mind.

"Oh, it will be some time before we get to those stages. I am more than willing to do any of them, or all of them... *with you.*"

Swallowing hard, Gregory stepped back and felt the door shut behind him. "Is this what Bishop meant about my dreams?"

"Yes and no," the sultry voice in the dark whispered. "She expected you to see a burning flame. You would know it was your aether and accept it. That is how novices are *supposed* to begin."

"Then why am I different?"

A throaty laugh filled the room, "Yes, you are smart to ask that.

But I won't tell you unless you can make me. Unlike the novice flame, I'm a bit more of a... *handful.*"

Gathering his courage, Gregory took a step toward the dark corner of the room. "Okay, if I have to."

A delighted giggle came from the corner, "Oh, yes! If you want to control me, you'll have to tame me first."

The room shuddered and the voice in the darkness sighed, "Alas, it won't be today, it seems. Grow in power if you want to see me again, dear one."

"What—?" Gregory asked, but the room began to crack and bright light surged forward.

* * *

"The tincture will heal him, sealing the wounds tonight, though the scars will stay with him for a long time," Bishop's voice said, jarring Gregory from the place he had been.

Sitting up, Gregory swayed in place, "I'm fine."

Soft hands grasped him and helped him stay upright. "You scared us," Amoria whispered.

"I didn't mean to. I heard the scream, and then the bane wolf came into view."

"You stopped it from coming after us," Eloria said.

"I'm glad, but I don't know why it came for me."

"It was after *you* because your aether is fresh," Bishop snorted. "They grow more powerful by eating hearts, and if that heart has been touched by Aether, they gain even more from it."

"Are there others nearby?" Gunther asked.

"I will be going to check shortly," Bishop replied. "We had no idea that any bane beasts had made it this far around the north edge. I will inform the academy so they can send some adepts to patrol this area."

"What about my son's fingers?" Gunther asked.

"The cost of having them regrown would be more than this village is worth. He'll have to learn to adapt. He does deserve compensation, though. The bounty on a bane beast of wolf size is five thousand vela."

The villagers nearby looked shocked, but she ignored them as she pulled out a handful of coins. Handing two to Gunther and two to Amoria, Bishop nodded. "There. The bounty is shared."

"What, not Greg?" Amoria asked, puzzled. "He was the one who held it for you?"

"I have taken his portion to help defer the cost of the tincture," Bishop replied.

"That's fine," Gregory said as he started to stand up. "I thank you, Proctor, for your help. We wouldn't have survived if not for your intervention."

Bishop eyed him for a moment before speaking, "You should rest. You lost a good deal of blood before I could see to your wound."

"We'll get him home," Gunther said, moving over to support him.

"We'll come with you," Amoria said, looking at her sister, who was fussing with Gunnar.

Tony grimaced but nodded to his daughters, "We'll see you tomorrow."

"We still leave at sunrise," Bishop told Gregory. "Make sure you are at the inn by then." Looking to Raymond, who had come out of his tavern because of the commotion, Bishop pointed to the dead bane wolf. "Salt as much meat as you can and bake the heart for me. I'll need it when I get back. Oh, and set aside its core." She flipped him a coin. "For the drinks and the work."

"Yes, Proctor," Raymond bowed before he bent to pick up the wolf. With a grunt of exertion, he hefted it onto his shoulder and staggered back toward the tavern.

"The rest of you may return to the festivities. The village will be protected," Bishop announced and began jogging toward the edge of the village.

"Come on, Gregory. Let's get you home," Gunther said, lending the young man a helping arm.

Yeva looked pale when they brought Gregory in. She flitted about, bringing wet cloths and hot tea to them when they were seated in the main room. Gunther escorted her away once she brought in food and a kettle of tea for the new adults.

The four friends had been mostly silent when they went inside the house. With the two adults gone, they relaxed. Eloria grabbed Gunnar and kissed him hard, and Amoria did the same with Gregory, much to his surprise.

When she broke the kiss, she leaned against him, "I thought you were going to die."

"I thought I might, too," Gregory admitted. "If I hadn't acted, though..."

"I would have died," Gunnar grunted. "Thank you for saving me."

"You saved Amoria," Gregory replied and held her tighter.

"You would have done the same if our positions had been reversed," Gunnar said. "I didn't even make it flinch when I hit it. I know it yelped when you did. Odd, that."

"I think it was the aether that hurt it, not me, which is what made it come for me instead of Ria and El." Gregory took his arms away from Amoria, as he recalled what her father had asked of him. "Though the day didn't go as everyone hoped."

"But your day is still good," Gunnar grunted, looking down at his three fingered hand. "Your dream was true."

"If I get the chance," Gregory said, "I'll do what I can to fix that." He glanced at Amoria from the corner of his eye, "I have to."

Gunnar grunted, shaking his head. "Like I said, you'd have done it if our places were reversed." Picking up his cup awkwardly with his left hand, Gunnar took a drink. "We have food and drink, so let us celebrate you."

The small celebration lasted for about five hours, with the four friends reminiscing. Eloria was the first to fall asleep, leaning against Gunnar. Gregory handed over one of the blankets that Gunther had left behind so Gunnar could get her settled.

Amoria yawned while Gunnar got her sister settled, "We should all turn in."

"Feels like one of our old sleepovers," Gregory chuckled. "That was years ago."

"Ten years ago," Amoria smiled softly, "in this very room."

"I'll see you in the dawn hours," Gregory said.

"You have a long journey ahead of you," Amoria said.

"Come on, you two," Gunnar chuckled as he pulled another blanket over himself. "If you keep talking, he'll end up being late."

Amoria and Gregory got themselves settled on the floor on opposite sides of Gunnar and Eloria. Snuffing out the lantern, Gregory lay in the dark. He kept replaying the bane wolf attack, and what had almost happened to Amoria. In time, his mind finally wound down and he was able to slip into sleep.

* * *

The soft, warm sensation of skin against his woke Gregory. "Huh?"

"Shh, you'll wake them," Amoria whispered as she began to plant kisses along his neck.

"Ria? What...? No, we shouldn't," Greg protested in a whisper, even though part of him was in full agreement with her.

"Greg, please," Amoria pleaded. "You'll never come back after tomorrow... no magi ever has. I know what it'll cost me, but I want this. I've wanted it for years. I know it'll be just for tonight, but it will help me because I'll know that you really did love me as much as I did you."

Her hands found his stiff flesh and his ability to make objections fled. "I don't want to hurt you, Ria. I promised your father."

"I'll stop if you tell me to," Amoria whispered and began to kiss his neck again, her hand stroking up and down his length. "Just tell me to stop and I will."

Gregory shivered as she worked him, "Promise me, Ria... Promise me that you'll try to find happiness after I'm gone."

"I will do my best to be the woman you would want me to be, Greg. My word."

"Oh, Aether," Gregory moaned lightly as he gave in to her demands. Wrapping his arms around her, he kissed her softly, tentatively. He knew that what he was doing would make her life hard, but he was unable to resist her desires and his own.

When they finally stopped, laying there covered in sweat, the pair felt awkward and unsure of what to say or do. Stifled moans came from a dozen feet away, making them both glance to the pile of blankets where Gunnar and Eloria were. Sharing amused looks, the two stared into each other's eyes before they came together again, more confident this time.

CHAPTER 6

"**G**reg, you have to get up," Amoria said, shaking his shoulder.

Jerking upright, Gregory grabbed her and squeezed her to his chest. "Thank Aether you're alright."

"Greg?" Amoria asked in surprise.

"The wolf—"

"It never got close," Gunnar said. "Nightmare?"

Letting go of Amoria as memory of last night flooded in, Gregory nodded, his face flushed in embarrassment. "Yes."

"I have travel food ready for you," Yeva said from the doorway. "You need to get moving. The sun isn't far from rising."

Pushing the blanket off, Gregory got to his feet with a wince. The bandage on his arm pulled at his skin. He unwrapped it, grimacing at the sight; wide, long, white scars marked his forearm.

"She was right about the scars," Gunnar grunted. "Looks like neither of us will forget the bane wolf." He held up the white nubs where his two fingers had been.

"Gunnar, take him to wash. Quickly," Gunther told his son. "The women will be ready by the time you finish."

"Come on," Gunnar said, "I have a basin in my room."

It did not take long to get clean, and afterward Gregory got back into the same clothes that he had worn the day before. He only had a couple of sets, and would be traveling all day. Returning to the main room, Gregory picked up his bag.

"Thank you, Mr. and Mrs. Emery," Gregory said, bowing to them. "I will always remember the kindness you showed me."

"You are a good man," Yeva said, giving him a big hug. "Do your best and stay safe."

The goodbyes were quick, and soon, Gregory was out the door with food in hand. His breakfast was day old bread and cheese along with a thick slice of dried meat. Amoria held his hand as they walked to the square, Gunnar and Eloria following them.

"Do you ever wonder why no one sees the magi off in any of the stories?" Amoria asked as they walked toward the tavern.

"No," Gregory replied. "I always thought it was to make parting easier for the families."

"That is part of it," Bishop added from behind them, making them all jump. "You are on time, good. I would have been displeased to be delayed."

Gregory looked back, his eyebrows rising. "Proctor, did you sleep?"

"No, I was busy," Bishop replied with a grim look. She smirked, "Looks like I wasn't the only one who had no sleep."

The four flushed and looked away from her, earning a chuckle.

"There are no more bane beasts currently in the area. The academy will still be informed so they can send adepts. This way, an event like yesterday's will never happen again. I'll go get my things and we will be on our way."

Passing them, Bishop moved as if she was having a pleasant walk, but her speed would have been hard to match at a run for Gregory. As they watched her go, Gregory wondered how long it would take for him to be able to duplicate that feat.

The group reached the inn just as Bishop left the building. She had a bag over her left shoulder and a fist sized object in her right hand. Her clothing was still dirty and covered in blood, and her face had small smears of both. Seeing them, she smiled and took a large bite of what she was holding.

"Good! Let's be going. We have many miles to cover, and novices always move slowly."

Gregory looked back at his friends. "Gunnar—"

"I'll look after her for you."

"We will," Eloria said.

"Ria..." Gregory said, touching her cheek gently.

"Go, be the magi you were always meant to be," Amoria said, her eyes bright with unshed tears. "You'll always be in my heart, but I will do as I promised."

He kissed Amoria hard, the kiss slowly becoming softer, before he stepped back from her. "Goodbye, Ria."

"Novice, time to go," Bishop said firmly, but not unkindly. "Start walking."

Choked up, Gregory turned away from his old life and started down the road toward the next village. The feeling of finality made him cold, even with the aether inside him keeping him warm.

Bishop left him to his thoughts, letting the pace be slow to start with.

Falling into step with her after a while, Gregory's eyes grew large when he realized what she was eating. "Is that the heart, Proctor?"

"Yes," Bishop chuckled. "It always shocks people when you do this. I tempered my impulse to eat it raw. You gain more aether that way, but non-magi tend to react badly if they see it."

"Would I gain aether if I did?"

She gave him a bloody smile as she tore another chunk free. "Yes, but it would be a greater risk for you, Novice. Your body is not tempered yet, and the aether of the bane wolf would run rampant through your system. You will address me as proctor or ma'am anytime you wish to speak with me. Understood?"

"Yes, Proctor."

"Good. Now save your breath. We'll be moving as fast as you are able." Bishop's easy pace grew faster until Gregory had to jog to keep up.

* * *

Gregory did his best, but he was never the best at physical exertion, having his mother's slight build. When he flagged for the third time, Bishop sighed.

"You'll have to do better," Bishop said, pulling some salted meat from her bag and passing it to him. "Chew and suck, do not swallow. It will dissolve with time."

Gregory took the meat with a puzzled expression and stuck it in his mouth. The flavor of the bane wolf was unpleasant, leaving a sharp and tangy taste on the tongue. He chewed slowly, hoping he would grow accustomed to it.

"Now *run*," Bishop said, prodding him sharply. "Run until I say stop."

Gregory started to jog, but Bishop did not let him stay at a jog. She kept prodding to make him run. Grimacing, Gregory stretched out his legs and began to run, wondering how long she would make him do this. Bishop stayed right behind him, a smirk on her lips as she finished the bane wolf heart.

Miles flew by, and Gregory came to realize he should not be able to keep the pace he was setting. He laughed when he realized he was moving faster than he ever had in his life, the joy of it making him grin.

It was almost an hour later when his legs suddenly stopped responding and he went head first into the dirt. Rolling to a stop, Gregory winced as he sucked in air, covered in sweat.

Bishop laughed when she came to a stop beside him, "Didn't realize the meat had vanished. Get up. We'll walk for a bit now."

Gregory grunted. His right knee felt stiff as he got back to his feet, but the sensation quickly subsided. He drank from his canteen as he walked, suddenly aware of being thirstier than he could ever recall. He checked to see if he was injured, but did not see any gashes.

"You need to keep better track of everything you are doing," Bishop told him. "You fell because the meat was used up and you didn't slow."

"The jerky did that...? Proctor?" Gregory asked, adding the title belatedly.

"Bane beasts have many benefits for the people who can touch aether," Bishop replied. "The drawback for you is that you can't ingest much of it without negative feedback. The jerky especially, because it wasn't prepared correctly. Out here on the fringes, that is to be expected."

"Proctor, how do I grow stronger?"

Chuckling, Bishop shook her head. "That is what the first year is about; learning, growing, and choosing."

"Will there be a time when I can ingest more of the wolf, or a better prepared version of it, Proctor?"

"The food at the academy is made to help you grow. You will learn to accept the aether it gives and store it for use when you wish instead of using it for instant energy to run."

"My aether mentioned needing to choose a path. Do you know what it meant, Proctor?"

"Choosing the way your aether grows. During the novice year, you'll have to pick between body, mind, or spirit."

"You said that hard paths make the best magi, Proctor. Which path is the hardest?"

"The hardest path is annoying those who are there to help you," Bishop replied. "Speaking of which, it's time to move fast again. You'll find out what academy encouragement is when you start to flag."

Gregory took off running, not wanting to find out before he had to. Bishop watched him run and nodded as she kept pace easily.

Asking about paths and which are harder than others? Maybe you'll be worth watching, even more than I had thought. Speaking to your aether though? Hmm... Bishop focused on Gregory, thinking.

* * *

Gregory coughed as he pushed himself back to his feet again. Sweat was pouring down his face. *She's a demon! She smiles every time she pushes me harder. Even the breathing techniques mother taught me can't help me keep up with Bishop's demands...*

"Come on, Novice. Your friend wouldn't have had as many issues as you are," Bishop said, chiding him for the tenth time as the sun began to descend toward the western horizon.

Gregory groaned. *If I slow again, she might not just prod me. That last strike was bruising.*

Bishop was beside him in an instant, her voice barely audible as she gracefully glided alongside him, "Worried about the next hit, Novice? Do you think it'll be easier than this at the academy? What I'm doing is *mild* compared to what is coming for you. You'll grow or break, but either way, you will serve the empire."

He winced, but did not reply. Instead, he kept putting one foot in front of the other. *Is she right? Or is this just her goading me to keep me moving?* Gregory waffled back and forth on the question as they rounded the curve in the road.

"There is Linom," Bishop sighed. "Walk and recover," she told Gregory. "I'll see you when you get there. I need to arrange our stay, but don't dawdle."

"Yes, Proctor."

Bishop nodded, her legs stretching as she began to run. Gregory watched her go in awe as chunks of dirt flew up behind her.

"Wonder if I'll be able to do that one day?" Gregory muttered.

He did not stop moving, but was grateful to finally have a chance to breathe and not get slapped for it. Thoughts of what the academy was going to be like filled his head as he closed in on the village ahead of him.

CHAPTER 7

Gregory woke slowly, groggily. The dream of a giggling woman using him for her own pleasure lingered in his mind. "What in Aether's name did I drink last night?"

The almost pitch black room held traces of dawn creeping through the closed shutters. Sitting up, he pushed the coverings aside. Stretching as he got to his feet, he winced. His legs were doing their best to support him after all the torture from the day before.

"We should be in the village all day for their age day," Gregory muttered as he started dressing in his second set of clothes. "I need to get some water and wash the other set."

When he was dressed, he left the room and met Bishop leaving her room. She nodded when she saw him, "Good, I don't need to wake you. You are to shadow me all day unless I say otherwise. We'll start with breakfast."

"Yes, Proctor."

Bishop moved past him, leaving barely an inch between them, and Gregory pressed against the wall to give her more room. Following her downstairs, he took the seat she pointed him to. She went to the bar and slapped it hard.

The innkeeper poked his head out of the back, the rebuke dying on his lips when he saw who it was. "Yes, Proctor?"

"Breakfast for both of us."

"You want me to use the meat you gave me?"

Bishop's easy smile dimmed, "Are you questioning my judgement?"

Going pale with beads of sweat forming on his forehead, the man shook his head. "No, never, Proctor."

"I recall your father," Bishop said easily, but her gray eyes looked like they were sparking with flame. "Does he still limp?"

Swallowing hard, the man bowed to her, "Please, Proctor, forgive me."

"Of course," Bishop said smoothly. "Today is a day of celebration and hope, not a day for pain and regrets. Make sure the food is prepared as I ordered. Go."

The man fled the room, and Gregory felt his own scalp prickle at the power that radiated from Bishop. Bishop watched the tavern keeper flee and moved over to sit with Gregory.

Seeing Gregory's frown, she shook her head. "Novice, you don't realize the power the magi wield, do you?"

Gregory frowned, "They protect the empire. Their power—"

"No," Bishop cut him off. "I meant power like I just exerted. Magi are listened to or there are consequences for those without power."

"What if the magi is wrong?"

"Magi can't be wrong," Bishop said simply. "It is only because of us that the empire stands. We protect the lesser people, and in return, they do as we require. Did you think me harsh with him?"

Gregory frowned, "I was always told the magi are the shield that protects us, but none of the rest."

"You know how the empire works though, surely? The strong are in charge, and those under them help as required."

"The strong lead," Gregory nodded. "That is true, but they guide everyone. They don't demand."

"Ah, the fringe is so different," Bishop said and a hint of wistfulness filled her voice. "This is why I am the proctor for the northern fringe."

"Proctor, why do you keep calling it the fringe?"

"The common name given to outlying villages such as yours. You are considered foolish and backward by most of the empire. You will need to be cool, calm, and ready for the barbs that come your way."

Fast footsteps announced the innkeeper as he brought over a tray and two cups of tea.

"You kept me waiting," Bishop snapped, her eyes cold.

"I'm sorry, Proctor," the man said, bowing, the tray still in his hands.

"Set it on that table," Bishop commanded. "Bring us a kettle of mint."

"Right away," the man said.

"Novice, enjoy the meal," Bishop said as she took a majority of the food. "After breakfast, we will walk around the village. I will leave you alone for an hour or two so I can check the surrounding area, so be on your best behavior."

"Yes, Proctor," Gregory said, wondering about Bishop's harshness toward the innkeeper.

* * *

After a silent breakfast, Gregory followed Bishop into the village. The villagers stared at them with a combination of fear and awe, and those who were coming of age stared at Gregory with envy. Bishop stopped and talked with the craftsmen and the elder of the town, inspecting the square where the stage and decorations waited.

Two hours after they had stepped outside, Bishop turned to him. "I'm going to check the area around the village to make sure no bane beasts prowl the area. While I'm gone, you represent the empire. Do not disappoint me."

"I'll do my best, Proctor."

Giving him a wintery smile, Bishop headed away, her hand

tapping the hilt of her sword as she went. Gregory watched her go and a feeling of anxiety crept over him.

Should I check the merchants? I have the money from the village, so maybe I can find something good. Yes... I should see about a new tunic, at least. My other one was pretty well destroyed by the bane wolf.

The first merchant had a collection of tinkered items for sale, from pots and pans to small blades, but nothing Gregory was interested in. The next merchant was a jovial fat man who laughed a lot. His cart was full of spices, herbs, and other cooking ingredients. Going to the third cart, Gregory felt hopeful, seeing the colorful cloth draped over the side of this wagon.

"Ah, are you seeking to buy something?" the lanky, bald merchant asked with a grin. "Perhaps something for a young lady? I have a number of dresses that would be well received." With a deft movement, he presented an emerald dress to Gregory. "Made with fine cotton."

Gregory shook his head. "You have it wrong. I have no woman to buy for." A pang of guilt made him think of Amoria and how that dress would make her face light up. "I hope to buy a tunic or two for myself."

"Ah, I can do that, young sir. My tunics are on the other side of my cart. I even have one made from a wonderful light blue silk."

"I need solid tunics that can stand the rigors of travel," Gregory said, following the merchant to the far side of the cart.

"Ah, travel tunics? Yes, I have a number of them, as well," the merchant said, his excitement dimming. "Here are a dozen. Let me know when you have found what you want."

Gregory thanked him and looked through the selection. After some time, he had two tunics; one light brown and the other green. "Sir, these two tunics? How much?"

"Seventy vela for both," the merchant smiled.

"That much?" Gregory said, thinking about all the time he had spent in the Delarosa's home. "The stitching is good, but not great, and the material would be better suited for the winter months, not the summer months that we are in."

The merchant stared at Gregory for a long moment. "You aren't from this village, are you?"

"I'm from Alturis," Gregory replied.

A dawning light began to fill the merchant's eyes. "Would you happen to know the Delarosas?"

"I do," Gregory admitted. "They are shrewd when it comes to cloth."

The merchant chuckled, "You were the one that hung around with their daughters. Why are you here and not there?"

"I'm on my way to train at the academy."

"Magi..." the merchant said softly.

"A novice," Gregory corrected. "I would be interested in buying them, just not for seventy."

"I meant no disrespect, magi," the merchant said humbly. "If I had known, I wouldn't have asked for so much to start. Forty for the both of them."

"I took no offense," Gregory said, handing over the forty vela. "These clothes are worth forty, at the least."

The merchant bowed his head, accepting the coins without counting them. "It is an honor to serve, magi. If you have need of more clothing, my family has a small shop in the lower ring of Wesrik. Tell them you spoke with Nicholas Lagrand."

"Wesrik is the home of the academy," Gregory said. "I'll likely be there in a week or two. Thank you."

"What is your name, so I can listen for news of your journey?" Lagrand asked.

"Gregory Pettit," Gregory replied.

"May Aether guide you," Lagrand bowed his head again.

"May the Traveler watch over your journey, as well," Gregory said.

Gregory headed for the inn to drop off his new tunics and to see about washing his old one.

CHAPTER 8

I can't believe Gunnar and Amoria each gave me half their reward from the bane wolf, Gregory thought as he hung up his clothing so they could dry. Never thought I'd see a five-hundred vela coin in my life, but now I have two of them.

"Novice," Bishop said, opening the door to the room, "it is almost time. Follow me."

"Yes, Proctor," Gregory said and finished hanging his clothing on the makeshift line.

Following Bishop out of the tavern and through the crowd to the small stage, Gregory realized how much bigger Linom was compared to Alturis. The square was packed with people, and the only reason they were able to move through it easily was because of everyone getting out of Bishop's way.

Making it to the stage, Bishop motioned him up behind her. She looked out over the crowd and waited for the noise to die down. "Linom, I have come to administer the ritual of Aether. Have those who would become adults form a line."

Five young adults stood off to the right side of the stage, waiting. The first in line was a waif of a girl who looked sickly. Bishop stared at her for a long moment before motioning her onto the stage. "Come, child. You will need to hold to your strength."

The waif swallowed hard as she stepped onto the stage. Kneeling before Bishop, the sickly girl bowed her head.

"Child, you come before me on the verge of adulthood," Bishop said. "Today is your age day, and you should rejoice. Today also marks the chance for you to join the ranks of the magi. Let us see if you have the spark of Aether inside of you."

Trembling as Bishop touched her head, the waif's voice broke as she spoke, "I'm ready to become an adult, Proctor."

"Aether, have you blessed this child with your grace?" Bishop asked the sky before a blue flame covered her hand, which looked to be gently cupping the waif's skull.

The frail girl bucked and screamed, her whole body bending in the grip of the proctor, who watched with no outward emotion. The scream cut off and the girl went limp in her hand. The flame vanished a moment later, and Bishop gently lowered the girl to the stage, her face solemn.

"Aether did not bless her. Mortum has welcomed her into his eternal embrace instead," Bishop said softly. "Frankan, come forward," she commanded, her voice firm.

A couple stepped out of the crowd, crying as they walked forward. Both the mother and father looked ill, as well. "Proctor," the father said, his voice breaking.

"My condolences. Your child has passed on before you. Remember her with love. She will be waiting for you." Extracting a coin from her pouch, she handed it to the mother. "For your loss."

Sobbing harder, the mother took the coin. Her hand clenched it tightly as she leaned against her husband.

"Elder Olitum, have someone help them with their child."

"Yes, Proctor," an elderly woman said, motioning to one of the burlier men to help.

When the body was removed, Bishop looked at the crowd again. "Tragedy of this kind happens infrequently, but it is still a danger during the ritual. Keep this in mind over the coming years. Let us continue."

The rest of the children came forward one by one, none of them becoming magi, but with no more deaths, either. When the last adult was helped down from the stage, Bishop spoke to the village again.

"No magi, but four new adults. Welcome them as citizens of the empire. Mourn the loss of today, and celebrate the passage of your children."

Stepping off the stage, Bishop motioned Gregory to follow her. A number of eyes in the crowd stared at him as he followed her. They went into the tavern before it began to fill, where she turned to him, "Rest, relax, and shop if you wish, but we leave at sunrise again. I will have dinner sent to your room."

"Yes, Proctor," Gregory said, bowing his head.

"Proctor, may I speak with you in private?" the mother of the dead girl asked. She had followed them, tears still falling from her eyes.

Bishop's gaze softened and she nodded, "Of course." She led the mourning woman up the stairs, speaking softly to her.

The door opened behind Gregory and admitted the villagers into the tavern. "Magi, will you share a drink with us?" a voice called out to him.

Remembering what Bishop had said earlier about representing the empire, Gregory smiled and said, "Of course."

"A round of ale," the speaker told the tavern owner.

Gregory managed to not wince as he moved over to the bar with the villagers. The hard stare from one of the new adults made the hairs on Gregory's neck stand up.

"You're from Alturis?" the young man asked bluntly.

"Yes."

"How many undertook the ritual?" one of the other men asked as he picked up a mug.

"About double those here."

"And you were blessed?" an older woman asked with surprise.

"Twenty years since we last had a magi from the village," Gregory said, not liking where the questions were going.

The villagers nodded, and the original speaker chuckled, "We produce one every five years, give or take."

"Probably be next year," another chimed in.

"Should have been this year," the young man said bitterly. "There's no saying who Aether will bless, but this twig was blessed, while a strong man like myself was not."

The other people at the bar looked a bit uncomfortable, but none of them rebuked him. Gregory had just taken the last mug, but held it.

"Otus, I don't want trouble," the tavern owner told the young man.

"My grandmother would not take kindly to you telling me what to do, and you know it," Otus fired back. "I'm having a discussion with the *magi*."

"Doesn't feel like a discussion," Gregory said, setting the mug back on the bar. "Sounds like bitter grapes."

"Feel special with your spark of aether?" Otus snarled. "Without it, I could break you, and you know it."

Gregory's jaw set, but instead of lashing out, he unlaced his sleeve and rolled it up his arm. "A bane wolf already tried breaking me, less than an hour past my blessing." The vivid scars stood out like beacons.

"He didn't mean—" the first speaker tried to calm them, but Otus was not having any of it.

"Ha, a bane wolf? You would never survive one," Otus jeered.

Gregory was torn; he wanted to shut Otus up, but he was not sure how that would look to Bishop or the villagers. It seemed the magi were usually feared and listened to, but the young man did not care.

"Believe what you wish," Gregory said, turning away and pulling his sleeve down. "I don't have time to deal with idiots."

A sharp intake of breath behind him was the only warning Gregory got before Otus hit him in the back of the head with his mug. Ale went flying as the two men went to the floor.

"What in the empire's name is going on!?" Bishop's voice cut over the sudden yelling from the spectators.

Otus did not hear it, raising his mug to bring it down on Gregory's skull. "Your aether is supposed to be mine! Give it back!"

The mug was almost to its target when it went flying away, deflected by a blue flame sword. Coming back to his senses and looking up from atop Gregory, Otus stared at Bishop. Freezing in place, he stammered, trying to form a sentence.

"I... no... Proctor... he...!"

"Attacking a magi, even a novice, is a crime," Bishop said flatly. "Get up, or be sentenced summarily."

Otus scrambled to his feet and began backing toward the door. "Proctor, I was defending myself! He—"

"Silence. Stop moving," Bishop commanded coldly.

Otus shuddered, spun, and fled. Before he could reach the door, Bishop was in front of it, looking like she had teleported across the room. Her empty hand caught Otus by the tunic, lifting him from the floor as if he was a small child.

"I *told* you to stop moving," Bishop whispered with malice. "Failure to listen to a proctor on age day is a serious crime."

"No, no! Stop it! My grandmother is the elder of this village," Otus cried as he physically tried to pry her hand off his tunic.

"Not after today," Bishop replied. "Can anyone here attest to what happened to the novice?"

"Otus picked a fight, upset that he wasn't blessed. When the novice tried to leave, Otus attacked him," the tavern owner said as the others all looked down.

"Lies!" Otus snarled. "Wilson is lying! You can't trust their family! You know that, Proctor... You've dealt with his family before."

"The Wilson family has learned their lesson," Bishop said calmly. "I ask again: will anyone here speak about what happened?"

One by one, the others gave the same story. Otus tried to disavow each in turn, trying harder to pry at Bishop's hand on his tunic. Gregory sat up, his head swimming.

"I shall bring this complaint to Elder Olitum. Stop trying to resist or it will be worse for you... *child*."

Otus gnashed his teeth and kicked at Bishop, "I'm an adult! I passed the ritual."

Bishop shook her head, ignoring the young man as he kicked and flailed at her. "A chance given and rejected? Pity. Today shall see two deaths, after all." She hauled Otus out the door, ignoring his struggles and protests.

Those left inside the tavern looked ill at ease and quickly left. Wilson frowned, but did not ask for payment for the ale. He knew he would have enough trouble shortly when Elder Olitum came to speak with him.

"Can I get some hot water and a clean cloth?" Gregory asked, using a table to steady himself as he got back onto his feet.

"Of course," Wilson said, fleeing into the kitchen.

"Guess I need to be more aware," Gregory muttered as his vision swam again.

"Here is the water and cloth," Wilson said, coming around the bar.

"Can you help me with the stairs?" Gregory asked slowly, his words slurring.

Wilson set the kettle and cloth on a table. "Of course."

Greg wobbled as he took a step toward Wilson. "Guess I shouldn't drink so much."

"Not from behind, at least," Wilson added as he gave the young man his shoulder.

Gregory started to reply, but instead, his eyes rolled up and he passed out. Wilson caught him and carried him up the stairs. "Daughter, I need a hand," he yelled downstairs.

* * *

"How is he?" Bishop asked.

"Asleep," the young woman, Victoria, replied softly. "He passed out when Dad tried to help him upstairs. Some of his aether was helping with the wound, I think. Blue fire would spark from the cut on the back of his head." Her voice was half amazed and half fearful.

"Unaided?" Bishop asked, moving over to the bed. Checking the wound, she grunted, "So it seems. Interesting."

"Proctor, what happened with Otus?" Victoria asked.

"He was executed for attacking me while I was looking into the attack against this magi. His grandmother joined him, and I had to appoint a new elder. Such a waste," Bishop sighed. "Those who don't respect the magi and the empire must be removed for the good of the whole. Not that a single non-magi is a threat to even a trained novice, but unchecked, it can cause unrest."

"Thank you for sparing my grandfather, Proctor. You were merciful ten years ago."

"I did what had to be done. No more and no less," Bishop told her. "Do you remember it well?"

"I do, Proctor."

"Will you stay and watch him for me?"

"If that is what you require."

"If he grows unwell, come for me, even if I sleep."

"As you command, Proctor."

"Tell your father that no reprisals will come to him for him telling the truth today. The new elder has already been told."

"Yes, Proctor."

Bishop left the innkeeper's daughter with Gregory. The girl, a year from the age day ritual herself, sat on the edge of the bed and gently stroked the hair of the sleeping boy, smiling softly at him. A tiny spark of blue tickled her hand and made her smile more.

"Maybe next year..."

CHAPTER 9

Days passed by as they travelled from village to village. Bishop fed him more bane wolf on the road between villages, to keep them moving faster. No more magi were blessed, but there were not any more deaths, either.

The sun was sinking toward the horizon when the walls of Tolkin came into view. Bishop slowed to a walk, with Gregory following suit. Bishop sighed and stretched. "I've been looking forward to a real bath."

"Real bath, Proctor?" Gregory asked.

"You've only ever had hip baths, right?" Bishop asked. "I hope every year that the villages get a little more advanced than they were the year before. Yes, a real bath and more. This one is special. A maid cleans you, then rubs you down with oil. I wonder if she still works at the inn..." She trailed off, smiling slightly at her thoughts.

"What of the ritual, Proctor?" Gregory asked.

"Every town and all the cities have a magus stationed in them. The new magi from them have already moved to the academy to get settled before the new year starts. You'll have a week at most to get settled, while others have been there for weeks or months, making alliances and learning how things work. Your home is in the cluster of villages that I visit last every year."

A single man in leather leaned against the wall next to the large gate, a pike propped against his shoulder. As they drew closer, the guard stood to attention. Bishop snorted, but did not speak as she walked past him.

"Do all the towns have guards and walls, Proctor?" Gregory asked.

"Yes. The villages should, too, but no one wants to pay for it," Bishop shrugged.

"But why do the towns and cities need them, Proctor?"

"Because bane beasts aren't always small, and sometimes because people don't think of the good of the empire, but only of themselves."

Gregory wondered what that really meant, but instead of asking, he turned his attention to the town. The buildings were much closer together than he was used to seeing, and the city itself did not smell like any of the villages they had gone through. He looked around with a frown when he realized that he had not seen any place for waste to be deposited in the town.

"There it is, the Proctor's Rest," Bishop smiled when a three-story building came into view. "We stay there tonight. Tomorrow, we will be taking a carriage to Kedlin City. That will be four days and a number of stops. We might be joined by another novice or two on the way."

Bishop led him inside and Gregory's eyes widened as he took in the interior of the inn. The place gleamed; lanterns hung from chains above the room, their bright light illuminating everything inside clearly. A plump matronly woman stood behind the bar, while two younger women moved from table to table, serving the guests.

"Samantha, done for the year?" the matron smiled when Bishop entered the room.

"Done, indeed," Bishop replied.

"You actually have one this year," the matron said, eyeing Gregory up and down. "A bit on the scrawny side. I'll do what I can to fatten him up before you take him away."

"I doubt you can, but you may try," Bishop laughed. "Is Lauren still here?"

"Of course. We were thinking you'd be in tonight. I'll arrange to have her ready when you finish dinner."

"We'll drop our things and come back down. Have Lauren ready to bathe me." Lips twisting into a smirk, she leaned in toward the matron, "Have Jess bathe the novice."

A booming belly laugh came from the matron, "Oh, up to your tricks again? Fine, fine. They have to learn sometime, and my girls are clean, at least." Slapping a bell on the counter, the matron waited a moment for a young boy to come out of the back room. "Rooms three and four, Gino."

"Yes, Mama," the young boy said, then turned and bowed to Bishop. "Please, Proctor, follow me."

"Lead us," Bishop smiled at the young man. "How have you been, Gino?"

"Well. Mama thinks I'm ready to study at the hall."

"Ten more years and you'll be going through the ritual," Bishop sighed. "Time flies. The hall will do wonders for you. If you are blessed, your learning will make the first year much easier. The one behind me hasn't had that luxury, and will have a harder time because of it."

Gino glanced at Gregory and bowed his head. "I hope you are able to overcome that hardship, Novice."

"I have had schooling," Gregory said with a frown.

"A single teacher in a small room *isn't* learning," Bishop corrected him. "What did you know of magi before I told you what I could?"

Gregory lapsed into silence, and Gino shook his head. "He should find a woman who will care for him."

Bishop snickered, "Listening to your mother's advice, I see."

"Mama is smart," Gino said with a pout. "Not many could run this place as well as she does."

"That is true, Gino," Bishop admitted as they reached the second floor. "She has held onto this place despite some very nasty problems. I have met few who can out stubborn her."

"Mama says she would have lost everything if not for you," Gino said shyly. "Said I should grow up big and strong to court you."

Bishop laughed as she stopped before the door with a three carved into it. "That sounds like her." Turning, she bent at the waist to speak on Gino's level, "Tell her that you are cute, but that it will not happen. Unless you are magi, it would never work out, and she knows that. Now go. The novice can find his room from here."

"Yes, Proctor," Gino said, and rushed down the stairs.

"Store your things, wipe the road dust off, and meet me downstairs for food," Bishop told him before she went inside her room.

Gregory bowed to her and walked into the next room. A bed, large enough for two to use comfortably, sat in one corner. A table and two padded chairs took up the middle of the room. The window was not wooden shutters like he was used to, but glass with curtains. A shelf ran under it, and a basin, pitcher, and small cloth were on it. An armoire stood against the wall near the door, and there was still plenty of room to move around.

"So much space," Gregory muttered.

He set his bag inside the armoire, then went to the pitcher. Clean water was waiting for him. Shaking his head, he poured some into the basin and quickly washed his face and hands. He used the cloth to dab at the worst stains on his tunic and pants, and gave his boots a fast wipe down.

When he was finished, he went downstairs and found Bishop at a table near the cold fireplace. The table was larger than needed for just two of them. Gregory had barely been seated when a maid was there with glasses full of some clear, crystalline liquid that Gregory had never seen before.

"Your meal will be right out, Proctor," the maid said, moving away without pausing.

"At high sun, the carriage will be here for us. Do not be late for it. Until then, your time is your own. Your food and drink here are paid for by me, so feel free to enjoy yourself one last time. Did you have any questions?"

"Will we be stopping at any other towns and cities on the way, Proctor?"

"Yes, but we will be stopping for the night only. When the sun rises, we will be traveling again."

"What would you suggest I see or do before we leave?" Gregory asked.

Bishop smiled, "A good question, Novice, but I can't give *you* advice."

Gregory silently thought for a while before he came up with another question. "What would you tell a younger you to see or do before leaving?"

"A better question. I would have told me to see the scrivener and ask about scrolls useful for novices. Picking up a short blade, long enough for defense but not long enough to be viewed as a weapon only, would have been a good idea. Telling me to savor the food and drink would have been good, too."

"Where are the scrivener and smith located, Proctor?"

"The scrivener is a block north of the square. The smith is two squares east from there," Bishop replied, her eyes going past him. "Here comes our dinner."

"Your meal, Proctor," the maid said, serving Bishop first.

The platter held a layer of finely sliced vegetables topped with what looked like most of some sort of bird. Gregory's platter was similar, but with less meat.

"Bane duck, with elixir-laced vegetables," Bishop sighed. "Nomia takes such good care of me when I stop here. Thank her for me."

"Of course, Proctor," the maid bowed before leaving them.

"Is this food dangerous for me?" Gregory asked.

"No. Nomia's cook is skilled. They have to be, since I visit. The meal will fill you to your breaking point, so eat slowly and let your aether process it. Savor it, in other words. Same with the wine; sip it slowly."

Gregory's eyes widened after taking a small sip of the wine, "What is this made from?"

"Rosem. The berries must be picked just before they fully ripen.

If they are picked late, the whole barrel will spoil. Rosem wine is good for helping the body process aether from bane beasts. Now *eat.*"

The moment the first bite hit his tongue, a shock of energy raced into him as the meat dissolved, leaving a hint of orange that quickly faded. Eyes wide, he speared some vegetables and ate them too. The shock of energy faded and a lighter orange flavor lingered. The aether inside him perked up without becoming active.

"This is similar to what you will receive in the academy... well, it's technically a bit better than a novice gets, honestly," Bishop said after swallowing. "Slowly, savoring it... that is the best way to enjoy this meal." She smiled, eating with a languid happiness.

Gregory did his best to eat as slowly as Bishop did, but it was hard because his aether was eager to have more of the feast.

The meal passed with a slow deliberateness that Gregory was not used to. By the time he finished, his aether felt full to bursting. Bishop pushed her chair back, "I'm off to use the bath. It'll be an hour, and then your turn will come. If you are going out, be sure to be back by then."

Finishing the last of the wine, Gregory watched her go. *Should I head to the scrivener first, or the smith?* After a moment's thought, he decided to visit the smith. He wanted to get a set of utensils, in case they were not supplied at the academy.

When he left the inn, Gregory saw that the streets were busier and the sky was starting to redden as the sun slid behind the horizon. He knew he was acting like an idiot, but he could not help but stare at the different clothes and buildings as he went by.

It took him five minutes to walk to the next square, passing a handful of other streets as he went. He had to pause as a group of men in dark red livery embroidered with flames marched past him.

"Wonder who they are?" Gregory muttered when he was able to cross the street.

"That was the resident magi's men," a stranger said, having overheard him and walking the same way. "New to town?"

"Yes. I'm passing through."

"Don't get on the bad side of them and you'll be fine," the man chuckled before turning down another street. "Good day."

"Good day," Gregory replied as he passed the scrivener shop. *Smith first, but at least I know where this place is now.* Seeing the sun sinking even lower, he hurried his pace, not wanting to miss his chance.

As he hurried down the street, several people watched him with various degrees of interest. Three men started to follow him, evil intent in their eyes.

"Fringe dweller," one of them chuckled to the other. "Not that he'll have much, but easy pickin's."

"Maybe," the second one snorted. "We'll at least have some fun hurting him."

When he reached the smithy, Gregory saw a man stepping out of the smaller building attached to the house. The man saw his hopeful expressions and snorted. "I just closed for the night."

"Sir, I'm a novice on my way to the academy," Gregory said. "I was hoping to buy a few items to make things easier for myself."

"Who brought you in?"

"Proctor Bishop."

A soft smile touched the man's lips, "Still doing the fringe walk, is she? I swear she enjoys it. I owe her a favor or two, so I'll help you." Turning back to the building, he pushed the doors open. "Come in."

Following the smith into the shop, Gregory waited while the man got a lantern lit. The reflective surfaces inside it focused the light on the counter. Behind the counter was a closed door, while the walls near the door had blades displayed on them.

"What are you looking for?"

"A short blade. Long enough to defend, but small enough to be viewed as a utility or dinner knife, and a set of utensils."

"I see you asked her the right questions," the smith chuckled. It took him a moment, but he retrieved a blade with six inches of steel above the hilt. The leather was plain, but finely stitched, and the blade shone, clearly indicating good steel masterfully forged.

"This is better work than I've ever seen," Gregory said in awe as he examined the blade.

"What village are you from?"

"Alturis."

"The ore for this blade came from there," the smith chuckled. "Good mine in that village. Not many impurities for me to work out. This blade is five hundred vela."

Gregory inhaled sharply before setting the blade down. "It is masterful work, but I can't afford that price."

"I don't barter," the smith said, "though considering your origin and who brought you, I will discount it to four hundred."

Gregory sighed, but he knew that he would need this blade from the hints Bishop had dropped over the last week. Pulling out the five hundred vela coin that Gunnar had slipped him, he set it on the counter.

The smith did not touch the coin, giving it a hard look. "Not many fringers have vela in that denomination."

"It was earned by slaying a bane wolf," Gregory replied matter-of-factly.

Eyebrows raised in surprise, the smith grunted, "A bold claim, but not one I'd expect you to idly bring up, which means this is part of the bounty."

"Proctor Bishop killed the beast and took the majority of it," Gregory said respectfully. "Those of us involved were surprised to get any coin."

"As you should be," the smith chuckled. "Any other proctor would have kept the entire bounty." He finally picked the coin up, handing Gregory two other coins in return. The new coins held the traditional holes in the middle denoting them as fifty vela each. "Was that all?"

"Bronze cutlery?" Gregory asked.

"Want to hide some of your origin?" the smith nodded. "A wise move. You should replace your boots, too. Let me get those utensils for you— fifty vela."

Gregory placed one of the new coins back on the counter, taking the cutlery in return. "Sir, would you be interested in buying this old blade?" Gregory asked. He knew that his old knife would mark him as out of place with its warped antler handle.

Examining it for a moment, the smith shook his head, "Not worth it, sorry."

"Very well," Gregory sighed, knowing it was not anywhere near as good as the blade he had just purchased.

The smith saw Gregory out before locking up again. As he turned toward his home, the smith caught sight of the two men following Gregory and sighed. After a moment's hesitation, he passed his house and headed up the street.

Gregory made his way back toward the scrivener's shop, hopeful it was still open. Halfway there, a small child stumbled out an alley in front of him, crying.

"Momma," the child sobbed, grabbing Gregory, "help Momma! Please." The small child tried to tug him toward the alley. "Please... help."

Gregory felt a pang, thinking of his own mother, and let the child guide him into the alley. As they reached the halfway point, the child let go of his sleeve and took off running. A man with a nasty smile stepped out, blocking the way as the child ran past him. Gregory looked behind to see two more, clubs in hand as they moved toward him.

"Give us what we want and no one gets hurt," the man in front said with a leer as he began to advance.

Pulling his old blade, Gregory did his best to sound convincing, "I'm a magi. Walk away, or else."

The larger man laughed, "Tell us another one, rube."

His aether churning in his chest, Gregory's hand tightened on the blade. "I don't want to hurt you."

"Tough. We *want* to hurt you," one of the men behind him laughed.

Fear crashed against him, but the burning aether pushed it away. Gregory felt a sense of calm envelop him. "Fine. I bet you're easier than a bane wolf."

Not waiting for the muggers to make their next move, he leapt at the big man. The mugger was surprised that the scrawny fringer attacked, but he pulled a cosh from behind him and deflected the blade.

"Eh, bunny has teeth, does he?" the mugger laughed and shoved Gregory back. "I'll enjoy this even more now."

The sound of feet rushing toward him from behind should have made Gregory worry, but he did not panic. The warmth of the aether in his chest soothed him. Bringing the blade up, he attacked the big man again. Aether flared inside him as his blade came down. The mugger went to deflect it again, laughing.

The laughter cut off abruptly when Gregory's blade cut cleanly through the cosh and lodged in the big man's chest. Gurgling, he clutched at the hilt and Gregory let it go, just as surprised at what had happened.

"Henrich!" one of the muggers shouted.

That was enough to snap Gregory out of his shock. He bolted past the dying man and out onto the street. Not pausing, he hurried away just as the sound of whistles started to blow behind him.

He ran the entire way back to the inn. Gasping as he stumbled into the tap room, he looked back along the street. There was no one chasing him.

"Is everything alright?" the matron asked from behind the bar.

"Yes..." Gregory managed after a moment. "Sorry." Keeping his head down, he hurried up to his room.

Gregory collapsed onto his bed, his aether churning inside him and making him feel ill. *What do I do? I killed him and ran. The whistles must have been the guard. Do I tell Bishop?*

A knock on his door made Gregory groan. Pushing himself to his feet, he winced at the tightening of his gut. A couple of unsteady steps brought him to the door and he opened it. Instead of her usual uniform, Bishop was wearing a robe, cinched tightly at the waist. Her hair was still damp, and Gregory figured her bath had just ended. "Yes, Proctor?"

"Let me in so we can talk."

Gregory held the door open for her, then staggered back to his bed. Collapsing onto it, he wheezed, his gut churning harder and faster.

"Did you use your aether?" Bishop asked.

"Didn't mean to, but yes," Gregory grunted.

"Tell me what happened," Bishop commanded as she moved over to the bed and began to gently prod him.

Gregory told her what had happened between hisses of pain as she prodded his gut. "I was about to come tell you, but you came to me first."

"It'll settle down shortly. You didn't do any damage to your core as far as I can tell, lucky for you. It is hard to control without training. I'm surprised you managed to escape unharmed."

"How did I cut through his weapon?"

"Aether can do many things. Using it without training can possibly damage your core, so try to refrain from using it without a trained magi nearby until you learn how to control it."

"I will do my best, Proctor."

"Rest. Your bath will be soon. Do not fight the maid and do what she tells you to do. It will help soothe your aether. Understood?"

"Yes, Proctor."

"I will see you at midday."

Gregory nodded, flopping back onto his bed when she left. The cramps in his gut did seem to be easing up, but it was not quick and it was not pleasant.

CHAPTER 10

G regory's pain had eased by the time there was a soft knock on his door. He answered, "Can I help you?"

A woman with fox ears wearing a maid outfit stood just outside. "I'm Jess, sir. I'm here to bathe you. Are you ready?"

"Umm, not sure what I need," Gregory admitted, staring at her in shock.

"A change of clothing is all," Jess replied. "If you want, we can have your boots and clothes cleaned and returned in the morning, as well."

"Oh, yes, please," Gregory said, turning to open the armoire. He rummaged through his clothes, trying to find a set that was not road stained.

"We can clean all of those if you wish, sir."

"Oh, that would be nice. Thank you."

Jess smiled, "It is our pleasure, sir. Just leave them next to the door, and I'll have them collected."

Finding a single change of clothes that were not dirty, he breathed a sigh of relief. He dropped his dirty clothing by the door and slung his clean tunic and pants over his shoulder, smiling at her.

"Follow me, sir," Jess said, walking ahead of him down the hallway.

Gregory was mesmerized by the red-furred tail that came out of a slit in her uniform. It gently swayed side to side, in counterpoint to her hips. "Miss... are you an eurtik?" he asked, unable to stop himself.

"My grandmother was, and as you can see, the blood runs strong in my family. Did you wish another to care for you instead?" Jess asked, pausing just in front of a door.

"Umm... no. I just... I've never seen anyone with eurtik blood before."

"You will see more like me, and even some purebloods, I'm sure," Jess replied softly. She opened the door and led him into the room beyond.

The room was tiled, dominated by a large bronze tub that was easily big enough for two people. Steam was drifting up from it and an assortment of soaps and oils were laid out beside it. Three fluffy cloths lay on a waist-high padded table that was across the room.

"Please strip and get into the tub," Jess instructed him.

Gregory stood there in shock, not quite sure he believed what he was hearing. "But, umm?"

"I know. You are a fringer and might not understand, but it is fine. This is one of my tasks."

Do not fight the maid. Do what she tells you, Bishop's voice echoed in his mind. Taking a deep breath, Gregory stripped and gingerly stepped into the tub. The water was right on the edge of being too warm, but he was grateful to not be on display. Sighing as he settled into the tub, he glanced back at Jess. His jaw dropped and his eyes widened.

Jess had stripped, leaving herself completely exposed to him. Her smile widened as she moved across the room to him, her hips swaying slightly as she walked. Eyes twinkling, she slowed her pace, taking her time getting to him. "Is this your first time seeing a woman naked, too?"

"Umm... uhhh... yes," Gregory stammered. His cheeks turned a bright red that had nothing to do with the heat of the bath. "You're beautiful."

Her laugh was light as she came to a stop beside the bath. "Thank you, sir, but there is no need for flattery. Would you prefer the orange, vanilla, or jasmine soap?" Taking each bar, she held them up for his examination as she knelt beside the tub.

Having trouble keeping his eyes off her body, he took each bar and sniffed it before handing them back. "Vanilla, please."

"My favorite," Jess purred and returned the other two to the small table they had been resting on. "Please slide forward some. I will be cleaning your back first."

Gregory did so, which removed her from his line of sight and allowed him the chance to calm down. Or it would have, if she had not stepped into the tub behind him. Her long legs slid to either side of him as she eased herself into the tub.

His mind going blank, Gregory did not say anything as her soft hands worked to lather soap across his back. Jess was silent, her touch soft, but firm enough to work the soap into his skin.

She leaned forward, and Gregory became aware of her small firm breasts pressing into his back. "Raise your arms, sir, please."

Gregory did so at once. Jess let out a pleased giggle as she reached out, working on his right arm first. When she had soaped that arm, she took his left arm and her fingers faltered for a moment.

"What happened to your arm, sir?"

"Bane wolf," Gregory replied. "I had to drag it off my friend."

"Barely an adult and a novice, and you fought a bane wolf bare-handed?" Jess asked, her voice curiously intent.

"It was that or death," Gregory replied.

"Your friend lived?"

"Proctor Bishop killed it once I dragged it off Gunnar."

"Still, it was very brave to grapple with one of them."

"I just did what was needed," Gregory said truthfully.

"As a hero would say," Jess whispered in his ear while she finished soaping his arm. "I will have to treat you extra special now." More of her body pressed against him as her arms went around his chest.

"Please enjoy your bath, sir." Soft lips brushed his ear, and Gregory shuddered.

Jess kept up with the same soft, gentle, and firm touch as she cleaned him. Gregory was having difficulty keeping his hands to himself. When she had him stand to wash his legs, he tried not to think of his erect cock pointing straight at her.

Her hands began at his calves and worked up his legs, but it was her tongue licking at his shaft that made him gasp. Gregory startled and looked down to see her peering back up at him through her eyelashes. She pulled back slightly, smiling, and took the head of his rigid shaft into her mouth as she continued to wash his legs.

"Oh, Aether," Gregory moaned, his legs trembling.

She giggled, clearly pleased by his reaction. Her head bobbed, slowly at first while she kept eye contact with him. After a few seconds, Gregory got an idea. Unable to resist, he grabbed Jess firmly by the head and began to rock his hips, forcing his cock in and out of her mouth. She moaned, the sound vibrating along his shaft. Her hands moved up his legs to fondle his balls.

The aether inside him settled down as he picked up the pace with his hips. After a few minutes, Gregory shuddered and pulled Jess tightly to him as he emptied his seed into her mouth.

Letting go of her, Gregory grabbed the edge of the tub and eased himself back into the water, his breathing ragged. Jess coughed for a moment before she leaned forward and kissed his cheek. "Well done, Novice. I hadn't thought you'd be that aggressive, but it is something I do enjoy. I am done cleaning you, so just relax while I get the next part ready."

Gregory laid back, letting the warm water cover him. He felt his aether subside, returning to the calm flame he was becoming more familiar with. While he lounged, he wondered about the flashes of insight he had started having. *I wonder if it's connected to you, Aether? I'll just need to ask when I speak with you again.*

Another thought occurred to him. *If this is a bath, I find myself liking them... but does that mean that Bishop...?* Gregory shut the train of thought down, not ready to consider that possibility.

"When you are ready, sir, we can continue," Jess said from beside the padded table.

"Huh?"

"The oil massage comes next. I just need you to come lie down over here for me." She patted the table. "Once the oil is done, we have a couple of other options which you might find appealing." A slow wink and smile made Gregory shudder as his blood again headed south.

Climbing out of the tub, he moved to the table and did as she requested. "I'd like to hear more about the options."

Warm breath tickled his ear as Jess leaned down to whisper to him, "This is just for tonight, but please, consider it my gift to a hero who risked his life for his friend. I'll be anything you want me to be, and I'll do everything you want."

CHAPTER 11

Stretching as he woke, Gregory felt like he could take on the world. The spot beside him was empty, and he sighed. Jess had told him multiple times that it was a one-time thing, but Gregory wished it could have been more. His time with Amoria had been wonderful; full of love, if a bit awkward, while his night with Jess had been one of lust and experimentation. He knew he would always be grateful to the both of them for showing him two very different sides to sex.

As he got out of bed, he saw that his clothing was just inside the door, folded and clean, and his boots were the cleanest he had ever seen them. He packed everything away and caught the faint scent of vanilla still lingering on his skin, making him think of Jess again. Shaking his head, he got dressed and left the room.

The common room was mostly empty, with just two old men sitting by the large window playing a game of Go. Gregory glanced at the board as he went past, but the game seemed to be evenly matched.

A maid bustled over almost as soon as he sat down. "Breakfast?"

"Please, and some tea, too?"

"We have mint, black, and orange," the maid offered. "Which would you like?"

"Mint, please."

The food was not as rich as dinner had been, but it still made his stomach and aether feel pleasantly full. He finished off the tea with a sigh. "I can't believe I'm going to eat even half as well at the academy."

Once he was finished eating, Gregory set off to the scrivener. The walk was uneventful, though Gregory could not help glancing at anyone who seemed interested in him. The door to the scrivener's was closed, but Gregory could see a man working through the large front window. Entering the shop, Gregory called out, "Excuse me, sir."

"I'll be with you in a moment," the balding man called back. "Feel free to look, but do not touch any of the books."

"Yes, sir."

The titles of many of the books made no sense to him, and he saw more than one that appeared to be in some other language. There were a few tomes in cases, behind glass. Gregory looked at the titles, wondering. *The Dryad's Kiss, Darkness Comes,* and *Temptation's Enticement* all had a certain tone to them, but Gregory could not believe stories of that kind would be written down.

"There we are," the scrivener sighed as he slipped away from his work bench. Moving the costly glasses from his nose, the man frowned at Gregory. "Have you come to the wrong shop?"

"No, sir. I am interested in a book or two," Gregory said. "Proctor Bishop suggested this shop to me."

"Must still be serving on the fringes," the scrivener muttered, then asked, "What books are you interested in?"

"Anything that will help me at the academy. As you stated, I'm from the fringes. I know that I could use help to catch up to the others."

Lips tight, the scrivener grumbled, "I can't do charity."

"I can pay some," Gregory said.

"Each book normally costs five hundred vela or more," the scrivener said bluntly. "Books are for the learned."

"I can afford at least one," Gregory said, pulling the lavender-scented five hundred vela coin from his bag. Gregory tried not to think of Amoria as he held out the coin that she had given him.

Seeing the vela, the scrivener frowned. "Bishop isn't one for charity, either. Where did you get the coin?"

"A bounty payment," Gregory bristled slightly. This was the second merchant who had implied indirectly that it might be stolen.

"Bounty for what?"

"A bane wolf. It wounded me and my friend, Gunnar Emery. We got part of the bounty because we were fighting it when Proctor Bishop showed up and dispatched it."

Seeing the scrivener's disbelief, Gregory rolled his sleeve up to show him the scars. When he saw the damage to Gregory's arm, the scrivener's lips pursed. "How many died?"

"None, but Gunnar was almost killed. I was able to pull the beast from him before the worst happened."

"Hmm. Novices who fight bane beasts and seek to gain knowledge before they arrive at the academy? I feel like this year's class will be interesting. I have a scroll and a book that you would find useful. The book is an in-depth history of the empire, and the scroll trains one in the beginning steps of the spirit path. Following its teachings will stop you from delving into body or mind paths. Which would you like?"

Gregory took a moment to consider before replying, "The history book, please, sir."

"A wise choice," the scrivener smiled.

Moving off to one of the bookshelves, he pulled down the book and a scroll, handing them both to Gregory. The book was called *Empire's Founding*. The scroll was blank on the outside as far as Gregory could see.

"I only have the vela for one," Gregory said.

"True," the scrivener said, taking the coin from him. "Consider it an investment for the future. Remember my shop if you need more in the future; Babel's Books."

"Thank you, Babel. I will."

"Keep them away from flame and liquids," Babel said sternly. "A ruined book is a travesty."

Gregory bowed to the scrivener, tucking the scroll into his pouch and the book under his arm. The scrivener smiled before dismissing him and going back to his work.

"Never thought I'd own a book," Gregory said, talking to himself when he was back on the street. The thick tome was heavier than he would have expected, but he could carry it without difficulty. "Or buy one... and from a scrivener, no less."

Gregory went back to the inn, intensely curious about what he could learn from the book and scroll.

* * *

The book turned out to be a dry recounting of the empire's founding. Gregory read through the first part, going back to reread a few paragraphs to understand them better.

War leader Toja didn't trust the eurtiks; their visage, which melded beast and human, seemed wrong to him. When the eurtiks sent an emissary to the king, war leader Toja had a dozen magi and a thousand men on hand, while the eurtiks sent a meager thirty. No one was prepared for the chaos that came.

The feast was the last bright point of the Kingdom of Welton. While everyone slept that night, the thirty eurtiks crept from their rooms for their real mission. Toja had remained awake, burning his aether, so the first shadow that tried to slip past him never made it— his flame blade cut it down. That roused the eurtiks and their true, savage nature was shown when they became wreathed in red flames.

Toja did everything he could, but his magi were ineffective against the eurtiks. The eurtiks had agility and strength far beyond normal men. Toja was hard pressed to save even himself. When the long night ended, the eurtiks were dead, but the entire royal family was, as well. Standing with the thirty survivors of his men, Toja declared a blood feud with the eurtiks. He gathered the wealthy and powerful from the city, forcing them to bend knee to him. With their backing, he declared himself the new king and started to build an army for the First Eurtik War.

Gregory paused as he finished the section of the book. *Toja, the Divine Emperor... he's been alive for all these generations. Magi can live far longer than normal, but here, he wasn't at the divine tier yet.*

Gregory wondered what that would mean for him. If he survived the academy, he would far outlive his friends. *Maybe that's why magi never come back... it would be hard to see friends and family dying while you still lived in your prime.*

"Hard at work studying?" Bishop asked, making Gregory jerk in startlement. He had not heard her approach. She chuckled at his surprise. "You'll have days of reading ahead of you. Hopefully, you can understand what you read. That will be critical."

"I'm doing my best, Proctor," Gregory replied. "The wording is... odd."

"The language is archaic and advanced," Bishop corrected him. "I'm reminded that your education is minimal. What book did you get?" Gregory told her the title and Bishop nodded, "That's a good start. We'll be leaving in three hours."

"He also gave me a scroll, Proctor," Gregory said, pulling the scroll from his pouch.

Taking it, Bishop opened it and read some of what was inside. "Tsk, he should know better. This is a scroll that will prejudice your path if you follow its teachings."

"What if I don't do what it says, but just read it to understand more, Proctor?"

Bishop paused, "A good question, Novice. If you can stop yourself from following the instructions, you would learn what the first steps of the spirit path entail. What you do with it is up to you."

"Thank you, Proctor."

When Bishop moved away, Gregory sighed. Focusing his attention back on the book, he continued to read, slowly and with difficulty, but with determination.

* * *

"It is time," Bishop said, startling him again.

Rubbing at his tired eyes, Gregory grunted, "Yes, Proctor."

Bishop chuckled, "You have ten minutes. The carriage is outside."

When he got outside, Gregory could not help but stare at the carriage. The whole thing was painted sky blue with silver trim, and the emblem of the empire was affixed to the door. He gave his bag to the driver to be tied with the other luggage atop the vehicle, but held on to his book. The interior had padded seats and curtains that were currently tied back to let the light in. Taking a seat next to the window, he placed the book beside him, content to rest his eyes for a moment.

"Already here? Good," Bishop said. "Driver, we are here. You may go." Hopping into the carriage, she shut the door. "You may read or nap. The next stop will be at Fentic, which will be just before sunset. Did you enjoy your stay?"

"The room and food were amazing," Gregory replied.

"And the bath?" Bishop asked with a twisted smile.

Gregory coughed and looked out the window. "Educational."

Laughing lightly, Bishop nodded, "I'm sure it was."

"I was wondering, Proctor, what became of the muggers?"

"The thugs who attacked you were taken before the city magistrate," she told him. "They are paying for their crimes now. Two of them, anyway. The other died from his wounds."

The carriage lurched as the driver cracked the whip and got the four horses moving. Gregory looked out the window, unsure of how he felt about what had become of the men who attacked him. His aether pulsed, and a happy feeling welled up inside of his chest.

"That kind of thing happens in the empire. You've been removed from it out on the fringe, but that and worse are common. Do you know what punishment the men who attacked you are likely to get?" Bishop asked as she settled back into the seat.

"No, Proctor."

"Servitude," Bishop replied simply. "They will be required to serve the empire for a set length of time. If they fail in their duty or commit another crime during that period, their lives are forfeit or they will become slaves. Have you gotten to that part of the history yet?"

"No, Proctor," Gregory admitted.

"You will. I'm going to rest for a bit. I didn't get much sleep last night," Bishop said, and leaned her head against the doorframe. "Don't worry about keeping it down; you won't bother me." A moment later, a soft and almost delicate snore came from Bishop.

Watching her for a moment, Gregory wondered what he should do. After a few minutes of watching the city go by, he picked the book back up and started reading again.

CHAPTER 12

The days flew by, as did the towns and cities. Gregory had at first been surprised at how fast the carriage traveled when they were between the various settlements. Bishop had answered his question with a simple, "Enchantment," before going back to her own amusements. They had changed carriages at Kendlin to the one that would take them to Wesrik. Gregory felt a bit of disappointment that no other inn they stayed at offered the same type of bathing that the Proctor's Rest had. He had noticed an increase in the number of servants with eurtik blood, and had even seen a couple of pureblooded eurtik working at the inns they stayed at.

With the carriage getting closer to Wesrik, Gregory asked a question that had been bothering him, "Proctor, I read in the history where the emperor instituted slavery and servitude. But, that was over a thousand years ago. Why is it still in place today?"

Bishop eyed him with a raised eyebrow. "That question would cause you a lot of problems if voiced in front of someone else. The answer is because once an institution is set up, it is hard to pull down. We've ingrained distrust and hatred of the eurtik into the very fabric of the empire. It isn't just the eurtik who are servants and slaves, though; it has spread as a way of keeping the peace. Do you know the difference between a servant and a slave?"

"Slaves have no rights; they are property and owned by the one who has their control rune. A slave who touches a control rune dies, and in the history book, it says that many eurtiks chose that death. The one who creates the runes can place restrictions on what the slave can and can't do, and pain is used as the control if they break their restrictions. Servants are constrained by the rules imposed on them when they became servants. They are still people and are to be treated well by their keeper. Servants are housed, fed, and cared for. If they aren't, then the servants are to be freed or their debt surrendered to another."

"The men who attacked you were forced into servitude as labor for the city. That is why the system is still in place. They will spend the next three years working off their crime. If they commit any other crime or fail in their duties, they will become slaves instead. Now, who can create a rune for slavery or institute the servant pact?"

"Magus and higher tiered magi can create slave runes, while adepts and higher can create the servant pact. Only a grandmaster and above can break a rune, but the pacts fade after a set time, or they can be broken early by a master or up."

"Correct. Now, how can you tell if someone is a servant or slave?"

"There is no way to tell for a servant," Gregory replied. "Slaves have a brand in the shape of their rune somewhere on their body, though it is most commonly on the arm or chest, Proctor."

"Well done. You are picking up your history well. I doubt any of that was covered in your village."

"It wasn't. We had no servants, slaves, or eurtiks. Have you known any half-bloods that weren't servants?"

"Many, though they have a rougher time of it than others."

"Are there any pureblood eurtiks who aren't slaves?"

"Besides babies? None. The law states that all purebloods must be bound to slavery for the good of the empire."

"But why? The Eurtik Empire fell nearly a thousand years ago. For a hundred years or two, it might have made sense, but now?"

Bishop shook her head, "Never say that to another person. You'd be viewed as an anarchist at best. Understood, *Novice*?"

Hearing the stress on his rank, Gregory bowed his head. "I will do as you say, Proctor."

"Have you looked over the scroll?" Bishop asked to change the subject.

"I did, Proctor. It focuses on how meditation can improve your aether. Refine the flame so it can burn cleaner, and use less aether for anything you need it to do."

"Every path likes to claim that it's the best of the three," Bishop replied. "The body path focuses on bettering your physical body to increase how much aether you can move through your body without stress. Detractors would say that the body can only be improved so far, and then you stagnate. The mind path devotes itself to learning. Increasing one's mind can help your aether grow, giving you more aether to use. But, while that can lead to fast growth at the academy, once outside of its walls, the rate sharply declines. The spirit path, as you stated, focuses on mediation and knowing oneself to increase aether, but others point out that it is the slowest growing path. No one of great note has ever used it to rise to prominence."

"How does one choose which path is right for them, Proctor?"

"The clans at the academy will each do their best to recruit you, but it is best to wait until you have been enrolled into the academy before you choose."

"Why is that, Proctor?"

"When you enroll, you will be taken to the Blade, which will let you know which magical path is yours to tread." Seeing his interest, Bishop decided to skirt the line of what she could tell him. "Everyone is predisposed to a magical path. Mine is physical enhancement, which is why I can do some of the things you've seen me do. Others are on the path of one of the elements: fire, water, earth, or wind; and some are set on the path of crafting: alchemy, enchanting and the like. Since my magic is physical enhancement, it was best for me to follow the body path, as together, there was an increased effectiveness."

Gregory stared out the window, thinking about how little he knew of his aether and what that might mean for him. The body path would probably be a bad idea; he was painfully thin, though that had begun to change over the last week with good food every day. Following the path of the mind would be interesting. He had discovered he enjoyed learning new things, though he worried about the drop off of growth that Bishop mentioned. Spirit he could not decide about. Meditating seemed like it would be a good path and easy to do, but the fact that no one in over a thousand years had followed it and made a name for themselves worried him.

"What is it you want from your time at the academy, Novice?" Bishop asked after the silence had lasted for over an hour.

"I don't know," Gregory admitted. "To grow stronger, to serve the empire, to be like Lionel Lighthand and the other great magi? I'm not even sure what the academy does, besides teaching novices to become magi."

"A blank slate," Bishop murmured. Clearing her throat, she spoke up, "The normal answers are power, prestige, and wealth. A few like to speak of helping the family they came from, while others are about helping grow the clan they join. It is a question that all novices confront in their own way. Why did you yearn so fiercely to be a magi?"

Another long silence fell as Gregory tried to find the right words to reply. *Why did I want it so much? I loved the stories that Mother told me, but it had to be more than that? Was it stubbornness? Wanting to prove everyone wrong when they told me it wouldn't happen?*

Gregory was still lost in thought when the carriage began to slow. Jolted from his thoughts, he blinked, looking out the window to see a tall white wall stretching into the distance.

"Wesrik," Bishop told him. "You've been thinking for over an hour."

"I'm sorry, Proctor," he apologized. "I still don't have an answer for you. I think it might have been a number of factors, but my mother's death played a large role in it. She always encouraged my childish whim, and then she was gone. It might have been the faint hope that, as a magi, I could find answers as to what happened."

"You held to it for years, against your father's objections and the villagers deriding your dream as fantasy. That determination will help you in the coming years. If you can hold to something as strongly as you did that wish, you will go far, Novice. I hope you find what you desire."

Bowing his head, Gregory felt humbled, "Thank you, Proctor. I will do my best."

"Good. Your mother would have wanted that," Bishop replied. "Now, turn your eyes to the city. There is only one city grander than Wesrik in all of the empire."

"Hikari," Gregory said the name of the capital on reflex.

"Yes. Wesrik has only a fourth of its population, but as home of the academy, it has almost equal sway in the empire."

Gregory looked out the window at the homes and businesses that spilled beyond the wall. The main road going to the city was paved, but he could see that other streets were dirt. Gregory noticed that even the outermost buildings were better built than the ones in Alturis, but they did not compare to what he could see inside the walls. As they neared one of the main gates, the carriage slowed even more, joining the queue of wagons, carriages, and foot traffic funneling into the city.

"How many people?" Gregory half asked as he stared.

"Thousands of times the size of your village," Bishop answered. "Wesrik was last known to house over half a million people."

Gregory blinked, not really able to comprehend a number that big. "How can that be?"

"Because here, the empire pours resources into helping the city run. You'll learn. All novices learn how the empire runs. As you advance, you'll also help the empire run."

Getting closer to the open gates, Gregory began to realize just how massive the walls really were. They were thirty feet tall and half that thick, and had been built of white stone that joined together with barely any seam visible between the stones. The carriage rattled through the corridor between the inner and outer gates. Gregory caught sight of metal grating that could be dropped to close the passage, as well as the numerous arrows slits and murder holes above them.

"When was the city last attacked, Proctor?" Gregory asked as they exited the tunnel.

"The last eurtik incursion five hundred years ago," Bishop replied, "if the histories are correct."

His next question was forgotten as the lower ring came into view. The streets were cobbled, and the buildings were constructed of wood or stone with slate roofs. His mind reeled, trying to think how much space even half of these buildings would take up in Alturis, and here, they were lined up as far as he could see.

"The lower ring, unlike the outer ring, is regularly patrolled and cared for. The cheapest of registered merchants can be found inside this ring. All kinds of goods, entertainment, and other distractions can be found here, for a price."

Eyes darting all about, Gregory noted that most of the buildings on the main street were businesses of one kind or another. The little he could see down the side streets and alleys hinted that that was where people lived.

They traveled on the main road as it wound to the north, the sun starting its descent as midday came and went. It took them over an hour to reach the next gate. The walls here towered forty feet into the air, while still being half as thick. Looking back, Gregory was able to see the slope of the ground which helped raise the second wall even higher. The gates here were thicker, and reinforced with bands of metal.

When they passed through the tunnel from the lower ring to the inner ring, Gregory's jaw dropped again. The inner ring had buildings of stone— mostly marble— with solid sloped roofs that would never have to worry about the weather. The wealth on display was hard for him to even think about. The buildings were larger here, taking up more space than in the previous ring, and the signs informed him that these shops were more ornate.

A four-story building that took up more space than any other stood almost isolated from its closest neighbors. The traffic coming and going from it was significantly less than any of the other buildings they had passed.

"Auction house?" Gregory muttered, puzzled by the unfamiliar word on the sign.

"The auction houses of the empire help facilitate the selling of goods not normally found in regular shops. Their goods can range from art, treasures, rare ingredients for crafts, or in the rarest cases, items of power from other kingdoms, ancient ruins, or from noble families who find themselves fading. Nothing inside those walls fails to impress those who go to bid on them."

"Have you ever been, Proctor?"

"Once, many years ago," Bishop said softly, her eyes going distant.

Seeing her withdraw into a memory, Gregory stayed silent, but he did notice how her hand touched the hilt of her sword. His focus shifted when he caught sight of the academy tower thrusting into the air inside the next ring of walls.

It took them nearly another hour to reach the next gate. The stone walls here towered sixty feet into the air, and the gates were no longer wood, but solid metal. Before them stood two dozen guards and a magi in emerald robes.

"Ah, it appears we are almost at the end of our journey together, Novice," Bishop said. "I will see you settled before we part ways."

"My thanks, Proctor."

As the carriage approached, one of the guards stepped forward to inspect it before he motioned to the gate. One of the massive winches atop the wall began to move, and one of the metal doors swung ponderously open for them.

Gregory felt the end of his old life and the start of his new one as the carriage rolled forward. Memories of friends, family, and even a lover flashed before him. Smile in place, Gregory felt his aether stir inside of him as they crossed the threshold of the academy grounds.

CHAPTER 13

The carriage came to a stop just inside the gates. Bishop got out, with Gregory close behind her. The driver was quick to hand down their bags, not wanting to delay them.

Gregory blinked at the large building just inside the gate that abutted the wall. Five stories tall, it was one of the tallest he had ever seen.

"Come on, Novice," Bishop said, shouldering her bags and already moving toward the building.

Gregory quickly picked up his bag and hurried after her, forcing his mouth shut. When he entered the building, he managed to not gape, but his eyes were still wide. The interior was all white marble with streaks of black and red. A number of small dark wood tables dotted the room, with cushions next to them. Decorative screens and potted plants helped break up the room, so it was not a massive cavern.

Gregory just managed to keep from bumping into Bishop when she stopped in front of a desk. The tall redhead sitting there turned to address Bishop first. "Proctor Bishop, you brought us one? First one in three years."

"John Hardin? I'm surprised you're still in this position," Bishop replied. "I wish it was more, but no one knows what Aether plans."

"I can't refute that," Hardin chuckled as he started to pull papers out of the desk. "Fill out the forms. You know the drill."

"Thank you," Bishop bowed her head, accepting the stack.

Gregory sat at one of the low tables with Bishop while she filled out the forms. His attention was drawn to the double doors when they opened again, revealing another proctor with a novice. The novice was slender, with pale skin and long platinum blonde hair flowing down her back. She glanced at Gregory with startlingly blue eyes, looking away when he smiled.

"Ah, Proctor Harrison. Unlike some others, you always bring us at least one novice every year," Hardin said in greeting.

"Some of us haven't been banished to the worst of the fringe," Harrison's voice carried a rough edge.

"Some haven't kissed enough polished asses to be rewarded with a more cushioned post, either," Bishop said as she filled out the next form. "I wonder when some proctors last had to defend their novices from anything more than salty soup?"

"Bishop," Harrison spat the name as he turned to sneer at her, "I didn't see you there. It must be your lack of standing, in all ways."

Bishop shook her head as she capped the ink and cleaned the pen nib. "Some of us aren't so lacking in motivation that we wish to be carried on the soft cushions of fat clans. When was the last time you even had to draw your blade, Harrison?"

"Three years ago, when some bitch made me challenge her," Harrison growled. "I've grown since then. Have you?"

"You could easily find out," Bishop said, rising to her feet fluidly and striding toward the desk Hardin occupied, "but I doubt you'll risk losing face to your clan again."

"At least my clan isn't a shell, forgotten and wasting away. Does your clan head even still draw breath? No one has seen him in twenty years."

Bishop did not reply, instead handing the papers to Hardin. "The forms. I shall take him to the Blade now."

"Protocol has changed since you last brought a novice," Hardin said stiffly. "You are to wait for a master to come for you and the novice."

Bishop's expression was bored as she received the new information. "So be it."

"If you will fill out these forms," Hardin told the other proctor, "I shall call for the master so both of your novices can go together."

With an annoyed grunt, the other proctor snatched the papers, ink, and pen from Hardin, then stalked off to one of the tables. The novice with him scurried after him, clearly uncomfortable. Bishop did not bother to watch them, but returned to the table she had been at moments ago. Gregory followed her, casting another glance at the other novice.

"Proctor," Gregory said softly to not disturb the others, "you fought him three years ago?"

"Challenges of honor are a common event inside these walls. Three years ago, he challenged me. I won, and he lost standing with his clan and for his clan."

"What about your clan, Proctor?"

"As Harrison said, my clan is a shell of what it was in years past. We've lost most of our standing, wealth, and more in challenges to other clans."

"You don't seem upset about it."

"I'm sad, but I can't change the past. No one can. I will do what I can for my clan, as anyone should. I hope one day that it will rise in prominence again, but at this point, it will likely fade into obscurity. As the youngest of my clan, I will probably be the last of it."

"And good riddance," Harrison said loudly as he went back to the desk.

Bishop's eye twitched, "Some people don't know when to be civil. It's like having a wild hound nearby— it howls and barks as if it's the biggest beast in the world, but turns tail and runs when a bigger threat comes near."

Harrison spun on her, the forms dropping onto the desk, forgotten. "Who is the dog? You don't bother to even defend your clan.

You're like a beaten cur that whimpers when someone passes by, never fighting for yourself."

"If you are confident, you may challenge me," Bishop said, her back still turned to him. "I will ignore those who aren't worth my attention."

"Bitch!" Harrison hissed. "I challenge you, then! Do you dare back up your barking?"

Gregory saw the smile that flitted across Bishop's face before it vanished. "I accept. Terms are as follows: swords only, no aether. The reward shall be the year's stipend. Do you still wish to press your challenge?"

Harrison's hand tightened on the hilt of his sword, his nostrils flaring as he breathed hard. "Accepted."

"Tomorrow. The arena, at high sun," Bishop said nonchalantly, as if the whole thing was beneath her notice. "I'll arrange a suitable adjudicator."

"Fine."

A door opening cut off any further conversation as a man in cobalt robes entered the room. He paused for a moment, taking in the atmosphere before sighing. "Proctors, did you arrange a challenge, again?"

"I was challenged, Master," Bishop said. "All I was doing was waiting for you to arrive."

"Lying bi—"

"*Proctor,*" the master said sharply, cutting him off, "there is a young lady present. Restrain your phrasing."

"Bishop misrepresents, Master, but yes, we have agreed on a challenge for tomorrow."

"If you would be so kind as to adjudicate for us, Master Damon?" Bishop asked, rising gracefully from her seated position and bowing, her right fist cupped by her left palm at chest height.

With another sigh, Damon shook his head. "I hadn't even thought you might bring a novice this year, Bishop, yet now I have a challenge to oversee in addition to my other duties. Tomorrow at high sun.

Now, put aside the differences you both have. Your novices need to be seen to."

"As you say," Bishop bowed again.

Harrison gritted his teeth, not saying anything as he bowed to the master.

Damon wore a small smile as he looked at the two novices. "Welcome to the academy, Novices. You have years of learning and growth ahead of you. During your years, you will befriend some, while making enemies," he paused to glance at the two proctors, "of others. Your old life is behind you. All that stands before you is your service to the empire and the joy of Aether."

Gregory got to his feet hurriedly and bowed like Bishop had. "Thank you, Master."

The other novice was quick to copy him. Her voice shook with timidity when she said, "Thank you, Master."

"Good, you are on the right foot. You will have a week before classes begin, but today is a joyous day, as we will see what your magic is. Follow me." Damon started for a door to the side of the room, his slippered feet not making a sound as he walked.

Gregory was quick to follow him. The other novice fell into step with him and the two proctors trailed them. The trip through the building took a few minutes, and involved going down a couple flights of stairs.

The sub-basement had a dozen iron doors, and two emerald-robed magi stood next to the largest at the end of the hall. Master Damon headed straight for them, and when they got close one of the two opened the door. The magi stood aside and bowed as Master Damon went through, followed closely by the novices and proctors.

Gregory's steps slowed as he entered the room. Jutting from the stone floor was a naginata, the blade sunk almost completely into one of the stone tiles. Dozens of different jewels were embedded into the silver bands near the head and endcap of the naginata. The blade and shaft were the blackest metal Gregory had ever seen, drinking in the light from the dozen lanterns that ringed the room.

"Aether's Blade," Bishop whispered reverently.

"Novices, remove your footwear and step forward to the line," Damon instructed.

Gregory blinked, pulling his eyes from the naginata. On the floor, a three-inch-wide slab of the same black metal was embedded in the floor, encircling the weapon. Quickly removing his boots, he stepped forward until his feet touched the line of metal. A shock of cold rushed into his body and made him shiver. Beside him, the other novice also shivered when she stepped on it.

"I want each of you to reach out and grasp the shaft of the naginata, one at a time," Damon commanded. "The gems will tell us your magic."

Gregory glanced at the other novice, who seemed afraid of doing as instructed. Taking a deep breath and reaching out, his hand wrapped around the shaft. His aether spluttered, dying down to the dimmest of banked coals, and his legs sagged. A wave of cold energy rushed up through his feet and into his body. When it reached his aether, the flame inside him roared to life, forcing his legs to straighten, then it rushed out through the hand touching the naginata.

The room was silent until the largest gem on the very end of the naginata began to pulse faintly with light. To Gregory, that moment seemed to take years. He watched as the gem began to glow, then brighten until it was almost blinding. Finally, after what felt like more long years, the gem's glow dimmed once more.

The three magi in the room eyed the gem with confusion. Damon spoke slowly, "I've never seen the ryuite glow, nor any gem glow that brightly. I need to see if it's recorded." As the last of the glow faded, Damon cleared his throat and spoke in a normal tone, "Novice, release the shaft and step back."

The moment his hand no longer touched the naginata, his aether returned to the small flame it had been. Staggering back a step, Gregory panted, feeling like he had just run for hours. He knelt on the floor, waiting for his strength to return to him.

The other novice was all but hyperventilating, but she reached out and grasped the weapon. The single black jade embedded in one of the silver bands of the naginata began to flicker. A soft glow grew in intensity inside the gem for a few seconds.

"A shadow," Damon whispered. "We haven't had a new shadow in a dozen years. Today is a momentous day, even considering her eurtik blood." Clearing his throat, he spoke in a normal tone, "Release the naginata and put your boots on, both of you."

When she released the weapon, the novice stepped back and stumbled. Gregory lunged over and caught her, setting her onto the floor gently. "You okay?"

"Dizzy... sorry. Thank you," she whispered.

"Release her," Harrison snapped.

Gregory gave her an apologetic smile and moved away. He pulled his boots back on, and was relieved to see her doing the same a moment later.

"Proctor, your novice will be sought after by many clans," Damon told Harrison. "I'm sure whoever she joins will be pleased with you, despite her heritage."

"Thank you, Master," Harrison smiled, bowing to the older man.

"Proctor, your novice strongly sparked the ryuite. Keep a close eye on him. What it means for his magic is unknown."

Bishop stared at Gregory for a long moment, her face blank. "I shall do as you say, Master."

"Come, the testing is over," Damon said, clearly eager to leave the room.

Gregory and the other novice pushed themselves to their feet and shuffled after Damon, both proctors following them. The door shut with a respectful snick when the guards closed it behind them and resumed their places before it.

Leading them back to the main floor, Damon bowed his head fractionally to the proctors. "See your novices to the dormitory and give them the information they require."

"Yes, Master," Bishop and Harrison said together, bowing to him.

"Novices, welcome to the academy. I shall pray to Aether for your success. Next week, your instruction begins."

"Thank you, Master," they said in unison, both of them bowing deeply.

Once Damon was gone, Harrison sneered at Bishop and Gregory. "I'm sure the ryuite is nothing of importance, Bishop. Don't think you've done something worthy of note. I'll be looking forward to tomorrow. Come, Novice. Keep up."

"Yes, sir," she replied softly, rushing after him.

Gregory watched him go and exhaled the anger he felt. "Has he always been so... unpleasant, Proctor?"

Bishop's lips twitched, "Harrison is who he is. Come now, Novice, I must see you settled, and then I can answer some of your questions about what your time will entail."

CHAPTER 14

G regory rubbernecked during the walk through the academy grounds, taking in everything he could. Bishop matched his pace, not hurrying him along. He did not understand why a plot of land with gravel, sand, and rocks had been raked. Another plot had small trees that had been shaped to look like normal sized ones, and a single man in an orange robe was carefully cutting pieces off one. A wooden bridge only wide enough for a single person took them over a stone-lined stream that was five feet wide. Multi-colored fish swam in the water, following the path of the stream.

They eventually came to a long three-story structure made of wood and white paper. He followed Bishop into the building, mimicking her when she paused just inside to remove her boots in favor of light slippers. They went past the front room and Bishop opened a sliding paper door. In the next room was a half-eurtik with furred round ears, sitting at a table.

"Proctor, another novice?" the woman asked, sipping from a cup of tea.

"Novice Gregory Pettit," Bishop said. "I'm to get him settled."

"He shall have the room next to the other new novice. Third floor, thirty-third room."

"Thank you, Keeper...?" Bishop let the sentence trail off in question.

"Keeper Dia, Proctor."

"Keeper Dia is the one who runs this dormitory, Novice. She is in charge of the servants, and her word is law inside these walls."

"An honor, Keeper," Gregory said, bowing formally to her.

A slight smile touched Dia's lips. "Thank you, Novice. If you have questions, you will find me here most of the time."

"Let's not take up her time. Follow me," Bishop said after the introduction was done.

Gregory followed Bishop to the third floor. They finally came to the room, which had a plaque on the wall next to it reading, "333." Opening the door, she motioned him inside. Gregory entered a square room marked off by the same paper walls that the entire structure appeared to be made of. It was twice the size of his old room; a mat and bedding were rolled up in one corner, and a low table and cushions sat in the middle.

"The wall across from you is the storage area," Bishop said as she placed her bags inside the door, taking a seat at the table.

Gregory moved to the sliding doors and found shelving reaching to the ceiling. On one of the shelves, there were two white outfits, some ink and paper, and a clear stone medallion in the shape of ten concentric circles. Putting his bag on the floor inside the closet, he closed the door and took a seat at the table.

"I will answer simple questions, but before that, let me tell you about what your first year will entail." Bishop paused, watching Gregory lean forward. "In a week, when instruction begins, you will have a number of classes. Since you reside on the third floor, your first class will be economics, followed by history, aether introduction, and physical conditioning. Physical conditioning is the only class that has all novices attending it at the same time. Each class is just short of two hours long, starting from the sixth bell. There is a break for an hour before physical conditioning so you can eat. If you require more supplies, speak with the keeper. She will impose a limit if she thinks you are being wasteful."

"Where can I get food?"

Bishop chuckled, "The mess hall. You'll find it easily if you follow your nose. You are allowed two meals and a small snack a day. Your medallion will get you your meals, and it tracks your growth."

"How should I divide up when I eat?"

"That is a good question. Break your fast before classes, snack before conditioning, and have dinner after. I found that to work best for me when I was a novice."

"Are there only novices in the building, Proctor?" Gregory asked.

"Mostly. A few apprentices might still reside within the walls if no clan has accepted them, and maybe an initiate or two."

"Is that normal, Proctor?"

"If they lack power or their magic is not sought after, there would be lack of interest from a clan. For this conversation, you may disregard my position."

"Wouldn't your clan accept them?"

"As the member is beholden to the clan, the clan is responsible for them," Bishop explained. "My challenge tomorrow is a good example; if I lose, it will cause loss of standing for my clan, making our position in bargaining with the other clans harder. That is why clans normally do not take the weakest, unless there is another reason. If the magi came from a wealthy background, they might be accepted, as that could open other avenues for them."

"The other novice... she has shadow magic. Why is that special?"

"Shadow magic has many uses, but the core of it is rooted in assassination and information gathering," Bishop explained. "Both of these things are highly sought after."

"How do I know what my magic is, if the master magi didn't?"

Bishop nodded slightly, "Another good question, Novice. You will have a chance during aether introduction to find out, unless Master Damon finds something hidden in the archives first. They show each magic in the class."

"Will he?" Gregory asked excitedly.

"Master Damon has been a master since my time here as a novice. He used to be the head assistant to the chief archivist. If anyone has a chance to find out what the ryuite represents, it is him or Chief Archivist Sarinia. I'm certain he will consult her if he can't find the answer himself. The one thing he hates is not knowing an answer."

"When we spoke of paths, you hinted that when I choose one, it will exclude the others. Why?"

"The number of magi who can grow their aether via multiple paths can be counted on the fingers of a single hand for the entirety of the empire. No one has *ever* managed to train using all three paths, except maybe the emperor, but no one knows, because he has never said."

"I need to choose a path to grow my aether?"

"Yes, but doing so before your magic is known might hinder your overall growth. If I had taken the spirit path with my physical enhancement magic, I wouldn't be able to do nearly as much as I do now."

"I should wait, then."

"That is the safest bet," Bishop nodded. "Unfortunately, that will likely put you at a disadvantage in the tournaments. You will be even further behind the others."

"Tournaments?"

"At the half year mark, the first novice tournament is held. It will help rank your class, and bring honor or dishonor to the clan you join based on your standing. There is a second tournament at the end of the year, as well. That one will help solidify your standing before moving onto the next tier. At the moment, all novices are supposed to be equal."

"But we aren't?"

"Not at all," Bishop smiled grimly. "Your past isn't supposed to matter when you arrive here, but as I said previously, having connections because of your birth still matter. You have none of that and an unknown magic. It will make people stand off until they know more. Use this time wisely."

Gregory lapsed into silence for a moment before he asked his next question, "Where are the books kept?"

"The archive... I could stop there, but I won't. It is located on the far side of the grounds from the gate. Respect anyone wearing black inside those walls; they are the keepers of the tomes. Any of them can help guide you to the right type of books, as that is part of their task. As a novice, the selection of books available to you will be limited, but it is a good place to learn."

"Is there anything else I should ask, Proctor?"

Bishop chuckled, "Do your best to make at least one friend, but be wary of false ones. Train as hard as you can in your chosen path, as well as physically. Study, and do not make enemies of the magi who teach you. Avoid as many conflicts as you can, but do not shy away from brutally putting down those that you can't avoid."

"You mentioned clans. Do I need to find one to join?"

"Clans pick who they want to join them. They will approach you. Joining a clan will get you help in training and a stipend for you to use."

"That would be helpful. Thank you, Proctor," Gregory said, bowing from his seat on the floor.

"I need to see about my own lodgings," Bishop said. "I will show you to the mess hall, if you are hungry?"

His belly growled, and Gregory blushed, "I will accept, Proctor."

Bishop laughed, "I remember what being young was like. Follow me, and don't forget your medallion."

* * *

The mess hall was a two-story building, with stairs on either side of the exterior that gave access to a balcony where magi in emerald, cyan, and cobalt were sipping tea or smoking. Gregory made out a set of large sliding doors in the middle of the balcony. "Where do those go, Proctor?"

"That is where the academy adepts, magus, and masters take their food normally," Bishop said. "No other tiers are allowed up there unless as the guest of a member of one of the aforementioned groups. The floor has a private kitchen where food is made to order, but only after the sixth bell. The first floor is different, and that is where your meals will be."

The interior of the mess hall was like nothing Gregory had seen before. Rows of low tables with cushions beside them filled over half the room. A half-wall divided the room, and the rest of the space was taken up by a large kitchen with four people working in it. Four eurtiks stood behind the wall, serving food to the magi who were lined up next to it.

Bishop joined the line of magi. She picked up a wooden tray and followed the person in front of her, and Gregory copied her. The first eurtik, a weasel, handed Gregory a small bowl of soup. The scaled one after him gave Gregory another small bowl containing salad. The third eurtik, a rat, motioned to the trays before him, which held a selection of cooked meats.

"Fowl?" Gregory said in question.

The eurtik smiled and placed a large serving of cooked fowl onto a plate, then passed it to the mink beside him.

"Rice," Gregory said, picking the same items as Bishop.

The mink scooped rice onto Gregory's plate and handed it to him with a smile. At the same time, she extended her hand to touch his medallion, which was glowing faintly.

"Thank you," Gregory said, returning the smile.

He followed Bishop to the side where pitchers and cups stood waiting on a small table with small baskets of utensils to one side. Gregory filled a cup with the same tea Bishop had chosen and picked up a set of utensils, as well. *Wish I had known they had them for use. I could have saved myself some vela*, Gregory sighed to himself.

He sat across from Bishop at one of the tables, and focused on his food. The soup was something he had never had before. It was thick and yellow, with bits of white floating in it. Covertly watching Bishop sip directly from the bowl, he did the same. The flavor of egg and corn washed over his tongue. It was warm, but not scalding, allowing him to enjoy it without pain.

His aether began to warm him from the inside as he ate. Unlike the meal at the Proctor's Rest, which his aether had accepted without reaction, this was different. His aether felt like it was burning the energy as it came into his core, making him a little uncomfortable.

"Hmm, potent," Bishop said, looking up at him. "Seems you are having problems. Sip the tea or eat some of the rice. Give each bite a chance to be accepted before eating more."

"Yes, Proctor."

Once he was doing as she said he was still uncomfortable, but it did not get worse. The meal took him longer than he would have anticipated, so he was glad he did not have to rush off to a class. *Make sure to give yourself lots of time to eat,* Gregory told himself.

When they both finished eating, Bishop showed him where the dirty dishes went. The otter eurtik took them with a smile. Exiting the mess hall, Bishop stepped aside and sighed. "That completes my duties as your proctor, Novice. I wish you the best in your education and path."

"Proctor," Gregory asked quickly, "would it be okay for me to watch your challenge with Harrison tomorrow?"

"It'll be held in one of the arenas," Bishop replied. "How you spend your time before classes start is up to you. Do your parents and village proud." With nothing else to say, she turned and walked off.

Gregory watched her go for a minute before he went back to the dormitory. The sun was setting, the last rays of sunlight supplemented by lanterns that had been lit while he was eating. He paused near a pool of fish. Gregory smiled when he spotted a much smaller fish darting among the larger ones. *That's how I feel, too,* he chuckled to himself before he started walking again.

CHAPTER 15

When he got back to the dormitory, he could hear voices from the left, just past the entry hall. Gregory put on his slippers and went that direction. Opening the door to the room opposite the one Keeper Dia had been in, he found a large room with five tables and cushions. Four of the tables had novices in white robes sitting around them.

"Another new face," someone called out, alerting the room that Gregory was standing there.

"New, indeed. He's still wearing his old clothing," another said.

"Just come in today?" a third asked, waving him over to a spot at his table.

Gregory gave the room a polite bow of his head before shutting the door behind him and moving to the offered spot. "Yes, just a few hours ago."

"Make sure you're in your robes tomorrow, or Keeper Dia will scold you," another novice at the table said.

"I remember my lecture," a third shivered. "Stay on her good side if you can."

"I will. Thank you," Gregory said.

"It's late for new novices to get in," a novice with a haughty bearing added from the nearest table. "Where are you from?"

"Alturis," Gregory replied.

"Where is that?" the haughty one asked with a smirk.

"Wait, I know," another novice at the same table said. "My father deals with ores. It's way out on the northwestern fringe."

"A fringer... yes, that explains things," the haughty young man snickered. "What magic do you have? I'm betting it's earth."

Gregory took a dislike to the novice. "Can't tell you."

"Oh, why is that? We're all taken to the Blade when we register. Or did whatever backwater proctor that found you forget to do that?"

Gregory's eye twitched, "The master didn't know."

The conversation in the room dimmed, and everyone was now interested in hearing more. The haughty novice sniffed, "Impossible. Master Damon is the foremost expert on the Blade."

"Hayworth, no one knows everything about it. It's Aether's Blade, for Aether's sake," the novice who had invited him to sit sighed. "Which stone was it?" he asked, turning back to Gregory.

"Ryuite. I'm Gregory Pettit, by the way," Gregory offered his hand.

"Nick Shun," the novice said, shaking his hand. "Sorry about the lack of introductions. Let me fix that," Taking a minute, he introduced Gregory around the table. "We mostly use given names, since we're supposed to *'all be equal.'*"

"What's your village like?" Michelle, the novice who had been lectured by the keeper, asked.

"Normal?" Gregory said questioningly. "It's a small village, smaller than any of the other places we went through on the way here. It has a mine, where most of the people work. The rest are mostly hunters or farmers. We have people skilled in the basic crafts, and a good clothier."

Hayworth snorted, "Good... so not worth using for the servants, you mean."

"What in Krog's balls is your problem?" Gregory snapped. "You don't even know me."

"Who would want to?" Hayworth hissed back, before he coughed and held up a hand as if in apology. "You do have a point, though. I should make allowances for a fringer. Your mother also being your older sister must have been hard enough. It has to be inbreeding; I mean... just look at you."

Teeth grinding, Gregory got to his feet, "What did you say, you—!"

The door to the room shot open and Keeper Dia stood there. She sternly cut Gregory off, "Fighting is *not* allowed inside the walls of the dormitory. If you have a need to fight, challenge each other and go to the arena."

Hayworth got to his feet. He had a sneer on his lips as he looked at the keeper. "If that is your word, *Keeper*," he said, his voice dripping with disdain. Hayworth headed for the door and Dia stepped aside when he got close. The others who had been at his table went with him.

When Dia looked back into the room, Gregory had calmed down enough to bow formally to her. "I apologize, Keeper. He insulted my mother. I will do my best to abide by your rules."

"Very good, Novice," Dia said, her gaze sweeping the room. "This room is for novices to use to relax, read, play games of chance, and even have debates, as long as they are kept civil. Good evening to you all," Dia said before she shut the door.

"Well, that was one way to make an enemy," Nick said. "Hayworth is an asshole, but one from a powerful clan, which is why he has friends and lackeys. You'll be having some difficulty in the coming year."

"I didn't even say anything to him."

"Didn't have to," Michelle sighed as she got to her feet. "Being a fringer is enough for him. If you aren't from wealth or power, you're either nothing to him or you're a target for his enjoyment."

"We should be going to get dinner," Nick said. "Would you care to join us, Gregory?"

"I ate before coming here. It was very good."

"We'll see you later, then," Nick said as they left.

Most of the others also left, talking about dinner. Discouraged, Gregory headed up to his room. *What the fuck is wrong with people?*

Gregory wondered as he climbed the stairs. *Why hate someone you don't even know?*

Lost in his thoughts, he did not notice that the door next to his room was standing open. Opening his own door, he was about to enter when a voice broke him out of his thoughts.

"Excuse me?" the soft voice called out.

Pausing, he looked over and saw the novice he had been with in the Blade room. "Did you mean me?"

A quick bob of her head and a small smile answered him before she said, "Yes. Do you have a moment?"

"Of course," Gregory said. "My room or yours?"

"Yours is fine," the novice said, shutting her door behind her and following him.

She was wearing the white robes of a novice, which covered her from the neck down and looked a little loose on her. Gregory shut the door behind her, moving over to take a seat at the table.

Giving her a smile, he introduced himself first, "I'm Gregory Pettit."

"Yukiko Warlin," she replied, taking a seat across from him and folding her legs underneath her. "I wanted to thank you for catching me earlier. I might have been injured if you hadn't, and it was rude of me to not thank you."

"Anyone would have done the same," he said.

"No, no they wouldn't," Yukiko replied.

"Why do you think that?"

"My heritage..." Yukiko sighed before meeting his gaze, her cyan eyes locking on his. "I have eurtik snow owl blood. It's only a little, but enough that many others would let me fall if they knew."

"I'd catch you every time," Gregory said simply.

Blinking slowly, Yukiko's head tilted slightly to the side. "You mean that?" A small smile started spreading on her face.

"My mother always said help those you can," Gregory replied, returning her smile. "Your heritage isn't noticeable, outside of your eyes." *Which are gorgeous*, he added in his own head.

"My eyes, my hair, and my pale skin make me stand out, bringing trouble," Yukiko sighed again, looking away from him. "Father took me on the road with him to help me avoid the troubles, which is why I'm here so late."

"Your father travels a lot? Is he a merchant?"

"Yes. Warlin's Mercantile. He does a lot of business in the east, along the Buldoun border. I almost missed the ritual altogether, but we were in Jezup when Proctor Harrison arrived, and father decided to have me do the ritual to become an adult. We never thought..." Trailing off, Yukiko's eyes began to fill with tears.

"You didn't want to be a magi?" Gregory asked, unsure of what to do for her. "I've wanted to be one since I was a child."

"I wanted to follow in his footsteps," Yukiko sniffled, doing her best to hold back her tears. "I'll never be a merchant now, only a magi."

"You can be both," Gregory said slowly. "Some of the clans are merchants."

Yukiko's smile dimmed, and her eyes crinkled in displeasure. "They aren't merchants, they are bullies. They use their power to intimidate others into doing what they want. They have no finesse, no soul for the deal."

"Oh," Gregory said awkwardly.

Yukiko looked at him again, "You didn't know that?"

Gregory sighed. *Might as well just tell her... it's already out.* Clearing his throat, he shook his head, "I'm from Alturis, in the northwest fringe."

"That explains why you are here so late, too," Yukiko said softly. "Jezup is on the eastern fringe."

"You're not from there, though."

"No, my home is... was... Tivano. Father will be heading home to tell Mother, if he isn't back already. I didn't get to say goodbye to her."

"Can't they visit?" Gregory asked.

"Only during the tournaments," Yukiko said.

"But they'll come. Your father obviously loves you a great deal if he went to such lengths to keep you with him and see you become an adult."

Tears began to fall, and Yukiko nodded, "Yes, he does. They'll both be here for the first tournament without a doubt, but I'm going to disappoint them."

"At least your family will be here," Gregory said softly, reaching out to gently pat her hand. "I doubt they will be disappointed if you do your best."

Sniffling, Yukiko met his gaze, "Yours won't come?"

Gregory looked away from her. "Father is a servant to the village for the next five years. Mother... died years ago."

"Oh," Yukiko whispered softly, "I'm sorry. I didn't mean to bring up—"

"It's fine, you had no way of knowing," Gregory said, cutting her off. Wanting to change the subject, he did so clumsily, "What do you think the classes will be like?"

Yukiko sniffled again as she forced her emotions down. "Tedious. History will be what we've been taught for years. Economics will be simple and repetitive. Aether introduction... I'm not sure about. Conditioning will be grueling."

"History might be more than you think," Gregory said, going to the closet to get his book. He set it in front of Yukiko, "I didn't know a lot of what's mentioned in here before I started reading it."

Yukiko opened the book and skimmed the first few pages. "Hmm, maybe you are right about that. I don't recall anything about the emperor being a war leader. Economics will still be trivial."

"To you, maybe," Gregory sighed. "You were raised around it."

Yukiko nodded, smiling again. "Maybe I can help you in that subject, then, as a thank you for your kindness."

"I won't say no. I have a feeling I can use all the help I can get."

"What about aether introduction?" Yukiko asked.

"I only know what Proctor Bishop told me. They'll teach us the basics of each kind of magic."

"Will they know your magic?" Yukiko asked.

"I don't know, but it's a new class for both of us, so maybe we can help each other?"

"Yes."

"As for physical conditioning, I'm not going to be good at it, either," Gregory admitted. "I was the weakest in our village... well, the weakest man."

"My heritage doesn't help me in that regard," Yukiko said.

"We can push each other, to help keep us motivated and working."

Yukiko's smile was strained. "Yes. I need to make sure Mother and Father are proud of me."

"I have a feeling you'll be able to do that pretty easily."

"I should get my things ready for bed," Yukiko said, rising to her feet smoothly.

"Yeah, uh... me, too," Gregory said. "I'm thinking of visiting the archive tomorrow, after the proctors' fight. Did you want to come?"

Yukiko paused at the door, "You don't mind?"

"I miss my friends," Gregory said on impulse, getting to his feet. "Having friends makes life better. Ria, El, and Gunnar would like you, too."

Yukiko had not turned to face him, but the smile in her voice was clear, "Might I go with you to the fight, as well? I would like to see Harrison lose."

Gregory laughed, "Me, too. Sure. If you want, we can make a day of it. Breakfast, see the grounds, duel, and then to the archive."

"I'll look forward to it," Yukiko said, opening the door. "Goodnight, Gregory."

"Greg. All my friends call me Greg."

"Goodnight, Greg. I don't have many friends, but you can call me Yuki, if you wish."

"See you in the morning, Yuki."

Greg shut the door after her and smiled as he went to the closet to get his stuff put away. *Looks like I made one friend, at least. Might want to tell her I already made an enemy... no reason for her to get tangled up. Maybe at breakfast tomorrow?*

CHAPTER 16

G regory yawned and sat up, sleepily rubbing his eyes. There was a bell chiming the hour, and Gregory listened to it. *Five? Might as well get used to being up at this time... going to need to be for next week.*

It took him longer than he would have thought to get into his new clothing; all of it was different from what he was used to. He was just finishing when a timid knock came on the paneling of his door.

"Who is it?" Gregory asked as he picked up his coin pouch.

"It's Yuki, Greg. I wasn't sure if you were awake yet."

Opening the door, he smiled at her, "Sorry, I was getting dressed."

Yukiko looked at his uniform and bit her lip. "Greg... umm... you're wearing it wrong."

"Huh?" He looked down at his clothing, unable to see any mistakes.

"Look at mine," she told him. She stepped back and spread her arms out for him.

Seeing the differences, he grimaced. "I see. Can you give me another minute or two?"

"Yes, it's okay. If you've never worn a kimono before, it can be confusing," Yukiko said, trying to help him with his embarrassment. "I'll be downstairs."

"I'll hurry," Gregory said, shutting the door as she turned to leave.

When Gregory made it downstairs a few minutes later, he found Yukiko pressed up against a tree a few feet from the dormitory. A couple of novices who had been with Hayworth were hemming her in place.

"Come on now, we just want to be your *friends*," one of the novices said with a smirk.

"We can help you," the other added.

"With what?" Gregory asked as he moved toward them. "Nothing she wants, obviously."

Both of the novices spun on Gregory, giving Yukiko just enough room to slip away. "Fringer...? Haven't figured out not to bother your betters, have you?"

"I haven't bothered anyone better than me yet," Gregory replied.

"Leave him, Skippy. He'll learn soon enough," one of them chuckled.

"Yeah, Hayworth will show him. Come on, Clement," Skippy nodded. "We'll just go back to talking to...? Where did she go?"

"Seems she didn't want to be bothered by her lessers, either," Gregory shrugged as he headed for the path to the mess hall.

"Fucking asshole. He'll get his," Clement muttered.

Once he was a little way down the path and away from the novices, Yukiko came out from behind a tree to join him. "Thank you. They surprised me while I was waiting for you."

"Then it's my fault to begin with," Gregory said. "Sorry."

"No, it's fine. They are unpleasant, but they didn't say or do anything to me."

"I'm glad. I'm pretty sure that fighting outside of challenges is frowned on."

"I don't know," Yukiko said. "Maybe we can find out today?"

"Maybe," Gregory agreed.

* * *

Breakfast was not as potent as dinner had been, which Gregory was grateful for. White rice, soup, fish, and pickled plums— it was a grander breakfast than he had ever had, even if it was odd.

The next bell rang just as he was finishing his food and Gregory shook his head. *Going to need to be faster with breakfast, or else I'll be late to class.*

"I'm glad class hasn't started yet," Yukiko commented. She had just finished eating as well. "Being late is unforgivable."

"Agreed," Gregory said. "We have a couple of hours before the challenge, and we need to find out where it's being fought. Maybe we should go over to the arenas and ask?"

"That is a sound idea," Yukiko agreed, getting to her feet.

"Let's get to it," Gregory smiled, copying her.

They left their dishes with the same cleaner as last night, and Gregory wondered about the eurtiks in the academy. *Why do they put up with the way they're talked about? They can't all be slaves or servants, can they?*

The walk across the grounds came with revelations for Gregory as Yukiko explained the different features that he had been puzzled about the day before. The rock garden was for meditation, and if not in use, could be changed by anyone to better help them meditate. The small trees were called bonsai, and it was considered an art form to grow them. The fish in the streams and pools were koi and were treasured, as they only thrived in aether rich environments.

Yukiko did her best to describe what each building they passed was used for. The tallest was the tower in the middle of the academy grounds. Reaching almost a hundred feet in height, it dominated the landscape. The council of the academy lived within its walls.

Gregory spotted what looked like a small cottage close to the tower wall. He pointed it out to Yukiko, "That's odd."

"I heard that those are the cottages for visiting magi that don't have a clan building inside the walls. The large building over there is a clan manor. The emblem tells you which clan."

Gregory looked at the two-story structure she pointed to. It was similar in design to the dormitory, but instead of wood and paper walls, it was built of stone. An emblem, depicting a gauntleted fist, stood out prominently against the stonework.

"The Hardened Fist. They are a clan that loves combat. Mercenaries mostly, they will fight for anyone, if the price is right."

"Not a clan that will be interested in me," Gregory said as they started walking again. "My magic is unknown, so it's unlikely to be good for combat."

"That is possible," Yukiko agreed. "Do you know what path you want to follow?"

"Proctor Bishop suggested I hold off deciding until my magic is known."

"I don't know what to do for mine. I'm considering waiting until classes start. Maybe the teacher will be able to help me."

"The archive might have information, too."

"Something for us to check on."

It took them another hour to make their way to the arenas. Four smaller arenas surrounded a larger one. Long buildings connected them, and Gregory wondered what they were for. As they approached the closest one, Gregory spotted an old man in a gray kimono sweeping the doorway.

"Excuse me, sir? I was wondering if you can help us?"

The man stopped sweeping and looked up. He gave the two novices a small bow, his expression serious. "How might Laozi help you?"

"Two proctors are supposed to be having a challenge in a bit, and we would like to watch. Do you know which arena we should go to?"

"It will be the arena directly behind me," Laozi replied. "Is that all you needed?"

"I wouldn't want to interrupt you," Gregory said.

"One must always take time to enjoy the company of others," Laozi smiled. "I do not mind a small delay if it helps you."

"We had questions about challenges, and what happens if you fight outside of a challenge."

"Do not fight outside of a challenge; the repercussions vary depending on who finds out, but all of them are bad. You might end up spending all your free time sweeping, for instance."

"But you can defend yourself, correct?" Yukiko asked.

"Defense is always allowed, but continuing the fight will make you just as guilty as the one who started it."

"Thank you," Yukiko bowed her head.

"As for challenges themselves, that is a long topic and has many nuances. I would suggest you visit the archive and ask for the current rules and guidelines, since they alter them as needed."

"Thank you for your time," Gregory said. He blurted out, "What tier are you, sir?"

"None. I'm merely a sweeper." Laozi bowed deeply to them. "I think I need to continue my work, lest I get in trouble." Putting action to words, he began to clean the front entrance again.

"Should we go and come back?" Yukiko asked.

"We can walk around the arenas," Gregory said. "I don't want to go too far and miss it."

The walk around the arenas did not take very long. The interior of each of the smaller arenas could hold over a hundred people, and Gregory figured that the larger one could probably hold a thousand. The raised seating around the arena would give everyone a good view of the sands inside.

A few minutes before the challenge was to start, Bishop walked out into the arena and began to stretch. Seeing Gregory and Yukiko sitting next to each other in the stands, she nodded to them. Gregory waved back to her, hopeful that she would win. Once she was done stretching, she sat in lotus position and closed her eyes. A minute before the start time, Harrison walked onto the sands, followed by Damon.

"I thought you might forfeit by not showing," Harrison laughed. "Glad I was wrong."

"Master, are you ready?" Bishop asked as she got to her feet fluidly, ignoring Harrison.

"I am ready to begin this challenge. The loser will be giving up their stipend for the year to the winner," Damon said. "The challenge will be blades alone— no aether. Do either of you wish to back out?" When neither spoke, he bowed his head. "So be it. To the middle."

Bishop and Harrison both walked to the middle of the arena, staying twenty feet apart, and Damon stood between them. "Bow to the spectators," Damon said. Harrison blinked, then turned to face them. His eyes narrowed when he saw Gregory next to Yukiko.

Both proctors bowed and turned back to Damon again. "Bow to the adjudicator," Damon said. Both did as he said, before facing each other again. "Bow to your opponent." They did so, and Damon stepped back a dozen feet. "Begin!"

Bishop did not move, but Harrison did, moving faster than Gregory could ever hope to. He closed the distance between himself and Bishop in a blink. The sound of swords striking echoed in the silence before the two separated.

"You have trained," Bishop said blandly. "Good, I worried you had grown lazy."

Harrison spat to the side, "I'm going to make you pay for the last time."

"Doubtful," Bishop said as she shifted her stance. "You'll need to train more. Come now, let's not waste the novices' time." Her words were calm and measured, as if she were discussing the weather.

"Bitch," Harrison hissed as he rushed forward again.

Gregory could not keep up with the speed, but the clashing of steel on steel was louder and faster than the first time. A minute passed before Harrison gasped and fell to his knees. Bishop tapped both of his cheeks with the flat of her blade, then the top of his head.

"Stop," Damon sighed. "Harrison is defeated."

"No," Harrison panted as he struggled to stand. "I can still fight."

"If she had been serious, your head would decorate the sands," Damon said sternly. "Do not disgrace yourself and your clan even more."

Harrison glared at Bishop, his left hand over his chest. The moment stretched out before he spun and sheathed his sword. "I'll send the vela to your lodging."

"Very well," Bishop said and sheathed her own blade. "Harrison, you fought well."

Harrison's shoulders became stiff and he walked faster.

"Did you need to needle him?" Damon asked.

"I meant it. He *has* gotten better. If we had used aether, he might have been able to win," Bishop replied. Turning to Gregory, she asked, "Did you learn anything?"

"You were too fast to follow," Gregory said.

"Control the battle," Yukiko said softly. "You baited him into the challenge so you could control the weapon."

Bishop nodded her head, "Correct. It isn't always about who is more powerful; knowing where and how to apply pressure can be the deciding factor. I had already won the moment he challenged me."

Damon shook his head, "I wish the two of you would stop this."

"We promised during our novice year to always make the other strive to be better," Bishop said simply. "I haven't forgotten my promise, even if he has."

"I'm going back to the archive," Damon sighed. "Good day, Bishop."

"Good day, Master," Bishop said, bowing toward his back.

"We were going to head that way, too," Gregory said.

"Learning is good," Bishop said. "I hope you both have a good day and year." Bowing fractionally to them once more, Bishop spun on her heel and walked away.

"She is better than any of my father's guards," Yukiko said softly. "Even without aether, she is someone to respect."

"I agree," Gregory nodded, recalling the bane wolf from Alturis. "Let's get going."

CHAPTER 17

The pair stopped for a snack at the mess hall before making their way to the archive. When they reached the building, Gregory slowed his pace. The archive took up a huge chunk of land and stood almost as tall as the sixty-foot wall.

"How many books and scrolls are inside?" Gregory whispered as he stared at the building.

"They say it's the biggest collection of works in the entire empire, even grander than the emperor's archive in the capital."

"So much knowledge," Gregory said in awe.

They could not help coming to a stop and staring around in awe when they went into the building. The interior was done in white marble that had streaks of black and red scattered through the stone. The wooden tables, shelves, and desks were all a uniform white, bordering on the unnatural. Lanterns illuminated the interior brighter than the sun outside.

"Might I help you?" a pleasant, if deep, voice asked from just off to their right.

"Umm, yes," Gregory said, turning to face the massive scaled eurtik resting behind a desk. "I'm interested in the current rules and laws for challenges."

"And I would like to see a book on the best paths for those who have shadow magic," Yukiko added.

"Shadow magic, hmm? It's been quite some time since we've had a novice with that magic. Follow me, please," the eurtik stepped away from the desk, his scaled tail dragging along the ground behind him.

Careful not to step on the archivist's tail as he led them past the first set of tables and desks, the pair looked around in wonder as they passed rows and rows of shelves filled with books and scrolls. When he went by one shelf, the eurtik picked up a large tome, but kept going with barely a decrease in his speed. Reaching the far wall, he bade them wait as he slipped into an aisle between the shelves and pulled out a much thinner book.

Coming back to where they were waiting, he took them over to a table and placed the books on it. "When you finish, leave the books. One of the archivists will put them back," he told them. "If you would like any other books, just find someone in a black kimono, or come see me at the front."

"Thank you, sir," Gregory said.

Bowing his head, the archivist gave them a toothy smile before heading back to the front. As he watched him go, Gregory wondered what animal he came from.

"I wouldn't have expected a crocodilian eurtik as an archivist," Yukiko murmured. "Maybe he also makes sure no one removes a book from the archive without permission?"

"Maybe," Gregory said, wondering what a crocodilian was, but set aside the thought to look at the thick book on the table. Opening it, he saw that it was a history of challenges, as well as the rules throughout the years.

"Challenges can be non-combative," he murmured in surprise, skimming through a few pages while he flipped to the back to find the current rules.

"What kind of challenges are those?" Yukiko asked, looking up from her own book.

"Go, chess, any number of tactical games... though there is a part about treasure hunts to solve disagreements, too."

"How would that even work?"

"The adjudicator sets up the hunt," Gregory said. "It was suggested that for such a challenge, the archivists at the academy archive be used."

"They are supposed to be neutral, and they would surely create an interesting hunt."

"What about your book?"

"It's very contradictory," Yukiko sighed. "One part of it says that body is the best path, because it will help with the majority of the physical demands that accompany shadow magic. The next part says that mind would be the best path, as it'll help me gather information more easily and quickly. The only mention of spirit is that it's only good for the least of shadow magic."

"Huh," Gregory grunted. "Not a lot of help, then."

"It does give me something to consider, although speaking to a user of shadow magic would probably be better."

"What would you ask them?" a soft, but firm voice asked from nearby.

Startled, as neither novice had noticed the presence of the black panther eurtik, their heads snapped in her direction. "Archivist," Gregory exhaled deeply, with his heart hammering in his chest, "you gave us a scare."

"My apologies, but thank you for not screaming." Moving toward them on soundless feet, the woman took a seat at their table. "What is it you are looking to find out from one who uses shadow magic, Novice?"

Yukiko slid the book to the woman in the black kimono. "This book seems to contradict itself. I would like to know which path different shadow magi have taken and what each offered that the others didn't."

"Would that not prejudice your own choice?" the archivist asked. "Should you not be looking for your own path?"

Yukiko frowned, looking down at the table. "Yes, but—"

"You don't wish to disappoint your family, friends, or clan," the archivist cut in.

"Yes."

"Then the answer you seek is simple," the archivist smiled. "Follow your instincts; your aether is likely trying to help you. If that doesn't work, then use the process of elimination. Body will help you with combat, so if you are lacking in that, it will also help you mitigate your weakness. Mind will help you learn and grow more than you could otherwise, and you'll find ways around fighting that way. Spirit can help you in other ways."

"What ways?" Gregory asked.

Raising an eyebrow at Gregory, the archivist shrugged. "That all depends on what she wants. The path of spirit is one of knowing yourself and building on that basis. I can offer you some scrolls that will outline what each path does in basic terms, if you'd like."

"Please," Yukiko said without hesitation.

"Very well." Rising to her feet with a grace Gregory had never seen, the archivist inclined her head a fraction of an inch to them. "I hope your time inside these halls is enlightening."

When the panther eurtik left the table, Gregory shook his head. "Did you feel that?"

"The small vibration? Yes. Maybe it was a purr?"

"Maybe."

"Did you learn anything about challenges?" Yukiko asked.

Gregory gave her a quick review of the things he thought were important. He was finishing when a timid-looking woman in an archivist kimono came to their table.

"The scrolls you asked for," the woman said, her buck teeth reminding Gregory of a mouse.

"What happened to the other archivist?" Gregory asked.

"She had other matters to attend to, and requested that I bring these to you."

"Thank you," Yukiko smiled.

"We are done with these two," Gregory said, closing the book he had. "Do we—?"

"I will take them," the woman squeaked. Picking them up carefully, she bowed her head to them before hurrying away.

"That was different," Gregory shook his head.

"I think she comes from mouse eurtik," Yukiko said. "It is very slight, like my own."

"That makes sense," Gregory agreed as he picked up one of the scrolls. "Let's go over these and see what they say."

* * *

It took them a few hours to read through the three scrolls. Each one extolled the virtues of the path it was dedicated to and outlined the basic steps to start down that path. The body path started with a few exercises that would help limber the body and get aether moving throughout the body more easily. The mind path began by doing simple math problems to get one used to processing information quickly, which was supposed to help them increase their aether. The spirit path scroll was a copy of the one Gregory had received from the scrivener; it instructed the magi to meditate. That was supposed to compress the aether, so they could use less to do the same job.

"In addition to what the paths do for aether, they also have physical benefits. Mind will let you track multiple things at once, helping you find a response sooner. Body hones the body to always be ready to attack or defend, making them instinctual. The odd one is spirit... it just lets you know yourself better, allowing you to ignore distractions so you can focus on whatever you need to. None of that will help me unless I know what my magic is, though."

"I still don't know which path I should take, either," Yukiko admitted. "Body would help make up for my slight frame in combat, but mind would let me keep track of goods and prices more easily. Spirit does sound strange, but something tells me I should follow it."

Gregory's vision wavered, and three copies of Yukiko stood behind her. The left was the most physically fit, but was covered in blood. She had a dead expression on her face, looking like she had given up on life. The middle image had a cruel smile and had a number of small puppets dancing at the end of strings tied to her fingers, making her seem like the spider in the middle of a web. The last vision was the same; Yukiko sitting across from him, except a happy smile touched her lips while shadows swirled around her feet like happy puppies. He knew with certainty that the visions represented what would happen if she followed the body, mind, or spirit paths respectively. He blinked repeatedly and the visions vanished, leaving him staring at Yukiko, who was looking at him with concern.

"Greg? Are you okay?"

"Sorry, yeah, I... uh... was just thinking. The archivist was saying that the spirit path would let you know yourself. Your gut is nudging you that way, and the scroll did say that the chance to grow was endless, unlike the other paths. It's just much slower."

Yukiko looked pensive for a long moment before she sighed. "You may be right, but I'll wait for classes to start. If we end up using the same path, we can train together."

"True," Gregory smiled. His stomach growled loudly. "Err, sorry."

"What time is it, do you think?" Yukiko asked as she stood and stretched.

"It is near the eighteenth bell," an archivist said as they went past the table.

"Dinner?" Gregory asked.

"I didn't think we had been here that long," Yukiko said. "Yes, dinner sounds good."

Leaving the scrolls on the table, the two novices started toward the exit. "Novice, wait!" a commanding voice called out loudly as they were nearing the doors.

Stopping, Gregory looked behind him with alarm, to see Master Damon hurrying his way. "Master Damon," the large scaled eurtik by the door said unhappily, "this is a place of quiet reflection. Yelling is prohibited as you well know, sir."

"Rafiq, I do know, but I had to stop him from leaving," Damon sniffed as he finally got close enough for polite conversation. "I need to know your lineage, Novice."

"My father is Carmichael Pettit, my mother was Marian Pettit," Gregory replied. "I lived in Alturis."

"What was your mother's maiden name?" Damon asked.

"I don't know, Master. It was never mentioned to me."

Damon grimaced, "Very well."

"Have you had any luck with finding out about the ryuite, Master?"

Damon's grimace deepened, "No. That's why I want your heritage. I'm hoping something there will help me, because magic talents are sometimes passed down through the mother's line. I'll need to send a message to Alturis to find out your mother's maiden name. That will be all, Novice," Damon dismissed them and went toward the stairs on the left side of the front room.

Rafiq watched him go, a soft chuckle escaping his scaled snout. "Haven't seen him that worked up in years. Sarinia will chew him out for yelling, but she'll be happy that he found something to occupy himself with."

Yukiko's stomach gurgled, and she blushed, "Dinner?" she reminded Gregory.

"Yeah, dinner," Gregory replied, a little distracted as they left the building.

* * *

The mess hall was busy when they got there. Seating was scarce, and the line in front of the eurtiks was moving slowly. Gregory looked at how busy it was and shook his head; there were more people in the mess hall than there were in his entire village.

"This seems to be the busy period," Yukiko said softly.

"It's moving steadily, though," Gregory added. "No one is lingering over their food except for the novices, but I think that's expected from the look of things."

"I see you're thinking the same thing we were," Nick said from behind Gregory. "Food would be a wonderful thing."

"Hey," Gregory said, turning around to give Nick and the handful of other novices a smile. "How have you been?"

"Bored," Nick laughed. "With days to go until classes start, there isn't much to do. We're going to get some sparring in after dinner. Want to come?"

"I'm not exactly skilled," Gregory hedged.

"No worries. Fureno back there is a complete loss."

"Fuck you, Nick," the boy named Fureno replied. "Not all of us had family that can do what yours can."

"Fair," Nick chuckled. "We can scale back and go over the basics. That'll give you a chance to not be completely lost when classes start."

"Is it okay if I come, as well?" Yukiko asked.

"Never say no to a pretty woman," Nick smiled widely, before his smile lost a touch of its luster. "I mean, sure."

"Finding a place for all of us to eat together might be a problem," Michelle sighed. "Maybe we should just meet at the training hall after dinner."

Nick looked over the room before nodding, "Yeah. Good call. If you can't sit with us, then just meet us there. Everyone got it?"

The five with him agreed. Gregory did too, but asked to make sure he knew the right building. "That was near the arenas, right?"

"Yes, right by them," Michelle replied.

"Sounds good," Gregory smiled. "I know where to go."

The line had kept moving, allowing them to pick up their trays and get ready to order. Gregory copied Yukiko, ending up with noodles in a brown sauce, pieces of beef sliced thin, a selection of vegetables with a butter herb sauce, and some tea. They were able to find a place to sit side by side. Gregory frowned at the two sticks that Yukiko had taken for cutlery instead of a fork.

Scooping the beef into the noodles, Gregory wondered why Yukiko did it, but he also realized she was likely to have had similar food in the past. He was surprised at how deftly she wrapped some of the noodles and picked them up with her sticks before they vanished into her mouth. Shaking his head, he took a bite of his own food. The sauce was creamy, but with a solid beef flavor. The noodles tasted like they were made from mushrooms. The small sliver of beef he ate made his aether flare before settling down, tempered by the sauce and noodles.

"I've never had anything like this," Gregory mumbled.

"It's stroganoff. It's popular in the east," Yukiko told him between bites of her own food. "Try the vegetables; they are good."

Gregory took a small bite of the vegetables, and was unable to identify the herbs. The vegetables were perfectly cooked, though, still firm with just a hint of softening. He thought that the way his aether reacted to them was unusual. The normal steady flame gave off tiny flares with each bite of the vegetables, which died down as he swallowed each mouthful. Enjoying the meal and not wanting to cause his aether to have problems, Gregory ate at a slow and measured pace, with Yukiko matching him bite for bite.

* * *

"Okay, now that we're all here," Nick grinned, "we can start. Gregory, Fureno, move over to the left for me. I'll get you two started on the basics. The rest of you, go ahead and pick out a partner and start on the drills."

Gregory watched Yukiko square off with Michelle before Nick stepped in front of him. "Okay, Gregory, have you had any training?"

"No."

"Then you and Fureno are evenly matched, since he only got here a week ago. He's about done with the first part, but he can still use some polish on breakfalls. Okay, so to start with, we're going to show you the right way to fall backward."

The two hours were physically taxing in ways that Gregory had never experienced. When they finally stopped, everyone was breathing hard and sweating. Groaning as he stood up, Gregory winced as his muscles protested.

"Good job, everyone," Nick said. "Baths are that way," he added to Gregory.

Gregory's eyes went to Michelle, Gina, and Yukiko, who were talking, and he looked back at Nick with wide eyes. "Baths?"

Nick smirked and waggled an eyebrow at him, "Yeah, we wish. It's segregated bathing. Come on."

The baths were radically different than any Gregory had seen before. Most of the room was dominated by a large steaming pool. In another part of the room, there was a long stone bench. A stack of buckets waited at the end of it. Next to those was a hand pump.

Unsure of what to do, he did what he had been doing: copying everyone around him. Stripping down, he set his clothes in an empty basket near the door. He pumped a bucket of lightly steaming water and found a spot on the bench that had soap on the shelf across from it. Using a wooden ladle, he poured water over himself before scrubbing up. As he rinsed the water off with the rest of the bucket, he was surprised that the others kept glancing at a wall.

"You're so pale," Michelle's voice drifted faintly to Gregory's ears. "Your hair is what I'm jealous over, though. That color—"

"The women?" Gregory asked Fureno.

"Shh," Fureno whispered, elbowing him. "They don't know we can overhear them."

Nick shook his head as he headed for the pool. "It's a small guilty pleasure," he told Gregory as he went past. "Come on, scrawny. The pool will feel great for your muscles." He paused and stared at Gregory's left arm. "What happened to you?"

"I was attacked," Gregory said, not wanting to expand on it.

"Sorry," Nick said, feeling like he had touched a nerve. "Come on, the pool is amazing."

The others grumbled when the conversation on the other side got softer and they could not hear it anymore. They followed Nick, with Gregory trailing all of them. The water was on the edge of being too hot, but as he sank into it up to his neck the warmth soaked into his tired muscles.

"Aether, that's wonderful," Gregory sighed. "Isn't this place too big for just us?" he asked after a moment.

"This is where we can train outside of class," Nick replied. "Everyone can use it, though some of the equipment is for more advanced tiers."

"I don't know if I could go back to a hip bath after this," Jason chuckled from off to the side. "Then again, we'll be magi, so we won't have to."

"Unless you end up a proctor on the fringe," Fureno said. "No offense, but the lack of comforts out there..." Trailing off, he shook his head.

"None taken," Gregory said.

"Aren't the people doing proctor duty on the fringe posted to those positions because they fucked up majorly?" Jason asked.

"Most of them," Fureno replied. "One of them asked for the post and has been doing it for years."

"Bishop," Gregory said. "She's been at the village every year since I was a kid."

"Yeah, that's her," Fureno nodded. "Rumor is she's a nut, that she enjoys being out there by herself."

Gregory frowned. Bishop had always been kind and respectful to everyone in all the years she had come to the village. "She's not a nut. She's always been respectful to us," Gregory said with a bit of bite to his tone.

"Easy, easy, Gregory," Nick laughed. "Fureno didn't mean it like that, did you, Fureno?"

Fureno shrugged, "Wrong word, sorry. I meant she's driven."

"Maybe I shouldn't have snapped. Sorry," Gregory said, though he meant it as much as Fureno did.

"See? We can all be friends," Nick laughed. "Now let's just relax and let the water soak in."

Gregory did as suggested. He closed his eyes and let the warmth of the pool seep into his aching muscles. Feeling his aether, he found it simmering at its usual intensity, no longer burning brightly like it had been two hours ago.

* * *

"You need to get out or you're going to become a prune," Nick laughed, snapping Gregory from his relaxed state of mind.

"Uh, yeah, sure," Gregory said, getting out of the pool. Catching the towel tossed to him, he dried off and got back into his uniform. "Umm, the uniforms... where do we wash them?"

"You don't," Nick replied as he finished getting dressed. "There is a white bag inside your closet. Put the uniform inside and set it outside your door. The staff takes them after sixth bell and returns them after midday. They'll put the clean bag inside your door."

"Does that include other clothing?" Greg asked.

"Yeah, anything you leave for them gets cleaned and returned."

"That will make things easier. I was going to ask for a larger basin tonight."

"Now I'm sorry I told you," Nick laughed.

Gregory was about to reply when the women came out of their bathing room. Yukiko was combing her hair out when she saw him, and gave Gregory a smile.

"I've been asked to join them again tomorrow," Yukiko told him, putting her comb away in her pouch.

"You, too," Nick chuckled, nudging Gregory. "You're invited back to train with us, too."

"Learning how to fall," Gregory rolled his eyes. "Great."

"Just tomorrow. After that, we'll teach you something different," Nick said with a grin.

"I don't trust that smile," Gregory muttered.

"He's smart enough to know when you're playing at something," Michelle said as she walked past them. Looking back, she gave Yukiko a smile, "See you tomorrow."

"Yes, I'm looking forward to it. Thank you."

"Anyway, see you tomorrow," Nick said quickly, following Michelle.

Gregory and Yukiko stayed where they were as the others left. "They seem like nice people," Yukiko said.

"Yeah," Gregory said, not so sure he agreed with her. "No one gave you any problems?"

"No, it was refreshing," Yukiko smiled. "I'm far from the worst in the group. Nick and Jason might be the only ones more skilled than me. That is Gin's fault... he always wanted me to be able to defend myself. I'm glad Father didn't stop him after he found out."

"While I'm learning to fall," Gregory sighed. "Let's head on back, shall we?"

"Learning to fall will help when you do fight. It'll help you get injured less."

"I know, Nick said the same thing. Makes me think the first year is going to be even harder than I thought."

"We will learn together," Yukiko smiled. "Friends make things easier."

Thinking of Gunnar and the twins, Gregory had a sad smile on his face. "Yeah... yeah they do."

CHAPTER 18

The next week flew by for Gregory; he would have breakfast with Yukiko, go to the archive and study, stop for a snack, then meet with Nick and his friends for sparring, before finishing his night having dinner with Yukiko. Having dinner after everything else always made him feel better.

Waking to the third bell, Gregory got out of bed and dressed. He gathered the paper, ink, and pen that had been in the room, double checking that he had everything he needed. Slipping into the hall, he gently tapped at Yukiko's door.

"I'll meet you downstairs," Yukiko called to him.

As he went down the quiet hall, Gregory wondered why the others were not already up. *Maybe they're just not as excited?* he shrugged mentally. Heading toward the front door, he was surprised when Dia stepped out of her room and into his way.

"Keeper?" Gregory questioned politely.

"Excited for today, Gregory?"

He gave her a broad smile, "Yes. I've been waiting for this day all my life."

"Very few wake this early," Dia replied, stepping out the front door. "I wish you the best day."

"Thank you, Keeper."

"Has everything been taken care of by my staff?" Dia asked as she pulled out a long, thin, pipe from her obi.

"I have had no complaints, Keeper."

"Very good." She placed a single finger over the now filled bowl of the pipe and a flame sparked from it. Sucking in, Dia exhaled a cloud of light purple smoke. "If you have any problems, please let me know."

"I will, Keeper."

"Greg, I'm sorry for the delay," Yukiko apologized when she came out of her room.

"It's fine, Yuki," Greg said. "Ready to go?"

"Good day to you both," Dia said as she stood there, smoking her pipe.

"Thank you, Keeper," the pair said together before heading toward the mess hall.

When they stepped into the mess hall, they saw four people already having breakfast. One was a magus, wearing a cyan kimono and reading a book as he ate. There was a bland looking man in an emerald kimono, who was staring at nothing and eating mechanically. Gregory and Yukiko met the sharp eyes of an older gray-haired woman in cyan, who glanced their way before she went back to her food, dismissing them as unimportant. The last one, another man in emerald, watched them with a curious expression until they left his line of sight.

"Early, novices. Never being late is good," the weasel eurtik behind the counter said as he gave them the first part of their breakfast.

"Wise to come before the crowd," the scaled eurtik agreed, dishing up the next portion.

"Best wishes on your first day," the rat grinned and plated them some fish, handing the plates to the mink beside him.

"May this meal sustain you during your classes," the mink gave them a bright smile, scooping rice onto the plates beside the fish. Her hand extended to hover over Gregory's medallion for a moment.

"Thank you," Gregory said, bowing his head to them, then going to get cutlery and a drink.

"A good day to you, too," Yukiko smiled as she followed Gregory.

With green tea to complement the meal, they took a table close to the cleaning area, putting them away from the adepts and magus. Gregory had gotten used to the breakfast meals, but wondered why it was nearly identical every day. Yukiko had told him that the soup was miso, and that, along with the fish and rice— white or brown— had been breakfast every day. The only change had been in the one side dish. The pickled plums were tasty, especially with the rice. The nori was odd, but okay. The one he did not care for was natto; the slimy texture put him off.

Gregory ate at the same slow pace he had gotten used to. The fish always made his aether flare up, while the other parts of the meal were there to help give him time for his body to accept the aether he was ingesting. *I wonder if it'll be covered in class today?* Gregory idly thought.

Gregory and Yukiko finished eating within a few seconds of each other, sharing a smile as the fourth bell started to ring. They had two hours before class started, giving them the time they wanted.

When they dropped off their empty trays, Gregory noticed the four magi who had been there before them were gone. The mess hall was busier now as magi of different tiers started to show up. As he made his way to the exit, Gregory did not see the man in the sunflower yellow kimono stick his foot out into the walkway to trip him. Gregory started to fall, but because he had spent the last week drilling how to fall, he managed to roll and come back to his feet.

"Watch where you're walking, Novice," the apprentice snorted.

Not sure what had happened, Gregory bowed to the apprentice, "Apologies."

Glaring at Gregory, the man's lips puckered, but he nodded and turned back to his meal. "Just watch your feet."

Yukiko frowned. She had seen the deliberate act, but had not been able to warn Gregory in time. Following Gregory out of the mess hall, she debated telling him.

When they were approaching the archive, Yukiko finally spoke up, "Greg, the apprentice in the mess... he tripped you intentionally."

"Huh? Why would he do that?" Gregory asked, confused.

"I don't know, but it was deliberate."

Gregory stopped walking and felt his aether burn brighter. *Why the fuck would an apprentice do that? It doesn't make any sense. Maybe he had me confused with someone else?* Sighing, he rubbed his face and let the anger go. "Doesn't matter. I'll just keep an eye out for him in the future."

"I will make sure to keep an eye out for him, as well," Yukiko said.

"Thanks, Yuki. Let's do what we came to do," Gregory said.

Entering the archive, they were greeted by a man with wolf ears on his head. "Back again, even with classes today?"

"We're going to read until fifth bell," Yukiko told him.

"Using as much time as you can," the man smiled as his ears twitched. "The books you used yesterday are on the table you normally sit at."

"Thank you," Gregory replied, bowing his head to the archivist.

"You're welcome, but it is Rafiq who deserves your thanks, not me. I merely did as he requested."

"I'll thank him later," Gregory said, "but you still have my thanks."

"You're welcome, Novice."

Going to the table they had used since the first day, the pair took their seats and dove into reading. Gregory was reading over a book detailing how vela became the standard currency of the empire, while Yukiko was working her way through the history book that was identical to Gregory's.

When the fifth bell rang, they put their books aside and rose to their feet. The black panther eurtik was coming their way when they stood up. "Should I have these books ready for your next visit?"

"That would be very nice," Gregory replied. "Thank you, Archivist."

"We appreciate it," Yukiko added.

"We don't get many novices who spend their time before classes studying as you have. Most of them focus on fighting only, so it is refreshing to see something different. Whatever book you were reading last shall be waiting for you every morning. Now, don't let me keep you. You have classes to get to."

Gregory and Yukiko bowed their heads to her. Gregory felt mounting excitement as they walked, though he was able to match the easy pace Yukiko set.

They were still half an hour early when they reached the class-room, but the door was open, so they walked in. Gregory was puzzled by the black wall at the front of the room, but chose not to comment. He followed Yukiko to one of the small tables that were spaced through the room, noticing that the cushions were only on two sides, so that every person seated would have a clear view of the black wall.

"Thanks for making the last week enjoyable," Gregory said.

"I should say the same to you," Yukiko replied. "That first day, I felt so alone until I saw you. You didn't make any comment about my appearance, then you caught me when I fell. Thank you."

Gregory was about to reply when the click of metal on stone got his attention. Looking back, he saw the gray-haired magus from breakfast. The old woman glanced their way, again dismissing them as she advanced to the front of the room. When she reached the front, she pulled a number of items from her pouch and set up the podium at the front of the room. She turned to the odd wall, holding a small white stick. Gregory's jaw dropped when she started writing.

"It's a blackboard," Yukiko whispered, seeing his shock. "She is using chalk to write on it. You've never seen one?"

Shaking his head, Gregory shut his mouth, glad no one else had seen his shock. "No. We didn't have anything like that."

"The best part is that with a cloth, the words can be erased so you can write on it again," Yukiko told him. "Dad sold a number of them to outlying villages."

"When class starts, you will *not* continue to prattle on, I trust?" the magus asked in a nasally voice.

"No, Magus," Yukiko said, bowing in her seat.

"No, Magus," Gregory added a moment behind her.

"You spoke of your father selling things. He is a trader?" the magus asked Yukiko.

"Yes, Magus. Hao Warlin of Warlin Mercantile is my father."

"He trades along the Buldoun border," the magus said after a moment of thought. "He is two decades removed from working with the Han Merchant Exchange."

"Yes, Magus."

A small smile touched the magus' lips. "He was very shrewd in his moves when he left the Exchange. You won't gain much from this class, but I will be calling on you often."

"As you require, Magus," Yukiko bowed again.

"And you, Novice?"

"I come from a village to the northwest, Magus. Alturis. No one in my family does any trading."

"Alturis? Aethite is mined there, along with high grade iron and a few other ores. Interesting... we don't get many fringers in the academy."

"Thank Aether for that," a snide voice chimed in from behind them.

"I will not abide disruptions in my class, even when the class isn't in session," the magus said sternly, staring at the newcomer.

"My apologies, Magus," the man replied. "I'll do my best to follow your instructions. I should sit in the back to keep the fringer smell from affecting me."

Gregory had turned to look at the novice who was now smirking at him. Voices and footsteps announced the arrival of the other students, stopping the tension from devolving further.

"Come in, find a seat. We start promptly at the sixth bell," the magus said archly.

Novices kept showing up in small groups, right up until the sixth bell. The moment the sixth chime sounded, the magus gestured at the doors and they slammed shut right behind the last novice.

"Tardiness upsets me, and that is *not* a good thing," she said sternly. "Welcome to economics. I'm Magus Marcia Han, and I will be your instructor for the year. This class is to teach you how economics work so you may better defend the empire against all manner of threat. Failure to complete this course satisfactorily will result in inel-igibility for certain posts in the empire, but you aren't mandated to stay. You may leave the class at any time, and even miss it entirely to better focus on other avenues, if you wish. Any questions?"

"Magus?"

"Go ahead," she motioned at the novice who had spoken.

"From your name, can we assume you are with the Han Merchant Exchange?"

"I am, and those who excel in this class could find themselves recruited by them or by other merchant groups serving the empire. Now, let us begin. We begin with the vela, and how this currency came to dominate the empire."

For the next two hours, Magus Han went over things Gregory had already learned from his time in the archive, but he was attentive and took notes of the small differences between what the magus told them and what he had read. Yukiko did not take any notes, but she did answer three questions put forth by the magus. That brought her to the attention of the other novices who had not seen her during the last week.

When class was dismissed, Gregory and Yukiko were one of the last groups out of the room. They had walked the routes to each class numerous times before, so they used some of the shorter paths they had found and ended up being among the first few into the next classroom. Sitting in the third row, they had a good view of the black-board and the severe-looking man in an emerald kimono.

"Wasn't he at breakfast, too?" Yukiko whispered to Gregory.

"Yes," Gregory said. "I think the four we saw were our instructors."

When the eighth bell rang, the instructor started talking, not caring that the doors were left wide open. "I'm Adept Thomas Martin, and I'm your instructor in history. Why are we teaching you history, some of you might ask? The answer is simple; those who don't know the lessons of history are doomed to repeat them. Now—" He cut off suddenly, his gaze narrowing at the door. "You are late,

Novice. *Come up here!*" The last three words held an edge that made Gregory's eyes narrow.

"I'm sorry, sir," the novice apologized and hurried to the front.

"You are late and disrupted my lesson," Thomas stated, his lip curling in displeasure. "You will complete an essay exploring why angering your instructor is an unwise decision, and you will hand it in tomorrow. Failure to do so will get you removed from this class. Understood?"

"Yes, sir," the novice bowed, then hurried to a table at the back of the room.

"Where was I?" Thomas sighed. "Oh, yes. None of you are required to be here. History is for those who wish to learn. You may leave the class at any time, but if you do, you'll never be allowed back in. Same goes if you fail an assignment from me. Failure to complete this course means that some postings in the empire will be denied to you. Any questions?" After a pause, Thomas smiled, "Good. Let us start at the very beginning, with Emperor Toja. Not as the Divine Emperor we all know today, but when he was simply War Leader Toja."

Gregory was quick to put his things away when class ended. Like economics, the class covered things he read over a week ago, so the only notes he had taken were the parts where Thomas discussed points that historians had contentious views on.

Gregory was almost jogging as he and Yukiko made their way to the next class. Yukiko giggled, "The next class isn't going anywhere, Greg."

"I know, but this will be new information," Greg said, but slowed his pace. "I'm hoping that maybe something will shed light on what my magic is."

"I understand," Yukiko said, touching his arm. "I'm excited about hearing more about shadow magic."

Grins in place, the two of them walked quickly to their next class.

CHAPTER 19

G regory approached the class area more slowly, since this class was held outdoors, near one of the walls. The patio had twenty tables set up in a long arc facing an open area. Setting out paper, ink, and pen, he looked at the teacher questioningly. The plain-looking man in the emerald kimono sat in a lotus position on a small stool, eyes closed and breathing slowly.

"I guess the magus who was reading is going to be our conditioning instructor," Gregory whispered to Yukiko.

"I believe this teacher must follow the spirit path," Yukiko whispered back.

"I do indeed," the meditating man replied, his voice as plain as the rest of him. "We will cover that when class begins."

Exchanging a glance, the pair stopped talking and made sure they were ready. The other tables filled rapidly as it got closer to the tenth bell. A minute later, the chiming of the academy bell began, and the teacher unfolded his legs, got to his feet, and stretched. Looking at the group, his eyes barely touched any of them. With a nod, he stepped farther back, so he was in the sun and not in the shade.

The moment the bells stopped chiming, he addressed the class, "Welcome to aether introduction. I'm Adept John Dunn, your teacher." His voice was nearly monotone as he spoke. "During the course of this year, I will introduce you to the three paths, as well as the known magics. This will involve a number of guests. Be respectful to them, as they are magi who have been in your place before. We are also lucky in that, at some point, we will get to see an unknown magic."

Hushed conversations sprang up at John's bombshell. He let them talk for a minute before he clapped his hands and everyone fell silent.

"Today, we will be focusing on the body path," John said. "We will discuss the different viewpoints of the path, both for and against it. We will also have a guest show you the basics of how to start on that path."

"Sir," one of the novices raised their hand and waited for John to acknowledge them. "Is it true that some can follow more than a single path?"

"The number of magi who have managed that is less than the number of novices in this class. No one, except maybe the Divine Emperor himself, has ever followed all three paths. Find the path you think best suits you and follow it. After you are comfortable with it, then and only then, should you think about attempting to start another path. Just be aware that you are all but doomed to fail."

Gregory's aether churned and flared briefly at John's words. Gregory frowned, wondering why it was acting up, but it subsided back to its base default state after a few seconds.

"I want you all to welcome Proctor Samantha Bishop. She has graciously agreed to be here as we speak of the body path." John's monotone voice had an edge of respect as he bowed to Bishop, who stepped past the novices and into the sun.

"Novices, I know many of you are wondering about the body path," Bishop said without preamble. "It is the most widely followed path in the empire. The reasons for this are that the body path will sculpt your body to be the best it can be, and it will help your aether integrate into your whole body."

"Is it only the body path that spreads aether throughout your body?" one of the novices asked.

"All paths will let you use aether throughout your body, but the body path makes it easier, faster, and makes it painless."

"Aether is the flame inside each magi," John continued. "If any of you tried to imbue a kick with aether right now, that flame could possibly damage your body. If you follow the body path, channels designed for aether will spread out through you."

"Doesn't that make it the best path?" another novice asked.

"Not at all," John replied. "The body path won't let aether augment your mind. Those who follow the mind path find that they can process information faster, and follow multiple threads at the same time without loss of understanding. That path is more useful to those who need to multitask. We will cover that more when we speak of the mind path."

"What about the spirit path?" another novice asked.

For a fleeting moment, a smile appeared on John's lips before vanishing. "It is unique, and is looked down on by those that follow the other paths. Again, we will cover it more in time. Today, we focus on the body path. Bishop," John bowed to her and stepped back again.

"The body path is a favorite for those who have physical enhancement magic, as the two dovetail nicely," Bishop said. "I myself am a user of that magic, and a follower of the body path. How many here are blessed with physical enhancement magic?" Six hands rose, and Bishop smiled. "You are the spears of the empire. Now, I know some of you are wondering how the body path really affects the body."

Most of the class nodded in agreement.

"Very well. I need a volunteer." Her eyes locked on to Gregory. "Novice, step out here, please."

Gregory felt dread start to build in his chest, but did as he was told. He stood next to her and waited. Yukiko smiled encouragingly at him.

"Now, strip," Bishop said as she began to pull off her own clothing, "just down to your small clothes."

Gregory blinked, staring at Bishop in confusion as she dropped her bag and sword. "Umm, Proctor?"

"What? Are you too shy for even that, Novice? I can ask your tablemate instead."

Setting his jaw, Gregory glanced at Yukiko, who had turned red. He began to take off the kimono.

"Don't gawk. The point is what the body path does, and that is all," Bishop said firmly, glaring at one or two novices who were smirking at her. They quickly stopped smirking when they saw the promise of pain in her eyes.

Once they were both in their underwear, Bishop began to speak again, "I was roughly the same size and shape as your peer, but I grew out of that by the end of the year. Raise your arms, Novice."

Gregory did as he was told, his face blank, his jaw set, and he kept his eyes off the others although he could hear their whispers when they saw the scarring on his left arm.

"As you can see, there is a lack of muscle definition. Now, look at my arms," Bishop raised her arms in the exact same way. "Do you see the definition of muscle, class? Now curl your arm, Novice."

Bishop led them muscle by muscle through the difference between their bodies. Gregory got a good look at Bishop, doing his best to keep his mind calm. Bishop in her underwear looked like she had been sculpted by a master crafter. Every movement left her flexing and shifting muscles on clear display. The scars she had criss-crossing her body were stark reminders of a hard life.

Once she was done, she picked up her clothing and began to dress. "You're free to cover up again, Novice."

Gregory dressed as quickly as he could before returning to his seat. He could feel the amusement of the others in class, along with the pity a few of them directed at him for his spindly frame. Taking a seat, he closed his eyes and tried to block out the embarrassment.

"Thank you, Greg," Yukiko whispered, "for sparing me."

Gregory nodded, "Welcome." Opening his eyes, he locked them onto Bishop, now fully dressed.

"That is the most obvious benefit to the body path," she said.

"There are degrees to how much your individual bodies will change. Not only are my muscles as perfect as they can be, my aether is in conjunction with them, as well. I will demonstrate a simple punch, with and without aether. Adept, do you have the display ready?"

"I do, Proctor," John said, bringing out a set of targets.

"The first target is one-inch thick wooden squares," Bishop said. "We have ten of them here." Standing above the stacked boards, Bishop focused on them. Breathing in and out steadily, she exploded into motion, her hand coming down square in the middle. The sound of breaking wood filled the silence, and the stack of boards fell away, all of them broken cleanly. "That was without aether," Bishop said before stepping over to the stone blocks stacked thirty high. "This is with aether."

The novices were silent as they watched her with breathless expectation.

Bishop breathed deeply again, and as she brought her hand over the stones, it was engulfed in blue flame. The flame deepened in color and blazed brighter. With no warning, she drove her arm down into the stone. The sound of stone shattering made everyone lean forward to see what had happened.

Stepping away from the broken bricks, Bishop flexed her hand. "Thirty stone blocks in a single blow. There is little difference between those stones and the walls you see around most cities. Now, for the last point, and this is for those of you with the same magic I have."

John brought out a training dummy made entirely out of metal. Wheeling it in front of Bishop on a cart, he unloaded it with a groan. "Here you are, Proctor."

Standing next to the dummy, she looked at the class. "A trained magi with physical enhancement can do amazing things, but most of it is geared toward combat. This is a dummy from the training hall— it survives even with adepts beating on it. That shouldn't be a surprise, because it is thirty inches of solid steel."

The class was dead silent as Bishop squared up to the target. Her breathing relaxed into the same deep pattern as before, and blue flame covered her arm from fingers to shoulder. With a sharp exhale, she drove her fist into the dummy. Stepping back, she turned it so they could see the hole punched clean through.

"*That* is what you can do if you reach the magus tier," Bishop said. "Sorry for the trouble, Adept."

"It leaves an impression," John said.

A number of snickers echoed through the class.

"I hate that joke," Bishop sighed. "Anyway, onto the basic training of the body path. Everyone, get up and move over here. This won't prejudice your path, so don't worry."

Over the next hour, Bishop ran the entire class through a basic stretching routine generally used for the body path. A few in the class felt their aether become more active, but most did not.

"Stop. Return to your seats," Bishop commanded. "Any questions before the class ends?"

"Are you seeing anyone?" one of the novices asked. His easy going smile and good looks made him seem like a playboy.

"I only date men," Bishop said firmly, shutting him down. "Anyone with an *actual* question?"

"Why would you recommend the body path over the others?"

"Good," Bishop gave the novice a smile. "Most of you will face combat; that is a given. Out of all paths, body is the most geared for combat. I would rather you all survive for many long years."

"If not body, would you have gone with mind?"

"I'm not sure," Bishop said. "Those who have physical enhancement magic would be foolish to take any other path. If I absolutely had to... maybe mind. I know a few mind path magi who can hold off multiple opponents."

"Class is done for today," John said. "You have a break before conditioning. I will see you tomorrow." He stopped talking, and the twelfth bell began to toll.

CHAPTER 20

"Novice, a word," Proctor Bishop said as Gregory gathered his things. Yukiko stepped to the side to wait for him.

"How may I help you this time, Proctor?"

"Do you know why I picked you?" Bishop asked.

"Because we had the same body type," Gregory recited what she had told the class.

"I could have picked any of the women in class as easily."

Gregory sighed, "Because besides them, I'm the thinnest, least muscled person in the class. It spared any of the women from baring their bodies to the rest of the class."

"Exactly. Most of them won't see it, but your friend with you does. Do you still think of your friend Delarosa?"

Gregory blinked. He was at a loss when he realized he had not been thinking of her nearly as often as he thought he would. "Occasionally," he said after a moment.

"A word of advice; relationships between magi and non-magi don't work out well due to the difference in our lifespans," Bishop replied, a sad smile on her lips. "You don't have to forget her, but you need to accept that fact."

"I will keep that in mind, Proctor," he replied, bowing to her.

＊ ＊ ＊

"Greg?"

"Huh?"

"Thank you again."

"It's okay, Yuki," Gregory said.

"Can I ask about the scars?"

"Bane wolf," he said, thinking back to the attack. Silence followed his two word answer and he sighed, then explained. They reached the mess hall just as he finished telling the story.

"Amoria... she is your—?"

"Friend," Gregory finished for her quickly. "One of my best friends. We can't be anything more, and she knows that. I made her promise to find happiness when I left. Magi loving non-magi never works out because of the difference in how long they live," he said, restating Bishop's admonishment.

"Oh," Yukiko said, "I see."

"Let's grab our snacks and get moving. We don't have a lot of time before conditioning."

"Yes."

After waiting in the line for a few minutes, they asked for a snack instead of a meal. One of the eurtiks handed them each a small sack. Taking the bags, they left the mess hall and headed for their next class. While they walked, Gregory pulled out one of the jerky cubes and began to chew on it.

When they reached the training hall, a note at the entrance instructed the novices to report to the orange arena. They picked up their pace, and located the arena with orange flags flying over it. They made it inside and an apprentice directed them out onto the arena floor. A handful of other novices were already waiting, and a few had snacks in hand, as well. Moving off to the side, Gregory took a seat and focused on eating, using the cheese and fruit to help temper the aether rush from the jerky.

More novices arrived, many of whom Gregory did not know. He called out to Nick, Michelle, and the others that he knew when they appeared. He tucked the empty snack bag into his pouch to return it later and got to his feet.

"How is your class?" Gregory asked when Nick got close enough.

"We're doing well. Glad we don't have all our classes with Hayworth. He's on the first floor, thankfully."

"Aether introduction was weird," Michelle said. "The proctor disrobing in front of us was rather shocking, and she made Fureno disrobe with her."

Fureno was a little red at the ears, "I didn't want to, but I wasn't going to argue with a magus. Now everyone thinks I'm the weakest one in our class."

"She picked Greg to go up with her for our class," Yukiko told them.

"Yeah, the thin guy over there... his arm is all scarred up," a novice's voice drifted over to them.

Gregory glanced over to see one of the other students from his class with a group of other novices. "*Great*. It's going to spread."

The bell sounded the thirteenth hour and as the last chime rang, a man in a cyan kimono walked out onto the arena floor. Gregory nodded; it was indeed the fourth person he and Yukiko had seen at breakfast. Instead of looking studious like he had this morning, he stalked forward like a hungry tiger. Gregory swallowed as he watched the teacher size each of them up.

"Fall in!" the man shouted.

Some of novices knew what he meant and quickly formed up into ranks before him. Gregory was doubly glad for his friendship with Nick, because he had explained this to Gregory over the last week. Now, Nick stood near the front while Yukiko and Gregory were farther back.

"Move it!"

The rest of the novices scrambled to get into lines like the ones that had already formed. Seven ranks of twelve novices eventually stood facing the magus.

"You will *always* form up like this when told to fall in, understood?"

A score of voices shouted back at him, "Yes, Magus!"

The instructor glowered at the novices. "You will always answer with a 'yes, sir,' or 'yes, Magus,' understood!?"

"Yes, sir."

"Yes, Magus." The echoed and jumbled voices yelled back.

With a sniff, the magus began to pace up and down the ranks. "I'm Magus Paul Erichson, and I will be your instructor for physical conditioning. If you displease me, you will be doing extra conditioning. Understood?"

"Yes, sir," came the loud reply.

Paul was swiftly in front of a novice in the front, almost nose to nose with him. "I can't hear you, Novice!"

"Yes, sir!" the novice yelled back.

"Most of you have never had any training, which means the first week is going to be torture for you. We will be working to get all of your weak, soft bodies into some semblance of healthy and fit. Twenty laps around the arena— run!"

Nick took off right away, and those behind him in line were quick to follow. Surprisingly to Gregory, Hayworth and the people with him did likewise. After a moment, the entire class was running. Paul followed them with a switch in his hand, swatting at anyone who was not running as fast as he wanted them to.

Feeling ready to collapse after the last lap, Gregory sucked in air like a bellows as he continued to pace. Even though aether churned inside him, his breathing was returning to normal faster than most in the class. Yukiko was pale, sweaty, and having trouble catching her breath, tripping and falling. Going to her side, he got her up and walking.

"Deep breaths," he managed to tell her. "It'll help. Mother taught me this as a kid."

Yukiko wanted to lay back down, but leaning on Gregory, she kept walking and doing her best to breathe deep. After a minute, she was feeling better and was able to walk on her own again.

"What's this? It's not time to nap," Paul bellowed. "Fall in!"

Less than twenty people were able to stand up straight. The rest were bent over, still gasping, or on the ground by the time they got into something resembling ranks.

"Pathetic! A mere twenty laps and you think you're done?" Paul scoffed at them. "Last five people not on their feet will be switched until they can stand."

Novices struggled harder to get to their feet, sucking in air. Paul was already among them and switching people before everyone knew it. Cries of pain filled the air until everyone was on their feet.

"Novices, you are here to be made into the weapons of the empire," Paul said, standing in front of the class again, his face grim. "Some of you might find some way to leverage a clan or family into sparing you the worst of it, but *all* of you will see combat, and at least half of you will die a bloody, messy death. The more you struggle and the more you fail, the more likely you'll be among the dead."

He let his eyes rove from one novice to the next, snorting. "I can guess who the unfortunate ones are going to be. But if you pour your heart and aether into training, you might— just maybe— survive. Now, spread out an arm's length apart from the people next to you, and again before and behind." He waited a moment for them to comply. "Passable. Now, first row, a step to the right. Third row, a step to the left. Fifth row, step right. Seventh, to the left." Walking down the length of the ranks, he nodded slowly. "We will begin stretching. We will start with this every day from now on. If you fail to keep up, you will have extra laps running."

* * *

Gregory felt his muscles burning. His aether was a dim coal inside him and his brain was full of fog when the eighteenth bell chimed.

"Dismissed until tomorrow," Paul said as he strode from the arena.

"He's a demon," one of the novices whimpered, forcing themselves upright.

"How are we going to survive this?" another asked in horror as they watched Paul leave.

"Yuki," Gregory asked, "you okay?"

"I feel faint," Yukiko replied as she slumped to her knees.

"Dinner. We need to eat for our aether," Gregory told her, holding out a hand.

Looking up at him, Yukiko nodded, "Yes, I know."

Taking her hand, he pulled her upright. "Bath first," he told her. "The water will help ease our muscles."

"He's right about that," Nick said with a nod, not looking as worn as they felt. "We're heading there ourselves."

"Okay," Yukiko added, leaning against Gregory. "Just go slow, please."

Making their way from the arena floor, Gregory was shocked to see how many novices were still sprawled in the sand. Silently thanking his mother for teaching him how to breathe to get his breath back as a kid, Gregory knew he would have been with them otherwise.

"We survived," Fureno mumbled, limping along.

"The first day," Nick replied. "Tomorrow will be worse. He was merely feeling us out today, finding out who could excel and who would collapse first."

"That doesn't fill me with hope," Gregory muttered.

"You stayed upright most of the time," Nick said with a respectful nod. "You'll be fine if you can keep that grit."

Conversation fell off as they made their way to the training hall and split into male and female groups for the baths. They spent twenty minutes soaking before more people began to show up. Taking that as their cue, the novices left and went to the mess hall. The nineteenth bell chimed as they made it to the door.

Inside, it was moderately busy, with two other groups of novices eating already. It was obvious they had skipped the bath, as dirt was smeared on cheeks, necks, and in their hair. Gregory went through the line almost in a daze, not recalling what he ordered, only that the eurtiks served him with smiles.

Taking a seat next to Yukiko across from Nick, Gregory blinked at his tray. One bowl held salad, while the omnipresent soup took up a second. Red meat sliced into thin strips was on his plate alongside brown rice. His cup was full of a sparkling yellow liquid that smelled of apples. Condensation was collecting on the outside of the cup.

Gregory was surprised at how long it took his aether to return to normal. It burned just barely brighter than usual, but he felt sated and content by the time he finished. Yukiko sighed appreciatively as she set her empty cup down.

"I feel exhausted," Michelle yawned. "I'm going to bed early tonight."

"A good idea," Nick nodded. "Greg, Yuki, we'll see you for conditioning tomorrow."

"Night," Gregory replied.

"Of course," Yukiko replied. "Sleep well."

Pushing themselves to their feet after the others, Gregory and Yukiko walked slowly to drop off their dishes. When they turned to leave, Gregory recalled the bag from lunch and turned it over. Yukiko followed suit, reminded by him.

"Many have forgotten. Thank you," the otter eurtik said with a smile. "Keeper Dia will be unhappy tomorrow."

"I'm glad it won't be us that caused her ire," Gregory replied as they turned to leave.

"Greg... would you like to stop by and play some Go before bed?" Yukiko asked, brushing some of her blonde hair behind her ear.

"Not tonight. I feel as exhausted as Michelle," Gregory replied, his eyelids feeling heavy. "Sorry, Yuki. Maybe tomorrow?"

"Okay, tomorrow. Thank you for helping me in class."

"I do what I can," Gregory smiled. "I'll need your help with economics."

"I'll gladly return the favor, then."

Gregory made it to his room in the dormitory, his steps dragging by then. He got his clothes set out for the staff, collapsed onto his mat, pulled the blankets over his head, and fell fast asleep.

CHAPTER 21

"Oh, that won't do. Come now, dear one, wake up," a hauntingly seductive voice whispered.

Gregory sat bolt upright, his heart pounding. His head whipped from side to side as he took in his surroundings. His panic subsided when he realized where he was. "Have I grown enough for us to talk again?"

"Enough for a short talk," the darkness whispered. "I never expected you to take two lovers, but you did. It's a shame you'll likely never see either of them again."

Gregory got out of the bed and noticed he was nude, "Umm..."

"What? I'm enjoying the view," light laughter circled him. "There is clothing in the armoire, if you insist."

Gregory opened the doors of the armoire and stared. Men's clothing hung waiting for him, each outfit different from the others. "What?"

"Just pick what suits you best," the darkness told him.

Gregory looked at the clothes for a long moment. There were kimonos of every color along with more ostentatious outfits, a suit of proctor's armor, and even a set of armor for the emperor's guard.

Stepping back, Gregory shook his head, "No. None of these feel right."

"Oh, dear one, you do so surprise me," the voice whispered excitedly. "Here, have these for now."

Gregory saw his novice kimono covering him. "Thanks?"

"You are welcome. Now, we need to talk about paths before these well-meaning, but flawed, individuals bias you. Train in any way you wish, or in every way all at once. Force your body to do as you command. Make your body, mind, and spirit all work together. You can, if you have the strength of will to make it happen. If you do, I'll give you a special treat," the last few words dripped with sexual tension.

Shivering as thoughts of decadent pleasure ran through his mind, Gregory exhaled slowly. "I see. That is motivation, even if this is only a dream."

"Only a dream... if that is what you wish to believe. They have no idea about what you can do and the records have likely been destroyed. I'll tell you more after the first tournament. Don't disappoint me, dear one."

"Wait—" Gregory began, but the room dissolved around him as a bell chimed three times.

* * *

Gregory woke with a shudder, sitting bolt upright when the third bell finished ringing. "Was that real, or a dream?" he asked the empty air. He got no response, so he forced himself to his feet and reached for his clothes.

He almost ran into Yukiko as the two of them left their rooms at the same time. "Morning," he said softly, stepping back so they were not on top of each other.

"Morning, Greg. You were right to decline last night. I fell asleep soon after getting in."

"I passed right out," Gregory said. "Breakfast and then the archive?"

"Yes."

They reached the mess hall in short order and the only other people eating were the four teachers. Those four looked at the two of them with varying degrees of interest before turning back to their own amusements.

While he was getting breakfast, the last eurtik smiled at Gregory. "I see you've already started to grow. Well done," she said with her hand hovering over his medallion.

"How do you know?" Gregory asked.

The mink eurtik indicated the medallion on his chest, "Another ring is empowered this morning."

Gregory looked down and blinked, wondering how he had not noticed before. Four of the ten circles were now faintly glowing with clear light. "Oh, um... right." Bowing his head to her, he picked out a cup of tea and went to sit with Yukiko.

"I didn't grow in power," Yukiko said softly, her medallion still showing the four circles it had before. "Did you pick a path already?"

Gregory paused, his fork of salad halfway to his mouth. "No..."

"You seem unsure," Yukiko replied.

"I think I'm going to try training all of them," Gregory said very quietly so his voice would not carry to the teachers.

Yukiko looked at him curiously while she continued to eat. After a few bites, she spoke just as quietly, "Why?"

"I think it'll work," Gregory replied.

Yukiko shook her head, "The teachers—"

Gregory lost track of what she was saying as he felt a crossroads open before him. He could try to convince her to join him, or not. The outcome of each was shrouded in darkness to him, but he knew that something pivotal hung on the moment.

"I can't rightly explain, but I think it'll work," he said as he came back to his senses. "Just trust me, with you and me both doing it, it'll work."

Yukiko blinked at him slowly, before she bowed her head. "I do trust you, Greg, I shall train as you do."

Gregory smiled and started to thank her, but he was distracted by another vision. Behind Yukiko stood a copy of her. Clad in darkness, her face was mostly obscured, but the image had a warm smile directed at him. Blinking as the vision vanished, Gregory sat there motionless.

"Greg? You need to eat if we're going to the archive," Yukiko said, breaking him out of his stupor.

"Oh, yes, sorry," Gregory said, starting to eat as fast as he could, but his thoughts were elsewhere.

Do I ask about it in the archive? Or would that be bad? The visions might not even be real... could just be wishes given form... I should wait, at least until my magic is known. With those thoughts running around and around in his head, he finished his breakfast.

They dropped off their dishes when fourth bell started to chime. More novices were arriving and there was a short line. On an impulse, Gregory got into the line again. Yukiko was watching him and standing off to the side.

"You've already eaten, Novice," the weasel eurtik said.

"I was hoping to get my snack now," Gregory explained.

"Ah. Yes, that is doable," the eurtik grinned. "See Velma." He motioned toward the mink at the end of the counter.

Gregory waved Yukiko over as he waited to speak to Velma. "Velma, we would like to have our snacks now. Is that okay?"

Her eyes were twinkling and she smiled as she handed two small bags over. Gregory and Yukiko each took one, thanking her and quickly left the mess.

"Jerky, cheese, and a piece of fruit. It will all keep easily," Yukiko said, checking the snack as they walked. "Why did you ask now?"

"So we won't have to go back there before conditioning," he replied. "I think having the extra time to rest might be better."

"We'll see today," Yukiko said.

They greeted Rafiq when they entered the archive. "Morning, Archivist," Gregory smiled.

"Morning to you both," Rafiq replied. "Your books are on the table you've been using. Do you wish for any other books or scrolls?"

Gregory almost asked for information on visions, but shook his head instead. "Not right now, thank you."

"Good studying to you both," Rafiq said, bowing his head to them.

"Good day to you," Yukiko smiled as she followed Gregory into the archive.

They got to their table and gave their attention to their studies. Gregory felt his focus narrow down to the book before him and nothing more. The text was slow and tedious, but it made sense as he read. The current chapter described how vela had been disputed as the currency for the empire; it had a dozen names before anyone settled on "vela" five hundred years ago.

Time ticked away as they learned, but the fifth bell chiming brought both of them out of their studies. Gregory realized he was a page from the end of the book so continued reading. When he was finished, he put the book aside.

"You finished yours, too?" Yukiko asked.

"Yes. I'm not sure any of it will ever be of use, but it was interesting," Gregory said as he got to his feet and stretched.

"I feel the same about history. Father always said history was written by the winner. I think I understand that better now that I've read this tome. There is nothing about any wrongdoing by the empire in the entirety of it."

"Because history *is* written by the winner," the panther eurtik said from a row of shelves nearby. "Winners do no wrong— they are the ones who were wronged and were only seeking to make the world better."

"Archivist," Gregory bowed his head, "we've finished with these books."

"Did you have a preference for your next study session?"

"I will leave that in your hands, as I feel you'll guide me better than I could," Gregory said, bowing formally to her.

A slight smile creased her muzzle, "I will do my best, but a direction would still be appreciated."

"I want to know more about the wars the empire has fought,"

Yukiko said slowly. "Surely there are other books that have a different view."

The eurtik eyed her, "I would advise you to rephrase that carefully if you were to say that to anyone else. Some might view it as disrespectful or even traitorous to the empire. *But*, I do have a book for you."

Gregory frowned as he thought about what he wanted, "A book on visions of the future, or maybe one about how someone who trained on more than one path managed it?"

The archivist nodded slowly, "Very well, Novice, I will find you something. I wish you both a good day."

Gregory and Yukiko returned the bow and left the archive, wishing Rafiq a good day as they went past him. The pair was silent as they walked the path to their first class, each thinking about what the archivist had said to them.

Yukiko broke the silence as they drew close to the classroom, "Greg, how do we know if your idea of training all three paths is working?"

"I don't know, but I think the hour of study every morning might count for the mind path. It's not what we read as the preferred training, but maybe it'll still work since we are expanding our horizons. I wanted the snacks early so we can meditate before conditioning to train the spirit path, and I'm fairly certain that conditioning will count for body. I hope that will at least work for the first steps of each, but we'll have to see what happens in the coming days to know if anything is working."

"Very well," Yukiko said. "Early mornings and early nights for the future."

"It does seem that way," Gregory nodded.

* * *

They took notes during their classes, doing their best to learn. When the break before conditioning came, they made their way to the training hall, then went to the green arena.

"Changing it each day to keep us off balance?" Gregory asked Yukiko while they sat on the arena floor to eat their snack.

"To trick some into being late so he can make an example of them, I think," Yukiko replied as she nibbled on a piece of cheese. "Your idea for snacks and meditation is even better now."

Gregory chuckled, "Even a blind squirrel finds a nut occasionally."

"What?" Yukiko asked.

"A saying Gunnar is fond of," Gregory laughed, and explained what it meant.

"I see," Yukiko giggled.

They finished their snack and no one else was there yet, so they each crossed their legs, closed their eyes, and concentrated on steadying their breathing. Gregory was not sure how long he sat there, but a memory came to him.

* * *

"Do you understand, son?" Marian asked.

"Yes, Mama," Gregory said, looking up at her with bright eyes. "I'm gonna be a magi. I can make things better."

Marian tousled the five-year-old's hair. "If that is what you really want, then you should. You don't have to be a magi, you can be like your father. Helping those close to you is just as important."

"Papa is strong," Gregory smiled. "I can be like Papa *and* a magi!"

Marian laughed, "Yes, that is certainly possible. I think you'll take after me more than him, though." Her eyes were sad as she gently brushed at Gregory's hair. "I hope I am wrong, but only time will tell..."

"Mama? Don't cry... I'll be a magi, don't worry," Gregory said, reaching up to touch the tears on Marian's cheeks. "I'll be the best magi."

Marian's eyes went distant and after a moment, she shook her head, "Yes... yes, you will." Hugging him to her, she kissed the top of his head. "With such joy and pain awaiting you, if I could only..."

* * *

"Greg, wake up," Yukiko's voice shattered the memory.

Blinking, Gregory shook his head, "Huh? What?"

"It's almost time," Yukiko said, looking at him with worry. "Are you okay?"

"Yeah, why?"

"You're crying," she whispered, reaching out to brush the tears off his cheeks.

He wiped at his eyes, trying not to be too obvious. "A memory... it's nothing." Getting to his feet, he looked away from her as the memory started to fade. "My mother was speaking to me as a child. I haven't been able to recall her face that perfectly in years."

"Ah, I apologize for interrupting you," Yukiko said.

"No, it's fine," Gregory said, turning back to her. "Thanks, Yuki."

She gave him a tentative smile, "You're welcome."

"He's here," Nick's voice carried across the arena.

Seeing Paul walking across the sands, the novices hurried to line up before the magus could call for them to do so. Gregory and Yukiko got into line just as his thunderous voice echoed off the walls, "Fall in!"

CHAPTER 22

The week became a blur to Gregory; waking, food, archive, classes, break and meditation, conditioning, then sleep. Twice he felt the mind path opening more to him. Body was being trained every day, but spirit had not shown him a second memory yet. Their teachers started to take notice of him and Yukiko, recognizing them from their early starts each day.

When he woke up, he got out of bed and dressed by habit, only stopping when he reached the door. "Wait. Today is our day off... I think?"

He opened his door almost on reflex when a soft knock sounded. Yukiko was standing there, wearing a dark blue kimono embroidered with white owls. "Greg... it's our day off today... why?"

"Reflex," Gregory sighed. "I'll change and meet you downstairs as quickly as I can."

"I'll be waiting," Yukiko giggled.

Shutting the door when she turned away, Gregory went back to the closet and got dressed in his best clothing. Looking at it, he frowned. *Plain, drab. This makes me look poor... well, I am, but it reflects on Yukiko now, too.* Tying his money pouch onto his belt, he felt the jingle of coins— not many but some.

When he made it downstairs, he found Yukiko and Dia speaking on the porch. "Here he is," Dia said. "I do hope you enjoy your day."

"Thank you, Keeper," Yukiko smiled. "We will do our best."

Dia just took a long drag on her pipe, watching as they went toward the mess hall. "The clans should be taking an interest soon. I wonder who will approach them first?" The light breeze did not answer her question, wafting the smoke away from her instead.

The mess hall was empty; the four teachers who were usually there were not present today. The eurtik working behind the counter waved them over. "I told you they would be here, Zenim," the weasel chuckled.

"So you did, Ravol," the scaled eurtik, Zenim, replied, handing over some vela.

"Betting if we would show up?" Yukiko asked as she took her offered breakfast.

"Yes. Today, many novices will sleep in," Velma replied. "You two are driven, though. We had doubts when he only thought you'd sleep."

Zenim shrugged, "Didn't lose much, at least."

Gregory shook his head, "Next time, tell me and we can work out a deal."

Zenim laughed, and the others joined in. "Have a good meal."

"Can we get our snac—?" Gregory started, but Velma was holding out the snack bags before he could finish asking. "Thank you."

"Thank you," the four replied, bowing their heads in almost perfect unison.

Taking their seats, Gregory was in thought. "Why did they thank us?"

"I forget you're a fringer, sometimes," Yukiko replied. "We treat them well, we are polite, and don't yell at or scold them. All of them have strong ties to eurtik blood, which means they are used to people looking down on them."

With a puzzled shake of his head, Gregory started to eat. He wondered about the eurtik and how they could accept that treatment after hundreds of years of servitude to the empire.

By the time he finished his breakfast, he had stopped thinking about it, instead turning his thoughts to his current reading. "Ready for the archive?"

"Yes," Yukiko smiled, getting to her feet.

"Let's go," Gregory smiled back as they headed out together.

It was not a long walk, and Rafiq grinned at them as they entered the archive. "I thought you two would be here, even with it being your day off."

"Good morning, Rafiq," Yukiko greeted him.

"No reason to break our routine. We'll just be going into town instead of class today."

"Interesting. That will still make you some of the first to leave the walls today. Your books are awaiting you. Did you need new ones?"

"I'm almost finished with the history I'm reading," Yukiko replied. "I have enjoyed seeing things in a different light. Maybe you can have another ready tomorrow?"

"Of course," Rafiq bowed his head.

"The scroll written by Lionel Lighthand has taken me a long time to work through," Gregory admitted. "If you have anything on future visions, though, I'd like to see it tomorrow."

Rafiq looked into the distance for a minute. "I'll see what can be done. Books like that are normally for more advanced magi."

"I see," Gregory sighed. "If it's not possible, then something on economics, please? The teacher is about to race off ahead of me. Yukiko and I haven't had much of a chance to study together, since we've been collapsing every evening after conditioning."

"I can do that," Rafiq replied. "Good learning to you both."

As they walked toward the table in the back, Yukiko glanced at Gregory, "We could study together tonight."

"After an hour of physical training," Gregory said. "We need to keep the training going."

"Yes," Yukiko nodded. "I've felt connections with mind and spirit over the last week. Body is being drilled into us... I wonder if the other novices are seeing that?"

"It's slight," Gregory said, "but it proves that training more than one path at a time is probably very possible. Some of it might be how much you can train in any given day, too. We're pushing as hard as we can and barely scratching all three of them."

Yukiko nodded, taking her seat at the table. "True, but maybe the next step on each path will make it easier to train?"

Gregory smiled, "Hope is good. It sustained me for years. I have a feeling it will only get harder and more intense, though."

Yukiko looked serious, "Then we will do more."

"Helping push each other and support each other."

Yukiko smiled brightly, then opened the book in front of her. Seeing her focus, Gregory unrolled the long scroll he was reading and settled in, trying to decipher the text written by one of the greatest magi of the empire.

* * *

Rolling the scroll up, Gregory set it aside, deep in thought. *Lionel states it's possible, but takes dedication... he trained both body and spirit. He was trying to merge the two by training them together, but hadn't yet been successful when he wrote the scroll. Can we do that...? How would we manage two, much less all three, together? They're all so different.*

Yukiko closed her book when she finished reading, only to look up and see Gregory lost in thought. She sat there quietly, watching him with a smile.

The chiming of fifth bell brought Gregory back, and Yukiko looked away before he could catch her watching him. "Guess it's time to go to the city," he said.

"Yes," Yukiko said, her cheeks turning a light shade of pink.

"You okay, Yuki?" Gregory asked, concerned for her.

"Yes," Yukiko repeated. "If you want to purchase anything while we're in the city, I can get you a good deal."

Thinking of his limited purse, Gregory nodded. "Thank you, I'd appreciate the help."

"Have a good day, Novices," Rafiq grinned as they approached. "Enjoy your day together."

"We always do," Gregory replied, missing the context.

Yukiko blushed again, "Friends always enjoy each other's company."

Rafiq's smile tilted into a suppressed smirk, and he said softly, "Yes. Some more than others."

Yukiko looked away from him, her cheeks burning hotter as she followed Gregory down the path.

* * *

At the gates of the academy, Gregory was surprised to be directed to one side of the giant gates. There was a small metal door guarded by six guards and an apprentice, and they examined the pair with curiosity.

"Going out on a date?" the apprentice asked with a smirk.

"We are going into the city," Gregory replied blandly.

"Early in the day, but it's allowed," the apprentice replied. "Novices are to be back by sundown, or they will face discipline."

"We understand," Gregory said.

"Sergeant, the door," the apprentice said.

"Open it," the sergeant told the man closest to the door.

With the metal door unbarred and opened, Gregory and Yukiko stepped out into the city. The door closed behind them with a firm thud.

Gregory looked around in the predawn light. "Not sure where we should be going besides down to the lowest ring."

"It's a walk to get there unless we can find a rickshaw," Yukiko said. "We can try to find one, because it will take us most of our time otherwise."

Thinking about the limited funds he had, Gregory frowned, but followed her. "Okay, but we should start walking just in case we don't find one."

"Agreed," Yukiko said.

They did not have to walk far before a man driving a rickshaw came toward them, clearly heading for the academy.

Yukiko flagged him down, and when the man came to a stop next to them, she handed him a coin. "We would like to be taken to the lower ring."

"Of course, mistress," the man bowed.

Yukiko got into the seat and Gregory followed her. He tried not to stare, as he had seen this vehicle during his trip to the academy with Proctor Bishop. The seat in the covered carriage was barely wide enough for them both, and once they were seated the driver mounted the device at the front and pedaled them down the gently curved incline toward the lower ring.

"How much do I owe you?" Gregory asked after a minute.

"Nothing. I was the one who wanted to take the rickshaw," Yukiko said, aware that Gregory did not come from money.

Gregory considered arguing, but he glanced at her and noticed her set expression. "Okay, Yuki. Thank you."

She smiled, "You're welcome, Greg."

The pair watched the streets roll by as the sun broke over the horizon. The empty streets slowly came to life, the traffic increasing as they drew closer to the lower ring gates. Sixth bell had just chimed throughout the city when they arrived at the gates between the upper and lower rings.

"Should we start here or at the lower gates?" Gregory asked her.

"Let's start at the bottom," Yukiko replied. "I doubt we'll make it around the entire lower ring, but we can try."

"I'm in your hands, Yuki. You have more experience in a city than I do."

Yukiko's cheeks pinked and she nodded. "I will do my best, Greg."

It took a few minutes before they were past the gate and into the lower ring. The rickshaw driver followed the long, spiraled, inclined main road all the way to the north gates. Yukiko had him stop a hundred yards short of them.

"We will disembark here, thank you," Yukiko called out.

"My pleasure, mistress," the driver bowed deeply to her and Gregory. "A pleasant day for you both."

Gregory whistled as he took in the view. None of the cities he had been in with Proctor Bishop had been anything like as grand as the city spread out in front of him.

"Are you looking for anything specific, Greg?" Yukiko asked, bringing Gregory's attention back to the street in front of them.

"Better clothes, maybe? Beside you, I feel like a beggar."

"A clothing store first? Very well," Yukiko said as she looked down the street. "Follow me."

Gregory fell into step with her. He was looking everywhere, trying to both take in the city and avoid another run in with muggers. After a few blocks, Gregory realized something that had been nagging at him.

"These shops are all pretty large, but the second levels are almost always smaller," he muttered.

"They're homes. They reside above the shops, or their apprentices do," Yukiko told him. "It is a common practice."

"Why are the shops so large?"

"They have storage space as well."

A stray memory came to him, "We should find Lagrand Clothiers. I ran into one of their family on my way here. He sold me this tunic, in fact."

Yukiko slowed her pace for a moment. "Okay." Looking around, she waved at a man in light armor bearing the empire's colors and emblem. "Sir, may I trouble you?"

"Yes, miss," the guard said, coming over to them. "How might I help you?"

"Where might I find Lagrand Clothiers?"

"Not far from here," the guard said, turning to face the direction they were heading. "Six or seven streets that way, on the left side."

"Thank you."

"You're welcome. Have a good day."

"You, as well," Gregory replied to the guard. "Well, that will make it easier to find. I'm not used to patrolling guards."

"They help people like us find our way, as well as deterring crime," Yukiko said as she started walking again. "Another expense of the empire, but one that is well spent."

CHAPTER 23

Gregory was interested to see that the sign for Lagrand Clothiers was a little more ragged than some others they had passed. Yukiko stood for a moment, looking at the exterior of the shop thoughtfully before she went inside. A small chime announced them to the staff.

"Welcome to Lagrand Clothiers. How can I help you?" a kindly-looking middle-aged woman asked.

"We're hoping to upgrade his wardrobe," Yukiko said plainly, motioning to Gregory.

"Of course, miss. Are you looking for multiple outfits or just the one?"

"Just—" Gregory began.

"At least three sets," Yukiko cut him off, her tone more assertive than usual. "He must look at least my equal."

"Yuk—" Gregory began again.

"Excuse us," Yukiko told the staff member, cutting him off again. Taking his elbow, she led him toward the door. "Greg, let me handle this. I come from merchants, remember?"

"Yes, but I don't have that kind of vela."

"We'll sort it out later. Trust me for now."

He wanted to argue, but seeing her earnest and hopeful expression, he bowed his head. "I'm in your hands, Yuki."

"Thank you." Giving him a bright smile, she turned back to the shopkeeper. "Now, as I was saying, three outfits, equal or better than what I am wearing. I would like two of them in Buldoun cotton, and a silk kimono for formal wear."

Gregory's eyes bulged at the word silk. He knew that the Delarosas only had it to work with once. They had made a dress from it that they sold to a merchant for hundreds of vela.

"We can do that," the shopkeeper smiled, picking up a bell and giving it a ring.

A tall man came out of a side door, "You rang, mistress?"

"Measure the gentleman. We will be doing three outfits, two in Buldoun cotton and one kimono in silk. Did you have a preference for colors?" the shopkeeper addressed the last to Yukiko.

Yukiko looked Gregory over. "Green, like his eyes, but don't overdo it. I want it to be subtle."

"Very well, miss."

"Sir," the tall man said, motioning Gregory to the door, "if you will follow me, we need to measure you."

Gregory looked at Yukiko, who met his gaze. After a few seconds, he followed the man into the back. They went into a hall lined with doors, and the servant led Gregory to the second room.

"Please, stand on the blue square," the man said with deference. "I'll have you measured quickly."

Doing as he was told, Gregory placed his stuff on the single chair in the room before stepping onto the blue square painted in the middle of the floor. The servant began to measure him, starting with his legs.

Gregory had been measured before, helping Amoria practice, and his mind drifted to an old memory. A traveling merchant had stopped in their shop about five years back and asked to have a new set of clothing made to order. The Delarosas had been more than happy to help him until the man began to strip. Tony, Amoria's father, yelled at the man to get him to stop. The merchant explained his normal tailor had him strip to be measured, but Tony had just sighed and explained it was not necessary, grabbing his tape to start the process once the merchant was dressed again.

"All done," the man said, stepping away and making notes. "Would you like something to drink while we get things ready?"

Blinking as he came back from the memory, Gregory shook his head. "No thank you, I'm fine."

"Very well," the servant said before stepping out of the room.

Gregory took a seat and closed his eyes. He knew it might take them a few minutes to find the right items, so breathing slow and deep, he tried to find the right meditative state. Calmness spread over him and memories came trickling back, until one filled his mind.

* * *

"Greg, why don't you want to consider it?" Amoria complained.

"Because I'm going to be a magi, Ria. I won't be here after next year," Gregory replied, his jaw set. "Your father wouldn't seriously take me as an apprentice, anyway. I know you think he would, but you're not being realistic. What future would you have with me? Gunnar would be a better bet, or even Stan! He's always had a crush on you."

Amoria's face went red, then white, before heating again. "You dumb asshole!"

"I don't see why you're upset. I've told you every day that I'm going to be a magi!" Gregory called after her as she stormed away.

* * *

The moment crystallized for Gregory and he knew now why she had been so upset back then. *It was right in front of me and I was too blind to see it. I was so caught up in wanting to be a magi that I couldn't see, or didn't want to see the truth. Ria, I hope you're doing okay and are doing what you promised.*

"Sir, we have a few selections for you to try," the servant said, coming into the room with a collection of clothing in his arms.

"Yes," Gregory said, blinking and wiping at his eyes. "Of course."

It took him a while to try on all the different outfits. Eventually, he settled on two that were off-white with green accents for the cotton. The last one was mostly green with white accents for the silk kimono. All of them were a little large for him, but he knew he had been putting on muscle and wanted to make sure he had room for growth.

"Are you sure these are the ones you want, sir?" The servant looked a little skeptical because of the looseness of the fabric.

"I've been putting on weight and will need the extra room," Gregory told the man.

"Very well, sir. The mistress has already paid for them and asks that you change into one before coming out. We will have the others sent to your abode, along with your current clothing."

Gregory held in the wince as he thought of what this was costing Yukiko. *I'll have to pay her back somehow.* "I'll wear this one," Gregory said, picking up the first outfit.

The servant had stared at the scars on Gregory's arm multiple times, but he had politely not asked about them while Gregory was trying on outfits. As he was bundling up the sets that were to be delivered, the servant did make a comment that made Gregory pause. "The mistress seems quite interested that you are her equal in appearance, sir."

"Yes... yes she is, isn't she?" Gregory murmured as he continued dressing.

"I will show you out," the servant said once Gregory was ready.

Yukiko was sipping tea and chatting with the shopkeeper when the servant brought Gregory out of the back. Her eyes lit up upon seeing him, "Very good. Thank you for your service," she directed at the shopkeeper.

"Please come back if you require anything else," the shopkeeper said, setting her cup down.

"We will," Yukiko said. "Are you ready, Greg?"

"Yes."

The pair left, unaware of the gossip that transpired behind their backs once the door was closed. The streets were becoming busy with people as the eighth bell chimed.

Gregory did not go far before he said, "Yuki, it's too much."

Yukiko looked away from him. "I don't think it is, Greg. We are partners in training, aren't we? That means we need to be on an even footing."

"We already are. Clothing doesn't change that."

"No, but it will make it easier for others to accept." Yukiko glanced at him, then away, "Please, accept it for now. If you feel the need to pay me back later, I won't fight you."

Gregory sighed, wanting to argue with her, but he saw her eyes and could not. "Yuki, if it had been just one outfit, I wouldn't say anything. But it wasn't— it was three, and one of them was even silk. I've only ever seen silk clothing once before, but I have a good idea of what it costs." Exhaling, he continued, "I'll accept them because you asked me to, but I will try to pay you back in time. For the silk, at the very least. Fair?"

Yukiko nodded, "Fair. I shouldn't have gone as far as I did. Forgive me."

"It's fine. If I could have, I might have done something similar in return," Gregory admitted. "I will hold you to not arguing when I try to pay you back."

"I will accept anything you wish to give me in return," Yukiko said, starting to walk up the street. "What else are we looking for on our day out?"

"That was all I could think..." Gregory trailed off as he looked down at his boots. They stood out badly against his new outfit. He could recall the smith telling him to replace them, but he had never gotten the chance. "A cobbler?"

Yukiko looked back, taking in his entire outfit and nodded. "Yes. I'm sure we will pass at least one this way."

"Okay," Gregory said, catching up to walk beside her. "Need to enjoy the little bit of free time we have."

"Yes," Yukiko said, giving him a smile.

They walked for a while before finding a cobbler. A gray-haired man sat behind the counter, tapping a hobnail into a boot heel when they entered. A chime sounded, and the man looked up once he was finished with the nail.

"How can I help you?"

"We need boots for him," Yukiko said, taking the lead again.

Looking at Gregory's boots, the cobbler nodded, "I'd say you do, indeed. I can get you into good boots today, or have a custom made set in a few weeks?"

"Today is fine," Yukiko said.

"Fine, have a seat," the cobbler said. "Be right there."

Taking a seat on one of the benches, Gregory wondered what this was going to involve. He unbuttoned his old boots and set them aside. The old man came out from behind the counter with a strange object in hand.

"Good, already got the rags removed," the cobbler said, pulling a stool over so he could sit in front of Gregory. "Give me your left foot."

Gregory watched as the cobbler manipulated a set of sliding wooden bars to measure his foot. He switched feet at the cobbler's command.

"Pretty standard. Let me see what I have on hand," the cobbler said.

When the old man stepped away, Gregory turned to Yukiko and held out his hand, "For the boots, since you're paying for them."

Yukiko hesitated, but took the vela. "I'll return any extra."

"I doubt there will be any," Gregory said. "Going to need a clan for the stipend, if nothing else."

"Yes," Yukiko agreed. "I had a good sized purse when I left with the proctor, but it won't last forever."

"Especially not when you buy expensive gifts for your friend," Gregory added with a grin.

Yukiko looked away from him, her cheeks heating. "You are showing me how to walk multiple paths. If anything, I owe you even more."

Gregory blinked, his mouth opening and closing. "Just thought of that, did you?"

"On the way here," Yukiko giggled. "So when I find a way to pay you back, you shouldn't fight me."

Gregory chuckled, then began to laugh, "Fine, Yuki, fine. You win."

Yukiko turned back to him, her cheeks still slightly flushed, but she was smiling broadly. "Good. I like winning a good haggle."

"Young love," the cobbler guffawed as he came out of the back with two sets of boots. "Ah, the wife will love this story later."

Gregory and Yukiko went scarlet, both trying to stammer out an objection.

"I've lived too long to think otherwise. If you're not lovers yet, then you're on that path already. Now, do you favor the black or the brown?"

Gregory exhaled heavily, "Black, please."

"Very good. Let's try them on," the cobbler said, taking a seat and getting them onto Gregory's feet. "Take a walk around the room."

Gregory did as he was told, keeping his eyes off Yukiko while his ears were still burning. The boots felt perfect, and when he came back, he took a seat. "Almost as if they were made for me."

"Naw, they're good, but custom made? You'd know the difference. Those fit like gloves for your feet."

"I'll pay," Yukiko said, moving to the counter. "I also want to ask about more formal shoes. Will you take my measurements?"

"Gladly," the man said, going to get his measuring device.

A bit later, they were back on the street, avoiding looking at the other because they could both clearly recall the cobbler's words.

"Yuki," Gregory said, broaching it first, "you're a great friend. Doubt I'd be this happy if you hadn't been here."

"I feel the same, Greg. However... I can't court you, even if I wanted to. I've been betrothed for nearly a decade."

Gregory felt his stomach fall, his mind going blank. "Oh. Yeah... Of course. I wasn't looking to court you," he said quickly. "Just wanted you to know that I'll be here as a friend as long as you want me to be."

Yukiko felt a pit in her stomach and she bit back her sorrow at his words. "I won't ask you to go. You really are a dear friend to me. I just didn't want you to think it was possible, only to have your heart crushed later."

"Yeah, I totally get that," Gregory said. "We should start walking back, maybe find a park to eat our snacks."

"Yes, that sounds good."

They set off walking side by side, each lost in their own thoughts.

CHAPTER 24

Gregory and Yukiko eventually came across a small park off the main road and settled down on the grass for their snack. It was earlier than normal, but it helped them break the awkward tension that had fallen between them. After they ate, they both sat in the lotus position and began to breathe deeply.

Gregory spent the next hour failing to fall into the meditative space he needed. With the chiming of the eleventh bell, he sighed and stretched. "Not today, it seems."

Yukiko sighed as she stepped out of her own trance. She had a pensive look on her face as she continued to look into the distance. "Maybe... but father would...? Maybe..." Her words were nearly inaudible as she mumbled them.

"Yuki, you okay?"

Blinking, Yukiko looked up at Gregory and smiled. "Yes. Sorry, I found a moment of clarity. Did you?"

"No. If we keep training, it might become easier, though."

"Yes. We still need to train body today." Getting to her feet, she looked at the park, "No one is here... should we use this place?"

"Stretching and running... the park is smaller... so, forty laps?"

"That would be close to right, but forty-two would be better."

"Forty-two it is."

Over the next hour the pair stretched, ran, and stretched again. When they finished, Gregory glanced at Yukiko, who was still catching her breath. "We haven't sparred at all since classes started. Want to walk me through some basics?"

Looking around and seeing the place still empty even when the twelfth bell rang, Yukiko nodded slowly. "I will show you a couple of basic attacks and blocks to counter them. When the thirteenth bell chimes, we should start back up toward the academy."

"Deal," Gregory grinned, settling into the balanced stance Nick had taught him.

The next hour flew by for Gregory as he copied everything Yukiko showed him, including a better stance. She was quick to correct his mistakes, and near the end of the hour, she even allowed him to spar with her. She won easily, but Gregory felt like he could almost see the tempo of the fight.

* * *

"You didn't want anything today?" Gregory asked when they started up the road again.

"Just to get out, see the city, and engage in a little commerce. Father always says if you don't use your knowledge, it'll fade."

"I can see that," Gregory nodded. "Does your father use the enchantment that the proctor carriages do?"

"We can't afford those. The great clans keep a tight hold on those to keep the most profitable trade to themselves. It requires a grandmaster enchanter to even attempt to make the tack that allows that to happen."

"Ah," Gregory said, "that would let them do long distance trading faster than the smaller merchants."

"Yes. As a result, the most perishable items are controlled by them."

Gregory lapsed into thought again. *If the great clans control perishable goods and anything that has to move quickly, they must be the ones who take the raw goods from the north into the cities. Those are worth more than any of the standard goods, which is how they stay wealthy and in power.*

"Oh, wait. I want to stop here," Yukiko said, moving toward a shop.

"Herbalist?" Gregory asked, following her.

"I'll be right out. Please wait here for me."

Gregory wanted to ask more, but leaned up against the wall instead. "Sure."

Yukiko vanished into the shop, leaving Gregory to watch the city go by. He noted two guards patrolling by themselves, as well as a few of the city servants moving down the street with their wheeled buckets, picking up after the horses.

"Excuse me, sir, would you like to buy a flower?" a young girl asked, coming toward him with a handful of flowers.

"What would I do with one?"

"Give it to a special someone, or your mother or sister, perhaps?" the girl gave him a dimpled smile.

Gregory smiled back at her, "How much?"

"Five vela?"

Gregory dug out a five vela coin, handing it to her in exchange for a single flower. "Thank you. May Aether watch over you."

"Thank you, sir."

"Urchin, I've told you before that you can't sell on the street," a guard said, coming toward them with a fast stride.

"Sir, I asked her if she would sell me one," Gregory said quickly. "It isn't her fault, but mine."

The guard turned on him, catching sight of the medallion around his neck. "Magi, the laws state no soliciting on the streets. We have squares for that."

Gregory bowed slightly from the waist. "Apologies, I will remember."

"Now, you—" the guard started, turning toward where the girl had been. "I'll catch her later," the guard mumbled as he moved off.

When the guard was farther down the street, the urchin girl came back and gave Gregory a smile. "Thank you, sir. Not many would try to help me. Did he say right? Are you a magi?"

"A novice, but yes. You better run along. He'll be looking for you."

"I will. Thank you again."

"Wait," Gregory said, stopping her from fleeing right away. "Here, take this. I'll take the rest of those in exchange."

"Yes sir," the urchin said, giving him all her flowers before looking at the coin. "A hundred vela? Sir, I—"

"Quick, run. Here comes the guard," Gregory said, looking past her.

With a gasp, the urchin bolted, and Gregory chuckled as she ran. Shaking his head, he looked down at the wilting flowers and sighed.

"I'm back, Greg... why do you have flowers?"

"Bought them off an urchin."

Yukiko tsked, "They always go for the soft touches."

"Maybe, but she seemed nice," Gregory said. "Anyway, have some flowers."

Yukiko took them on reflex. "What? I—"

"The urchin said to give them to a friend, and you're my only friend here, Yuki."

Yukiko looked at the sad wilting flowers, and smiled softly. "I accept, since there are no other friends nearby."

"Get what you needed?"

Yukiko's cheeks tinged with pink briefly, "Yes."

Gregory kept a knowing smile off his face. He remembered Eloria and Amoria wanting herbs during certain points every month, too. "We should get moving again. Have to make it back before sundown."

The sun was low in the sky when they arrived at the postern of the academy. A knock on the metal door caused it to be opened, but the guards on duty stood in their way, different than the ones who had been there when they left. The magi on duty was an irritable-looking man in an orange kimono.

"Medallions?" the magi snapped at them.

Both presented their medallions, and the magi grumbled. He waved the guards away so the pair could pass, "Novices on their days off..."

"Thank you, sir," Yukiko said, giving the initiate a bow of her head.

The initiate gave her a slight nod in return, going back to a bench to sit. "Clear the gate, please."

"Dinner?" Gregory asked, his aether still low from their sparring earlier.

"A good idea," Yukiko agreed. "Maybe we can study afterward?"

"Sure, we can use my room," Gregory said, knowing that Amoria had always been picky about him going into her room.

"Very well."

As the pair approached the mess hall, a familiar voice called out to them, "Greg? Almost didn't recognize you."

"Nick," Gregory replied. "How have you been?"

Nick's smile was wide, "Good. My father just happened to be in the city. You should come by my room later tonight. I have gifts from my father to the people who have been friendly with me."

"We'll stop by," Yukiko smiled. "We're on our way to get food."

"I'd join you, but I just recently ate at Zerig's," Nick smiled, but when neither reacted, his face fell slightly. "It's one of the best places to eat outside of the academy."

"Oh," Gregory said, "I'm sure it was a good meal, then."

Nick sighed, brushing at his elaborate silver-trimmed, red silk kimono. "Yeah. Anyway, I'll see you both later."

Yukiko's smile waned once Nick left, "I've never understood the need to flaunt wealth that way. Father always said that it was foolish. There are easier ways to let people know you are well off than that."

"Huh, I wondered why he'd mentioned it."

"Wanting to show off," Yukiko sighed. "Let's eat."

The meal was as delicious and aether-filling as ever. The two of them felt more awake and refreshed than they had all week as they walked back to the dormitory. Gregory realized he had seen very few novices during the day. During dinner, there had been only five other novices in the dining hall.

Reaching the dorm as the eighteenth bell chimed, he exchanged his boots for slippers, and the voices from inside the common room were noticeable. "Guess we're not the only ones full of energy," Gregory chuckled.

"We weren't run ragged," Yukiko said, "even though we probably did more than they did."

"Fair point, Yuki. Let's see if Nick is in his room. We'll stop by on our way up to my room."

Muted voices could be heard from inside the room, so Gregory knocked on the wood panel beside the door. "Nick?"

The door opened to reveal Fureno, Jason, Michelle, and the others all sitting around the room. Nick gave them a wide smile, "Come on in. You are the last two, so I can give out the gifts now."

A small cheer from the other novices filled the room, and everyone crowded one side of the low set table that had a few bags on it. Nick took his seat on one side, facing the others. "Okay, Father wished me to convey his thanks to the people who've made my time here better. I have a gift for everyone, but a few special gifts, too. First, the gifts for everyone."

Fureno, Jason, and a couple others leaned forward a bit more. Gregory, sitting off to the side, wondered what the big deal was. Yukiko watched the room with a knowing expression.

"First, we have something from Yomba's Alchemy; aether growing powder," Nick said as he pulled vials out of one of the bags. "These are guaranteed to stimulate your aether as you sleep, so take it before bed tonight." He uncorked one of the vials, and the scent of unknown herbs filled the air briefly before he recapped it. Nick handed them out one by one, smiling broadly.

Gregory thanked him and tucked the vial into his pouch. Yukiko was a little slower accepting it, but did as well.

"Next, I have certificates for a massage at Felina's Spa," Nick grinned. "I'm sure we can all use them next day off."

"Damned right," Jason laughed. "Man, it's been months since I was there last."

Michelle's smile was a little wooden, "Felina's? Nick, really?"

Nick blinked, then started laughing, "Oh, don't worry, she has male masseuses, too. They'll work those *kinks* out of you."

Michelle's cheeks heated, "I will decline."

"I'll take hers," Fureno offered.

Nick shook his head at Fureno, but addressed Michelle. "Michelle, come on, don't be like that. We're all adults. There's nothing wrong with a little enjoyment here and there. Besides, you can enjoy just the basic massage. It's up to you."

Yukiko drew in a sharp breath as realization dawned on her, but it was inaudible to everyone but Gregory. Glancing to the side, she saw Gregory looking at her with a questioning gaze. She shook her head, and put a smile back on her face.

"Fine, but unlike you, I'll *just* be having the basic massage," Michelle sniffed.

"Of course," Nick grinned as he handed her a small scroll. "Just do what you enjoy."

Gregory took the small scroll and tucked it into his bag, wondering if he was understanding the context completely. *I can ask Yuki when we go study.*

"That's it for everyone," Nick said as he set aside every bag but one. "However, I have two special gifts. Michelle, Father wanted you to know he's appreciative of you keeping me focused." Pulling a box from the bag, he slid it to Michelle.

Michelle frowned as she looked at the small rectangular box. Opening it, she blinked, her cheeks heating again. "I can't—"

"It's fine," Nick said, cutting her off. "It's not from me. It's from my father as a thank you, so it doesn't violate any rules about accepting gifts from another besides your betrothed."

Michelle touched the object inside the box. "I'll ask Mother. If she agrees, I'll accept it."

"Fine," Nick's smile grew wider. "I'll look forward to seeing it on your neck soon."

Michelle blushed deeper, tucking the box away.

"The other one is a more formal gift," Nick said, turning to face Yukiko. "On behalf of the Eternal Flame clan, we extend this gift to you, Yukiko Warlin. We'd like you to join our ranks." Nick pushed another similar box to her.

Yukiko shook her head, "I can't accept."

Nick frowned, clearly peeved at her instant rejection, "Why not?"

"I have not yet made a decision as to which clan I will join. As such, it would be wrong of me to accept this gift, since I might not join your clan."

Nick chuckled, "Oh, I see. Then accept this as a token indicating our desire for you to join us."

Yukiko looked at the box for a long moment, then took it, slipping it into her bag without opening it. "I accept it as a token."

Nick looked a little upset at her reaction. Gregory was unsure about what had just transpired, besides Yukiko being asked to join a clan already.

"Now that gifts are done," Nick said, trying to regain his footing, "let the celebration of friendship begin."

Fureno put a couple of bottles on the table.

Yukiko rose to her feet, "I'm sorry, but it has been a long day and morning comes early. I must depart."

Gregory got to his feet beside her, "Thank you for the gifts and for inviting us, but she is right."

Nick's smile thinned, "I see. Very well. We'll see you in conditioning. Goodnight to you both."

"Goodnight," Yukiko said, bowing slightly at the waist.

"Night," Gregory echoed, bowing a bit more than Yukiko had.

Gregory had a couple of questions, but waited for them to enter his room before he spoke. "Yuki, what was that all about?"

Yukiko went back into her normal demeanor and sighed. "He is trying to buy allies. The powder is worth over two thousand vela for each vial. If Felina's is the sort of place I think it is, it's less a bathing house and more an oiran house. The gift... more like leash... is to tie me to their clan before others can even bargain. This might be part of why he's been so friendly to us."

Gregory looked lost, "He was pleasant and nice to me even before we had talked. The gifts might have been pricey, but like you said, maybe he just likes to throw around his money."

Yukiko shook her head. "No, they are bribes to keep people close. Did you not note that Jason said it had been months since he'd last been to Felina's?"

"Yeah? Umm, what is an oiran house?" Gregory asked.

Yukiko blushed, then saw his obvious confusion. "Right, I forget with you at times. What is the right way to say it...? Oh yes... it's a... whorehouse, but higher priced than you could imagine." Pulling the scroll from her bag, she read it. "Much higher priced. This is a blank ticket for the bearer to indulge as the guest of the Eternal Flame clan."

Memories of Jess at the Proctor's Rest flashed through his mind, causing his cheeks to flush. He had another reaction, making him glad he was sitting. "Oh, err... sorry."

"As for the leash..." Yukiko slapped the small box on the table and opened it. Nostrils flaring, she grimaced, "They don't skimp on their pets." Pulling out the silver and sapphire pendant, she squinted at it. "I think it's enchanted on top of the craftsmanship."

Gregory could only blink upon seeing the necklace. He knew it would have cost more than Alturis was worth. "Pet?" he asked when he could think.

"The Eternal Flame is a clan devoted to keeping eurtiks in their place. They don't mind using those of mixed blood, but they are kept on a strict watch. They must not have realized my heritage yet, or they are looking past it because of my magic."

"Are you sure? Maybe Nick really is just friendly," Gregory said, but the words felt wrong to him even as they came out of his mouth.

"No. They will stay friendly, but the relationship will cool now. Just watch," Yukiko said as she put the pendant away. After a moment, she shrank in on herself and glanced at Gregory with guilty eyes. "I'm sorry, Greg."

"Huh? Why?"

"They will distance themselves from you, too."

"No," Gregory said. "If they do, it isn't your fault, Yuki. It'll just prove you were right, and frankly, I don't have any real love for people who think less of you just because one of your ancestors was a eurtik. Even if your mother was full eurtik, I'd still be right here with you."

Yukiko stared at him, seconds ticking by, and her eyes started to glisten. Looking down, she coughed, "I see. You're the best friend I could have hoped for, Greg. Thank you... for being my friend."

Gregory reached out and tapped her hand with his. "Partners in training *and* friends, right?"

Yukiko looked up, her eyes still glimmering with unshed tears. "Yes. We should get some more study in before bed. You wanted help with economics, yes?"

CHAPTER 25

When the third bell rang, Gregory was out of bed in seconds, feeling energized and ready for anything. Getting dressed more quickly than normal, he paused to make sure his kimono was correct before grabbing his bag and heading for the door. As he opened it, he came nose to nose with Yukiko, who had just raised her hand to knock.

Stepping back, Gregory coughed, "Morning, Yuki."

"Morning. Should we go?"

"Yeah, let's do it."

They gave Dia a bow as they went by. Dia, sitting on the porch smoking, waved to them and watched as they headed toward the mess hall, smiling.

Breakfast was the same as it had been, though Gregory and Yukiko were done eating and walking to the archive before fourth bell rang. Gregory wondered about that as they walked. *Maybe the powder is helping us process the food easier? We'd have just been finishing, but instead we're ten minutes or more ahead of where we were last week.*

Rafiq smiled and bid them good morning when they entered the archive. "Your new books await you, Novices."

"Thank you, Archivist Rafiq," Gregory replied.

Yukiko bowed her head, "Thank you."

"You may use just my name. The books you requested are being considered by the chief archivist," Rafiq told Gregory. "It might be a few weeks before we can supply the first choice you asked for."

"Thank you, and please thank them for me," Gregory bowed his head. "I'll muddle through economics until then."

"Very well."

Once they were at their table, the pair settled in and dove into their selected books. Gregory went slowly; the subject matter was denser than he anticipated, making it harder for him to understand all of it. Yukiko was absorbed in her book, the pages turning slowly but steadily.

Fifth bell rang, snapping them out of their studies. Gregory blinked and shut the book with a sigh, "That is hard to work through."

"The history in this book is a middle ground between the others I read," Yukiko said. "If you need help, I can answer questions while reading."

"Maybe tomorrow," Gregory replied, stretching as he stood.

As they were leaving the archive, Rafiq stopped them to ask if the books were what they wanted. After a brief exchange of thanks, they were on the path toward their first class of the day.

* * *

Gregory managed to keep up with Magus Marcia as she went over economic theory, but he struggled at points. *Going to need Yukiko to help clarify some of this*, he thought. *Maybe we won't be exhausted tonight.*

Yukiko was bored in history, and Gregory was not much better off as they listened to Adept Thomas talking about the First Eurtik War. Gregory noted the absence of two novices from their class, and both of them wondered if it was even worth going to for the two hours— they could study history on their own in the archive if they wanted.

As they left history and went toward aether introduction, Gregory was frowning. "Yuki... should we drop history for more time in the archive instead?"

Yukiko was silent for a few minutes as she considered the question. "We lose posting opportunities that way... but I don't know which ones. We can ask Rafiq. Maybe he'll know, and then we can make that decision."

"Okay."

When they reached aether studies, they wondered about the extra people. One dozen apprentices, two adepts, and a magus, most of them with clan emblems on their kimonos, stood beside Adept John. One of the apprentices was the man who had almost tripped Gregory a few days ago.

When the bell chimed for the class to start, the fifteen magi silently lined up, facing the class with John standing in front of them. "Welcome back, Novices. Today, you will see basic magic in each known branch. Be attentive, and if you have any questions, wait to ask them until after all demonstrations are finished."

Seeing that he had their rapt attention, John turned to the left side of the line of magi. "Jubal, you may begin."

The first apprentice stepped forward. "I use enchanting magic, which can't be seen, so I don't have anything to demonstrate. I can, however, explain how it feels."

Gregory's hand was starting to cramp halfway through from all the notes he was taking. The first few were crafting magics, and they talked instead of showing their magic. The magi after them gave demonstrations of the basic magic they all learned first, from creating a small breeze to lighting a candle.

"Trade off? We can copy from each other later," Yukiko whispered, watching him flex his hand.

"Agreed," Gregory whispered back as the water magi separated salt water into pure water and salt.

The magus was the last one to step forward, his face impassive as he looked over the classroom of novices. "I'm Magus Aldum, and I'm a magi of shadow." Turning to face Yukiko directly, Aldum smiled, "I am no longer the last shadow magi the academy has seen. The first magic a shadow magi learns is how to blend into shadow, letting it cloak them. I'll use as little aether as possible to give you an idea of what it looks like at your tier."

The class had looked at Yukiko and began to murmur, but fell silent and went back to watching Aldum. John opened a large parasol and held it up so the shadow fell over the area where Aldum was standing.

"First, connect to your aether and try to direct your shadow to pull in toward you." As he spoke, his shadow contracted toward him. "Once that is happening, you want to bring it into contact with the shadow you wish to blend into. You should be able to feel that shadow and yours— now mix them to form a shroud."

The class murmured as Aldum's form began to fade into the shadow of the parasol, making him difficult to discern. Yukiko was watching intently, and Gregory scribbled notes since she was observing.

"That is the first magic a shadow magi should be able to use. From there, well, depending on the clan and your path, things open up," Aldum chuckled as he vanished completely.

The class leaned forward, trying to find him.

"The Whispering Darkness clan will send someone to talk with you soon," Aldum said from behind Yukiko. "Do your best to learn all you can."

Every novice jumped when they realized that the magi had seemingly teleported to stand behind Yukiko. Yukiko gasped, her heart racing, but she nodded once. "I understand and will listen to the offer."

The adepts that had come to teach looked annoyed, but did not voice any objection. John stepped forward, looking stern. "Magus Aldum, talk of clans is forbidden during class."

Aldum's smile never wavered as he walked past Gregory and Yukiko. "I forgot. Apologies."

"It isn't me you need to apologize to," John said in his normal monotone. "It'll be the council."

Aldum's smile vanished, his face going cold. "You'd report my mistake, even after the apology?"

"Rules are rules, Magus," John replied with a shrug. "What are we without them?"

Lips tight, Aldum snorted, "I see. I should expect no less from a member of the Shining Light clan."

"This has nothing to do with clan affiliation and everything to do with rules," John said evenly. Turning to the class, John continued as if the conversation was over, "You are invited to speak to whomever has the same magic as yourself. We are a quarter hour from the end of class."

Magus Aldum sneered at John before stepping to the side. The novices had separated, each of them going to speak with the magi who had similar magic. Gregory frowned; as he gathered his notes together, he realized that no one here had talked about anything besides the already known types of magic.

Yukiko put her notes in order and looked at Gregory. "Do you want to copy these while I talk with Magus Aldum?"

"Please. If I have time, I'll make duplicates of mine for you."

"Thank you," Yukiko said, pushing her notes to him. "Now to see if he will talk about magic or just try to sell his clan to me."

"Good luck," Gregory said, watching her for a moment before he started to copy her notes.

As Gregory finished with Yukiko's notes, Adept John came over to him. "Novice, do you not wish to speak to any of them?"

"It wouldn't do me any good," Gregory replied. "Master Damon hasn't been able to find out what my magic is yet."

"I thought you were the one," John said. "You are a mystery that many clans are wondering about. I hope that is solved quickly. Without knowing what your magic is, it'll be hard for you to find the best path, which will stunt your growth."

Gregory's pen paused as he started to copy his notes for Yukiko. "I hope that an answer will come soon, as well. I can only do the best I can until then."

"Aptly said," John nodded, a faint smile appearing briefly on his lips. "Good day, Novice."

When the bell rang, announcing the end of the class, Gregory had just finished copying his notes for Yukiko. Putting their notes in order, he got his stowed as Yukiko came back to the table. "You okay, Yuki?"

Yukiko's frown lessened, "Yes. He didn't give me much to go on, and he sidestepped most direct answers. Thank you for the notes," she smiled at him as she put the papers away. "Time for our snacks and meditation."

"And then conditioning," Gregory's voice was pained, as was his smile.

"I wonder what he's planning today?" Yukiko mused as they started to walk toward the arenas.

"Running and stretching," Gregory grumbled.

"Yes, but he might also start us on sparring," Yukiko added. "We only have five months until the first tournament. We'll be fighting before that happens."

"Maybe," Gregory nodded. "It would be a welcome change from just running and stretching."

"I wonder if we'll still feel that way after class," Yukiko added.

* * *

Gregory sighed as they walked toward the mess hall, "Well, the answer was 'no.' Instead, we got even more exercises."

"It wasn't as bad as it could have been. We didn't skip a day."

"True. Most of the class seemed to struggle today, even Nick."

"Yes," Yukiko said. "How do you feel?"

"Not as tired as normal," Gregory said. "Is that the powder Nick gave us, or just because we're improving?"

"Perhaps both," Yukiko suggested. "Do you want to study economics a bit more tonight?"

"For a half hour, maybe. We still wake early."

"We do, but extra study is good for us, too."

"True," Gregory smiled at her as they reached the mess hall. "Before that, food."

Yukiko's stomach growled at that moment, and she blushed lightly. "Food sounds good."

CHAPTER 26

T he rest of the week was what had started to become routine for them, with only one major change. They left the history class as they had found out it would only disqualify them from positions in the academy or capital. They spent that extra time studying in the archive instead.

Up at the third bell as usual, Gregory put on the second outfit Yukiko had bought for him on their last day off. *We're going down to visit Felina's and have lunch somewhere. I still don't know how she talked me into that... I feel like I'm taking advantage of her. She insists that she's the one who owes me, but...* The tap on his door ended his train of thought.

He picked up his bag and opened the door to see Yukiko waiting there for him. "Sorry, Yuki, I'm ready now."

"It's fine, Greg. You look good."

Gregory brushed at the outfit, "Thanks. You do, too."

Yukiko pushed a few strands of her hair behind an ear, "Thank you."

"We should get going," Gregory said quickly.

As they were exiting the dormitory, Dia stopped them. "Novice Warlin, a moment, please."

Yukiko looked at her curiously. "Yes, Keeper?"

"I received a few scrolls for you last night, but you'd already gone to your room, so I held onto them. Please wait a moment." Dia clapped her hands twice and a rabbit eurtik appeared from the dormitory. "Bring me the scrolls for Warlin."

"Right away," the eurtik replied before hurrying off.

They only waited a minute before the servant came back with six scrolls. "I believe they are invitations from various clans asking you to visit them today," Dia said. "They at least had the decency to wait until a day off to request to speak with you."

"Thank you," Yukiko said, putting the scrolls into her bag.

"Good day to you both," Dia said as she took a puff on her pipe.

"Keeper," they said together, bowing.

"I wonder who you'll pick," Dia murmured, exhaling a thin line of purple smoke as they walked away.

* * *

Breakfast was the same, but the teachers not being there was different. The cooks greeted them with smiles and wished them a good day. Once they had finished, they headed for the archive to study. Greeting the eurtik on duty by the door, they went to their table and dove into their respective books.

When fifth bell rang, both of them closed their books. Gregory was still lost in thought over the last portion of the economics book as he got to his feet.

"Greg?" Yukiko asked.

"Sorry," Gregory smiled at her with chagrin. "I'm good, just trying to understand it all. I'll ask tonight if I can't puzzle it out."

"Okay," Yukiko replied as they headed for the door.

"All done?" the bull-horned eurtik asked.

"Yes. We'll need new books tomorrow," Yukiko replied. "Rafiq knows which ones we are looking for."

"I will inform him," the eurtik bowed his head.

"Thank you," Gregory replied for them. "Have a good day."

"You as well, Novices."

The walk to the postern gate was quiet, but they caught sight of a few people taking different paths. "I enjoy the mornings," Yukiko murmured as they walked. "It's peaceful."

"Not like later when everyone is bustling from place to place," Gregory agreed. "The city will be even busier, which brings it back into perspective."

"True," Yukiko smiled. Her smile slipped when she saw who was waiting with the guards on the postern door.

Magus Aldum stared at them as they approached. "Novices, going into the city?"

Gregory did his best to not stare, but knew he was failing. "We are, sir."

"Be back before sundown or you shall face discipline. Sergeant, open the door."

Gregory and Yukiko exchanged a look as they walked toward the street, wanting to find a rickshaw. "Do you think that was because of...?" Yukiko trailed off.

"Yeah," Gregory nodded. "Also explains why he gave us the stink eye. Probably blames us for him being there. Oh, what about the scrolls? What do they say?"

Yukiko grimaced and waved down the first rickshaw she saw. "I'll read them as we go down. Do you want to train physically first to make the massage better?"

"Go to the park for a couple of hours... that at least lets the businesses open for the day."

"From what I've heard from Michelle, Felina's is open all the time," Yukiko sniffed.

"Still good to get our training done first. We don't have anything else to really do today."

"There is one other stop I want to make, but we can do that afterwards," Yukiko told him as she climbed into the rickshaw. "Take us to a secluded park, please."

The driver's lips wavered, the smirk coming and going as he bowed to her, "As you wish."

Gregory winced internally at the phrasing, but got in next to Yukiko. *At least no one else heard that,* he sighed to himself.

The driver did not take them far, pedaling barely a dozen blocks away down a number of side streets. The park in its entirety was about the size of one of the small arenas, but different thanks to the dense tree line that helped set it apart from the surroundings. Inside the tree line, there were more hedges and trees to separate the park into smaller sections. In the middle of everything, there was a gazebo with a table and bench.

With the sun starting to lighten the sky, they did their stretches in preparation for running and sparring. As they went through the routine stretches, Gregory felt his aether stir and move with his muscles. When he began to run, his aether dimmed, helping him keep the pace longer and easier.

Smiling as he ran, Gregory was surprised when Yukiko matched him stride for stride. When they finished the laps, Gregory was a little winded, but nowhere near as badly as he had been two weeks prior. Sixth bell was chiming when he finally caught his breath.

"Did your aether move, too?" Yukiko asked as she caught her breath.

"Yes. I was wondering how you kept up with me, but figured that had to be it."

"This means we're on the first step of the body path now," Yukiko said a little hesitantly. "I haven't felt the mind path at all, besides some things becoming easier to comprehend. The spirit path, I've felt brief moments of when we're meditating."

"The same for me, but I'm certain the mind path is working," Gregory said. "I doubt I would have understood half of what Magus Marcia teaches if not for it and you."

"Are you good for a little sparring?"

"If you'll explain some of the attacks and defenses you use," Gregory chuckled. "At least Magus Paul said we'd be starting that next week."

"Yes, we'll need all the time we can get if we want to do well during the tournament."

"Ready when you are," Gregory said as he set himself to defend.

* * *

The seventh bell ringing brought an end to their sparring. Gregory felt an ache in his muscles, and he smiled at Yukiko. "Managed to tag you once."

"Yes, you pick things up faster than I anticipated. Are you ready to be pampered?"

"Yeah. Oh, you never did tell me what was in the scrolls."

"As Keeper Dia thought, they are invitations to stop by and speak to the clans about joining them. Some are offering gifts just for stopping by."

"Are you?"

"No," Yukiko said firmly. "The opening offer is never the right offer, and by not replying, they have no idea of how much value I place on myself. That will make it harder for them to find the right way to approach me."

"Yuki, clans are helpful. Everyone has said so," Gregory said as they left the park. "Why aren't you at least talking to them?"

Yukiko's jaw set, "I have my reasons. Please let it be for now."

Seeing her dig in her heels much like Amoria used to, Gregory shrugged. "Fine. If you want to talk about it, I'll listen. Just keep that in mind."

Yukiko sighed, glancing at him then quickly away. "I will. Thank you, Greg."

Back on the main street, they found the city had started to wake up. Yukiko flagged down another rickshaw and instructed the driver to take them to Felina's Spa. The rickshaw driver delivered them to a four-story structure that took up most of the block it occupied. The exterior was done in a rose-colored stone that seemed to soak up the sunlight.

Yukiko paid the driver, and they walked up the low, wide stairs to the double doors. The doors were some golden wood that had a single stylized 'F' carved in the middle of each. Entering the building,

Gregory's eyes widened slightly at the amount of subdued wealth on display. The floor was rose marble and the walls were paneled in the same golden wood as the doors. Two golden lanterns affixed to the wall behind the counter across from the door easily illuminated the entry room.

"How may I help you?" the woman behind the counter asked. The makeup she wore helped emphasize her deep blue eyes, and she was wearing an elaborately decorated kimono.

"We have come to see about being cared for," Yukiko said as she presented their scrolls.

The woman read the scrolls and her smile widened, "I see. Esteemed friends of the Eternal Flame are always welcome here. Please go through the door. Your needs shall be taken care of."

"Thank you," Yukiko replied as she moved toward the door.

"Thank you," Gregory said and followed her.

The next room they entered was a large lounge. Three women and one man were in there, relaxing. The moment they walked in, those four people all rose to their feet and bowed to them.

Gregory shut his mouth— his jaw had dropped open when they went into the room. The large golden chandelier in the room had a dozen lanterns that filled the room with light. The chairs and sofas were well-padded and covered in velvet. The four people in the room were all wearing brightly-colored kimonos with intricate artwork sown on them.

"Welcome to Felina's," one of the women said, moving in front of the others by a few paces. "How might we serve you today, mistress and master?"

Yukiko glanced at Gregory and whispered softly, "At twelfth bell we are going to eat. Don't forget, please."

"I won't," Gregory said. "That's a while away…"

"You might never see anything like this again, so you should enjoy it." Yukiko's smile was wooden as she spoke, "Don't forget to meditate, either."

Gregory took a deep breath, "Training. I won't forget, Yuki. If they do dual massag—"

"I can't," Yukiko cut him off gently.

"We do have a room with a silk divider so the mistress can be in the same room. It keeps the propriety of the woman sacrosanct, but allows for you to converse."

Yukiko looked at the woman and hesitated. "Does the room include a bath and laundry?"

"It can be made so, if that is your wish."

"Our conversation will be held in confidence?" Yukiko asked.

"No conversation that takes place inside these walls is repeated," the woman replied.

"Yuki, if you aren't comfortable, we can split up."

Yukiko glanced at him. "I'd rather not, but I have restrictions I have to abide by. Unless you'd rather be alone with one of them."

His mind went to Jess back at the Proctor's Rest and what that might mean here if he was alone. Seeing Yukiko's uncertainty, though, he shook off that thought. "Rather train with my partner."

Yukiko stared into his eyes for a long moment before her smile thawed. "Very well, Greg."

"You've decided?"

"The joint room with the divider," Yukiko said firmly, though her voice held a hint of a tremor. "I will have you care for me, and the one you choose for my friend."

"Nisha, you are to care for the master," the woman said, addressing another of the women in the room. "If you will both follow me, I will take you to your room. Would you care for tea, sake, or other refreshments?"

Yukiko's smile grew slightly, "Whatever is the best you have for novice magi."

The woman smiled, "As you wish, mistress. I'm Mitzi. If you need anything, please let me know."

The room they were led to was divided by a wall similar to those in the dorm, but made of silk panels instead of paper. Each side contained a tub large enough to relax in, as well as a waist high table. Nisha guided Gregory to the right, motioning him to the tub.

"If sir is willing to disrobe, we can start with the bath. This will allow us to get your clothes laundered while the massage takes place."

Gregory caught the same words directed at Yukiko, as the silk wall did little to mask the sound. He thought back to Jess again and knew that if he was not in the room with Yukiko, he could easily have had the exact same experience again. Exhaling deeply, he stopped thinking about her, though with some difficulty.

"Of course," he told the servant.

"Did you wish for me—" the woman began with a knowing smile on her lips.

"As formal as possible, please," Gregory replied before she could offer.

"As formal as you can," Yukiko's voice came through the silk. "I don't wish to cause my friend any discomfort."

The idea of Yukiko naked and enjoying Mitzi flitted through his mind, and Gregory swallowed hard. *Damn, this is going to be hard*, he sighed to himself before looking down. *Yeah, like that.*

Once the initial awkwardness was over, Gregory was able to relax. Nisha stayed clothed while she bathed him, her hands firm and warm as she cleaned him. She did not stray from work, for which Gregory was grateful and saddened by at the same time.

"Did you wish to soak for a bit first, sir?" Nisha asked once he was clean.

"For a few minutes, please."

"Greg?" Yukiko called to him.

"Yes?"

"Have you considered which clan you're interested in joining?"

"I don't know anything about them, and none of them have approached me."

"We should have the archive give you books about the clans so you know more than just what they'll try to tell you."

"That isn't a bad idea," Gregory agreed. "I had no idea that Nick's clan was so slanted."

"Most clans have an agenda one way or another. The trick is knowing what they really favor and if you can accept that."

"What about you?"

"I'm waiting for the right clan and moment," Yukiko replied. "There are a few I will have nothing to do with, as I can't stomach what they represent."

"Let me know which those are, so I can avoid them, too."

"I will." Those two words held a happiness that even Gregory could hear.

"Meditate during the massage?" Gregory asked.

"A good idea. Mitzi, we'll be meditating during the massages. Take your time, and try not to disturb us as much as you can."

"As you require, mistress. Would you like some more helitop tea?"

"I'll have some after the massage."

CHAPTER 27

G regory felt good when they left the room. He could feel his aether compress while he meditated, and was certain that he had started on the path of spirit. *Two paths have begun, but can I continue to grow them together? And what of mind?* Gregory wondered as they followed Mitzi and Nisha to the entrance.

"Greg," a familiar voice called to them when they reached the lounge, "and Yukiko. With two of the women, no less. My goodness."

"Nick," Gregory chuckled, "I can't say you have much room for talking there."

Nick smiled broadly from his place among three of the oiran. "Well, *someone* had to keep them company with the others all engaged. Besides, I was waiting. I heard that guests of mine had come in before us."

"Thank you for the gift. It was pleasant," Yukiko said. "It will make visiting the other clans today both easier and harder."

Nick's smile thinned a little before widening, "Just keep the Eternal Flame's generosity in mind."

"I shall," Yukiko bowed her head to him. "We have people to see, so apologies that we can't stay and talk longer."

"It's fine," Nick assured her. "Greg, stop by my room tonight. I'm having the guys over for some cards."

"Cards?" Gregory said.

"Oh, right, sorry, I forget. There are a number of games of chance that we play with cards. I take it your village didn't gamble that way?"

"The little gambling that went on was betting on Go or bones."

"Don't worry, we can teach you. Most magi play a variety of card games, so best to learn now."

"Michelle and the others won't be there?" Yukiko asked.

"I believe they're having tea," Nick chuckled. "I'm sure she'll invite you once she gets a chance. Don't let me keep you. Go and enjoy the day."

"Have fun," Gregory said.

Nick winked when Yukiko was not looking his way, "I'm sure I'll manage."

Leaving the building, they paused once they were on the street. "Where to?" Gregory asked as twelfth bell chimed.

"I heard of a good place near the gates to the lower ring," Yukiko told him as she waved down a rickshaw driver. "Before we go there, though, I have another stop on the way."

"Okay," Gregory said. He did not pry further, seeing that she wanted to keep it a secret.

"Yes, mistress?" the rickshaw driver asked when he came to a stop in front of them.

"Hemet's, please. I'll ask you to wait for us, as we'll be going to the Golden Boar after that."

"As you wish, mistress," the driver smiled.

It took a little more than ten minutes for them to stop next to an understated shop. The building gleamed as the sun shone off the immaculate white stone. The sign outside the shop declared it Hemet's Curiosities.

Following Yukiko inside, Gregory glanced back to see the driver putting an orange flag atop his rickshaw. *Must denote that he's waiting or something similar*, Gregory thought.

The interior of the shop was sparse; a counter took up one wall, behind which was a door, and two tables filled up most of the small area in front of the counter. A bald man with a long, thin, white beard stood behind the counter, his hands hidden in the voluminous arms of his kimono.

"Welcome to my shop. How can I help you two today?" the old man asked politely, his smile professional.

"I have an item I need you to check for me," Yukiko said as she approached the counter. "I am also counting on your discretion in this sensitive matter."

"You wouldn't have come to me if it was otherwise," Hemet replied.

Pulling out the case that Gregory had seen last week, Yukiko placed it on the counter. "This was a gift of enticement, but I need to know more about it to properly judge the worth of the gift."

Hemet's eyes flicked to Gregory for a moment before he opened the case. "Hmm, this is master quality at the very least." Hemet produced a monocle and placed it in front of his right eye. "Yes... high master quality, or maybe even lower grandmaster quality." Turning the necklace over, Hemet tsked upon seeing the small flame emblem emblazoned on the inside of the necklace. "It is a good piece. It will allow one to conjure a globe of fire once, until it recharges."

"Useful for the upcoming tournament," Yukiko nodded.

"Ah, a novice. I had thought so," Hemet nodded. "It could give you the edge to clear a tough fight, yes. It is well known that only the Eternal Flame produce these necklaces. They only give them to members in good standing and those they dearly wish to recruit."

"How much will you buy it for?" Yukiko asked.

Gregory blinked, not having expected her to sell it.

"Not many of these are around. To sell it would give away that I bought one recently."

Yukiko laughed lightly, "We both know that you transport items that you wish to distance from yourself to other cities and towns. I expect you to take that into account when stating your price."

Hemet's eye twinkled, "Ah, someone who knows the dance, and

so young, too. If only I was two hundred years younger. Fine, I will give you twenty-thousand vela."

"Thirty."

"Twenty-five, and no more."

Yukiko bowed her head, "As you say, but would you consider forty if it was in trade?"

Hemet's professional smile became real, "Thirty."

"Thirty-four, to undercut what I would normally ask for in return, out of courtesy."

"Accepted, with no vela exchanged."

"I would like to see what you would suggest for two novices who will have a very difficult time in the tournament."

Hemet's eyes darted to Gregory, the smile becoming knowing. "Very well. What magics do you both possess?"

"I have shadow magic and his... is unknown," Yukiko said.

Hemet blinked slowly, before his lips pursed. "Interesting. That makes this more of a challenge. Please be seated. I'll be back shortly."

When Hemet went into the back, Gregory was confused on what he should be feeling. He wanted to argue with Yukiko for what she was doing, but he also wanted to thank her for doing so much for him.

Yukiko stood at the counter, not turning to face him. "Greg? I touched the spirit path today. I could feel it, truly feel it. That means I've touched two so far, so please, don't fight me on this. It is a pittance compared to what you've done for me."

Gregory shook his head with a sigh, "But I haven't done anything, Yuki. You've done that all on your own." Moving to the side, he sat at one of the tables. "I haven't done anything to match this."

"No. You've done more than I can say. I would never have tried to reach for two paths, much less all three, if not for you. I tried because you told me it was possible. I put my faith in you, and it's been true. This barely scratches the debt I feel I owe."

"I feel I owe you, you feel you owe me... makes it hard to know what to do," Gregory chuckled awkwardly.

"Maybe we don't try to keep track," Yukiko said with a weak

chuckle of her own. "Father would be appalled at that idea, but if we're going to be partners, it makes the most sense."

Gregory felt two paths open before him again. One where he disagreed and they quarreled, causing their friendship to fade and break apart by the end of the year. In the other, they stood back to back and faced all comers with smiles on their faces, while wearing sunflower kimonos.

"Kind of makes the choice easy," Gregory muttered.

"What?" Yukiko asked, turning to him with worried eyes.

"Agreed, Yuki. No scores kept— only helping each other climb higher."

Her cyan eyes stared into his for a long moment, her cheeks heating. "Agreed, Greg. We'll climb together, no matter what others might think."

Gregory felt like he was missing part of what she was meaning, but before he could question her, the door opened and Hemet came back into the room.

"I have a few items for you to consider," Hemet said, laying a display case on the counter. Seven rings were contained within the velvet-lined, glass-topped case. "The first are simple; they will help you recover from fatigue and minor injuries," he pointed at two plain silver and onyx bands. "These will allow you to manifest your aether into attacks," he pointed to three rings in sequence, "kick, punch, grapple. Each of them is good as long as you have aether to fuel them. This one," he pointed to an odd-looking reddish metal band, "blocks pain for a short time. It will block all pain, even fatal pain, making it both a curse and blessing. The last one is for you, miss." Hemet smiled as he pointed to a band of mottled gray, "This will allow a shadow magi to shift from one shadow to another, but only as long as it has enough aether. If it is fully imbued, it can be used three times before it is drained. It normally takes a magus days to give it a single charge. A novice like you would take months."

"I think that item would take all of my potential trade," Yukiko said with a smile.

"Not many shadow magi, and most of them can do it without my trinket," Hemet shrugged. "It was a bad buy on my end years ago. I would let it and one of the lesser rings go."

"That doesn't make things even," Yukiko murmured.

"How is the ring charged, sir?" Gregory asked from his place at the table.

"Pouring your aether into it, which is why it'll take her so long to charge it. It is fully charged currently."

"Anyone can put their aether into it?"

"That is correct."

"Take the offer, Yuki," Gregory said. "That ring will help you more than any of the other rings. One of the lesser ones is more than enough for me."

Yukiko frowned, but sighed, "If that is what you want, Greg."

"It's a deal, then," Hemet said, unlocking the case and extracting the two rings. "The lesser recovery ring can be used multiple times, but like hers, it requires charging. This one pulls aether from the environment, and while at the academy, you should be able to use it every hour."

"How much for the match to that ring?" Yukiko asked.

"Normally, ten thousand vela. I'll let you have it for eight if you can pay it by the end of today."

"Will you take a bond for the eight thousand?"

"A bond? Backed by whom?"

"Warlin Mercantile."

Hemet eyed Yukiko for a long moment, "I'd want to verify the bond."

Yukiko nodded and pulled out a scroll, "I'll need a pen."

Hemet placed a pen and ink on the counter. "Before you put ink to parchment, may I see it?"

Handing it over, Yukiko smiled at him. Hemet looked over the scroll, then placed his monocle on for a moment before nodding. "Always a pleasure doing business with someone backed by the empire."

Yukiko wrote out the amount and signed the bottom of the scroll. She nicked her thumb for a drop of blood, which she smeared next to her name. The scroll glowed golden for a moment, and she handed it to Hemet. "Done."

"Three rings," Hemet said, handing over all of them. "Please come back again if you require anything further."

"I shall," Yukiko said as she took the rings in hand. "Ready, Greg?"

Gregory had risen to his feet, but stayed back when she had pressed for more. "Food, right?"

"Yes."

"I'm ready, then."

Once outside, Yukiko put two rings on and handed him the other one. "Now we'll have a slightly better chance during the tournament. Try not to use them before then. That way, it'll be a surprise to those we face."

"Sounds like the best idea," Gregory said, slipping the ring onto his left index finger. The band vibrated for a second, then shrank a little to fit him perfectly. "That was odd."

"It is normal for enchanted items, otherwise none of them could be made except to order."

"More to learn," Gregory said as they climbed into the rickshaw that had been waiting for them.

CHAPTER 28

The rickshaw dropped them off outside the Golden Boar. The tavern was lively when they entered. Seeing a table for two on the far side of the room, Yukiko headed for it with Gregory trailing her.

"Bit pale for my taste, but cute..."

"Her boyfriend is a twig. Bet I could break him and have her..."

"I think she's tainted, eurtik b..."

Snippets of conversation reached Gregory's ears as he crossed the room, and his hands tightened as he continued walking. Yukiko's pace never faltered, though her smile waned a little when she heard them.

"Idiots... pale of skin and hair? That has to be the new novice up at the academy that has all the clans clamoring for her. I wouldn't..."

They reached the table and sat. It was only seconds before a man in an embroidered kimono came to their table. "Welcome to the Golden Boar. Can I get you something to drink, and perhaps something to eat?"

"I'd prefer for our drinks to compliment the meal," Yukiko replied to him. "What do you have available?"

Seeing her medallion, the server bowed his head slightly. "Magi, we have pheasant over rice with infused herbs or bane boar grilled with chunks of spiker fruit and served with buttered noodles. The other options aren't aether infused, if you'd like to hear them?"

"That's fine. We need as much aether as we can get," Yukiko said. "Greg, did you have a preference?"

"The boar sounds interesting."

"Two of the boar, with whatever beverage will best suit the meal," Yukiko told the server.

"Yes, mistress."

The server walked away, and Gregory glanced around the room to see most of the patrons involved in their food or conversations. "What have you got planned after this, Yuki?"

"Originally, I was thinking of going back to the academy for more study or training, but since we've come to our agreement, I'm thinking of being as bold as my father."

Gregory frowned, "Huh?"

"Visiting the clans that sent me messages and seeing what they have to say. I'll accept any gift they wish to give and use that to help us gain better footing. I also need to stop at a courier to send messages to my parents."

"Are all of them inside the academy walls?"

"Yes, which means a stop at a courier's office before we go back," Yukiko replied.

"Your wine," the server said, coming back to the table with two glasses and a bottle. Opening the bottle at the table, he poured some for Yukiko and presented the glass to her.

Yukiko took the glass, swirled it around, sniffed it, sipped, then nodded. "Yes, this will do."

The server poured for each of them and left with his head bowed. Gregory picked up his glass and sniffed at the wine. The scent was complex, and he was unfamiliar with most of the spices. Sipping it, he discovered that the predominant flavor was orange, reminding him of a dessert his mother had made for him once.

"Reminds me of oranges," Gregory said after his sip.

"Mostly orange, as well as spices that mell..." Yukiko trailed off when she saw Gregory staring at her. "What?"

"Something you learned from your family?"

"Yes. You have to know what the wine is made of to better sell it."

"You know so much more than I do," Gregory smiled wryly. "I'm lucky you're here to teach me."

Yukiko looked down, a touch of pink showing on her cheeks. "I'm just as lucky that you enjoy my company. You heard them, didn't you?"

Gregory's smile slipped for a moment. "Idiots," he said softly. "Your heritage doesn't make you— only you can do that."

Yukiko looked up to speak, but closed her mouth. A moment later, the server was beside the table with two plates. Placing one before each of them, he bowed his head. "Please enjoy."

The scent hit Gregory's nostrils like a punch. His mouth started watering and his stomach growled. Coughing, he pulled out the cutlery he had made sure to bring with him. "Let's eat."

Yukiko had almost the same reaction so she did not argue, pulling out her own set of cutlery. The two of them sat there in silence, the sounds of a busy tavern washing over them as they ate.

The spiker's sweet-tart nature made the bane boar's flavor more potent, but also helped mellow the influx of aether that rushed into them with each bite of boar meat. The buttered noodles helped to blunt it even more. Gregory was surprised to find that the butter sauce had the same tangy flavor of spiker fruit. The wine softened the tartness of the spiker, adding a bit more boldness to the boar.

Gregory and Yukiko lingered over their meal, enjoying the new flavors. Both of them sighed when it came to an end and, sharing a content smile, they just stared at each other for a moment.

"Would you care for orange tart or chocolate cake?" the server asked, breaking the moment.

"I'd like the chocolate. What about you Greg?"

"Orange tart, please."

"And two of the bitter bean, please, with sugar and butter on the side," Yukiko ordered.

"Right away," the servant smiled as he took away their empty dishes.

"Bitter bean?" Gregory asked.

"It's a popular drink in Buldoun. It will refresh you and leave you ready to do more work after the meal. It's actually more prominent than tea in Buldoun."

"How different is it there?" Gregory asked.

Yukiko went silent for a bit, thinking. "We never went far past the border. Buldoun and the empire are tentatively at peace, and have been since the last war fifteen years ago. We only visited Blum, a small city two dozen miles from the border."

Gregory finished his wine while he listened to her relate the differences in architecture, clothing, and culture. Full-blooded eurtik were treated almost as badly as in the empire, but those of mixed blood were tolerated better.

Yukiko broke off her explanation when the server came back with their desserts and bitter bean drinks. Gregory took a sip of the drink at Yukiko's urging and nearly gagged at the bitter taste.

Yukiko was giggling as she added two scoops of sugar and one of butter to hers. "That is why it's called bitter bean."

"Very apt," Gregory said, copying her additions to the drink and taking a hesitant sip. "That's much better."

* * *

Instead of taking a rickshaw back, Gregory and Yukiko decided to jog to the academy. Halfway up, Yukiko asked Gregory to stop just outside of a plain-looking structure with a five-story tower. Following her in, he stepped into a large room with over a dozen desks scattered about, each one with a sign hanging over it. One side of the room had a long counter with stacks of paper on it.

"I need the paperwork to send two missives to Handa province," Yukiko said without preamble upon reaching the central desk.

"Do you have them ready?" the man asked, not looking up from his paperwork.

"No. I'll need paper and ink, as well."

A frown flickered across the clerk's face, then his expression was neutral again. "Use the counter over there." He motioned to the counter with paper on it. "Fill out these two forms." He took papers from stacks on his desk and thrust them at her without looking. "Once you have all that in order, see the Handa province desk."

"Thank you," Yukiko said, taking the forms and moving toward the counter.

"I need a form to send a letter to Alturis in Saito province," Gregory told the man.

"Here is the form," the man said, thrusting another paper at him. "Same instructions as the lady, but the Saito desk."

"Thank you."

"Sending a letter home?" Yukiko asked softly when he joined her.

"Figured I might as well let them know how I'm doing."

Yukiko smiled, "Good."

Gregory got the form filled out with minimal questions to Yukiko. Taking a blank sheet of paper from the pile on the counter, Gregory thought for a few minutes, then started writing.

Gunnar, how is the married life going? I'm sure if you aren't married by the time this reaches you, you will be soon. Things are good here; I've made a friend, you'd all like her. Her name is Yukiko Warlin, and she's the daughter of a merchant family. We've been helping each other study and train. The twins would like her, too— she's soft spoken, but can be surprisingly aggressive when it comes to commerce.

The academy is different. We have classes, but we can drop them if we want. The only drawback is that we won't qualify for some posts after our fourth year, depending on which class is dropped. I did drop out of history since it wasn't teaching me anything. I'm using the time to learn more about trade. Ria and El would be shocked at how much I understand now.

Speaking of Ria, how is she? If she hasn't started looking for someone, please help her. I know El will, but I'll not even be able to get back for years, if at all, and as a magi, my lifespan is going to far exceed hers if I get through training.

I need to thank you both for the money. I used it to help get me here and

purchase some much needed things. You didn't have to do it, and I'll find a
way to pay you back.

Is my father okay? I know he was bound in servitude to the village, but
is he still sober? Is the mine still doing well? I know it hasn't been that long,
maybe it will be by the time you read this, but please tell me what is going
on there.

I'll do my best to write you after the first tournament for novices. We
have one midway through training and another at the end of the first year.
I hope to hear back from you before then.

Your best friend still,

Greg.

He signed the letter and sat back to wait for the ink to dry. "I'm
done, Yuki."

"Fold it this way, then take it and the form to the right province
desk," Yukiko told him as she folded her letters.

"Meet you by the door?"

"Yes."

Gregory approached the Saito province desk, giving the woman
manning it a pleasant smile. "Excuse me, miss, I wish to send this
letter."

Taking the forms, the clerk frowned, "Alturis...? Oh, the fringe?
Not many letters go that far out. It'll take some time to reach that far.
Cost is also higher since none of the regular couriers go that far."

"How much?" Gregory asked.

"Three hundred vela, I'm afraid."

Gregory blanched, but dug out what amounted to most of his
coin. "Here you go."

The clerk took the money and looked at him curiously, "What's a
fringer like you doing all the way here?"

"Novice magi."

"Should have marked it on the form," the clerk sighed. "See this
box here?" She showed him the place he should have marked.
"Check that next time, magi. Even novices pay less." She handed him
back half of his money. "There. This will go out in the next week, but
as I said, it'll take a while to get there."

"Thank you," Gregory said, bowing to her. "I understand and will remember."

"Very good. Have a good day."

Gregory nodded, heading for the door. He did not wait long before Yukiko approached him. "Back to jogging?"

"Back to jogging, and then to see the clans."

CHAPTER 29

When they made it back to the academy, the two novices were breathing fast, but they were not as winded as they would have been last week. The apprentice on duty had the guards let them in while giving them an appraising look.

"Which clan first?" Gregory asked as they started walking down one of the paths.

"Smallest to biggest. Raises the stakes on each one in turn," Yukiko replied. "That means the Saito Clan is first. We'll talk for a few minutes and leave, but they won't have anything to gift— they're too small a clan. When we visit the Gelta Clan after them, we can mention we came from them."

"Which makes them want to do something more than the previous clan to win your favor. I see."

"You pick up on the nuances faster than a fringer should, Greg."

"Thanks... I think?"

"It's a compliment. Father won't believe you're a fringer when he meets you."

"Meeting your father?" Gregory asked with surprise.

"He'll want to know who's been taking care of me while I've been here. That won't be until the first tournament, though. I wonder if Mother will come? I hope so."

Gregory stayed silent, wondering if it was alright for him to meet her parents. *That's what you do if you are courting someone from a different village... Stop being stupid, Greg, she is just doing what she needs to. Her father is going to be very curious about the guy she's been hanging around with. Need to make sure to give a good impression so he knows that everything is okay.*

"Here we are," Yukiko said, approaching a small single story building.

Ringing the bell attached to the front post, they waited. A few minutes later, the door opened to reveal a middle-aged woman in a cyan kimono. There was an embroidered open palm clearly visible on her sleeve. "May I...? Oh, Novice Warlin, please come in."

"Thank you," Yukiko replied, bowing formally to her. "My friend, Gregory Pettit, is with me."

"By all means, please come in," the magus said, ushering them inside.

The magus escorted them to a meeting room, and tea was brought in as soon as they were seated. "We weren't sure you would respond to our invitation, much less show up the day after," the magus explained.

"I have a number of invitations to visit other clans," Yukiko said kindly. "I'm seeing them in the order that I read them."

"Of course," the magus replied. "Saito Clan can't really compete with the larger clans in terms of generosity, a point I'm sure you are well aware of. Unlike them, however, we do actually care about those in the clan, and we have a shadow magi that is more than willing to train you personally."

"That is very generous. I doubt many ranked magus or above would take me under their wing."

"In any of the big clans like the Eternal Flame or the Han Merchant Exchange, that is doubtlessly true. That is one of the reasons you should consider all your options before choosing."

"A wise point," Yukiko agreed, sipping her tea. "I understand we can't officially join clans until after the tournament."

"That is true, but our door is open if you would like to discuss joining us."

"I will undoubtedly do so in the coming weeks, Magus...?"

"Oh, I forgot my manners. I'm Magus Anita Alon."

"I do need to ask if your clan is actively feuding with any others. It would be bad for me to join a clan that is in the middle of a crisis."

"Currently, we do not have any feuds," Anita replied, but her eye twitched.

"That is good. Thank you for the tea, Magus. I must be going, I intend to also visit other clans today. If time allows, I will stop by in the coming weeks to speak further."

"I will look forward to it," Anita smiled.

Once they were outside the clan building and walking to the next, Yukiko sighed. "Lying about the feuds... she had been doing so well until then. All clans have a feud of one type or another going. No doubt they wish another shadow magi to help them gather more information to build themselves up."

"Most of the meetings are going to be like that one?" Gregory asked.

"The first few, yes. Once we speak to the White Eagle Clan, things will become much more involved, since they and the larger clans will start trying to outright buy my allegiance."

"I feel out of place coming with you."

"No, you are necessary. How they treat or ignore you will speak volumes about what they are thinking."

"Okay. If I'm being helpful to my partner, then I'll continue."

"Thank you, Greg. I'll try not to draw it out too long, but it's best to see what might be arrayed against us later."

* * *

True to her words, the next two clan visits went much like Saito Clan's meeting. Both of them promised more than just a shadow magus to teach her. Gregory could only marvel at how eager or desperate each clan seemed to be to get Yukiko.

When they reached the White Eagle Clan's manor, Gregory stared at the black marble building. The only decoration was the white eagle emblem that adorned the front of the building, and the intricately carved door that was just under the eagle's talons.

Yukiko rang the bell and the door was opened by an initiate. "How can we help you?" the initiate asked with a raised eyebrow.

"I'm Yukiko Warlin. I was asked to come," she presented the scroll.

The initiate read the scroll with a frown. "Please wait here," he said before shutting the door on them.

Gregory winced, "He's going to pay for that, isn't he?"

"If I act offended, as I properly should, then yes," Yukiko replied. "Please don't hold what happens here against me, Greg."

"Going to play into it?"

Yukiko gave him a small smile before she erased it from her face and put an angry expression on. "Asking me to come, then keeping me waiting on the front step? I won't stand for this. Come with me," Yukiko said a little loudly as she spun on her heel to leave.

Gregory followed her without comment. A gust of wind nearly knocked them both over when they reached the path away from the building. Staggering, they managed to keep their footing and saw a man in a cobalt blue kimono standing in front of them.

"Apologies for the rude manner of getting in front of you and for the rudeness of our initiate. I'm Master Quinn Marzden, head of the White Eagle Clan here in the city. Please, Novices Warlin and Pettit, come inside and let us talk."

Yukiko smoothed her kimono before replying. "Master, I appreciate the gesture, but today is not the day to make amends. I shall return next week to speak with you."

Marzden's lips twitched downward, "That would be less than desirable, as you are surely on your way to speak with the Han Merchant Exchange and possibly even the Iron Hand clans."

"Indeed," Yukiko bowed her head. "Both have expressed interest in meeting me, and are likely to show a bit more *decorum* when I show up at their door. I suggested next week, as right now, the foul taste in my mouth left by that initiate is strong. Next week, it will be mellower, and will allow for a more productive meeting."

Marzden glanced at Gregory before putting his focus back on Yukiko. "I see. Your father has surely taught you how to be unmovable when needed. Very well. I shall look forward to next week." With a slight dip of his head, Marzden stepped aside for them. "Until then, may your training be vigorous and true."

"Good day," Yukiko said, bowing formally.

"Good day, sir," Gregory echoed, mirroring her bow.

As they left the area on their way to the Iron Hand manor, Gregory exhaled slowly. "Damn, Yuki, do you have ice for blood? I could feel his aether pressuring you."

Yuki stopped walking and leaned against Gregory. "No. My knees would have been shaking if I hadn't locked them. I hope there are no other masters to speak with. Talking to a magus is difficult enough."

"You had me fooled," Gregory said, supporting her for the moment. "Want to call off the last two?"

"No, because next week, we will have even more to deal with. I need to see this through and project confidence the entire time," Yukiko whispered as she finally pushed herself away from him. "If you weren't here to support me, I'm not sure I could."

"I couldn't at all," Gregory replied. "Let's get it done, then we can relax and study."

Yukiko's lips turned upward in a smile. "I'm sure it'll be tea for me and cards for you, but we can study some, as well."

"Good," Gregory said. "I'd rather study, but seeing what Nick has to say will be interesting."

"Indeed."

When they arrived at the Iron Hand manor, Gregory had finally stopped being surprised at the sheer wealth involved in the structures. The Iron Hand manor looked to be more barracks than manor, but the stonework itself was still worth more than his birth village.

"Stop, you aren't one of ours. Who are you, and what brings you to our door?" a balding, heavily muscled magus asked from beside the front door.

"I'm Yukiko Warlin, and this is Gregory Pettit. I was invited to come speak with the clan." She held out the scroll she had received.

"Ah, the shadow magi," the man said, eyeing the two of them. "You could both use some hard training to fill out. The commander will wish to speak with you. Follow me."

The interior of the building was as spartan as the exterior. They passed two doors before their guide knocked on the third one. When a voice called for him to enter, the magus opened the door and motioned them inside.

"Novices Warlin and Pettit, sir."

The heavily scarred man behind the desk looked up as they entered. Gregory's eyebrows went up when he saw the network of scars beside the man's eye, along with the deeper one that ran above and below it.

"I know we sent an invitation to Novice Warlin, but I don't recall inviting you, Novice Pettit."

"He is with me," Yukiko replied as she took a seat. "I'm sure you've heard of him, even if you haven't decided if you should approach him yet."

The man wearing the cobalt kimono behind the desk nodded, "Accurate. Very astute to have figured that out before speaking with us. I'm Master Yong Chen, Commander of the Iron Hand in the city. I'm not one for wasting time, unlike most of my contemporaries— we'd like you to join us, Warlin. The Iron Hand is hard and unyield-ing, but we never leave one of our own to fend for themselves. We won't give you false praise, try to buy you, or pressure you. What we will do is give you the best training we can. In return, you will fold into our clan as is fitting for one of your magic."

"The Iron Hand is well known as the main fighting force of magi within the empire. You've been the spear point of every war for the last hundred years."

"As we need to be. The other clans would let the empire crumble if it aided their petty disputes. Our founder knew that a solid, reliable clan would be needed for the emperor to keep the empire solid. We uphold that ideal to this day."

"I'm not one to seek combat," Yukiko said honestly. "I doubt I'd fit into the clan as well as you hope."

"We were uncertain. Your performance during conditioning puts you in the top ten, but conditioning isn't the same as combat. Magus Erichson spoke well of both of you, so we knew we had to act, let you know our interest before all the other clans closed in. Please keep the option of joining us open. We'll be looking forward to the tournament."

"I will do so," Yukiko bowed in her seat. "I wish you a good evening, sir."

"Good evening to you both. Pettit," he called as they stood up, "we'll be keeping our eyes on you, too. If your magic turns out to be combat related, we'll be talking again."

"Yes, sir."

"Dismissed," he said, turning back to his reports.

Walking out of the building, they gave the magus at the door a polite nod. Once they were down the path and heading toward their last stop, Yukiko shook her head. "I would still take them over the Eternal Flame, but not by much."

"They seem very rigid," Gregory added. "That explains why Magus Erichson is the way he is."

"Yes. Last stop is the Han Merchant Exchange. This is the one that will be difficult for me. Father used to be part of their clan; not as a magi, but as a trader."

"If you can face down two masters today, you can handle this, too, Yuki."

"With that kind of confidence, I'll have to," Yukiko replied with a smile.

* * *

The Han Merchant Exchange was the second largest clan manor inside the academy walls, only slightly smaller than the Eternal

Flame manor. The walls were golden marble, and the exterior fixtures were a shining silver that were already lit as the sun sank toward the horizon.

A couple of adepts were smoking from a hookah on the front porch. Seeing them coming, one of them set aside his pipe. "Novices Warlin and Pettit, we've been expecting you. Please, follow me. Magus Han is waiting."

Yukiko bowed her head to the adept, "We follow."

Gregory did his best to hide his discomfort at putting on silken slippers upon entering the manor. The wealth displayed inside the Han manor was more than the last two clans combined, and it was hard for him to ignore.

They were led through a series of hallways before they came to a halt next to a door. The adept knocked, then entered the room. "Novices Warlin and Pettit, Magus."

"Send them in. Arrange for refreshments."

"As you require," the adept bowed deeply before he stepped back for them to enter. "Please be seated. Refreshments will be along shortly."

Entering the room, they found Magus Marcia Han sitting behind a large dark oak desk. She gave them a pleasant smile, unlike her usual frown during class. "Novices, I figured we'd be having this conversation today. Sit, and let's wait for refreshments before we begin with business."

"As you wish, Magus," Yukiko bowed in her seat.

"Thank you, Magus."

It was only a few moments before there was a knock on the door, announcing the arrival of a servant with a loaded cart. "Mistress, the refreshments, as ordered."

"Serve."

"Would you prefer tea or something stronger?" the dark-haired servant asked them with a polite smile.

"Tea," they said in unison.

"We have a variety of delicacies if you'd like some, as well."

"No, thank you. The tea is enough," Yukiko replied.

"I'm good, too, thank you."

The servant served them, then bowed and stepped back to stand against the wall. Marcia sipped her tea, waiting for Yukiko to speak.

"Magus, I received a scroll asking me to come speak with you," Yukiko said after a minute of enjoying her tea.

"Shadow magi are coveted by all the clans, as I'm sure you are well aware of by now. As one of the great clans, it behooves us to approach you early and make you aware that the option of joining us is available. I understand you had a half dozen scrolls delivered last night. Knowing your family, I expect you waited to speak with me until last."

Yukiko took another drink before replying, "One should always look at the lowest offers first."

"Yes. You can use it to strengthen your position in bargaining. We weren't sure if novice Pettit would be with you or not, but I thought he would. The two of you seem... close."

Yukiko's back went stiff, "We are friends and have been helping each other study."

"That would explain how a fringer is able to keep up with my lectures." Marcia turned her gaze to Gregory, "Has it been difficult?"

"I've been learning a lot, Magus. Difficult paths are the best paths for growth."

Marcia's lips twitched and one eyebrow rose. "Goodness, I didn't expect you to know and understand that truth yet. Many novices balk at how hard we push them to learn. Though I hear you have both left the history class."

"We've learned more through the archive than from Adept Thomas' lectures," Gregory replied.

"Yes; sadly, many are leaving his class. Only those dedicated to certain posts are staying. I have been glad to see you both remain in my class, even if Novice Warlin does get bored easily."

Yukiko gave a polite smile, "I find it interesting, Magus, but I've just heard and seen much of it firsthand. I take notes on the differences between what you teach and what I learned from my father."

Han's brow furrowed for a fraction of a second. "Indeed. Speaking of your father, he has done well since leaving the clan. Several people were surprised at how quickly and strong his enterprise has grown. I've looked into how and why he left our clan. Do you think he'll attend the tournament?"

"I hope to see him there, Magus."

"Good. I shall send him an invitation to tea during that time. Now for the real business: enticing you to join us." Marcia looked at the servant, who pulled a six-inch square box from the lower shelf of her cart. "Take this with you. The contents are yours to use as you see fit. Just consider that things like this are commonplace for those who help the clan advance and grow."

Yukiko accepted the box and placed it in her pouch, which it filled entirely. "I won't be surprised to find that this easily outstrips the gifts the Eternal Flame gave me last week."

"You do understand. Good." Marcia looked back to Gregory, "Your magic is problematic, Novice. Master Damon still has yet to find any lead on what the ryuite means. If we had even a hint, we'd likely be lavishing you with similar gifts, depending on what your magic is."

"I'd be honored, Magus. I hope the master will find out soon so I can seek guidance on how to use it."

"The hands-on aether introduction classes should be starting after next week. I'm sure that many people will be interested in knowing what happens during those classes."

"As will I, Magus," Gregory said wryly.

"Sadly, I do need to finish preparing for tomorrow. Take your time to consider our offer, and if you have any questions, come by again."

"Thank you, Magus," Yukiko replied. She bowed formally.

"A good evening to you, Magus," Gregory said as he bowed deeply to her.

"Show them out," Marcia told the servant. "I'll see you both in class."

CHAPTER 30

After dinner, Gregory and Yukiko were on their way to the stairs in the dormitory when one of the staff appeared in front of them. "Novice Warlin, Keeper Dia would like to see you."

"Greg, will you take this to your room? I'll be right there," Yukiko asked, handing him the box.

"Sure. See you in a few."

Making it to his room, Gregory set the box on the table, got his things put away, and set out his soiled clothing for the cleaning staff. He took a seat and looked closely at the box that Magus Marcia had given Yukiko. The box itself was crafted of some dark wood, with a hinge of burnished bronze. There was no lock on the box. The desire to open it was strong, but he resisted, as it was not his.

Yukiko entered the room a minute later, shutting the door behind her. She was holding another clutch of scrolls. "More clans to see next week, though many will give up after hearing what the Eternal Flame and Han Merchant Exchange have already offered me."

"You didn't seem interested in any of them," Gregory said softly.

"No, none of them have offered sufficient inducement yet."

"Afraid to see what you consider sufficient," Gregory chuckled.

"That necklace was worth more than many in my village will see in their lifetime."

Yukiko looked down, "I... I didn't mean..."

"It's fine, Yuki. I don't take offense. You're worth more than that bauble. Whichever clan gets you is going to have an edge; that's why they're all trying to get you. There's nothing wrong with being wanted or trying to get as much as you can for yourself."

Yukiko's cheeks were pink, "Let's see what's in the box, huh?"

Seeing her desire to change the subject, Gregory nodded. "Yeah, let's see."

Opening the box, Yukiko's lips pursed as she pulled out a few pouches. Each had a small card attached to it that Yukiko read aloud, "Somnia leaves: to help your aether grow while sleeping, place a single leaf under your tongue when you go to bed. Ring of the mind: wearing this ring will aid the wearer in connecting to the mind path. Scroll of the shadow magi: this scroll instructs a shadow magi in how to pull shadows around yourself easier and more quickly."

Gregory's shock at each gift grew, and he was shaking his head when she finished pulling the items out. "They're trying to prejudice you to the mind path and have given you a technique to help with your magic. How expensive are scrolls like that one?"

"Ones aimed at helping a novice perfect their first magic are expensive, but not overly so. The ring is worth more monetarily... and maybe we can both use it, trading off every day?"

Gregory was about to object, but he closed his mouth and shook his head. "If that is what you think is best."

Yukiko gave him a soft smile, "Thank you for not fighting me."

"What about the rest of this stuff?"

"We'll split them."

"Understood," Gregory said as he accepted the leaves she gave him.

There was a knock on the door a moment later, and Gregory went to answer it. "Michelle?"

"I was looking for Yu— there she is." She looked past him to

Yukiko, "I'm having some of the girls over for tea in my room. I'd like it if you came."

"I will be there after we finish studying. It'll be about an hour from now, if that's okay?"

"You two study much too hard before we have any clan to worry about. We'll keep a spot open for you."

"I'll be there."

"Great, see you later."

Gregory sighed as he closed the door after Michelle. "I guess that means cards for me with Nick and the other guys. I don't even know what that means."

"I can show you the basics. We have an hour, and it is a type of learning for you," Yukiko smiled. "Bring me a couple pieces of paper and some ink."

* * *

An hour later, Gregory knocked on Nick's door. Nick smiled when he opened the door. "Was wondering if you were going to show. Greg's here, guys. We can start up the game."

"I don't have a lot of—"

"I got you covered," Nick laughed. "Come on in."

Gregory entered the room to find all the guys Nick hung out with already there. A couple of open bottles were on a side table, along with an assortment of snacks. Fureno moved over a little, making room for Gregory.

"We were about to start without you," Jason smirked. "Figured you might be... *up* to things with Yukiko."

Gregory frowned, "Yuki and I are just friends."

"Just friends who shared a massage at Felina's," Fureno snickered.

"Guys, stop busting his balls," Nick laughed, seeing Gregory starting to get upset. "They had one of the split rooms."

"Really?" one of the others asked. "The way you two are always together, I was sure you'd made a move on her."

"She's betrothed," Gregory said stiffly as he took a seat. "We're just friends and helping each other train."

"I'd like to help her train," Fureno snickered. "*Physically* train," he said, wiggling his eyebrows for emphasis.

"Damn man, you got it that bad?" Jason asked, seeing Gregory's brow furrow as he glared at Fureno. "I mean, she's got the exotic look: pale skin and hair and bright eyes, but come on. It's only us guys here. No need to get pissy. Surely you and your friends back home used to compare the women."

Gregory sighed, "Sorry. It's true that Gunnar and I used to compare the twins."

"Twins?" Nick asked, his eyebrows rising as he grabbed a deck of cards. "Twins are fun if you get them together. How were they, the twins?"

"Beautiful," Gregory said, without pausing. "Ria and El are the best-looking women in the village. Gunnar and El were courting when I left."

"What about the other one? Ria? You ever *get close* to her?"

Gregory looked down, "That isn't—"

"I'd say yes," Fureno snickered. "Look at that blush."

"Okay, come on, we're playing cards," Nick chuckled. "Jason, hand out the vela. You can back out at any point and keep the vela, but I'd prefer you try to win as much as you can."

"Never played cards," Gregory said. "I could use a little help."

Nick grinned, "Friends help each other out, don't they? Jason, give him the notes I had you make."

Gregory studied the sheet of paper that Jason handed him. It listed the best winning hands for the game, and the rules of how to play the game *Trade and Barter*. The players were dealt three cards, starting with the oldest player. He could trade a vela to the pot for a new card, discarding one of his old ones as he did, or he could barter, trading a card with the player of his choice— without payment— who had not knocked on the table yet. Play continued until two players knocked on the table, at which point, cards were revealed and the one with the best hand took the pot.

"We normally play this at higher stakes, but because you were joining us, Nick made it lower so you'd feel better about it," Fureno said, looking at the stack of twenty-vela coins as if they were trash.

Gregory looked at his stack of two hundred twenty-vela coins and shook his head. "What stakes do you normally play with?"

"Hundred vela coins," Jason admitted. "We come from different backgrounds, though," he added with a shrug. "No one can control where they are born or to whom."

"Right, sorry," Fureno said with a pained grimace. "Didn't mean it the way it came out."

"We ready?" Nick smiled, trying to push past the awkwardness. "Ante your coin."

Hours passed as they played, coins flowing back and forth across the table. Gregory did poorly to start with; his hands at the end always ended up just a little worse than the others. As the second hour passed, he started to gain ground. Luck was part of it, but he started to understand what each player valued and was likely to trade away.

Banter at the table stayed away from the subject of women for a while, instead centering mostly around the teachers and classes, with a few conversations cropping up about family. The only drinks in the room were alcohol, and Gregory sipped at his single glass sparingly while the others imbibed with less reserve.

As the second hour was coming to a close, Fureno brought the topic of women up again. "Remember the crazy proctor?" He snickered, "I mean sure, she was crazy and had a lot of scars, but damned if she didn't look good when she stripped down. I can imagine having her working for me."

"I like my women softer," Jason said. "Michelle is a good example. If Nick wasn't bent on trying to get with her, I'd be making my own play."

"Feel free," Nick chuckled. "I'm not serious. She'll be a hard one to pin down, though. She is semi-serious about staying chaste for her betrothed. I think she'll break by third year. From what I've heard, her betrothed has been seen visiting a few places he should know better than to be seen at. Once that comes to her attention..." Shrugging, he laughed, "Well, she'll be easy for at least one night. You or me, doesn't matter. Have to let my friends have their own fun, you know?"

"If that's the case, I'll just start laying the groundwork. I already have Melody interested, but she won't be hard to convince. Her family could use anything I let fall to them, and she knows that. At least she'll be smart enough to stay as a mistress and not make a scene. I like the game of conquering tough women, and Michelle will be that."

"The chase is the best part," Nick agreed as he knocked on the table. "I mean, collecting at the end is fun— a lot of fun— but the chase is just more exhilarating."

"You should go for Yukiko, then," Fureno snickered. "*That* would be the hard chase."

Nick's lips thinned, "You know how I feel about... I mean, Gregory has his sights set on her. Don't you, Greg? It's okay to admit among us." Nick's tone shifted hard in the middle of his sentence.

"She's betrothed."

"Yeah, but if she crept into your room tonight, would you tell her no?" Jason pressed.

Gregory looked away, "I... wouldn't. I'm not trying to win her affection, though. We're friends and training partners only."

"What if she *didn't* have a betrothed?" Nick asked. "You'd be considering it, wouldn't you?"

"If horses had wings, we'd all be able to fly," Gregory shrugged.

"You wouldn't know this, but past agreements get annulled when one joins the Eternal Flame," Nick commented. "If Yukiko were to join the clan, her betrothal would be broken."

If she isn't betrothed, maybe we could... His thoughts were derailed when Jason knocked on the table, indicating the end of the hand.

Gregory handed his cards to Fureno, knowing he had not won. The chime of the twentieth bell made him blink at how late it was. "I need to get going. The day comes early."

"Of course," Nick said. "Take your coin with you."

Gregory moved to put it into his bag before he realized he was not wearing it. "It was your coin to begin with," he said as he got to his feet. "Thank you for inviting me. I'll see you later."

"At class, if not before," Nick said. "Good evening, Greg."

"Night," Gregory told the room.

Yukiko's room was dark when he went past it. *Maybe she's still having tea? I hope she doesn't stay out too late. If what Nick said is true, it'd be possible that maybe I could...* Putting the brakes on his thoughts, Gregory rubbed at his face.

"It's not going to happen. She is a friend, and that is all," Gregory mumbled to himself as he got ready for bed.

Retrieving one of the leaves from his closet, Gregory thought about it and Yukiko. Shaking his head again, he stuck it under his tongue and went to bed. *Dreams are nice, but some of them will only ever be dreams*, he thought, darkness creeping up over him to pull him into slumber.

CHAPTER 31

Waking as the third bell tolled, Gregory got up and dressed, feeling energized and ready for the day. When he stepped out of his room, he was surprised that Yukiko was not there. Knocking lightly on her door, he heard her stir inside. "Yuki, it's third bell."

There was a scrambling sound from inside before the door slid open an inch, revealing Yukiko's disheveled hair and one bright eye. "Sorry, Greg. I'll be as quick as I can."

Gregory blinked and forcefully pulled his gaze back to her face, his cheeks red, "Um, yeah... um... I'll be downstairs."

"I'll hurry," Yukiko said again as the door slid shut.

Gregory stood there for a long moment, the image of Yukiko in a thin silk shift seared into his mind. Her pale skin reflected the low light in the hall, clearly revealing more of her figure than Gregory had seen until that moment. Gregory exhaled deeply and made his way to the stairs, wondering if her skin felt as silky as he thought it did.

Exiting the dormitory, he took a seat on the bench and tried to center his mind, but the image of Yukiko in her nightgown would not let him. Gregory groaned in frustration, gripping his knees painfully hard.

"There *is* a place for that kind of thing, Novice. You can always use the one around back," Dia's voice came from a few feet away.

Gregory jumped up from the bench, his face turning bright red. "No, I wasn't! That—"

Dia laughed lightly as she lit her long pipe. "Relax, I'm aware. I was just making a joke. You seem rather on edge this morning... and without your companion. Did something happen?"

"No," Gregory said quickly, "nothing," he added with a pause.

"Then she is merely delayed. No reason to be upset. Unless she's going to join a clan that you aren't invited to?"

"No, she hasn't decided on a clan yet."

"I figured as much. She comes from a shrewd family, and she would be foolish to decide on a clan before all options are on the table, even if two of the five great clans have already approached her."

"Are you part of a clan, Keeper?" Gregory asked.

Dia paused, eyeing him before shaking her head. "I'm merely a keeper. I have no clan affiliation. No keeper can be part of a clan, as it would bias us."

"Ah, right," Gregory said.

"You should take the time to study the clans before you decide on one. Most novices don't and the rest are already spoken for, like your friends Nick and Hayworth."

"Hayworth isn't a friend, but he has thankfully left me alone except for some comments during conditioning. Nick is a... friend..." Gregory trailed off as he said it, the word not sitting right on his tongue.

"An ally, perhaps?" Dia asked, blowing a smoke ring.

"An ally, certainly," Gregory agreed, the words not fighting him that time.

"Five months until the tournament... much will change between now and the day after," Dia said idly. "The day after the tournament, novices may formally accept the invitation of a clan and leave the dormitory. Until that day, you're all here together to build friendships and convince others to join the clan you might be backed by."

"Have the other novices been getting invitations like Yukiko?"

"A little less than half have received at least a single scroll, but that will change in the next two months. None will be as sought after as much as your friend, except maybe you. No ties to any clan and a mystery magic that still has Master Damon in a tizzy? Many are biding their time since they won't want to invite you if your magic is underwhelming."

"Don't want to buy a pig in a poke?" Gregory asked with a snort.

"They rather the cat was out of the bag, first," Dia smiled. "I haven't heard that idiom in years. Many novices don't realize that they are doing exactly that with the clans."

Gregory frowned, but before he could say more, Yukiko came rushing out of the door. "Greg, I'm sorry—!"

"Woah, calm down, Yuki," Gregory cut her off. "It's okay, let's get walking. Did you bring your comb with you?"

Yukiko was flushed and nodded, "I did."

"Brush as we walk?" Gregory asked, stepping toward the path.

"Have a good day," Dia said as she went and took a seat on the bench.

Yukiko bowed to Dia and pulled her comb from her bag, working to get her hair manageable. "Thank you, Keeper. You as well."

"Thank you for the conversation, Keeper," Gregory said, bowing to her.

* * *

Yukiko was not complaining, but Gregory could tell she was upset. "Yuki, you okay?"

"Yes... no... maybe," Yukiko sighed as she jerked at a knot.

"I'm not going to press, but if you want to talk about it, I'm here."

Exhaling deeply, Yukiko calmed more as she continued untangling her hair. "Thank you, Greg. It was just the girl-talk last night, and I didn't realize how late it was getting until the last bell tolled."

Gregory noticed the dark circles under her eyes and nodded, "Okay. Don't worry if you nod off at some point. I'll wake you."

Yukiko snorted, "I figured you would. How was your time with the guys?"

"We played a different game of cards, and I did horribly to start with. I started getting the hang of it before I left."

"Have a good time, then?"

Gregory considered the question for longer than he should have needed to. "Not enough to want to do it every week. Would have been more productive to study with you."

"Oh? I thought maybe you'd be able to get things off your chest that you couldn't with me."

"Can't think of anything I wouldn't tell you that I would them."

Yukiko's smile slipped a little, "Oh. I see. Maybe they were wrong, then."

"They were wrong?"

Blushing, Yukiko put her comb away and pulled out a hair clip to gather her long, flowing hair together. "You know, I've never had many friends, so last night was different for me. Someone said that when guys get together, they talk about women... in a certain way."

Gregory coughed and looked away from her, his ears starting to burn. "It happens," he admitted.

"Did anyone say anything about me?"

"Did anyone say anything about *me*?" Gregory countered.

Yukiko looked away, "Fair. I'm sorry."

"No worries, let's eat," Gregory said as they reached the mess.

* * *

Rafiq greeted them with a smile when they stepped into the archive after their breakfast. "Morning to you both. We have books ready for you."

"Can I get a book that describes each clan?" Gregory asked. "I need information before the tournament."

Rafiq nodded, "I can arrange that, if you'll give me a few minutes."

"Two books, please," Yukiko said. "We can read and compare notes," she told Gregory.

"Makes sense."

"I shall have them brought to you shortly."

"Thank you," they said together.

A man with yellow, square-pupiled eyes brought them two books a few minutes later. Bowing to them, he withdrew without speaking. They dove into the material, eager to find out more than they had known before.

The clans have been around for generations, three of them founded just after the First Eurtik War; The Eternal Flame, Han Merchant Exchange, and Aether's Guard. While the Aether's Guard clan has been all but forgotten, the other two have built themselves into part of the five great clans of the empire.

The five great clans are made up of...

* * *

Gregory frowned when the fifth bell chimed. Closing the book, he looked up and saw Yukiko blinking slowly as she closed her book. "You okay, Yuki?"

"Tired and annoyed at this book," Yukiko replied. "It reads more like a recruiting guide than anything useful."

"Mine was more about the history of the five great clans," Gregory added. "Let's get going; don't want to skip class."

"Right," Yukiko yawned, covering her mouth with a hand. "Let's go."

"Books to your liking?" Rafiq grinned.

"I almost feel like you're having a joke at our expense," Gregory said.

"I'll have different books for your next study session," Rafiq's smile grew wider.

"Something based more in fact and less to sell the clans to us, please," Yukiko requested.

"I'll see what I can do," Rafiq chuckled. "Have a good day in class."

* * *

Yukiko started to nod off three times in economics, getting nudged awake each time by Gregory. Magus Marcia noticed, and sent a withering glare Yukiko's way.

When they got back to the archive, Rafiq had different books waiting for them. Gregory dug into his, but after a few minutes a soft snore made him look up. Yukiko was passed out beside her book, her face blank as she slept. Looking around, he did not see anyone nearby, so he sat there for a minute just watching her sleep before sighing and going back to his book.

When the ninth bell rang, Yukiko jerked awake, looking around wildly for a moment.

"Have a good nap?" Gregory asked, looking up from the book.

"I... you could have woken me," Yukiko pouted.

"You needed the sleep," Gregory replied evenly, meeting her cyan eyes. "I was looking after my partner. No one came near, so no one knows you slept." Yukiko looked slightly mollified until Gregory added, "Until you began to snore."

Her cheeks flushed and a look of horror spread across her face. When Gregory began to snort, trying to hide his laughter, she glared at him. "You made that up."

"Only a little. Your snoring was very soft, and I almost didn't hear it."

Yukiko pouted again, "That was mean."

"Friends poke at each other with harmless jokes, Yuki. Do you think I'd make that joke to Nick, Jason, or Michelle?"

Lips twitching, Yukiko was conflicted about whether she should frown or smile at him. "I guess not."

"I wouldn't. I'd only make that joke to Gunnar, El, or Ria, and now, you."

She did smile then, "Okay. I accept it as a joke."

"We have a little under an hour before we have to make it to aether introduction. Did you want to start that book, or take a leisurely walk that way and not have to worry about hurrying?"

Yukiko glanced at the book in front of her— which was still on the first page— and sighed. "I think it would be best to walk."

"I'll tell you about what I've read so far," Gregory said as he shut his book and got to his feet. "I'm not fond of the idea of joining the Iron Hand... this book is not flattering to them."

As they were leaving, Rafiq gave them a nod, "Better books?"

"Much," Gregory said. "I appreciate it."

"You are welcome. I wish you both a good day."

"Good day," they replied as they left the archive.

Stepping out into the sunlight, Yukiko sighed and stretched a little. "I do feel better for having napped. Thank you for watching over me, Greg."

"You'd have done the same for me. Let's go this way today. We have time and I want to see if it connects around."

"Oh look, it's the fringer," a snide voice snickered. "What were you doing in the archive, fringer? I'm sure the books in there are well beyond you."

Gregory looked back to see Hayworth and his friends coming toward them. "Hayseed? I would have thought you'd be in aether studies."

Hayworth's nostrils flared at being called "Hayseed," but he did not respond to it, just sneering at Gregory instead. "I have had private tutors for that for the last three years. That class is for dullards and fringers."

"What brings you to the archive?" Yukiko asked in a neutral tone, though Gregory noticed her hands were clenched.

"I've had a request to see some more advanced scrolls and have come to check on them," Hayworth told Yukiko civilly. "You really shouldn't stand too close to him. He's from the fringe, likely infested with all manner of vermin."

"I find him to be cleaner and better mannered than some others here," Yukiko said with a smile. "Have a good day."

Gregory turned with her, walking away from the shocked Hayworth. Once they had put some distance between them, Gregory snorted, "I thought his eyes were going to pop out of his head."

"He was being a prig," Yukiko grunted. "Self-important assholes deserve to be reminded that people don't like them."

"Father's guards teach you that word?"

"If Father knew half of what they taught me, he'd either be horrified or proud."

"Hayworth is going to be one of those that will cause us trouble later," Gregory said as they crossed a foot bridge.

"That's a given, considering his attitude toward you."

"Thanks for having my back."

"As you had mine earlier."

CHAPTER 32

Taking their places after the last class let out, Gregory waved to Nick and the others as they left. Nick looked surprised to see them, waving back as he went by. Adept John raised an eyebrow when they entered, but did not say anything, taking a seat in the sun and waiting for the class to arrive.

"We're supposed to try using magic today, aren't we?" Gregory asked.

"That is what he said last time we had class. I'm excited to practice."

Gregory's smile slipped, but he forced it back in place. "I'm sure you'll do great."

"Greg, I didn't—"

Clapping a hand on her shoulder, he shook his head, "I know, Yuki, it's fine. Master Damon will figure it out eventually. Until then, I'll take notes."

"Actually, I want you to attempt to use *every* type of magic," Adept John said, his eyes still closed. "If you can use the magic, it'll work, and if you can't, nothing will happen. It is another way of testing for magic, but this method hasn't been used in generations, not since the

Second Eurtik War, in fact. Master Damon requested I have you try this to aid him."

"Okay," Gregory said, feeling a bit of excitement spark inside of him. "I'll do my best."

The rest of the class started showing up and taking their seats. An undercurrent of excitement was palpable as the students chattered amongst themselves. When the bell chimed to indicate class was starting, Adept John got to his feet. "This week, you will be trying to use the most basic form of your magic. To that end, I'm going to put groups of you in different areas, so you can train without disturbing each other."

It took a few minutes for the class to move to their assigned areas. Yukiko was off to the side in the biggest area of shade. Most of the class had been separated to the four corners of the yard where the elements had been placed, and the physical enhancement magi were set in the middle. The crafters stayed at their tables, with Adept John handing out small items for them to work on.

Gregory stayed seated to start, making notes as he watched each group in turn, but he kept glancing over to Yukiko. Yukiko smiled broadly after about ten minutes when the shadows around her began to move to her will. Gregory watched intently as she used her aether to command the shadows. When he started to look away, he thought he could see small strings of blue aether between her and the shadows. Blinking in surprise made the faint blue lines vanish and Gregory frowned.

"Do you see it, Greg?" Yukiko called out, looking back at him.

Gregory put a smile back on his face, "Yup, definite movement. Good job."

Pleased smile in place, she went back to focusing on the magic. Gregory put his notes away and got up, moving over to where the alchemists and enchanters were sitting. One of them looked up at him questioningly when he got closer.

"I'm just curious as to how it works," Gregory said. "Crafters have always had my utmost respect."

"I don't mind," one alchemist said as she ground up some leaves in a pestle. "Not much to see with us, though. Mostly manual work until we start combining things."

"Ours is all mental imagery," an enchanter sighed as he set aside the plain brass ring in front of him, rubbing his forehead. "I need to take the mind path, it looks like."

"Mind if I come back in a bit to see more?"

"You're the one who doesn't know their magic yet, aren't you?" the alchemist asked.

"Yes."

"You must be hoping they find out soon. The clans are already asking about people, and they start accepting them after the first tournament. Some are already getting interest from the great clans, I've heard."

"I'm very hopeful," Gregory admitted. "I'll come back. Good luck with your project."

Moving over to the two magi who had wind magic, he watched them keep a leaf in the air with short bursts of aether. As he turned to walk away, again he thought he saw small strings of blue aether going from the novices to the air under the leaf, but it vanished the moment he turned back to see them.

Am I imagining it? Or am I seeing the aether being used by people? Gregory wondered as he moved over to watch the water magi separate pure water from salt water.

After about five minutes of not seeing anything, he moved to where the single earth magi was making small holes appear in the ground before filling them in again. Again, no blue threads appeared as he watched, so he walked over toward the fire magi, who were lighting and snuffing out candles from a few yards away.

Shaking his head, he finally turned toward the five magi using physical enhancement. Gregory watched as each struggled to summon aether to coat various parts of their bodies.

"It is time for you to try to mimic them," Adept John said, coming up behind Gregory.

"I'll start with the wind magi," Gregory said.

"Very well. Good luck."

Gregory felt his aether start to stir each time he tried to mimic one of the groups, but each time, it settled back in place and nothing happened. When the teacher called an end to class, Gregory was disappointed but not entirely surprised.

"Maybe tomorrow will be different," Yukiko tried to cheer him up as they headed for the arenas.

"Maybe," Gregory agreed, though he doubted it. "You seemed to be getting better control as class went on."

Yukiko smiled, "You think so?"

"Yes. By the end of the week, you might be able to completely cover yourself."

"Thanks, Greg." The happiness in her voice was joined by a little extra bounce in her step.

* * *

When they arrived at the blue arena, they took their seats against one of the walls and started eating their lunch. Gregory finished before Yukiko and settled himself into a lotus position, closing his eyes to meditate.

"Oh, before I forget, Greg."

Opening one eye, he saw Yukiko holding out a ring to him. "Trading off every day."

"Oh, okay. I thought we'd trade off in the morning, but this works, too." Taking the ring of the mind, he slipped it onto his left hand. Closing his eye, he missed Yukiko's smile.

Slipping into the right mind frame, Gregory felt his focus pulled to his aether. He stood inside a cavern, the fire before him slightly larger than a campfire and burning brightly. *Guess this is how I interpret my aether when meditating*, Gregory thought as he looked at the cavern. The light from the fire illuminated the stone walls, and Gregory watched the shadows flicker along them. *Too much to ask to have Yukiko step out of those and join me, isn't it?* The flames seemed to flicker like laughter, and Gregory shook his head.

The shadows dancing on the wall eased his thoughts, except that every once in a while, he thought he saw something odd. After a few minutes, he got up to examine the wall. A thin hole had been dug out of the stone, smaller than his pinkie in diameter. Frowning, he began to walk around the cavern and he found more of them. *Weird... I wonder what the holes mean. Maybe I can ask Rafiq tomorrow about spirit caverns.*

"Greg, you awake?" Nick's voice echoed throughout the cave.

Blinking, Gregory found himself seated against the wall of the arena with Nick standing a few feet from him. "Huh?"

"Napping?"

"In a way. What did you need?"

"On our next day off, the guys are going into town for some fun. Thought you'd like to join us." Nick glanced at Yukiko. "It's guys only."

Gregory scratched his chin, feeling the vaguest hints of stubble there. "Tell you tomorrow?"

Nick rolled his eyes, "Need to check with her first? Come on, man, you can have a day away from her. Neither of you will die."

"I just can't remember if Yuki and I were going to visit the scrivener this coming day off or the following one. I don't want to cancel a plan already made," Gregory lied.

"That's fair. Tell me tomorrow, then. Might want to wake up, though. Class will start soon."

"Got it," Gregory said, uncrossing his legs.

When Nick walked away, Gregory reached out and tapped Yukiko's knee. "Yuki, class should start soon."

"Understood," Yukiko replied.

"Need to talk to you after class about next day off."

"Something happen?"

"After class," Gregory murmured, his eyes going to Nick and friends.

"Very well."

Magus Paul Erichson strode out onto the sands of the arena floor as the thirteenth bell chimed. Seeing the novices already lined up, he nodded, "Good, do that every day. Before we get to the real fun, we'll start with stretching and running." Before he could say anything more, the novices spread out like he had them doing for the last few weeks. He grinned momentarily when they moved into position without command. "We'll start with…"

The next hour was dedicated to stretching and running, leaving some in the class panting and drained. Paul shook his head, "I see that some of you still need to work on the basics. Too bad for you we're moving past that. Now fall in."

The handful of novices who were all but dead managed to pull themselves up and into ranks. A couple of others helped them, lessening the time it would have taken otherwise.

"Now, how many of you have had some training?" Paul asked. Half the class raised their hands, Gregory among them. "You novices move behind me. The rest of you, fall in."

Those who did not have any training in combat formed new ranks before him, while the others formed ranks behind him. Gregory noted that the ones still standing in front of Paul were the novices who did the worst on conditioning.

Paul turned to the novices who had been behind him. "Pair off. You're to spread out and spar to your best ability. My assistants will be around to help give you pointers." Dismissing them, he spun back to the other group, "Okay, you sorry sacks; first, we get to work on falling."

Gregory and Yukiko stepped away from the others, automatically pairing off with each other. Taking a spot near where they had meditated, Gregory noted that Nick and the others were the ones closest to them. A handful of magi in emerald kimonos began to walk among the pairs, watching as the fights began.

"Glad we've done this before," Gregory said as he settled into a defensive posture.

"Now we get serious," Yukiko said as she settled into a similar stance. "This is our best chance to learn and grow for the tournament. I hope you forgive me."

Gregory was about to reply when she rushed him, her steps light and balanced. Not used to her being so aggressive, Gregory was forced onto his back foot as he deflected her initial attack. Yukiko capitalized on that, going down to sweep him, before springing onto him and striking his chest right below his neck.

"Point, and ably done," a clear resonate voice said. "Break and square again. What is your name, Novice?"

"Warlin, Adept."

"You have good speed, and you outclass your opponent."

"Thank you, sir."

"Novice, just because she is a woman doesn't mean you can go easy," the adept told Gregory. "Defend and attack as if your life depends on it. It will later."

"Yes, sir," Gregory replied as he got to his feet.

"Carry on," the adept said, turning to watch another group.

Settling into the same defensive stance, Gregory could see the worry in Yukiko's eyes. He gave her a small shake of the head and extended one hand slightly, beckoning her with a smile. "Can't learn without failure."

The worry vanished, suddenly replaced with happiness, and Yukiko settled into her own stance. "Here I come."

For the next hour, Gregory lost every single match against Yukiko. His body was battered and his ego deflated. Seeing the looks of pity from the others did not help his mood any, either. Yukiko walked with him, but stayed silent as they headed for the baths.

Leaving the bath after getting clean, Gregory leaned against the wall, going over every loss to Yukiko in his mind. When she left the building, she looked for him, worried he had left without her.

"I'm right here, Yuki," he said softly, pushing off the wall to step next to her.

"I thought—"

"That I left you? Not going to happen that easily," Gregory said evenly. "My pride is in tatters, and my body is bruised, but I'm learning. Partners learn from each other."

Mouth opening, Yukiko started to say something before closing her mouth and shaking her head. Taking a deep breath, she started again, "You are a great partner, Greg. Dinner?"

"That's why I was waiting," he smiled. "On our fourth match, you snagged my sleeve and used that as the contact to pivot me into a clinch before throwing me. Can you show me that throw later?"

"Of course. What did you want to talk about earlier?"

"Nick said that he's getting the guys together next day off and wants me to go with. I told him we were going to the scrivener either this day off or next, and I had to ask which it was. I didn't want to lose the day of training with you, but also think it might be educational to go with them."

"That would explain why Michelle asked me about next day off," Yukiko nodded. "I can't tell if they are serious in being friends, trying to recruit us, or trying to drive a wedge between us."

"Go with them this time and find out?"

"Okay, but we keep the morning schedule and then study more after dinner."

"Deal, Yuki."

CHAPTER 33

The week flew by for Gregory— he only briefly saw the thin blue lines once more during aether introduction. Once again, it was only obliquely, so he was still wondering if he was actually seeing the lines or just imagining them.

He was frustrated that he continued losing to Yukiko during conditioning. He knew he was getting better over the course of the week because she had to work to get him down, but he had not managed a single score on her. The adepts came by and gave him pointers that helped him along with Yukiko's advice, but he felt that he was not learning fast enough.

Their time in the archive before class and in the open period they created helped the two of them get a better feel for the clans over the course of the week. The five great clans did great things for the empire, but also seemed to care more for themselves than anything else over all. The smaller clans had all started off as satellites of the five great clans, but slowly found their own ideals.

Gregory was struggling in economics class, but he discovered that he was not the only one. Only Yukiko and Samuel, the son of a well-known blacksmith, were able to understand everything Magus

Marcia threw at them. Gregory was getting a handle on it after classes, as he and Yukiko would review the material for a half hour before bed.

They had breakfast together as normal on the morning of their day off before they went to the archive. Gregory had not yet read about a single clan he would have liked to join, and he had finished two books on them. Yukiko said she had not found the clan for her yet either.

Entering the archive, they were surprised to see Rafiq there. "I thought today was your day off?" Gregory greeted the eurtik.

"Someone fell ill," Rafiq shrugged. "I'm only filling in for a few hours. Did you need new books today?"

"Yes..." Gregory said slowly, wondering how to phrase his request. "I meditated the other day and found myself in a cavern with a flame. Is there anything that will help me understand it more?"

"Spirit path," Rafiq said, looking surprised. "I'll pull a scroll for you."

"Oh, I was wondering about that," Yukiko said. "I saw that place yesterday."

"Both of you are following the spirit path? Hmm, I shall bring a collection of scrolls for you to look through. If you are just seeing the cavern of aether, you still have time to choose another path. Keep that in mind."

Gregory tried not to smile, "Understood. We'd like to know more about the cavern."

"Very well. The scrolls will be delivered shortly."

The friends had barely taken their seats when an archivist brought them a pair of scrolls. Gregory thanked the mouse-eared eurtik and opened the scroll that had been handed to him.

If you are reading this, you are one of the few who have embarked on the path of spirit. It is the least celebrated path in the empire, and roundly criticized by the great houses as inferior to body or mind. They have a single point correct— it is slower than the other paths. They have managed to marginalize it over the last few centuries, which is a pity.

You are reading this for advice, though, not to listen to an old man ramble on about the follies of youth. The archivists would only have given you this scroll if you've seen the cavern of aether we all have inside of us. Only those who tread the spirit path see the cavern and can understand the majesty of it.

Let's start at the beginning: meditation is the key to the spirit path.

Gregory was lost in the scroll when a hand touched his shoulder and broke him out of the moment. "Huh?"

"Seventh bell," Yukiko told him. "We have a little over two hours to get the physical training in before you're supposed to meet up with Nick at the eleventh bell."

"Right," Gregory replied, rolling the scroll closed.

Rafiq was not at the front when they left, and both were quiet as they began the walk to the training hall. The morning sun was just starting to cast light when Gregory broached the subject of the scrolls.

"What did yours say?"

"The scroll I read seems to have been written a couple hundred years ago," Yukiko sighed. "Some of the phrasing is difficult to parse. The bit I could make out talked about the cavern only being seen by those who are on the spirit path."

"Mine said the same thing."

"The fire inside the cavern is directly tied to your aether. As you expand your aether, the fire grows, but slowly. The spirit path is dedicated to having your flame as dense as it can be."

"The scroll I was reading mentioned channels in the walls. Did yours mention them?"

"No."

"The author seems to have been between spirit and body paths when they wrote it. He hypothesized that the channels were made by the body path, making it easier for the flame to travel to different parts of the body. As the writer worked on the body path, the channels grew a little deeper and wider, but the cavern became harder to connect with."

"I think I saw them," Yukiko said, excitement coloring her tone. "They weren't big and barely indented into the walls, but there were clear, obvious indentions about as deep and wide as my pinkie's last knuckle."

"I saw similar ones," Gregory agreed. "What if it helps create the channels for aether to flow through the body easier? That could explain why body path followers can use less aether to get the same effects as other paths when it comes to fighting."

Yukiko considered the implication as they walked. "If the body path does create channels for the aether, and the spirit path lets you contemplate your aether and how it works, what does the mind path do?"

"Maybe that'll be in one of the next scrolls we read?"

"Perhaps," Yukiko agreed. "Ready for training?"

"Can we go a little slower so you can explain why I lose each time? The adepts don't want you to, but they won't be here to stop us today," Gregory asked.

"Does it bother you?" Yukiko asked as they stepped into the training hall and saw that no one was there. "Losing to me all the time?"

"A little, but not because it's you. It's because I should be good enough to be your partner."

Yukiko's eyes sparkled and she swallowed hard. "I'll do my best, Greg."

"So will I, Yuki."

Trading their shoes for slippers, they went to an empty room to face each other in. Gregory focused, studying Yukiko as she settled into her preferred stance, trying to find a weakness he could use.

* * *

Tenth bell brought them to a stop, both covered in sweat and panting. Gregory shook his head in frustration as he got off the floor again.

"You are improving," Yukiko said.

"Still haven't managed to put you down," Gregory grumbled. "Feel like I'm being toyed with."

"No," Yukiko said quickly, holding out her hand, palm toward him. "I have to work hard to stop you. Believe me, Greg."

Exhaling to try get rid of his frustration, he nodded. "I do, Yuki. I'll see you for dinner and study, right?"

"Yes, I'll be at the dormitory by the eighteenth bell."

"See you then," Gregory replied, making his way to the showers to clean up.

"Greg..." Yuki called after him hesitantly.

"Yeah?" Pausing in the doorway, he looked back at her.

"Do you need any vela for today? I have some if you need it."

Gregory stopped his first reply, which was tinged with his frustration. Seeing her worried eyes, he shook his head, "No, Yuki. Nick said it was all taken care of."

"Oh. Okay. Umm... are you considering joining them?"

"The Eternal Flame?"

"Yes."

"Not at the moment, though Nick wants to make it hard by being as friendly as he is. I doubt there'd be any..." He trailed off as he thought about what Nick had said about Yukiko's betrothal being voided if she joined.

"Any what?"

"Huh? Oh, sorry. Any reason to join. I do want to join a clan where I know someone to make things easier."

"So do I," Yukiko murmured too softly for Gregory to hear, before she cleared her throat. "I was just curious. I'll see you tonight."

"Yeah. Have fun with Michelle and the others."

"You, too."

The eleventh bell was chiming when Gregory met up with Nick and the others by the main gate. "Sorry for the delay."

"It's fine. Fureno just got here, too," Nick shrugged. "Now that everyone is here, we can get going." Gregory turned to start for the postern gate when Nick stopped him. "The carriage is waiting for us this way."

Following Nick and the others, Gregory was surprised to find a stable tucked away behind a screen of trees a few hundred yards away from the main gates. Nick motioned to a carriage, and the group moved to the side. The bright red carriage came to a halt near them, the emblem of the Eternal Flame emblazoned on the door.

"This will take us where we need to go. Everyone in," Nick said, opening the door. "Time to show you another perk of joining the Eternal Flame."

The carriage was large, but it was a little crowded with them all inside, so Nick had Fureno go ride with the driver. Fureno grumbled but did as he was told, and a few moments later, the carriage started to roll.

"Surprised I wasn't the one to ride with the driver," Gregory said as the carriage paused for the gates.

"Fureno knows propriety," Nick shrugged. "He's along for the ride currently, but he needs to improve in conditioning and in magic. We can't just have everyone join the clan, after all."

"I didn't think any novice could join a clan until after the first tournament."

"*Officially* join," Nick chuckled. "My family has been with the Eternal Flame since its founding. Everyone knows that I'll be joining them as soon as the rules allow. It's your good fortune to be in the same year as me."

"You're scouting the novices for those who'll fit in, making it easier for the clan later."

"We all help the clan as we can," Nick grinned. "Was glad you decided to join us. Thought for sure you were going to decline and stay at Yukiko's beck and call."

Gregory frowned, "I don't stay at her beck and call."

"Seems like it to us," Jason snickered. "You even let her thrash you in sparring *every day*."

"I don't let her thrash me; she's just more skilled," Gregory said tightly.

"Maybe you should partner up with Jason or Fureno, then," Nick suggested. "I understand the attraction you have to her, but it's not good to let a woman you're interested in unman you over and over again, especially in front of others."

"Maybe," Gregory said grudgingly.

"We heading to—" Jason began to ask, but Nick cut him off.

"Of course. Have to let the others see one of the major perks of joining the clan."

CHAPTER 34

The carriage came to a halt outside a grand manor. Gregory looked at the massive structure with awe and trepidation. The motif told him it belonged to the Eternal Flame, but the craftsmanship and material it was made of boggled him.

"The Manor of Flame," Nick smiled as he nudged Gregory. "This is where those of the clan can find rest and relaxation while in the city, and those in training can use it on their days off. The rooms inside can be claimed for just a day, or up to a year, depending on what the magi of the clan needs."

"What is the red crystal that the columns are made of?" Gregory asked.

"Lava stone. When aether is added to it... easiest to show you." Moving over to one of the columns, Nick touched it reverently. A few heartbeats later, the red crystal began to glow with red light. Stepping back and wiping his brow, Nick grinned, "I can manage that, at least. It'll glow for an hour, maybe."

Gregory stared at the red column, which now looked as though it had living flame inside of it, illuminating the area. "That must be something to see after nightfall."

"When they're all lit, it can be mesmerizing," Nick chuckled. "We have permission to use the manor all day. Do mind your manners if you see other magi, though; they are full members of the clan."

Gregory nodded, pulling his gaze away from the column to follow the others. *They are one of the great clans, but it seems a waste to use aether just to make the columns light up. Why don't they try to improve the outskirts of the empire, instead? Why don't any of the clans?* In the front room, the others were exchanging their boots for silk slippers. Gregory did the same, noting the clan emblem emblazoned on the silk.

Once everyone had slippers on, Nick addressed them formally. "Welcome to the Manor of Flame. You are guests inside these walls. I'll give you all the tour before I turn you free to enjoy your day."

Gregory frowned briefly. *Why invite us if we're going to be left to our own devices?* The frown vanished as he followed the others. The manor had dozens of rooms that offered various distractions: two small archives, a game room where some magi were playing cards, an indoor hot spring and outdoor pool, and a handful of small sparring areas, two of which were in use. There was a dining area that was staffed with full-blooded eurtik in maid outfits, waiting to serve them.

"There you have it. Enjoy the day. I'll be collecting all of you an hour before sundown so we can make it back to the academy. If you need anything, just ask one of the slaves, and if you want *that*, go upstairs and find a room marked with a red light that is uncovered." Nick grinned, "No one here will comment on what you get up to."

Fureno laughed as he headed for the stairs, "Might as well go see what's on the menu."

Jason shook his head, "He's so simple. I'm going to see about joining the card game. Anyone else want to go?"

"I'll come with," Nick said, a couple of the others chiming in. "Greg?"

"I want to take a walk through the whole place again... it's daunting."

"If it's the coin, I can lend you some," Nick said, seeing his reluctance.

"Maybe after the walk."

"As you like. Just make sure to enjoy yourself. I'd hate for the clan's name to be lowered because you didn't."

"I'm sure I'll find something to keep me interested."

"He might just want to sneak upstairs without us all knowing," one of the others snickered. "After all, he—"

Jason elbowed the man in the stomach, "We're going."

Grumbling and rubbing his stomach, the man complained as they left. "Why does he get special tre…"

Gregory had walked away from them, not wanting to get involved. *Why do people always want to pick fights? I was telling the truth, and I might well have gone up there to at least see what it was all about, but damned if I'm going to now.*

Pausing outside of the sparring areas, he watched two magi fight. Neither were in the colored kimonos that denoted their rank, but he figured they had to be magus at least. One of them kept taking to the air in short flights while the other flung fire at him. Gregory blinked when one of the small firebolts vanished as it reached the edge of the area.

The fight ended a moment later when the magi in the air was hit by a firebolt. Screaming in pain, he landed and tapped the ground. "Damnit, I forgot how much that hurts."

"Just be glad the area has healing enchantments or that arm would be badly damaged," the fire magi chuckled. "Things would have been different if we hadn't been in here, anyway. You're hemmed in by the enchantment, so you can't go too far any one way without leaving the area."

"True, but I need to work on dodging in tighter conditions, which is why I asked you to help."

"Enjoy the show, boy?" the fire magi chuckled, seeing Gregory.

"It was an honor to watch two magi of your strength spar," Gregory replied, bowing to them.

"You one of the ones with Shun's grandkid?"

"Yes, sir."

"A novice, then. Maybe a recruit," the wind magi smiled. "What magic do you possess?"

Gregory grimaced, "Unknown."

Both the magi exchanged a look, but the fire magi spoke up, "You're the one, huh? Want to spar a little? No aether, just unarmed?"

"I'm lacking in that area, sir," Gregory said. "I wouldn't pose any challenge for you."

"Not what I was saying. I was giving you the chance to have some one-on-one tutelage."

Gregory blinked, not expecting the magi to offer him instruction. "If you are willing to do so, I would be foolish to decline."

"You two have fun," the wind magi said. "I'm going to get something to eat. Used a lot of aether in that fight."

"Have one of the slaves bring me a snack and some infused tea. He'll need it."

Chuckling, the other magi waved as he headed inside, "Sure, sure."

"Alright, novice, what is your name?"

"Gregory Pettit, sir."

"I'm Magus Ashon, and I'll be your instructor for now. The Eternal Flame, for all the bad that is said about it by our foes, always raises up those who deserve it. The strong rise— it's the way the clan works."

"Yes, sir."

"Now, let's see your basic stance."

* * *

Greg was panting and on his back when Magus Ashon declared their sparring over. "You have a surprisingly good basic understanding for a fringer. They're either teaching novices better than when I was there, or you have a gifted teacher. Try to drill those attacks I showed you a little every day."

"Understood, sir," Gregory grunted as he pushed himself to his feet. "Thank you for your time," he finished with a deep bow.

"You should get cleaned up before enjoying the manor. Come on, I'll show you the way."

He was shown to a room that he had not seen before. Gregory stripped down like Ashon was, dropping his stuff into a basket. Entering the connecting room, Gregory found a bathing room with a tub big enough for a half dozen people. What he had not expected was the naked cat eurtik who rose gracefully to her feet from where she had been kneeling in the corner. Gregory swallowed as he realized that pure-blood eurtiks were not always completely covered by fur; the woman in front of them was fully exposed.

"Slave, to work," Ashon grunted as he took a seat at a shower. With a glance at Gregory, Ashon chuckled, "She isn't that kind of slave, though I believe her sister is upstairs. Now, sit down so she can do her job and we can relax."

Tearing his eyes away from the slave, Gregory sat on the stone benches. "I can clean myself," he coughed, reaching for the soap.

"Nonsense," Ashon said. "This is her task, unless you don't care for her. She can get a different slave if that is the case. Is the otter taking care of the female side today?"

"She is, sir," the slave replied in a soft tone. "Do you wish me to get her instead?"

"No, no, everything is fine," Gregory said quickly.

"Start with the novice; he seems a bit nervous," Ashon snickered.

Gregory did his best to ignore the small touches of her naked skin against his as the slave washed him. She was efficient and business-like as she deftly cleaned him.

"You're done, sir."

"Thank you," Gregory said as he went to the tub. The steaming water felt wonderful as he slipped into it. Leaning against the wall, he let the hot water soak into his muscles.

"The manor on the academy grounds isn't this luxurious," Ashon said, breaking the silence. "It's not bad, but there are no bath slaves there, and no pleasure slaves, either. Though we do see a number of apprentices and novices on their days off."

"It has an archive and training areas?" Gregory asked about the two things he cared about.

"Not to the same scale, but yes. Also has a gaming room, where many stipends change hands."

"I'm not good at cards, so it'd be a place I'd likely avoid."

Ashon laughed, "Knowing your weaknesses is good. Fixing them is better."

Gregory could not argue with that so he did not try, instead sinking farther into the water.

* * *

When the bath ended, Gregory thanked Ashon again before heading for the small archives. The only person in the room was a duck eurtik wearing a butler outfit, who bowed to Gregory when he entered.

"How may I assist you, sir?"

"I wanted to see what books and scrolls were available to read."

"We have books and scrolls across a wide number of subjects. If you have a preference, I can find something suitable."

"Anything on spirit path training?"

The eurtik's brow furrowed, "No, sir. That is an inferior way to train."

"I'll leave the choice up to you, then."

"Very well. Please have a seat, sir."

Gregory took a seat in a well-padded chair at a desk. The cushion sank under him, and Gregory idly mused that this must be what sitting on a cloud felt like.

"This is a book recounting the greatest members of the clan," the eurtik said, placing a tome before Gregory. "Would you care for anything else, sir?"

"Not right now, thanks."

"Just ask, and I'll take care of anything you need, sir."

"Got it."

Gregory skimmed the book, not bothering to truly read the flower-laden prose that was written as if the author believed that the people he was writing about could do no wrong. He was not sure how long he skimmed, but he closed the book and stood when his stomach rumbled.

"Are you done, sir?" the butler asked, appearing just a few seconds after Gregory closed the book.

"Yeah, need to get a snack," Gregory said. "Thank you for the recommendation."

"You're very welcome, sir."

Gregory went to the dining room, where he found Nick and Jason talking to an older man whose solid gray temples gave him a refined air. Jason nudged Nick and gave Gregory a smile, waving him over.

"Greg, come on over. Looking for a snack, are you?"

"Yeah. A pleasure to meet you sir," Gregory said, bowing to the older man, "I'm Gregory Pettit, a novice at the academy."

"I'm aware of who you are," the old man replied, his tone cool and firm. "Has my grandson been helpful?"

Seeing Nick straighten a little, Gregory smiled. "Nick has been very helpful, sir. He's been showing me how generous the Eternal Flame can be to those who join it."

"Yet he still hasn't caught the specific individual I have tasked him to recruit."

Nick's smile was wooden, "Yukiko is considering, Grandfather. I'm sure she will join us after the tournament. Greg is likely to, as well. Isn't that right, Greg?"

"The Eternal Flame has been the most helpful clan I've been approached by," Gregory said carefully, though truthfully. "I wouldn't have expected a clan as venerable or powerful as this to take an interest in me."

"That wasn't a flat acceptance of the clan," the old man frowned.

"I can't see the future, sir. I would hate to say yes, only to find that something else forces circumstances in a different direction. The Han clan has spoken to me, and I feel as if the other three great clans will also before the tournament ends."

"You think any of them can do more for you?"

"I can't say, sir. I find it hard to believe considering everything, but it isn't impossible. It's why I've been so hesitant to accept Nick's generosity."

"Surprisingly well spoken for a fringer," the old man said as he rose to his feet. "I shall leave you with my grandson."

"Have a good day, sir, and thank you," Gregory bowed deeply to him.

Once the old man left, Nick exhaled deeply. "I didn't expect him to be here today."

"I should have waited another few minutes to come looking for food," Gregory added, taking a deep breath after the unexpected encounter.

"Could have been worse," Jason shrugged. "Take a seat, and one of the servants will bring you something. Nick, we should go check on the others."

Nick glanced at Gregory before nodding, "Yeah. Have a good meal, Greg. Glad to hear you're thinking about joining us." Pausing, he leaned on the table and lowered his voice, "If you can get Yukiko to join us, you'd find the clan to be *very* appreciative. Something to keep in mind."

Gregory sat there for a long moment, until one of the eurtiks brought food and drink to him. *Do they really want me, or are they just using me to try to get Yukiko?* That thought would not leave his head as he ate.

* * *

Gregory spent the rest of his time inside the manor in the garden meditating. He had trouble focusing, so he did not find the cavern of aether, but he did manage to eventually calm his mind.

When they left the manor to return to the academy, Gregory volunteered to ride with the driver. The driver was taciturn, only replying to questions with one-word answers and not starting any conversation.

When they got back to the academy, the others all headed for the dormitory since they had eaten at the manor. Gregory wished them a good night, and saw that Yukiko was waiting for him.

"You're sparring with me tomorrow, right, Greg?" Jason asked in front of Yukiko.

"I'll spar with you during class tomorrow," Gregory agreed.

Yukiko's lips turned down briefly before going back to neutral. When they were alone and walking toward the mess hall, she spoke up, "Greg? Did something happen?"

"A lot of insinuations," Gregory sighed. "I'll explain in my room later," he added, looking around idly.

Seeing him look around, Yukiko nodded slowly, "Okay."

"How was your day?" Gregory asked.

"We spent time at a tea house," Yukiko said. "After that, we went to a training dojo where the teacher drilled us for two hours. Finally, we went to a bathhouse. We got back just ahead of you."

"I got more sparring in, too," Gregory said. "One of the magi of the Eternal Flame taught me some things. I need to practice them to drill them into memory. This is yours for tomorrow," Gregory added, handing back the ring of the mind.

"Thank you," Yukiko said, slipping it onto her finger. "Have you noticed it helping at all?"

"Maybe? The days I've worn it, economics feels slightly easier to grasp. Not sure if it's working or if it's just in my mind, though."

"We'll find out over the next few weeks," Yukiko said.

* * *

Dinner was good, filling for both body and aether. They did not linger over their food since they wanted to get some studying in, though they did not rush either.

Once they were back in his room in the dormitory, Gregory sighed. "I'm not sure Nick is actually a friend, after all."

"Will you tell me what happened?"

Gregory recounted the events of his day, including the conversation where Nick admitted to being the front to find novices to join the

Eternal Flame clan. "Not sure if he's a friend, if he just wants me to join the clan, or if it's all just a ploy to get me to convince you to." Next he told Yukiko about meeting Nick's grandfather.

Yukiko sat there for a long moment in silence, clearly thinking about what she had heard. "Do you want to join them? That's still something that needs to be answered."

"I don't know," Gregory admitted. "They are powerful, but... the way they disregard the eurtik bothers me. Maybe it wouldn't bother me so much if I had been born closer to the center of the empire, but it does. Many of the clans seem to hold similar views, though, if less aggressively."

"There's something else, isn't there?" Yukiko asked, watching him.

"How do you know?" Gregory sighed.

"Body language. Father was teaching me to follow in his foot-steps. I might not have had many friends, but when it comes to knowing that someone is holding back, I can see it." Gregory did not reply, but his grimace proved she was right. "You don't have to tell me, Greg. If you want to though, I'll listen."

"It's said that preexisting agreements become null and void when one joins the Eternal Flame. Is that true?" Gregory asked slowly, looking up from the table to meet her gaze.

"They are a powerful clan, one of the five great clans. They have the power and wealth to pressure people into relinquishing prior agreements. I wouldn't say it's entirely guaranteed, though."

Gregory nodded with a deep sigh. "That makes more sense."

"Why?"

Gregory looked away from her, "It's not important right now. We should do our studying before it gets too late."

His attempt to switch the subject was obvious and Yukiko wanted to press him, but she gave him a soft smile. "Of course. I'm teaching you how to manipulate a market."

CHAPTER 35

The second month of training passed, and Gregory and Yukiko kept to their routine, with a few slight differences. During physical conditioning, they fought someone other than each other every other day. Yukiko held her own against everyone but Nick, who beat her soundly, but not as badly as she had been beating Gregory. Gregory steadily improved during class, occasionally able to manage a score or two against Yukiko when they fought.

More clans contacted Yukiko, including the other three great clans; Eternal Blossoms, Yamato Shipping, and Swift Wind. Each of those invitations were accompanied by presents, but nothing as lavish as the Eternal Flame or Han Merchant Exchange had given her. She divided the gifts between herself and Gregory.

Gregory found himself picking up economics a little easier by the end of the second month. Yukiko praised him and pressed him to learn even more difficult topics. During aether introduction, Gregory glimpsed the lines of aether from time to time, but only obliquely and never for long. His magic remained a mystery, to the growing frustration of Adept John.

Settling in for the night after another satisfying, if grueling week,

Gregory wondered what Yukiko had planned for tomorrow. Nick had asked them to have dinner with his group, but she had declined, explaining that she had already made other arrangements, and that they could not this coming day off. Closing his eyes, he snuggled into the blanket a little more, ready to see what tomorrow would bring.

* * *

Blinking, Gregory looked around. He was in an opulent room, not in his bedroom or anywhere else he had ever seen. The floor was black marble shot through with gold. The walls were covered with rich silk tapestries, showing various eurtik and humans using aether side by side. The far side of the large room was shrouded in darkness.

"Welcome home," the silken honeyed voice that had only spoken to him a few times flowed out of the darkness. "You are growing, and growing fast. Tomorrow, when your medallion has another ring glowing, people will begin to take notice."

Gregory looked down at his chest and saw his medallion glowing with five circles lit. The clothing he was wearing was not the white of a novice, but the indigo robes of the divine tier. He was also bulkier than he was in real life; not overly-muscled like Gunnar, but still far more than he currently was. "Why am I wearing the kimono of the emperor?"

"It suits you, or it will," the sultry voice replied. "I look forward to you reaching that stage. We have a lot of work ahead of us. Your magic has been leaking at the edges, and I've noticed that the archivists haven't figured it out yet."

"You know what it is, and can help me?"

"After the first tournament, as I've said before."

"Why not now?" Gregory asked.

"Because you aren't ready yet. Everyone here needs to accept you as you are, not for what you can be. You've seen how they circle around Yukiko— they won't just circle you. They will press any way they can find once it becomes known what your magic can do."

"Why? What is it that would make them take such measures?"

"After the tournament we will talk about it, but for now, you need to sleep. Yukiko went through some trouble to arrange tomorrow."

"What? How would you know?"

Sultry laughter echoed all around him as the darkness rushed forward, swallowing him whole. Gregory tried to fight off the drowsiness that assailed him, but his limbs grew heavy and his eyelids drooped.

"I'll beat you nex—" he muttered as he tried to fight it off, but his words slurred as sleep overcame him.

* * *

Third bell chimed, waking Gregory abruptly. Jolting upright, he rolled out of bed and got dressed by habit. They were still following their morning schedule of breakfast and study, so once he had everything ready, he opened his door, coming face to face with Yukiko.

"Morning, Yuki."

"Morning, Greg. Are you ready for today?"

"I don't know, because you haven't told me what we're doing," Gregory replied with a wry grin.

A soft giggle escaped her, "You'll have to wait and see. First, we're having breakfast and studying."

"Let's get to it," Gregory said, heading for the stairs.

As they exited the dormitory, Dia greeted them. "Morning, Novices. Did my staff handle your requests?"

Yukiko bowed to Dia formally, "They did that and more. They and you have my thanks, Keeper."

Dia smiled gently, "You're welcome. I'm interested to know how it is received. You won't mind if I ask later, will you?"

"No, you may ask."

"I hope your day is full of excitement and learning."

"Thank you, Keeper," Yukiko said, echoed by Gregory.

As they walked toward the mess hall, Gregory chuckled, "I was wondering how you set things up without me knowing about it ahead of time. I hadn't thought about asking the staff at the dormitory."

"I hope you'll like it. I know it's early by a week, but I wanted to do something for your birthday."

Gregory's steps faltered, "How did—?"

"Dia. I asked her if she could find out for me." She looked away from him, "I hope it was okay. I just wanted—"

Gregory put his hand on her shoulder gently, and she stopped speaking. "Yuki. It's okay. I just hope you didn't get carried away. When is your birthday? I'll have to figure out a way to pay you back."

"A week after the tournament," Yukiko replied softly. Looking up, she found him waiting to meet her gaze.

"Good thing I have time, then," Gregory smiled. "I'm going to need it to figure something out, I'm sure." Letting go of her, he motioned with his chin toward the mess hall. "First, some food."

"Yes," Yukiko said happily.

The eurtiks greeted the pair with smiles, "They never fail to show," the rat eurtik, Steva, chuckled. "Novices, your meal and snacks."

"Thank you," Yukiko smiled, pulling her medallion out.

"Fifth circle? You are advancing quickly," Velma smiled as her hand hovered over the amulet for a moment.

"I have a good partner," Yukiko replied.

"I'd say so," Velma said when she handed Gregory his meal and passed her hand over his medallion the same way. "Both of you have reached the fifth circle. Impressive, especially since he'd been third circle and you fourth at the start of the year."

"A partner who pushes you to learn helps," Gregory smiled. "Have a good day."

"You, as well," the four cooks replied together.

Taking their seats, they dug into their meals. Silence settled over them as each concentrated on eating and fueling their aether. Gregory finished a little ahead of Yukiko and looked puzzled.

"We finished faster because we have grown in power. Our aether can adjust to the food more quickly," Yukiko told him.

"Ah, right. That makes sense... Hm, I wonder if I'll see the cavern today? The channels have been growing steadily, if slowly, and the fire seems to be growing in size ever so slightly, as well."

"I was going to ask," Yukiko replied as they handed their empty dishes off. "Have a good day," she told the otter eurtik, Quilet.

"You both, as well," Quilet replied, bowing to them.

"Archive?" Gregory asked as they left the mess.

"Until seventh bell, then we need to go back to the dorm to grab some things before we go into the city."

"Mysterious, but okay," Gregory chuckled.

Entering the archive, they were greeted by the female panther eurtik that had talked to them over a month ago. "Morning to you both," she greeted them with a smile. "How goes your studying?"

"Slowly. We've been looking over how each of the paths start," Gregory replied. "It seems there have been a number of people who started on two paths, only to have one of them fade away."

"Indeed, that has been the case over the last few hundred years."

"Rafiq mentioned that scrolls written by those who did attain two paths are not available to novices," Yukiko said softly. "Are they available to apprentices?"

"If scrolls like that exist, they would likely only be available to adepts and above. If there are even any here in the archive. I feel many scrolls of that sort would be in private collectors' hands."

"We have scrolls waiting for us today, though we'd like to continue to look into more of these types."

"I will make sure that it is taken care of. Have you finished with economics?"

"My partner is teaching me that subject," Gregory said.

"Very well. Have a pleasant time," the eurtik smiled.

"You, too," Yukiko replied as they headed for their table.

* * *

Seventh bell had them both stretching as they got to their feet. "They aren't getting any less tedious, but this one at least talks about how the fire and cavern grew in size as they advanced down the mind path. They lost the ability to see the cavern shortly after that, though," Yukiko sighed.

"I'm still seeing the cavern, but I don't think it's grown any."

"I'll be checking next time I see it."

"So," Gregory said with a sardonic smile, "any hint on what we'll be doing, and what I need to get from the dormitory?"

Yukiko's face lit up and she shook her head with a soft giggle. "Not yet. As for what we need to pick up, it should be ready for us when we get there."

"Still keeping it shrouded in mystery, huh?"

"It won't last too much longer, but I want to keep it for as long as I can," Yukiko smiled.

* * *

Back at the dormitory, Gregory was surprised to see one of the staff waiting with a basket, which was promptly handed to Yukiko. He raised an eyebrow, but Yukiko shook her head and walked toward the postern gate after thanking them.

Yukiko flagged down a rickshaw as soon as they left the academy. When the driver came to a stop, she stepped forward and whispered to him before handing over some vela. Nodding, the driver motioned her and Gregory to the seats. Gregory shook his head, chuckling as he took his spot beside Yukiko.

The rickshaw took them through a maze of side streets until he reached a manor. "Your destination. Do you wish me to wait?"

"We'll be here some time, so you are free to go," Yukiko replied.

"Good day to you both," the driver said, leaving them standing there in the early morning light.

"Okay, so...?" Gregory asked leadingly.

"We go say hello." With a light laugh Yukiko went up to the front door. "It's only polite."

Following her, he examined the structure as much as he could, his brow furrowing slightly. *Not as extravagant as the other manors I've seen here, but in good condition. Not many windows, and the walls look surprisingly thick. I don't think this is a manor like the others, it just uses the appearance of a manor as a disguise. What do you have up your sleeve, Yuki?*

It took a few minutes for the door to open. An older man with a patchwork of scars on his left cheek and a deeper one above his eyebrow stared at them for a long moment. The glare he had been wearing slowly faded, replaced with a smile. "Yu, I thought the letter was fake," the man's voice was respectful, and he dipped his head to her. "What can this old man do for you?"

"Gin, you are no longer a family retainer, so I come to you as a friend. My letter explained what I was hoping," Yukiko bowed formally to him as an equal.

Gin's icy blue eyes went to Gregory, making the young man feel like he was being sized up. "This is your... *partner*?"

"My manners," Yukiko gasped, stepping sideways so the two men could see each other with her out of the way. "Gregory Pettit, this is Gin Watashi. Gin was my father's chief guard for many years before I was born and a number of years afterward. Gin, Greg has been my only friend and has been training me in ways other magi would be jealous of. I owe him a debt that I will never be able to repay."

Gin's right eyebrow went up, making his left dip and deepening the scars on that side of his face. "That is..." Gin's frown deepened more, "Training her in ways...?"

Gregory almost took a step back at the sheer bloodlust radiating off the old man in that moment. Gin seemed more dangerous than the bane wolf that had scarred him. Instead of flinching or looking away, the novice stiffened his back and lifted his chin, meeting the icy blue eyes with a steady gaze. "We are attempting to walk all three paths. It's supposed to be impossible," Gregory said simply.

"Gin, stop it," Yukiko said, stepping between them. "Greg is my dear friend, that is all."

Gin took his eyes off Gregory at her words, missing the flicker of disappointment in Gregory's eyes. "If you say it is so, Yu, then it is so. It has been three years since I've done as you're requesting. Can you afford my prices?"

"I will make sure you are paid after the tournament, if that is acceptable."

Gin's lips pursed before he sighed. "I could never tell you no, but... I will test you both first. If either of you is not up to my standard or close to it, I will not accept either of you."

Yukiko hesitated and bowed, "Armsmaster Gin, we submit ourselves as students to your training."

Gregory blinked upon hearing the title Yukiko used, bowing quickly to him. "Armsmaster, we submit ourselves to your training."

"First, the test," Gin sighed. "Follow me."

CHAPTER 36

Following Gin into the manor, Gregory was surprised at the spartan interior, which was completely at odds with every other manor he had been in. The walls were dotted with weapon displays, and Gregory had a feeling that they were not for show.

"Master, the room is ready," a feminine voice came from behind them, making Gregory and Yukiko tense up briefly.

Gregory looked back at the rabbit-eared woman who was now following them. She wore a kimono, but she had a short, slightly curved sword on her left hip. The hair on her head was cut short, much like Gin's, the same dark brown as the fur on her ears.

"Thank you, Inda. Please prepare the tea for after the test."

"As you wish, Master," the woman replied before the shadows swallowed her and she was gone.

"A shadow magi?" Yukiko asked.

"Yes and no," Gin replied evenly. "Inda is able to use aether, but never went through the academy, as she was not born in the empire." Stopping next to a set of paper sliding doors, he opened them, revealing a training room. The walls were lined with various wooden weapons, and the center of the room was barren of anything but mats.

"I'll test you one at a time. Gregory, you are first. Drop your things and go to the center of the room."

Yukiko took his things and set them beside her as she took a seat near the doors. Sitting cross-legged, she watched intently so she would know what was coming.

"You may stop the test at any time," Gin told Gregory. "It will end when you tap the mat three times. We will spar until you call for a stop. We'll keep it unarmed for now, because that is the basis for many of the weapons in this room."

Gin stepped to the center of the mat, facing Gregory, and bowed from the waist at a slight angle. Gregory returned the bow, then settled into the defensive posture Yukiko had taught him. Gin eyed the stance for a moment and glanced at Yukiko. Turning back to Gregory, Gin took a different stance. "Begin when you are ready."

Gregory did not want to be the first to attack, but Gin left him with no option. Shifting forward and remembering to keep his pace balanced, Gregory closed the distance between them slowly. Gin did not move— he waited patiently, watching him intently.

Getting to the distance he needed, Gregory launched his first kick. Gin barely moved, his own leg coming up to block his attack, before he stepped in, his hands blurring as he struck. Gregory grunted when Gin's hands struck him four times, but managed to block the last couple. Blocking the attacks let Gin get closer; old hands gripped the young man's kimono and with a pivot, Gregory was airborne briefly.

With a thump, Gregory hit the mat and rolled. Getting back to his feet, he found Gin almost on top of him. "Krog's balls," Gregory hissed when the old man attacked him again.

* * *

Gregory gasped as he pulled himself back to his feet. Sweat and blood dripped from his face when he turned to face Gin again. His ring that helped heal and keep him going had been depleted during the session.

"Greg—" Yukiko began, but was silenced by Gin.

"Silence, Yu, or leave. Every potential student must decide when they cannot fight anymore." Gin said the words softly, but forcefully, his gaze never leaving the young man in front of him.

"Not done," Gregory muttered, brushing at the blood leaking from his nose.

Gin bowed his head, "Then come. You have yet to land even a single strike."

As he closed on Gin with slow steps again, Gregory blinked because he knew what was about to happen. Following the images that came to him, his right hand flashed out and Gin grabbed it, pulling Gregory in. Dropping his weight, Gregory tried to sweep like he had earlier, but Gin jumped the attack while holding his arm. Gregory had a feral smile as he pushed off the ground before Gin could land. Slamming his body into the old man, the pair tumbled to the ground. Gin grunted, not expecting Gregory to land an attack on him. Even surprised, Gin had the experience to deflect Gregory's attacks as he released the young man's arm and rolled out of the attempted clinch. As he rolled away, Gin felt a stinging strike to his cheek. Getting to his feet, Gin touched his cheek and felt the tenderness.

"A strike," Gregory panted as he got back to his feet.

"Indeed," Gin nodded. "Now, I will go faster. Are you ready?"

"No," Gregory replied honestly, settling back into his defensive posture, "but I'm not stopping yet."

"Very well. If you are rendered unconscious, we will stop."

* * *

Yukiko glared at Gin when Gregory collapsed unconscious to the mat a few seconds later. "Gin, was that necessary?"

"Yes. He is stubborn, which is good and bad. He should have

stopped after landing the strike, but he wouldn't... because you were here."

Yukiko hesitated, "Because of me?"

"He couldn't risk looking weak before you, Yu. I knew you would have trouble with some things, being on the road with your father all the time." Gin sighed, "Inda? Take the young man to rest."

Inda dropped from above, landing beside Gregory. "As you wish, Master." Gathering Gregory into a princess carry, Inda stepped behind Gin and vanished with Gregory.

"Indara, please clean the mat so I may continue the testing."

Another bunny-eared woman entered the room, cloth and pitcher in hand. She quickly and deftly removed the sweat and blood from the mat, then bowed to Gin and left.

"Now, Yu, it is your turn. I will not be as soft as I was when you first started to learn. You will be just another potential student. Are you ready to face this test?"

Yukiko placed her things neatly beside Gregory's and rose to her feet. Her face was calm as she stepped toward the mat. "I am, Arms-master. Before we begin, I have to ask: did Greg pass your test?"

Gin shook his head, "You will only know after the test is over."

Settling into a different defensive stance, Yukiko nodded. "Then let us begin, sensei."

"Very well, Yu," Gin bowed to her. "Let's see if my son taught you more after I left."

* * *

Gregory clutched his head as he woke up. "Ugh, what happened?"

"You fought the master," a soft voice said from beside him. "Drink this."

Gregory slowly opened his eyes and saw the bunny-eared woman offering him a tea cup. Taking the cup, he sipped at the liquid that turned out to be a mild broth. After a couple of swallows, his headache subsided, becoming a dull ache instead of pounding, stabbing pain. "Thank you."

"You're welcome."

A pained whimper from beside him had him look over to see Yukiko waking up on a mat a few feet from him.

"Excuse me," the woman said as she shifted to Yukiko. "Drink this," she advised her, presenting her a cup as well.

"It helps," Gregory added when Yukiko took the cup.

"Now that you're both awake," Gin said, coming into the room, "we can talk. Thank you, Indara."

Indara helped both of them into a sitting position before moving behind Gin. Yukiko's headache faded as she sipped the drink. Gregory finished his cup, setting it beside him.

"I will accept both of you as students. Yu has a better grasp of how to fight, but that is a given considering her prior training. You, Gregory, have the spirit to fight, but lack the skill. While Yu and the academy have started your training, it isn't enough. Every day away from the academy, you will come here at the eighth bell. We will stop two hours before sunset so you may refresh and make it back before the gates close. During the week, you will find an hour every day, at the very least, to drill what I teach you. You should consider doing two, Gregory."

"Thank you, Armsmaster," Yukiko said, bowing deeply from her seat.

"Thank you, Armsmaster," Gregory echoed her.

"Once I'm sure you have a better grasp of the basics, I will teach you weapons. That's still a couple of months off, but you will be learning them. Now, a question: how did you know what I was going to do when you managed to strike me, Gregory?"

Gregory paused. "Intuition. I just knew what your escape would be," he answered slowly.

"Hmm," Gin said, staring at him, "very well. I've known a few men who had an instinctive feel for combat. We'll see if it is the same for you. Do either of you have any questions?"

"Do you think this will help us during the tournament?" Gregory asked.

"If you give me everything you have, yes. You will easily place in the top eight, maybe even the top two, if you apply yourselves."

"Master," Inda said, appearing behind Gin, "am I to train Yu in shadow magic, as well?"

Seeing Yukiko lean forward in clear anticipation, Gin chuckled. "We might be able to arrange that for the daughter of my old friend. Teach her only what she could learn from the academy for now. We don't want her using some of your techniques before the tournament."

"Yes, Master." Inda stared at Yukiko, "I will give you a scroll. You need to memorize it. Practice it when you are alone." Yukiko started to speak, and Inda smirked, cutting her off. "You may practice when he is present, but only him."

"As you command, sensei," Yukiko bowed.

"Yu, Inda will be your trainer. She is my most adept pupil, even better than my son," Gin said. "I will train Gregory. Every training day will end with you two sparring to compare how well you are learning."

Gregory winced; he knew that their day off would be the hardest day of the week to endure, but he also knew that he would learn faster and better during that time. "I look forward to it, sensei."

Gin chuckled, "All new students say so. We'll see how you feel after a month."

"Master, tea and food are ready," Indara said, coming into the room.

Gregory blinked as he looked at the two bunny-eared women. They looked nearly identical, the color of their fur and hair being just a shade different.

"Thank you, Indara. Come, we shall have a rest, then we will start from the beginning to fix the flaws that are there before we advance. The first thing to do is get you changed into a gi so your kimono can be washed."

Getting to their feet, Gregory and Yukiko followed Gin. Yukiko whispered as they went down the hall, "What do you think of my surprise?"

"I would never have guessed," Gregory chuckled softly. "We might surprise everyone in a few weeks."

"Good," Yukiko smiled.

* * *

They were exhausted when they made it back to the academy, but they both had smiles on their lips. The adept on the gate looked at them with suspicion, but let them in.

"Food first, or dormitory?" Gregory asked as they walked past the guards.

"Food. We can study after dinner. We don't have anything that has to be stored right away."

"It was a fun day... painful and exhausting, but fun. Thank you, Yuki. I wonder though... Yu?"

Yukiko blushed lightly, "My parents, Gin, and his son called me that. The others called me 'Little Miss.'"

"Greg," Nick's voice broke the tranquil air, "heading for dinner?"

"Yeah," Gregory replied, looking over his shoulder. "You all heading that way?"

"We already ate, going to get some sparring in. Care to join?"

"Did sparring earlier," Gregory replied. "Going to eat, and then study."

"Sparred earlier?" Jason asked, "Didn't you go into the city?"

"Yes," Yukiko replied with a smile. "I hope you all had a good day."

"It was a good day. The food was amazing. Maybe you can join us next time," Michelle said.

"Maybe... let us know. We have some things already planned," Yukiko said honestly. "If it doesn't interfere with our plans, we'd be happy to join you."

"We'll see you later, then," Nick said as they turned down a path leading toward the training hall.

Watching the other group walk away from them, Gregory gave Yukiko a puzzled glance. "We aren't telling them? Why?"

"Because if we don't join them, they will be adversaries instead of friends."

"They can't be both?" Gregory asked.

"Maybe, but I don't think Nick is one to take rejection well."

Gregory considered her statement and, thinking of Nick's grandfather, could not refute her assertion. "You may be right. Guess we'll find out in three months."

"I hope I am wrong," Yukiko added as they approached the mess hall. "I truly do."

CHAPTER 37

They knew they would need to adjust their schedule; after conditioning, they had been having dinner before getting a little more studying in. Now that they had become Gin's students, they went to a training hall after conditioning and worked on what he was teaching them for an hour, ate dinner, then went back to their rooms and collapsed into bed.

A little over two months passed in a whirl of motion to Gregory. Between classes and training with Gin on their days off, every waking hour of every day was filled with something to be done.

Even with everything going on, Gregory was starting to realize that he cared for Yukiko as more than just a friend. The last few nights, his dreams had a decidedly lustful tone centering on her, making waking up and leaving right away a bit problematic.

Nick and his group invited them out every week. They declined the invitations every time, which was starting to strain the friendly relationship between them. The sparring in conditioning class had started to take on a darker tone as the tournament drew near. Accidents happened occasionally, where a novice would go too far and injure another student enough that the healers were needed. Next week would be the last week before the tournament, and Gregory had a feeling that change was coming.

Bedding down for the night, he was looking forward to training with Gin tomorrow. The armsmaster had promised to start them on a single weapon when they had seen him last week. *Need to progress faster... Yuki has had magic training and has really advanced in shadow camouflage and that shadow bind thing she's learning. Aether, why do I have to wait to learn what my magic even is? I'm sure it has to do with seeing the strands of aether when people are using theirs... I guess I'll find out soon. I mean, I've gone this long without knowing.*

* * *

The ornate room surrounded him again when he opened his eyes, the darkness on the far side of the room shifting slowly. "Guess I unlocked the next circle?"

"You have indeed, dear one," the honeyed voice from the darkness said happily. "Six circles and not yet to the tournament? You've caught up with the others in your class. Yuki has also unlocked her sixth circle. She is such a good match for you— you've done well to nurture her."

Gregory's jaw set, "I haven't nurtured her, we are partners."

"Partners," the voice said, clearly implying the things that Gregory had started to want. "Yes, partners would be good. Do you think she'll be like Ria, or more like Jess?"

Memories from both his past lovers flitted through his mind, causing rising problems. Coughing as he looked away, he blinked when the room suddenly had a sleeping mat in it. Yukiko lay on it, a simple sheet pulled up to her shoulders as she looked at him with trepidation and desire. "Yuki?" Gregory asked in shock.

"Greg, we shouldn't," Yukiko said, looking around the room. "Oh, it's a dream...?" A happy smile came to her, "I can have what I want in my dreams, at least." Looking up at him, she let the sheet fall away from her chest. "Will you come lay with me, dear one?"

The rising problem was now a hard thing to ignore, and Gregory realized he was naked as he stood there. "I want to," Gregory said, taking a step toward her, then stopping. "This is too much. Stop it."

Puzzlement filled Yukiko's face before she vanished, along with the sleeping mat. "If you wish it, though you are only denying what you both want. You might need her shoulder, at least, today. We'll talk again after the tournament. I hope you'll be prepared for the change that is coming."

"Not going to give me a hint?"

"Do you think you can make me, dear one?"

Gregory gathered the flame inside of him, which had grown over the last two months, and wrapped it around him as he stepped toward the darkness. "Yes."

A happy laugh and clap came from the darkness he advanced toward. "Good, good! Keep that spirit. You'll need it in the years ahead... however..." the words trailed off as the darkness surged at him, enveloping him.

Gregory struggled, but it felt like the weight of the entire world was crushing him. His aether spluttered, then vanished completely as the darkness crashed down on him.

* * *

Third bell brought him awake, springing from bed and getting dressed almost immediately. His moment with the darkness was nearly forgotten in his excitement to begin learning a weapon from Gin. He slowed a little as he realized his clothing— which had been loose on him four months ago— was starting to feel snug. Looking at himself, he could not help but smile. *Would Ria and the others even recognize me as the same person now?*

A soft tap on his door got him moving again. "Be right down, Yuki," he said loud enough to be heard, but keeping his voice down so as not to wake any of the others.

Once he had his things together, Gregory hurried down to find Yukiko and Dia talking together softly. The moment he stepped out the door, they stopped and looked at him. Yukiko had a light blush and quickly looked away while Dia had an amused smile on her lips.

"Sorry for the delay," he said, wondering what he had missed.

"You two have a good time," Dia said, taking a seat, her lit pipe held in one hand. "And, Yuki, most times dreams are just that: only dreams."

"We should get going," Yukiko said as she stepped away from the dormitory.

"Good morning, Dia," Gregory called to the keeper as he hurried after Yukiko. "What was that about, Yuki?" Gregory asked after they had been walking for a bit.

"Just asking her some things. Nothing of import," Yukiko said, looking away from him.

"Sounds like a dream. Had an odd one myself last night," Gregory said, deciding to chance things a bit. "Never seen a room so richly furnished in my life, but that wasn't what caught my eye the most." He paused there, letting out a wistful sigh.

Yukiko's steps faltered for a second before she matched his pace again. "Oh? What caught your eye?"

Gregory looked away from her, "Beauty that I couldn't begin to even wish for. Perfection given form, at least in my eyes."

Yukiko stopped walking for a moment. "I saw something similar. It's been dominating my dreams for the last few nights. Last night, for a few moments, it felt different... it felt real."

"What if it had been?" Gregory asked.

"I would have felt horrible, since I'm still betrothed," Yukiko said sadly. "If I wasn't..." Shaking her head, she looked away. "If wishes were horses, I'd own a stable."

Gregory's heart twisted and he did his best to keep a smile on his face. "Yeah, so would I." Clearing his throat, he changed the subject. "I'm going to need new clothes soon. I've grown bigger, and these are getting too snug."

Yukiko's face flushed deep red before she shook her head. "Oh, yes, of course. You even got them a little loose, but you've been putting on muscle over the last few months. The difference is there to be seen. I wonder if your friends back in Alturis would even recognize you?"

Gregory chuckled, "Had that same thought this morning. Need to see if Gin will let us out a little earlier so I can arrange for new clothes."

"We'll ask him," Yukiko nodded. "If not, I can probably arrange something. You liked the colors you picked last time?"

"Yeah, thought they went pretty well with yours," Gregory replied. "Made me feel like we were a coup... a team."

Yukiko pretended not to hear the slip, "I'll take care of it if we can't leave early, but I doubt we'll be able to today, with weapon training starting. Gin has been impressed with how fast you're coming along. Inda told me last week that he's been smiling more over the last few months than in all the years she's known him."

"Huh," Gregory said as they reached the mess hall. "Let's eat and head to the archive. We need to get our studying in early."

* * *

Rafiq greeted them when they entered, "Morning to you both."

"Someone sick again?" Gregory asked.

"Indeed, like I was three days ago. They covered for me, so now, I do the same for them. How goes your studying?"

"Well," Yukiko smiled, "we finished the scrolls yesterday. Do you know—"

"New ones already await you," Rafiq cut in. "One of them is a surprise for you," he nodded to Gregory, "from Chief Sarinia. Treat it with reverence, Novice."

Gregory bowed by reflex as Rafiq exuded power for a moment. "I have always treated the books and scrolls with care."

"Which is why this exception is being made," Rafiq replied. "Do not mention it to anyone else, either."

Curiosity and excitement surged in Gregory and he bowed before hurrying toward the back of the archive. Yukiko blinked and went after him, while Rafiq watched them go with a smile.

I hope you know what you are doing, Sarinia. This treads very close to breaking the rules, Rafiq thought as he watched the two novices hurry away.

Sitting down at the table, Gregory slowly reached for the scroll that had been left for him. Yukiko took her seat, watching Gregory intently, not bothering to reach for the scroll in front of her. Gently unrolling the scroll, Gregory noted the aged look to the vellum and made sure he was exceedingly careful with it.

If you are reading this, then you've managed to combine two paths. I don't need to tell you how rare this is: only a handful of my peers have managed it, and none in the last hundred years. It always seems to be spirit, with either body or mind. Seeing the cavern and being able to see the growth of the other path makes it easier, or used to. Those who have come close recently say the cavern vanished for them, which isn't surprising when their clans force them to focus on the other path and abandon spirit entirely. Walking two paths isn't possible if you aren't training them equally; that makes it difficult, as it takes immense dedication to walk even a single path. To walk more than one, you need to believe and be dedicated to working on both of them, equally. On top of that already steep challenge, it feels as if the empire is actively trying to stop others from walking more than a single path, as well. I'll be surprised if this scroll is ever read after I hand it to the Chief Keeper of the academy archive.

Gregory looked up from the scroll and saw Yukiko watching him. "This scroll came from someone who managed to combine two paths."

Yukiko leaned forward, "Does it tell you how?"

"I'll find out."

Yukiko shifted around the table to sit beside him. "I'll read with you."

Gregory nodded. His desire to know more overrode the warmth of her leaning against him to read the scroll with him.

CHAPTER 38

S eventh bell brought them both out of their reverie, pulled from the scroll by the bell. Realizing what time it was, Gregory carefully rolled the scroll even though they had to hurry. "We need to hurry."

"I'll head to the gate to get a rickshaw," Yukiko said, getting to her feet and hurrying off.

Gregory slowed so he would not damage the scroll. *They know*, he suddenly realized. *The chief archivist knows, or is guessing, and this scroll shouldn't be given to Novices. Does it mean they are an ally, or they are setting us up?* Mulling over the thought he sealed the scroll into its case and set it aside. Shaking his head, he got to his feet and headed for the door.

"Greg," Nick called out as Gregory walked quickly down a path, "hold up a moment."

Gregory paused, unhappy at the delay but trying to stay friendly. "I need to get going, Nick. What do you need?"

"Odd to see you without your shadow," Nick chuckled.

Gregory's smile faded, "Yuki went to get a rickshaw for us, we have to be somewhere soon."

"Look, I know you like her, but you also need to consider your future. Next day off the clan is holding a party for those they want to join the clan."

"Before the tournament?"

"It's for those they know they want to join regardless of how they place in the tournament," Nick grinned. "You're invited, and you can bring Yukiko if you'd like. I've talked with Grandfather, and if she joins with you, we'll be willing to let you be her handler. Something like that wouldn't normally be allowed, but we figure you'd appreciate being the *firm hand to guide her*," the last few words were dripping with innuendo.

"I'll let you know," Gregory said. "I have to run, if I don't want to be late. Later." Gregory shook off Nick's hand and took off at a steady jog down the path. As he left, he could feel Nick's eyes on his back the entire way.

Yukiko was waiting for him at the gate. They climbed into the rickshaw and the driver got them moving. "What delayed you?"

"Nick," Gregory said gruffly. "Pressure is starting now. The clan is holding a party for those they want to invite on our next day off. I was invited, and told that I could bring you as well." He paused, wondering if he should say the last bit, before he exhaled and told her. "Said that if we both join the clan, I'd be your handler for the clan."

Yukiko stiffened next to him, "He said that?"

"Yeah."

Yukiko fell silent for a moment, before she spoke slowly. "Did you agree?"

"To the party? I told him I'd have to see if I could make it. Frankly, that last bit pissed me off. He was all but promising you to me, as if he could. Asshole. As if your feelings aren't even a consideration." Gregory discovered his hands were clenched, and forced them open. "Not going to the party, though, is going to make it clear that we're not with them. Over the last few months things have gotten colder, but they're at least willing to pretend to be our friends."

"Did you want to join them?" Yukiko asked. "If it wasn't for me, would you join them?"

Gregory started to immediately reject her idea, but stopped. Instead he took a minute to seriously consider her question. "No. While they do have a lot to offer, no, I don't think I would. All the staff in the manor are eurtik, and I think they're slaves, not just servants. I still don't like that divide, and they seem to love it."

"We'll have to find a clan to join right after the tournament," Yukiko said. "One of the other four great clans would be best to avoid strife."

"None of them have approached me," Gregory said, shrugging a little. "They'll take you though. Which is good, it'll mean you won't catch the shit as bad."

"But..." Yukiko began but trailed off and shook her head. "We'll talk about it later," she said instead as they came to a stop before Gin's home.

"Okay."

Yukiko knocked on the door, to have Indara open it for them. "Close," Indara said as the eighth bell chimed. "You had better hurry and change."

The two of them hurried inside, changing their shoes for slippers. It did not take them long to change from clothes into gis. Stepping into the training room, they found Gin and Inda waiting for them with disappointed looks. The pair took their places before Gin, and bowed to him.

"I had thought you were serious about weapons training," Gin said, his disappointment palpable.

"We are, Master," Gregory said bowing low. "We were detained by a member of the Eternal Flame clan, who is trying to recruit us."

"I see. And?"

"We were invited to a party next week."

"Before the tournament? They only do that for those they are serious about," Gin said with one eyebrow rising the tiniest bit. "I shall clear the—"

"There's no need," Yukiko interrupted him. "We won't be attending."

Gin's eyebrow raised even farther, "Oh? Which clan are you thinking of joining then?"

"We haven't decided," Gregory admitted. "The Eternal Flame, though, isn't suitable for either of us."

"I know why it isn't for Yu, but why not for you?"

"Because of how they view Yuki."

Gin snorted and laughed, "Yes, I can see that. Very well. I will send a letter to the clan head explaining why you will be missing the party. That might buy you a little leeway, at least."

"Thank you, sensei," the pair said in unison.

"The weapons are ready," Inda said.

"Good, we can start then," Gin nodded. "Everyone has an affinity for certain weapons, based on their personality and body type. The open cases around the room have been enchanted to help you realize which will be easiest for you to learn. Open yourself to the feeling, and check each weapon. Once you have gone around the room, come back here."

Bowing, the two novices rose to their feet and went to check the weapons. Yukiko went left and Gregory went right. He stopped before a war axe, and felt repulsed by it. Shaking his head, he continued around the room. The tetsubo was slightly more tolerable than the axe, but not by much. A little better than the last two, the tonfa and kama still did not feel right. The katana and wakizashi felt better, as if they could be used. Gregory's steps slowed when he reached the su yari and naginata; the feeling from them was warmly welcoming, as if they were old friends waiting for him. The feeling was stronger from the naginata than the su yari. None of the other weapons felt as right to him, though the bo felt almost as good as the su yari.

Moving back to the middle of the room, Gregory knelt again, resting on his shins, as Yukiko moved to the last weapon box. She joined him a moment later, kneeling as he did.

"What weapons felt right to you, Yu?" Gin asked.

"The shuriken, tonfa, and wakizashi felt right to me. The katana was close."

"And you, Gregory?"

"The bo and su yari felt good, but they were far overshadowed by the warmth of the naginata."

Gin's eyebrow went up, but he merely nodded. "I see. Inda, you'll be taking Yukiko and teaching her the art of the blade. Have your sister drill her on the shuriken."

"As you wish, Master," Inda bowed to him.

"I will be teaching Gregory the way to properly wield a naginata. We will pause for midday as normal," Gin said. "Make sure to spend the first two hours on unarmed combat."

"Yes, Master," Inda replied. "Yukiko, follow me."

"Indara, return the cases to the vault," Gin said, and the door opened to admit her.

"As you wish, Master," Indara said, moving to close and secure the cases before she started to move them out of the room.

"Let us begin the training," Gin said, getting to his feet.

* * *

When the sparring was over, Gregory was dripping sweat, but he was not exhausted like he had been months before. What surprised him more was the fact he had landed a couple of clean hits on Gin— not enough to stop the flow of combat, but still more than he would have ever managed months before.

Training with the naginata began in a similar manner that the unarmed training had; with stances. Gin drilled the five basic stances into him, nothing more than each stance and flowing from stance to stance as each was called out.

Gin watched the young man handle the practice naginata, his face carefully blank, as he kept calling out the forms. Gregory felt as if the weapon was part of him as he moved from form to form.

When Gin suddenly called out a stance he did not know, Gregory's body moved into a form Gregory was not familiar with, but felt correct. When he finished the attack, Gregory stopped and blinked. "Huh? What happened there?"

"That should be my question," Gin muttered. "You are moving as if you've held a naginata for years. I'll see what you can do now." Gin took another practice naginata and two helmets off the rack, then stepped onto the mat. "Debilitating strikes stop the bout," he said, tossing a helmet to Gregory.

Gregory fumbled the helmet for a second, but caught it. "Understood." Getting the helmet on, he took up the standard ready posture that Gin had taught him.

Gregory breathed slow and deep as he waited for Gin to start. The nerves he felt when normally sparring were missing. He felt at peace in the moment, even though he was standing across from an armsmaster.

"Fight," Gin announced.

Gregory shot forward, the naginata lashing out. The clack of wood on wood came fast as Gregory pressed the attack and Gin defended, giving ground and circling as he went.

With the masks on, Gregory could not see Gin's expression, so he could not see the surprise written across the old man's face. The fact that he was pressuring the armsmaster did not register as Gregory kept the attack going, his naginata continuously in motion as the fight continued.

The seconds became minutes as the two moved back and forth across the room. Gin was finally able to press his own attack, forcing the younger man to defend. Deep laughter bubbled up from Gin as he felt a rush of exhilaration at having someone keep pace with him. Gregory laughed as well and the moment stretched out between them.

The minutes seemed to elongate as the pair flowed across the floor. Gin knew he had to end it, and with a win, or he would lose respect from Gregory. Forced to act, Gin gave up two minor hits, wincing when each connected, but that gave him the positioning to drop his weapon and grab Gregory. Before the young man could react, he found himself flying across the room. Landing with a thud, Gregory gasped as the breath was knocked from his body.

Gin was above him a handful of seconds later, his wooden blade tapping Gregory's prone body. "Finished."

"You... dropped... your weapon?" Gregory gasped out.

"To secure the victory, yes," Gin said, pulling off his helmet. "If it had been more than just you, it would have been too risky to do. Since it was just us, it was worth it to win."

"I didn't think... to try using unarmed... as well," Gregory admitted, trying to catch his breath.

"If you had, I might have lost," Gin admitted. "You are a savant when it comes to the naginata. You are my equal with that weapon in hand. It is either instinctual, or perhaps you are a reincarnated soul who used one extensively in the past."

"I haven't felt like a reincarnated soul," Gregory said as he sat up, finally getting his breath back. "If I was, I don't think I'd make so many mistakes."

Gin chuckled, "If that were true, we'd know easily who was and who wasn't. There is nothing I can do to train you with a naginata, though we will spar at least an hour every week."

"Thank you, Sensei. I will do my best to not disappoint you."

"We'll see," Gin grunted. "Take the weapons and helmets back. Pick up a bo and come back to the mat."

* * *

When they stopped for lunch, Gregory was humbled by how badly he used the bo, especially compared to the naginata. Gin had been even tougher on him. Gregory did his best to learn, aware that much the same thing should have happened with the naginata as well.

Indara served small snacks and tea in the stone garden. The two novices had learned how to eat and meditate at the same time, which let them get all their training in for the day. The down side was that neither heard the conversation held by Gin and Inda.

After the break, they all returned to the training room Gin had been using with Gregory. For the next two hours, Gregory and Yukiko sparred with each other in unarmed combat. Yukiko was impressed by how much Gregory had improved. She would have been hard pressed if she had not improved as well, but even then, their sparring was now more even than it had been in the past.

Gin and Inda commented, pointing out their errors and flaws after each round. Gregory and Yukiko took the information in, doing their best to improve during the hours they sparred. Gin made them stop and wash up before sending them back to the academy. Watching them leave, Gin looked pensive.

"Indara, bring me paper and ink. I feel the need to write a few letters."

"As you wish, Master," Indara said, appearing behind him.

CHAPTER 39

Gregory and Yukiko walked side by side, crossing the grounds of the academy to the mess hall. Gregory was still musing on his ability to wield a naginata with such ease. Yukiko broke the companionable silence after a few moments.

"Greg, you've improved so rapidly. If it wasn't for Inda's training in shadow entanglement, I'm not sure I could win as often as I do against you."

"You're still winning half or more," Gregory replied. "Gives me something to keep striving for."

"You'll easily surpass me by the end of the year," Yukiko sighed. "I'm not sure I'll be a partner at that point."

"Yuki, you're improving fast, too. Remember how you did yesterday? You led Nick the entire time you sparred. You didn't do that the first time."

Yukiko nodded slowly, "You're right. It just feels like I'm losing ground compared to you."

"Or I'm finally becoming your equal?" Gregory suggested another way to view it.

Yukiko's frown became a smile. "Equal. Yes, I want you to be."

"I'm trying, Yuki, I am."

"Food, then studying, yes?" Yukiko asked.

"That is the plan," Gregory chuckled as they reached the mess hall.

* * *

With dinner done, the two friends headed back to the dormitory. "Our increased aether makes it easier to eat," Gregory said. "I barely have to slow down anymore."

"Yes, and after another circle or two, we'll be able to eat more quickly. That'll give us even more time in the morning and evening."

"More time for studying," Gregory grinned.

The front room was noisy when they entered the dormitory. Shaking his head as he changed his boots for slippers, he wondered if the happy sounds would continue after next week. They had only taken a couple of steps when Dia's door opened.

"Novices, a moment," Dia said as she left them at the doorway. She returned a moment later with a scroll and a small wooden box. "These came for you." Handing Gregory the scroll and Yukiko the box, she smiled. "I wish you both a good evening."

"Thank you, Keeper," they said in unison, bowing to her.

They glanced from the scroll, to the box, and finally at each other before quickly going upstairs to find out what they had. Sitting down at the table in Gregory's room, Yukiko set the box in front of her. "You first?"

"Okay," Gregory said, opening the scroll. He glanced at the first few lines, "It's a letter from Gunnar." He rolled it back up. "What about you?"

"You're not going to read it?" Yukiko asked.

"Later. It'll be mostly gossip about what's going on back home. I'm more interested in what that box contains."

"Okay, but after we know, you should read the letter."

"Deal."

Yukiko pulled the box to her and shook her head. "Too much, Father." With a sigh, Yukiko took out her knife and pricked her thumb, pressing it to the front of the box. There was a distinctive click before Yukiko lifted the lid.

"How was that locked?" Gregory asked.

"A blood-lock. Only those who are blood-related by a single degree can open it. They are norm..." Yukiko began to explain as she pulled a scroll out of the box first, setting it beside her, but she trailed off as she stared into the box.

"What is it?" Gregory asked.

Yukiko shut the box, shaking her head. "My father is insane."

Gregory chuckled, "What is it?"

"Money. More than he should have sent. It explains the blood-lock."

"Is it that bad?" Gregory asked puzzled. "It means you can get more things to help, right?"

"Possibly," Yukiko said slowly. "I need to read the scroll."

"I'll read mine, too," Gregory said, picking his up off the table. "Study afterward?"

"Yes," Yukiko replied distractedly as she picked up the scroll, broke the seal, and unrolled it.

Gregory worried for her, but followed his own suggestion and began to read the scroll from Gunnar.

Greg, we were surprised to hear from you. How is the academy? I'm sure things have happened since you wrote us. I'm not sure how to break the news to you so, I'm going to be blunt.

Ria is married to Stan. Two days after you left, she went to him and demanded he court her, and married him a week after that. I was pissed off, but El explained it to me; told me that you told Ria find a good husband. Still beat on him a bit, but I didn't break anything. I think she could have picked better if she had just waited a bit first, but both her and El have shouted me down over that repeatedly.

Your father is working for the good of the village as a servant. He hasn't touched a drop of alcohol since you left. He moved in with my family and gave us your old house in return. Said a growing family needs a home. Don't worry, I made sure your room was cleaned before El stepped foot in it.

The village had a visit from a trader named Lagrand about a week after

you left, and he has entered a deal with Ria to purchase clothing from the
Delarosas. Not sure what the deal is, but everyone seemed happy about it.

Not much else has happened here— you know as well as I that Alturis
doesn't change. Oh, well, not true. Today, we found a new vein of ore, so the
mine is still good for the next decade, at least. I'm working alongside both of
our fathers, so I'll be able to keep a good eye on him for you.

Now for the best news: El is pregnant. Ria turns out to be pregnant, too.
Before you go thinking that Ria's kid is yours, she wanted me to tell you
that the timing is not right. Wish it was your kid, but that wouldn't be
right to Ria. Keep your chin up, and we hope to hear back from you after
the tournament. You damn well better show them what an Alturis man
can do.

Oh, and you don't owe us anything. If you hadn't been there, we all
know what would have happened. Just do your best, and maybe visit us if
you ever get the chance.

Gunnar, El, and family.

Gregory felt drained, and his heart ached unexpectedly. *Ria... I*
hope he is good to you... I hope your child is as beautiful as you. Closing
his eyes, he took several deep breaths to control the emotional
turmoil that swirled inside of him.

"Greg?" Yukiko asked softly.

"Sorry, village gossip. Everything is fine," he said, but he could not
force a smile to his lips.

"Something is bothering you," Yukiko said, shifting around the
table to sit beside him. "I'm here if you want to talk."

Gregory slid the letter over in front of her, "Go ahead and read it."

Yukiko picked up the scroll, reading it slowly, before she set it
back down. "They are moving on with their lives, and that bothers
you?"

"Yes and no," Gregory sighed. "I don't know. I always wanted to be
here and I knew things would change after I left, but I guess I also
hoped they would still be the same."

Yukiko leaned into his side gently, "I'm jealous, myself. Your
friends obviously still care about you. It must be nice."

Gregory's arm went around her waist without thinking, holding her like he used to with Ria. "You have a friend— a true friend— in me, Yuki. I'll always care about you."

"Promise?" The word was a bare whisper leaving Yukiko's mouth.

"Promise, Yuki. I'll always care for you."

They sat there for a while before Yukiko sighed, "We need to study."

"Yeah," Gregory agreed, but he did not move.

"Maybe in a bit?" Yukiko said softly.

"In a bit is fine with me."

The pair stayed that way until the next bell rang the nineteenth hour. Yukiko was the first to move, letting out a regretful sigh. "We have an hour before we need to sleep."

Letting her go, Gregory exhaled sadly, "Yeah, work to do."

Yukiko shifted back to her side of the table and put her scroll back in the box, setting it on the floor beside her. She did not look up at Gregory, "Grab your papers. We'll get in what we can."

"Yuki," Gregory said gently, waiting for her to look up, "thanks."

She gave him a soft smile, "Just as you'll always care for me, I'll always care for you, Greg. My word on that."

The moment stretched as he stared into her cyan eyes and felt something he had not ever felt before. Heart beating faster and his mouth going dry, he just stared into her eyes.

"Greg?" Yukiko asked when he continued to sit there.

"Huh? Oh, um, yeah," he stuttered. He got up awkwardly and went to retrieve his notes so she could teach him more on trade.

* * *

The hour felt like it passed too quickly for Gregory. "Guess it's time for bed," he sighed as the twentieth bell chimed.

"Tomorrow comes early, and we have more studying to do. That scroll needs our attention; if we can combine two of the paths, we'll grow even faster. Since we'll have at least one of the great clans upset with us, it would be best if we do all we can."

"You're right," Gregory said. "You never told me what your letter said."

"It was from my mother," Yukiko said hesitantly. "She'll be coming with Father to the tournament. She's making arrangements to meet the day before the tournament starts. You're asked to come, but you don't have to if—" Yukiko started to speed up at the end, but Gregory cut her off.

"I'd love to, if you want me there."

Yukiko's hesitant smile grew wide, "I'd like you to come, yes. It'll be at a tavern, so food will be part of it."

"Can't say no to free food, can I?" Gregory joked.

Shaking her head, Yukiko gathered up the box and scroll. "See you in the morning. I hope you have pleasant dreams." The moment she finished speaking, her face flushed red and she hurried to the door. "Goodnight."

Mention of dreams brought back the memory of Yukiko nude in bed and asking him to join her. Taking a deep breath, he wished her a goodnight.

As he put things away and got ready for bed, Gregory had to wonder about what the day had thrown at him. He had grown in power, learned he was skilled with a naginata, and found out that Ria had done as he had asked and moved on with her life.

Guess that explains what the darkness was talking about last night, Gregory thought. *Doesn't explain how she knows things or how that bit with Yukiko in my dream happened.* With a sigh, he got comfortable on his mat. *I think I love her. Maybe even more than I loved Ria, and that's silly. I knew Ria for years and Yuki for only a handful of months... Not that it matters, can't be with either of them. Ria got married and is going to have a kid, and Yuki is promised to another... I wonder what her betrothed thinks of her being a magi?*

With that thought circling his brain, Gregory exhaled deeply and rolled to his side, hoping that sleep would claim him before too long.

CHAPTER 40

Their routine continued normally, except for a bit of tension between Gregory and Yukiko. Both of them kept shooting glances at the other and getting caught at it occasionally. Together, they continued to read through the scroll teaching them how to combine body and spirit training.

In economics, Gregory was able to understand and keep up with Magus Marcia as she lectured. Aether introduction was different, as Adept John had some of the students try combining their magics together. The wind and water magi managed to bring a brief rain down on the area. Those who did not have magic that could be combined with others practiced like normal. Yukiko kept her shadow bind magic to herself, not wanting to tip her hand before the tournament, so she just worked on concealing herself in shadow. Gregory watched everyone, taking notes on what each novice was able to do and remembering it for next week.

During the hour before conditioning, Gregory and Yukiko tried to follow the steps from the scroll, walking through the simple exercises while meditating. The moment eluded both of them, but they were confident they would be able to manage it with more practice. With the movements being slow and controlled, they could even practice in their rooms if they wanted.

It was conditioning that had the biggest shift from the standard day. When the class was pairing off for sparring, a novice Gregory had never talked to stepped in front of him.

"Spar with me?" the man asked bluntly, making it more statement than question.

"I'm going to spar with—" Gregory began, but another student had stepped in front of Yukiko and was asking to fight her. They exchanged a look and shrugged. "Sure," Gregory said, facing the man in front of him.

The first round was slow as Gregory and his opponent sized each other up, but Gregory knocked him down once they started in earnest. The man got right back to his feet and came back for more. Taken by surprise, since normally taking a person down was seen as a win and the sparring partners were supposed to square off for the next round, Gregory did his best to defend against the onslaught. A number of hard strikes connected with his chest, making him wince, but he managed to put the other student down again.

"You're supposed—" Gregory began to say, but again, the novice came off the ground to attack a third time.

The adept closest to them intercepted the student and put him on the ground, holding the novice's arm up and behind them. "You are breaking the rules of this class. The tournament is not until next week."

"Yes, sir," the novice on the ground spat.

A cry of pain came from behind the adept, and he released the chastised novice to find out what had happened. Yukiko stood back, her eye discoloring and her jaw set as she stared at the novice clutching his arm.

"What happened?" the adept said, going to the injured novice.

"He didn't reset after I bested him. Instead, he attacked again and gave me this," Yukiko gently touched her eye. "I reacted without thinking. I believe his elbow is broken."

"Fucking bitch," the novice on the ground spat. "Filthy half-bloods shouldn't even be allowed to learn magic."

"Quiet," the adept snapped at the novice. "You are going to the healers." Looking back, the adept stared hard at the novice Gregory had put down. "You will take him."

"Yes, sir," the novice replied, but his lip was pulled back in a sneer.

"The rest of you, back to sparring," the adept said, moving to Yukiko. "How bad is that?"

"It'll be fine. I don't need to see the healer, sir."

"Very well. You two square off."

Gregory nodded, moving into position in front of Yukiko, "Yes, sir."

* * *

When class ended, Gregory was slow in gathering his things. He wanted the rest of the class to leave before he spoke to Yukiko. "Yuki, are you okay?"

"It'll heal," Yukiko said, touching her sore eye, which was gaining even more color.

"Not what I meant. You can use your ring now that class is over."

Yukiko exhaled deeply, "It hurt more than I expected. I'd gotten used to people not knowing or mentioning it. Being with you all the time made me hopeful that maybe things were different."

"Fuck them," Gregory said simply, touching her shoulder. "We'll show them that you're worth a thousand of them. We'll take the top two spots in the tournament and make all of them cry. An uneducated fringer and a filthy animal will show them that they are below us. Won't make our time here any easier, but it'll put them all in their place."

Yukiko snickered softly, "You're not uneducated, not anymore."

"And you were never filthy, nor an animal, Yuki." Gregory squeezed her shoulder gently. "They're jealous and will say anything they can to hurt you to make you doubt yourself. Personally, I think you're the most amazing person I've met here."

"You're the only one who feels that way," Yukiko said and looked down, her cheeks heating.

"I doubt it," Gregory said. "Come on, let's get a little training in before dinner, then we get to study."

"Yes."

Leaving the arena, the pair headed toward the training hall. They were planning on using one of the rooms for trying to combine their paths before using the baths. Approaching the building, they paused, as a number of novices were exiting after having used the baths.

"Greg," Nick said, turning with his group toward the two of them, "about the party; are you coming?"

"I'm sorry, Nick, but my sensei has refused to give me the day off," Gregory said.

"Sensei? Who's teaching you, and what?" Nick asked, surprised. "Is that what you've been doing every day off?"

"Yes. Combat and Gin," Gregory replied, giving as little information as possible.

"That'd explain how they've both improved so quickly," Jason said. "If you just opt to join the clan, though, we can get you a better instructor."

Yukiko stifled a laugh, which made her the center of attention. She gave them a smile, "Armsmaster Watashi is hard to beat for instruction."

"He hasn't accepted students in three years, and certainly never a novice," Michelle said flatly. "His rates are exorbitant, as well."

"That is roundly true," Yukiko replied, her smile vanishing. "He was also the head of my father's guards for a number of years."

Nick's easy-going smile was nowhere to be seen. "Why didn't you tell us? We would have joined you."

"I had a hard enough time convincing him to accept myself and Greg," Yukiko replied. "If you know him, you know that he handles instruction one-on-one, not as a class."

"But he's teaching both of you," Fureno pointed out.

"He is teaching Greg. His assistant is teaching me," Yukiko said.

"I see," Nick said stiffly. "Then you won't be joining the Eternal Flame?"

"That's still up in the air," Gregory said, trying to buy time. "I've had no one else approach me to this point."

"I have not ruled against it," Yukiko said a second after Gregory, "though having eurtik in my heritage makes me a little leery, considering some of the stories I've heard."

Nick stared at them for a long moment before his easy-going smile came back. "Well, if you're busy, you're busy. We'll be talking again after the tournament."

"I'll be looking forward to it," Gregory said. "We're going to get cleaned up, see you later."

"Night," Nick said as he led his group away.

In the training hall, the two friends found an empty room to use. "Well, I guess that answers the question about his friendliness," Gregory sighed. "He's going to hate us after the tournament."

"Yes. First for beating him, then again when we turn his offer down."

"Still need to decide who we're going to join," Gregory said as he began to stretch.

"That is the difficult part," Yukiko agreed. "An hour, then bath and dinner?"

"Yeah," Gregory said. "I thought I almost had it earlier."

"As if you could see it just out of reach?"

"Yeah."

"Me, too," Yukiko said as she positioned herself to start. "Maybe this time."

"Maybe," Gregory echoed her.

* * *

The rest of the week continued in normal fashion until the day before their day off. Breakfast had been good, and they had finished reading through the scroll a few days ago. Instead of turning it back in, they both decided to go over it again.

Economics, their study period, and aether introductions yielded nothing new to them. Gregory caught sight of the blue threads twice more, once seeing thick strands wrapped around a shadow near the wall, where it had a clear view of the novices. The moment he thought he saw the shadow magi, his vision of the threads vanished.

During their hour of rest before conditioning, both of them felt the flow of spirit and body connecting. Each of them was inside their aether cavern, still performing the techniques outlined in the scroll. As they watched, large embers left the fire, drifting to the deepening channels, and wisps of smoke drifted out.

They came out of their trances when other novices began showing up. They did not have a chance to compare experiences, but the smiles both of them wore were enough for them to know what had happened for the other.

All during the week, Gregory and Yukiko turned down all other requests to spar and fought each other exclusively. They kept to the basics, feeling the number of eyes studying them.

Heading for the training hall after conditioning, they were whispering to each other about their success combining the paths when two other novices rushed them from a clump of shrubs. Neither was prepared for the attack, but they managed to defend themselves, earning minor bruises in the first clash. The two attackers rushed back in only to find Gregory and Yukiko set and ready.

"Stop!" The word cut through the air like a blade, but the attackers did not heed it.

Gregory and Yukiko resisted the attack and turned the tables. Both assailants slammed into the ground almost at the same instant with gasps of pain. Backing quickly away, Gregory looked over to see Magus Paul striding toward them, his face dark with anger.

"I told you to stop," Paul thundered at the novices on the ground. "You two, what happened here?" he demanded of Gregory and Yukiko.

"We were heading to the baths when these two rushed us," Gregory explained. "We defended ourselves twice." Gregory turned his cheek to show the red mark and scratch he had received from the first attack.

"That is what happened, Magus," Yukiko confirmed.

"Considering I saw their second attack and they didn't stop when commanded, I'll accept that version of events. It isn't unusual for novices to try removing competition before the tournament, but normally it is done with more finesse. It gets worse after the tournament, too. Now move along."

"Thank you, sir," Gregory bowed, mirrored by Yukiko.

The pair hurried away as Paul grabbed the two attackers by the backs of their necks and hauled them upright. "You two are going to have a hard time of it."

"But, sir," one of them protested, but Gregory and Yukiko did not hear the rest as they entered the building.

"Guess we'll need to be even more aware of our surroundings going forward," Gregory grimaced.

"Are you okay?" Yukiko asked, looking at the red line on his cheek.

"Yeah," Gregory said, gently prodding his cheek. "Damned cheap shot."

Yukiko frowned, "Assholes, trying to do that."

"They interrupted our conversation," Gregory said when they found an empty room. "Let's see if we can do it again."

"Greg," Yukiko said slowly, "tomorrow, we'll have to leave training a little early."

"Meeting your parents," Gregory nodded. "I remember."

"We'll bring our silks with us to change into after training."

"That formal?" Gregory asked with hesitation.

"Yes."

"I'm not sure they'll still fit," he mentioned, thinking of his other clothing.

"They were exchanged the other day. Didn't you notice?"

"Uh, no. I take it the staff at the dormitory did it?"

"They undertook the errand I asked of them. Lagrand Clothiers were happy to help with exchanging the items."

"When did you manage that?"

"I told you I would take care of it last week," Yukiko said, looking away and smiling.

"Some days, Yuki, I wonder if I can ever keep up with you," Gregory said as he walked to the middle of the room and took up the beginning stance. "You ready to start?"

"Yes," Yukiko replied with a grin, "let's improve ourselves so much that our peers are left far behind."

"Sounds good."

CHAPTER 41

Waking when the third bell chimed, Gregory was quickly dressed. He threw his bag over his shoulder and opened his door to see Yukiko closing hers. "Morning, Yuki."

"Morning, Greg," Yukiko replied, her smile uncertain. "Thank you for coming to meet my parents."

"I'm happy to put their minds at ease," Gregory said. "Let's get going. Gin is going to put us through the wringer, I'm sure."

"I'm not so sure. It is the day before the tournament starts," Yukiko disagreed. "We'll need everything we can bring for this coming week."

"We've had more training than the others. Well, most of the others. I'm sure Nick, Hayworth, and at least a dozen others have had personalized training, as well."

"Yes, and they'll all have tricks of their own, like our rings."

They exchanged slippers for outdoor shoes and left the dormitory. Dia was on the porch, smoking. "Morning, Keeper," Gregory and Yukiko said in unison.

"Morning, Novices. Keeping to your schedule even with the tournament starting tomorrow?"

"Yes, and we'll try to keep it even during the tournament," Yukiko replied. "We'll get our studying in early and avoid any needless conflict this way."

"There is that," Dia nodded. "My staff are doing their jobs, I hope?"

"They have gone above and beyond for me," Yukiko replied, bowing to Dia. "I'm very grateful."

"I've had no complaints," Gregory added.

"Good. When will your parents be stopping by to see the dormitory?"

"My father won't be here," Gregory replied a little stiffly.

"I'm not sure, Keeper," Yukiko replied. "I'm sure Mother will wish to see the rooms, at least."

"I shall look forward to meeting her," Dia smiled. "Good day to you both."

"Good day, Keeper," they said in unison, bowing together.

* * *

The cooks wished Gregory and Yukiko a pleasant day while serving them breakfast, and reminded them not to overdo anything since the tournament was tomorrow. They ate as quickly as they could and were heading for the archive before an hour had passed.

A short mouse eurtik was at the front desk when they entered. "Morning, Novices. You didn't leave us any instructions about what topic you would like to pursue next," he said.

"I'd like to see something on advancing the mind path, please," Gregory told him.

"Yes, that's a good idea," Yukiko nodded.

"Very well. I shall bring what I can," the man replied.

Gregory and Yukiko went to their table and took their seats, waiting for the books or scrolls to arrive. It was only a couple of minutes before the eurtik brought them two scrolls and left. The friends thanked him and began to read their respective scrolls.

The mind path is one of learning, growth, and advancing through intel-

lect. Starting the path is easy; read, learn, and memorize. Continuing the path can be daunting, though, as it requires a thirst for learning. Much like a fire, it must be fed constantly. If you fail to feed it regularly, the fire will dim and possibly go out. The easiest way to make sure you are maintaining is to work on logic puzzles. This step is best done with a helper. Listed below are sample puzzles that will help keep your mind sharp. Don't think these are where you should begin and end; you must still push to learn more, to understand how things work, and to find better ways of doing them.

Gregory looked over the puzzles, having never seen anything like it before. He was so intent on understanding how they worked and solving them that he almost missed hearing the seventh bell.

Gregory put the scroll down reluctantly, then sighed and rubbed at his eyes, suddenly feeling the strain of concentrating for so long. "This is going to take me a little while to work through."

"Okay. I think I can understand this one," Yukiko said as she rose to her feet.

"The scroll I've got is saying to use logic puzzles. The downside is that to properly use them takes two people: one to make them, then the other to solve them. The simplest is something called 'Magi Squares,' a three by three grid with nine squares in each grid. Each line, row, and box are to contain numbers from one to nine."

"That's what my scroll is saying, too. I've seen them before. Father used to do one every morning. He might have old ones that we can get from him. If we use charcoal pencils, we can reuse them and take turns doing the same puzzles."

"That would be good, but it also helps if we create them ourselves and trade them. Creating them is apparently harder than solving them in some cases; you have to remove enough to make it difficult to solve, but not so much that it's impossible."

"Hmm, that's a good point," Yukiko said pensively. "We can do both. I'll still ask him to send his old ones to us with the ink removed. He always did his in ink to make him go more carefully, so as not to make mistakes."

"Have a good day," the eurtik at the desk said. He smiled as they left, having overheard their conversation.

"Good day," they replied, unaware that they had been overheard.

Gregory and Yukiko stepped out of the building, and the panther archivist appeared behind the eurtik manning the door. "They seem to have understood the scrolls and are planning on using the knowledge."

The eurtik jumped with a squeak, "Chief, I wish you wouldn't do that to me."

"But it lets you know you're alive," Sarinia purred. "They are using the combined path scroll I gave them access to and looking to incorporate advanced mind path teachings."

"But they can't possibly manage that," the eurtik said, frowning.

"This knowledge is to stay only with the eurtik staff. Understood, Simon?"

"Yes, ma'am," the eurtik replied, bowing his head, even though his boss was behind him. "Do you really believe they are—"

"I'm not sure. Our oral histories only hint that two have ever managed it. Maybe our legend is coming true, which is why the knowledge stays with us."

Looking at the closed door, Simon bobbed his head. "I wouldn't believe that he..." Simon trailed off when he felt the presence behind him vanish.

* * *

Gregory and Yukiko arrived at Gin's before the eighth hour chimed. Indara opened the door, welcoming them as she always did, but her normally stoic expression was replaced with a smile this day.

"The master is waiting for you. You brought bags?"

"They contain our clothes for dinner tonight," Yukiko explained.

"You should hurry. It's almost time to begin," Indara replied just before the eighth bell began to ring.

"Going," the pair said as they hurried down the hall to change.

They slowed when they entered the training room. Another older man was sitting with Gin, sipping tea. Inda stood with her back against the far wall, clearly ready to serve. Moving to their normal spots, the two novices took their seats, bowing to Gin and his guest.

"Today is a half day," Gin said without preamble. "I understand your family is here, Yu. My son has told me they will be here for the week."

"They plan to attend the tournament, then," the other man nodded. "Good. Parents should watch their children aspire to greatness."

"I'm sure they also wish to discuss her training partner and her marriage, which has been delayed due to her being a magi," Gin added.

Yukiko's face went blank, and Gregory struggled to keep a frown from his.

"Yu, you will be training with Inda until our usual break. I will make sure the bath is ready for you to clean up and change, as I'm sure you've brought clothing to change into."

Yukiko bowed, "Thank you, Sensei."

"Inda, take her. Make sure you work her hard today, on both counts."

"As you wish, Master," Inda said, crossing the room.

Yukiko rose gracefully to her feet and followed Inda, leaving the three men alone in the room. Gregory felt like a bug being examined by the man, who had not been introduced yet.

"This is my old friend, Egil. I invited him here to test you. This is selfish of me, but I want to see what you can do, Gregory. What happens next will not help you for the tournament, but I believe you will place in the top eight regardless."

"If that is what you believe, Sensei, then I believe it as well," Gregory said, bowing to Gin.

"Are you sure, Gin?" Egil asked. "I'd hate to harm him before the tournament. The magi place so much weight on them."

"It'll be with the practice naginata, but if an injury occurs, I've some salves and potions that will heal all but the most grievous wounds. "

"Expensive," Egil grunted as he stood up, "but if that's what you want."

Gregory inhaled sharply as Egil stood up. The man was bigger than Gunther, yet moved with more fluidity than anyone he had ever seen.

"Don the masks and take up the training weapons," Gin said as he moved out of the way. "Indara... thank you," he finished as Indara was there to remove the tea things. "Gregory, hold nothing back. Egil will do his best to kill you, which means serious injury even with the practice weapons. You should be aiming to do the same in return."

"I know what you said, Gin, but looking at him, I find it hard to believe." Egil chuckled as he donned a helmet and picked up a wooden naginata.

Gregory got to his feet and went to take a helmet and blade from the racks. Crossing the room, away from Egil, he put the mask on and turned to face the large man. "Thank you for your tutelage, sir," Gregory said, bowing from the waist.

Egil bowed slightly, "Let us see if Gin is losing his grip on reality or if you are truly talented."

"Hold only when I call or before you deliver a finishing blow," Gin said. "Face me, bow." Both men turned to Gin and bowed formally. "Face each other, bow," Gin commanded, and they did. A moment of silence stretched out, with both men adopting ready stances. "FIGHT!"

Egil dashed across the floor, intent on ending the fight quickly. Gregory held his ground, deflecting the first three attacks in quick succession before he countered with his own strike.

Egil blocked the blow and sprang back, settling into a defensive posture. "Good. You can at least follow the simplest of attacks and even know when to counter. Now let's see if you can keep up."

Gregory did not speak, focused entirely on the fight. His body felt like it hummed with eagerness. He darted forward, the naginata spinning as he brought it around in an advanced attack.

Egil laughed as he blocked and countered, only to be deflected in turn. The two of them clashed time and again, neither finding the opening needed to land a blow. Seconds turned into minutes as they moved back and forth across the mat. Minutes began to stretch, and Gregory felt his aether keeping him fresh, banishing the tiredness from his limbs as quickly as it came.

"Damned magi," Egil grunted. "That's the problem when fighting them if they've followed their damned body paths. It's been fun, but I need to end this."

Gregory was forced backward as he deflected and countered the flurry of attacks from Egil. He knew the older man was giving him everything he had. Egil managed to speed up somehow, and Gregory found himself running out of room. His foot came down off the mat, causing him to stumble. The wooden naginata slammed into his helmet hard, making his vision blur as he fell backward.

Egil backed off when Gin called for him to stop. Gregory groaned as his vision swam and multicolored lights danced before him. Pushing the mask off, Gregory rolled to the side and vomited.

"I hit him harder than intended, it seems," Egil said pensively.

"Indara, bring him the potion, please."

Gregory managed to get to his hands and knees, his head still swimming, as he finally stopped vomiting. Panting, he inhaled sharply when a hand was thrust under his nose, the scent from the open vial helping his head settle.

"Drink," Indara said softly as she pressed the vial to his lips.

Gregory used a shaking hand to take the vial and, tilting his head sideways, guzzled the lilac-colored fluid. When he finished drinking, his vision cleared, and he felt shame for having vomited.

"Wipe," Indara said, handing him a damp cloth when she took the vial from him.

Doing as instructed, Gregory wiped his mouth, removing the remnants of his disgrace. "Thank you, Indara."

"Gregory, put your helmet and weapon away and join us," Gin said, not unkindly.

Not looking at the two older men, he did as instructed. Taking his seat, he finally looked up to find them both waiting for him. "I'm sorry, Sensei."

"Surprised you only vomited and didn't pass out," Gin said. "Egil has killed men with that blow before, though he did try to check it."

"I got caught in the moment," Egil admitted, looking a little ashamed. "Gin was right about you. Do you know who I am?"

"A friend of Gin. That is all I know, sir."

"I'm retired now, but I used to be the head of the Han Merchant Exchange's guards. I held that position against everyone who tried to replace me, including a number of magus and master tier magi."

Gregory's jaw dropped, and he just stared at the old man.

"If you had any combat magic and had used it, you would have won easily," Egil said seriously. "I was pressed to the limit of my skill even to hit you. Though you would do better to remember your surroundings in the future. I only won because you tripped. Admittedly, I was aiming for that to happen, but if you had known, you might have been able to find a way out of it."

"I think he's either an old soul or the most gifted natural I've ever encountered," Gin told Egil. "What do you think?"

"You only just gave him a naginata. That isn't a gifted person. He is obviously a reborn soul. All souls are reborn, but few hold on to any of their old talents when they come back. If he takes a naginata into the tournament, he'll win easily, even if they do try to stop him with magic."

"How would I stop them?" Gregory asked, his head spinning as he tried to process what they were saying.

"Training and practice," Egil chuckled darkly. "All magi give away that they are going to use magic. You need to watch them, know when those moments are coming and what they can do, and react accordingly."

"Do you think he'll be able to do what I asked you about?" Gin asked Egil.

"Yes, if he can get them to agree to use the naginata. I doubt it will work more than once or twice, unless their hubris gets the better of them." Egil stared at Gregory hard, "He's just average unarmed or with other weapons?"

"He learns faster than any other student I've trained, including my son and Inda," Gin shrugged, "but yes. If I had three years, I could make him equal to even the emperor's guards. I doubt I'll get that time, though."

"Sensei?" Gregory asked, interrupting the two old men for a moment. "Why would you not have the time? I have three more years of training here."

"Because whatever clan you join will force you to learn from their teachers," Gin said. "They won't want you to learn from another, to start with."

"If I remain without a clan—"

"Do you want a road of pain?" Egil cut him off. "Life without a clan's backing is walking over coals while carrying a great burden."

"The hardest paths make the best magi," Gregory said on reflex, recalling Bishop's words.

Egil began to laugh, "Oh, he'll give them fits if he lives."

"Gregory, what clan are you considering?" Gin asked seriously.

"None. I will go where my... friend goes."

"You're going to follow Yu?" Gin asked.

"We are partners," Gregory replied, meeting the challenging gaze without flinching.

"What clan is she going to join?" Egil asked.

"She hasn't told me," Gregory replied.

"Yu..." Gin sighed, shaking his head. "Let us focus on what the tournament will require. Egil, do you wish to stay?"

"I wouldn't miss it," Egil chuckled.

"Very well. Since Indara is done cleaning, we can continue with training."

CHAPTER 42

Gregory did not use the bath, opting instead to just shower and get dressed. The silk kimono was just about perfect for him. The colors were almost identical to the first one he had had, which had never actually been worn. Breathing deeply and trying to quell his nervousness, Gregory waited for Yukiko to join him.

The door to the parlor opened, bringing him to his feet. The words of greeting caught in his throat as Yukiko entered the room. Her hair was done up in two buns on the sides of her head, held in place by combs shaped like owls. Her silk kimono was in the same colors as his, with a design of white owls in flight amongst bamboo. Small touches of makeup helped accentuate her lips and eyes.

Yukiko came to a stop, her cheeks growing warm, "Greg?"

"Oh, um... you look beautiful, Yuki," Gregory fumbled as he looked away from her, his ears starting to burn.

"You look quite handsome, yourself," Yukiko smiled. "The carriage is waiting for us. Shall we?"

Gregory gave her a tentative smile, "Yes."

As they were leaving, Gin appeared from another room, wearing a traditional formal kimono. Two swords were through the obi at his waist. "I've been asked to attend as well," Gin told them. "Inda, are you ready?"

Appearing from his shadow, Inda replied, "I'm ready, Master." Her kimono was black with white decorative scrollwork along the left sleeve, and she had a wakizashi through her obi.

Gregory figured the crest on the carriage that awaited them had to be the Warlin family crest. It depicted a snow owl perched on a chest. The footman was waiting beside the door, helping them inside before he secured it and jumped onto the back.

Gregory noted that the footman, while carrying no weapons, had heavily scarred hands and his smile was stiff. *Clearly not just a servant, but a guard for the carriage if things go wrong. I wonder where the weapons are hidden?*

Yukiko and Gin made small talk, focused mainly on Gin's son, Lin. Gregory did his best to stay calm, repeatedly telling himself he was going to meet Yukiko's parents as her friend and training partner and nothing more. That helped, but also tore at his heart with each repetition.

The carriage paused at the gates between the inner and lower rings, prompting Gregory to wonder where they were going. Several minutes later, the carriage came to a stop outside of a tavern. Gregory was not sure what to think of the name of the place, Stabled Hunger.

Following the others inside, Gregory's neck started to itch when he saw the thirty armed men sitting and talking casually in the main room. None of the others seemed at all concerned, though; in fact, Gin headed for a middle-aged man, who stood up smiling.

"Father," the man said, bowing to Gin and then embracing the old man. "It is good to see you."

"I see you haven't gone soft. Good," Gin said stiffly as he slapped Lin hard on the back, the lacquered metal of Lin's armor ringing from the hit.

"Before we get started, Father," Lin said, turning to Yukiko. "Yu, your parents are in the private room. Jento will show you the way." One of the other men rose to his feet and bowed.

"Thank you, Lin," Yukiko smiled. "Greg, if you—"

"Yu, your parents wish to see you alone first," Lin said, cutting her off. "We will keep your... *friend* company until he is sent for."

Yukiko went still, staring hard at Lin for a long moment. "I see. Very well, he is in your care. Greg, please give me a few moments with my parents. It shouldn't be long."

"Take your time, Yuki," Gregory said. Thirty pairs of eyes focused on him when he used his nickname for her. Feeling the pressure of those gazes, Gregory smiled, "I'll be in good hands."

Yukiko looked around the room and everyone looked away as she turned her gaze to them. "I will try to make it brief." Yukiko followed Jento, leaving Gregory with the guards.

"Greg, is it?" Lin asked bluntly, glaring at Gregory.

"Gregory Pettit, sir."

"What is your relationship with our Yu?"

"She is my friend and training partner, sir. I met her on our first day in the academy, and we have been beside each other every day since."

"You think you're her equal?" Lin asked, moving to stand a few feet in front of Gregory.

"I'm not sure, but she wishes for me to be and I'm doing my best to make it happen."

"Lin," Gin said from off to the side, in an idle tone, "did you bring any training blades?"

Gregory's eyes went to Gin, confused by the question, but he did not say anything.

"Of course. We'll still be training, even while here."

"Pick five men. Give them any weapon you want, give him a naginata, and see for yourself if he is worthy of standing beside her."

Lin frowned, turning to his father with a searching gaze. "You can't possibly think a novice can—"

"Do it," Gin said simply, but the words carried steel.

"I won't unless he agrees. Yu would be unhappy if he gets hurt."

Gregory felt that moment of divergence, and two paths before him. In one, he declined, and the guards refused to accept him as worthy of Yukiko, regarding him with disdain that Yukiko's parents eventually echoed. The other showed him standing, bleeding but unbeaten amidst almost a dozen armored guards. Bowing his head, Gregory silently asked Yukiko to forgive him. "I'll accept."

The room had been quiet before, but went dead silent when he spoke. Ten men got to their feet, clamoring to be the ones to fight him and breaking the silence. Lin looked from Gregory to Gin with a questioning gaze for a few heartbeats before he nodded. "Fine. But we'll make it all ten, unless you wish to retract your bravado."

Gregory looked at each of the ten men, all of whom seemed personally affronted. "They must all wield swords, and I, a naginata. If that is acceptable, then yes."

"I'd prefer it if you didn't damage my business," a stocky man said, coming down the hall toward them with a fast gait. "Use the yard out back if you're going to do this. I'll send for a healer, too, but I'm not paying for them."

"I'll give five thousand vela to anyone who can stop him," Gin said. "However, you must each give up five hundred if you lose."

Lin snorted, "Father, you go too far. I'll pay their losses. I'll give you a thousand vela each if they are all defeated, but only then."

"Accepted," Gin said. "The money will go to him, not to me."

Everyone in the room was now watching intently and trying to figure out the trick. Lin laughed, "Fine, but no aether is to be used to injure my men."

"Agreed," Gin replied. "Gregory, this is your chance."

Taking a deep breath, Gregory bowed to Gin. "I am indebted, sir. Please help me explain it to Yuki later."

Gin chuckled, "Fair. I will take the blame for this."

"Hintle, go get blades for you and him," Lin snapped. "Everyone not fighting stays here; we are still on duty."

Those not fighting grumbled but took their seats while the ten men chosen to fight Gregory went for the door. Gregory shook his head, trying to figure out how it had all spiraled this quickly. With Gin's backing and his vision of what the future might be, he felt that it was at least possible for him to succeed.

Gregory found himself in a courtyard behind the tavern. Each of the men fighting him had taken a wooden sword, while Lin held a practice naginata in his hand, which he offered to Gregory. Gin came out behind Gregory with Inda trailing him.

"Rules?" Gin asked as Gregory took the weapon from Lin.

"If you get hit hard enough in a place that a real weapon would damage, you must react accordingly, so the 'loss' of arms or legs is possible. Any direct hit to the head means death. No offensive aether is allowed, either."

Gregory stretched to make sure he was limber, but also to find the extent of his movement in the silks. Satisfied that he was not going to be hindered, he faced the rough semi-circle of men, taking the basic ready stance.

"Don't kill him," Lin told his men. "Yu will be beyond upset if that happens, but since a healer is on the way, you can have some fun."

"I'd ask the same, Gregory, but don't let the possibility hinder you, either. I'll make reparations if things go too far," Gin told him.

"Master Gin, you go too far," one of the men snapped, rushing forward ahead of the others.

Gregory barely moved, countering the attack with ease. The wooden blade of his naginata slapped the side of the man's head and he dropped to the ground, groaning. Gregory stayed where he was, focused on the remaining nine, who all looked a bit more serious now that one of them was already gone.

"We have numbers, at least," one man said. "We can overwhelm him."

Gregory's hands shifted on the haft of the naginata as he waited for them. *If they're out of synch, I can shift between them, but if they come as a cohesive unit, I'll lose.*

The men started forward in step with each other and Gin grinned. "So you're all aware, he fought Egil to a standstill earlier."

The men looked at each other, uncertainty now on their faces. They fell out of step, and Gregory took that opportunity to attack. The naginata spun as it shot forward and three of the men fell before the others even knew what was happening. Defending as they retreated, the six remaining men no longer looked relaxed.

"Father, you could have mentioned that earlier," Lin sighed. "We might have skipped this if you had."

"No. Doubt about his ability to stand beside Yu would have remained. He's taken out four of your men in less than a minute and hasn't been touched yet. This was needed for him to be accepted by you and your men."

"Did he use aether against Egil?"

"He doesn't know what his magic is," Gin chuckled. "Once he finds out, he'll be in a tier all his own."

Gregory half-heard the conversation as he pressed the attack on the remaining six. They spread out, trying to circle him and Gregory was forced to give some ground to keep them from getting behind him. The next minute took all of his concentration, keeping track of his opponents and the battlefield. The six fell one by one, though the last two managed to injure him before they fell. Using the haft of the training weapon, Gregory remained standing over the fallen. His kimono was askew and blood dripped from his arm where a strike had opened a gash.

"The winner is Gregory Pettit," Gin said simply.

The street gate opened and a young woman with a horse tail and ears led a grumpy-looking woman into the yard. "Oh... my," the young woman gasped upon seeing the ten men slowly pushing themselves upright.

"Goodness, all of you stay down until I look at you," the healer said as she rushed forward. "What kind of foolishness happened here?"

"Training," Lin said shortly.

Gin motioned Gregory over and had Inda wrap his arm in a bandage coated with some green paste. Once she finished, she knelt and pushed his kimono and pants out of her way to see his knee, which was already purpling. Taking a bottle from her belt pouch, she poured a bit of light green liquid onto her hand and spread it over his knee. Gregory hissed as he felt his knee pop, but a moment later, the pain vanished and he exhaled in relief.

"He is fine, Master," Inda declared as she got to her feet and wiped her hands with a cloth.

"Lin, they are calling for him," another guard said, sticking his head out the door. The guard's mouth fell open when he saw his friends being treated and Gregory standing there seemingly unharmed.

"Understood," Lin said. "You should take a moment to repair your outfit," he directed at Gregory. "I'll make sure the vela is gathered before you leave today."

"Is there a place for me to dress?" Gregory asked.

"If you'll follow me, sir," the young woman said, her tail flicking in agitation.

She led him to a small room with a cot in one corner. Gregory closed the door and made what repairs he could to his kimono. When he came out again, Lin and the young woman were waiting. The woman ducked into the room while Lin led him down the hall to a set of sliding double doors.

Knocking once, Lin opened them and stepped aside. "Sir, your guest, Gregory Pettit."

CHAPTER 43

Gregory entered the room to see a stern-looking man watching him with inscrutable eyes. Beside him sat a smiling woman who strongly resembled Yukiko, but with graceful age wrinkles at the corners of her light blue eyes. Yukiko had her back to him, her shoulders stiff. "It is an honor to meet you, mister and madam Warlin. I'm Gregory Pettit, Yukiko's friend." Gregory's words were stiff and formal, exactly as he felt the moment needed.

"Come, sit," Yukiko's mother said with a smile. "Our daughter has been telling us about you."

Gregory moved to take the seat beside Yukiko. "Thank you," he said, bowing his head.

Hao Warlin did not smile as Gregory sat. "Yu has said you've been at her side every waking moment since she came to the academy. How did that come to be?"

The oppressive weight brought to bear by a concerned father settled over Gregory as he met Hao's dark brown eyes. "I saw her when we went to have our magic tested. I caught her when she fell. She approached me later that night as I returned to my room, and we struck up a friendly conversation. The next morning, I helped her get away from two overeager novices and again we started talking. We've been training side by side every day since then."

"It matches her tale, though with less praise for your actions than Yu gave us," Yukiko's mother mused with a knowing smile. "Where are our manners, dear?" she said, giving Hao a pointed look before facing Gregory. "I am Yoo-jin Warlin, and my husband is Hao Warlin. It is a pleasure to meet a friend of our daughter."

"Jin," Hao sighed. "We need to—"

"Nonsense," Yoo-jin cut him off. "Can you not see how uncomfortable you are making our Yu? We can just ask simple questions. There is no call to treat him like a debtor coming to ask for more time."

Hao's jaw tightened, but he did not gainsay his wife. "Gregory, tell us what your days with Yu are like, won't you?"

Gregory shot a glance at Yukiko. She did not look at him, sitting still and serene like a lake during winter. Not seeing any hint of what he should do, he gave them the flat truth of the matter, describing their days at the academy as well as their days off.

"Yes, I owe Gin a considerable sum," Hao said tightly. "My daughter didn't even try to negotiate the price."

"We needed his tutelage," Yukiko said suddenly. "I'm sure he'll barter with you, Father."

"I would pay any price for you, as you well know, Yu. I'm not sure how I ended up paying for your... *friend*." The last word was punctuated by Hao's frown.

"I owe him a debt, and this is but the very tip of that debt," Yukiko said, sounding as if she had already said the phrase often.

"I would like to hear more about what he is doing to warrant such repayment," Yoo-jin said gently. "She hasn't told us much, and your description of your studying didn't help in that regard," she told Gregory.

"How much do you know about magi and the paths to train?" Gregory asked.

"Evan, please," Yoo-jin asked. A person Gregory had not been able to see until then stepped away from the wall behind her.

The person's skin went from the same color and texture of the wall to normal, save that his eyes were purple. "Mistress, the magi of the empire believe that the way to build one's aether is by focusing on specific paths; body, mind, or spirit. Few in their history have managed to walk two paths at once, though among those who study the empire, it is thought that the emperor himself has managed to combine all three. Current thought in the empire is that it is foolish and a waste to attempt to walk more than a single path and it's practically impossible to do so, in their estimation."

"That is what we know," Yoo-jin said simply.

"Evan isn't a magi from the empire is he? He's like Inda," Gregory asked. No one replied, but Yoo-jin's smile grew at his question. "Very well— it is possible to walk more than a single path. Yuki and I are doing so."

Hao's eye twitched when Gregory used his nickname for Yukiko. "Oh? And you've had tangible results?"

"We have," Yukiko answered before Gregory could. "What is me being able to train twice as well as any other magi worth, Father?"

Hao leaned back, staring at his daughter for a long moment. "I sense a trap in those words. Good. You haven't forgotten everything I taught you."

"I ask that you answer the question, Father."

Yoo-jin sighed, "She is as stubborn as you, dear. If you do not answer, she'll stop cooperating, as well."

"Very well. I'm going to remove the familial aspect, though. If you were a normal magi, who I had a vested interest in..." Hao paused as he looked up at the ceiling for a few moments. "I'd consider it worth about a tenth of my proceeds for the year if they were under contract for at least five."

Yoo-jin nodded, "I agree. That changes since it is our daughter, though; it becomes worth more."

Yukiko smiled broadly, "This cannot leave the room. It would be detrimental to me if it became known." Seeing her parent's interest and Evan fading back against the wall, she looked over her shoulder to Lin, who nodded. "Very well. Gregory isn't just training with me on two paths, but all three. Without him, I would never have touched two, much less all three paths." Seeing both of her parents lean back with furrowed brows, she continued, "Now what is that worth, Father?"

Minutes went by before Hao spoke again, "How? How is he specifically tied to this?"

"He was the one who forced me to accept that it could be done. He's led the way for every exercise and attempt to push the boundaries. I would be average and either completely isolated, or forced into a clan like the Eternal Flame, if not for Gregory."

"Do you concur with her view?" Yoo-jin asked Gregory.

"Not exactly. Yuki believes in me more than I do. I did tell her it was possible and asked her to join me in attempting it, but she has been just as focused on the goal as I have been."

"Modesty is good, but when dealing with merchants, it can be a fatal flaw," Yoo-jin told him. "Can it be proven in any way?"

"It'll become clearer as the year passes. We're increasing our ranking faster than the other novices," Yukiko said, pulling out her medallion to show them. "This is the highest circle anyone has reached in the novices to this point, but many were only a single circle back when the year began. We were two and three rings back. Before the end of the year, we will have passed through the novice rings and begun on the apprentice rings. We've found a way for body and spirit to work in unison, and we'll be working on folding the mind path in next."

Hao stared at the medallion, "By the end of the year? You are sure?"

"Yes."

"Hmm," Hao nodded. "Very well. The cost of Gin's tutelage is far outweighed by this. And so much more. You have been correct in your assessment, Yu. If you are going to stand out that far, though, you will become a target, will you not?"

"Yes. After this tournament, the clans choose which novices to accept. Greg and I have not chosen a clan. You know of the great clans and why I won't choose any of them. The lesser clans would get overpowered and bow to them if we joined one of them. That leaves me lacking in many ways. Some can be fixed by the proper application of vela, but others cannot."

"Gregory, will you not be joining a clan?" Yoo-jin asked.

Asked the question flatly, Gregory answered truthfully, "I will go where Yuki goes."

Yukiko turned on him, her mouth opening and closing, clearly lost. "Is... is that why... you haven't chosen?"

"Yes. We are partners. We agreed, and we can't continue to be so if you and I go different ways."

"Greg," she grabbed his forearm. Gregory hissed in pain as she squeezed the wound there. "What?" Feeling the bandage under his kimono sleeve, she pushed it out of the way, exposing the bandage. Her face went white, then red in anger, and her chair shot backward as she spun on Lin. "What is this?"

Lin stiffened in the face of her anger. "Yu, I can—"

"No evading, Lin. Why is he injured? He was in perfect health when we arrived. Now his arm is bandaged." Looking back at Gregory, she scrutinized his clothing, letting Gregory see how serious she was, before she spun back to Lin. "His silks are marred as well. What did you do to him while I was speaking to my parents?"

Lin did not back down, instead pressing into her verbal attack. "Nothing to concern the young miss. He hasn't complained about anything. You seem to be trying to make an issue out of nothing."

Yukiko took a step forward, her jaw set, "*Nothing*? He is injured. When is it *nothing* if a guest of ours becomes *injured*? I left him in your care, and now he is injured and his clothing is damaged."

A knock on the door made her pause, and it opened to reveal Gin. "Excuse this old man, but I think I need to step in here."

Yukiko's ire went from Lin to Gin without dimming in the least. "What did you do, Gin?"

"An object lesson in who is fit to stand beside you," Gin said steadily as he shut the door behind him. "He fought ten of the guards." He paused, looking intently at Hao and Yoo-jin in turn. "He defeated all of them, and not one-on-one, either. He had only a practice naginata in his hands and no armor while they had their armor and practice swords. His knee was injured and his arm. His knee is healed already, and his arm will be by the end of the day."

Yukiko worked to conceal her astonishment, her emotions fluctuating wildly.

Hao spoke into that moment, "Bested all of them?"

"Earlier today, he fought Egil to a standstill with a naginata," Gin said. "Gregory is without a doubt among the best wielders of that weapon in the empire at this time, and in a few years, he will eclipse all others."

"What did Egil have to say?" Yoo-jin asked curiously.

"He concurred with my assessment," Gin replied. "Considering the restrictions placed by the academy, it is my opinion that Gregory is the best person to have at Yu's side. He will keep her safe and do everything he can to protect her. I'm willing to go so far as to say that he is as worried for her safety as either of you are."

"Yuki," Gregory said softly, "everything is fine. You've hurt me worse than this during training, and I'm as equally at fault. I agreed to the match in the yard. If you are going to chastise him, you must include me, too."

"I see." Yukiko's shoulders slumped, "You're really okay?"

"Not entirely. I'm worried for you."

With her cheeks flushed, Yukiko returned to her seat, not meeting his gaze. "I'm sorry for my outburst. It is wrong of me to act in such a way."

"Yu, we should leave your father and the others here. We need to speak privately concerning the matter of betrothal," Yoo-jin said, rising to her feet. Her face and tone were carefully neutral.

Yukiko's face froze and the color drained from it. "Yes, Mother." Rising from her seat, Yukiko looked down at Gregory, her eyes glistening with unshed tears. "Greg... I am sorry."

Gregory thought hard, trying to figure out what she could mean. Watching the door close behind Yukiko and her mother, he felt his heart clench as understanding came to him.

"Hmm. Yes. Talks," Hao said gruffly.

Gregory closed his eyes, taking a deep breath before he turned back to Hao. When Gin and Lin took seats beside Hao at the table, Gregory wondered exactly what was coming.

"Yukiko has been betrothed for nearly a decade," Hao said, his expression serious. "Her betrothed is Dan Yulin, the heir to the Yulin Merchant empire in Buldoun. Has she mentioned this to you?"

"She has told me repeatedly that she is betrothed, sir. Not to who, nor any other specific."

"What of you?" Lin cut in. "Where do you come from? Who are your parents? Do you have a betrothed?"

"I come from Alturis. My mother died when I was a child and my father is currently a servant to the village. There is no one waiting for me," Gregory replied, feeling his hopes diminishing with each word.

"A fringer with no family of note," Hao said flatly.

Gregory stiffened at the words. "Do only those born into privilege and power have substance in your eyes?" Gregory asked harshly without thinking.

Hao's eyes narrowed, "My daughter is the only thing besides my wife that matters in the world. All of my accomplishments are to ensure they are well cared for and safe. Evan was a street rat, and he is one of my most trusted employees."

"Then why can't a fringer be as trusted?" Gregory asked bluntly.

"He has a point, Hao," Gin nodded. "I've worked with them every week, and I can say that he has shown no inclination to tarnish Yu."

"Ten men," Lin added. "Not trash, either, but my men. Father and myself would be hard pressed to do as much, and to be standing at the end with only two wounds? He's by far better able to protect her than anything we can arrange for her inside the walls of the magi."

Hao looked thoughtful for a long moment. "You both raise valid points. I need to seek my wife's council before—"

"We have returned," Yoo-jin said as she came into the room. "Has anything drastic occurred?"

"No," Hao said. "I was about to seek your council, dear one."

"Ah, a good idea. Step out of the room with me. Evan, Lin, Gin, all of you come as well," Yoo-jin said as she moved to stand beside the door. Yukiko came into the room, her head down.

Gregory wondered what was happening, but could not ask any questions before everyone was gone, leaving him alone with Yukiko. He went to her, coming to a stop a few feet from her. "Yuki, are you okay?" he asked when she stayed by the door, her face hidden from him.

"I am not sure. I've had news about my betrothal."

Gregory's heart clenched, his final few hopes falling away. "Oh. I'm sure you will be happy. No man could have you as a wife and not feel as if the world smiles upon him."

"No man?" Yukiko said softly, her voice hitching. "I have one question that I need an honest answer to, Greg. Will you do that for me?"

"I'll always be honest with you, Yuki."

"If I asked you to flee with me, to run from this place, leaving behind the academy, to spirit me into the northern wilds, would you?"

Gregory inhaled sharply, unsure if he was hearing her right or if this was a test. Shaking his head, he did as he had promised and answered honestly. "I want to, Yuki. My dream of being a magi has met another dream and I've found it to be the lesser of the two. I can't, though; it would destroy your family and I know you love them. I can't cause you that pain."

"If not for my betrothal... would you..." Yukiko tried to ask the question she wanted the answer to, but she could not bring the right words forth.

"Yes. No price would be too high," Gregory said, his throat dry as he forced the words out. "I know that it—"

Yukiko was suddenly in his arms, her soft lips on his. Gregory pulled her tightly to him and returned the kiss, as he had time and again in his dreams over the last few months.

Breathing fast when the kiss ended, Gregory stared into Yukiko's cyan eyes with fear and hope. "Yuki?"

"My betrothal was absolved," Yukiko whispered. "Being married to a 'magi of the empire' was too much for him. I can accept my heart now." Leaning forward, she kissed him again, gently, sweetly, hopeful.

Gregory returned the kiss in equal measure, his heart pounding as he felt his dreams burst forth into reality. *If this is a dream, please, Aether, let me die before I wake.*

Gregory and Yukiko stopped kissing, but did not step away from each other when the door opened, knowing they had already been seen. "It seems you're right again, dear one," Hao sighed.

"It was painfully obvious to me, but men can be slow to see," Yoo-jin smiled. "I thought she was going to be upset by my news, but it turns out our little girl has turned out to be just like me. She found her heart all on her own and only tried denying it for our sake."

"Your father hated me for years," Hao said, glaring at Gregory. "I should keep that tradition alive." His lips trembled as he fought to keep a smile off them.

"Father," Yukiko sighed, "no."

"It seems we are going from one betrothal to another," Yoo-jin said, looking at Gregory. "I do take it that you would be amenable to that?"

"I have no bride price," Gregory hated to say it, but he did.

"Teaching her how to combine all three paths is bride price enough," Yoo-jin smiled. "She will be unique, alongside you, in that regard."

"I told you that we would be equal partners," Yukiko whispered.

Gregory chuckled, "I could never have hoped that this is what you had in mind."

"We shall have the official announcement dinner on the last night of the tournament," Hao said. "I trust you to do what is right and proper, Gregory."

Releasing Yukiko, who he had been holding the entire time, he bowed to Hao. "Yes, Father."

Yoo-jin laughed loudly at that, "Oh, he will fit in fine."

Hao blinked, shaking his head. "I can feel more hairs turning gray already."

CHAPTER 44

T hird bell woke Gregory from his dreamless sleep. Moving on auto-pilot, he got dressed and ready for the day. Opening the door, he met Yukiko, who was leaving her room at the same time. "Morning, Yuki," he said with a soft smile on his lips, memories of the day before flooding his mind.

"Morning, Greg," Yukiko beamed at him. Fidgeting, she asked the question that had plagued her all night, "You do mean it, yes?"

Gregory leaned in and kissed her cheek, "Yes. Or do you have second thou—"

Yukiko kissed him full on the lips, silencing him. She stepped back quickly, her cheeks burning. "Sorry. It doesn't do for public displays of affection, especially not before the announcement." She turned to the stairs, "It's just been so difficult not accepting my feelings for the last five months. I want to experience everything now, now that I can."

Gregory had fallen into step with her after a second of motionless shock. "Your father asked me to do what is right, Yuki. As much as I would love to spend the days secluded with you, we have goals to meet."

"Yes. I'm doing my best, dea... Greg," Yukiko coughed and corrected herself.

"Things will be easier after the tournament," Gregory said. "Six days of fighting, then the normal day off. The first three days will be difficult; three fights a day to find out who will advance to the top eight spots, then a single fight each day to advance again."

"Father will be meeting with Magus Han today, and Mother will be viewing the dormitory," Yukiko said as they put on their outdoor shoes. "We have to be at the training hall by seventh bell to find out when our bouts are and against whom."

"Morning, Novices," Dia said as they left the dormitory. "I shouldn't be surprised that you're awake this early, but with the tournament, I thought you might take the morning off."

"No reason to shift our usual routine," Gregory said.

"My mother will be by after my bouts today," Yukiko told Dia. "She is quite eager to see the rooms."

Dia nodded, "I'll be dealing with a number of visitors over the next few days. I look forward to meeting her. Not many have treated my staff as fairly as you have."

"We'll see you later, Keeper," Gregory said, bowing his head to her.

"Good day, and good luck," Dia replied, blowing a smoke ring.

"Did she seem happier than normal to you?" Gregory asked as they walked to the mess hall.

"A bit. Maybe it's the thought of getting rid of so many novices."

Gregory snorted, "Good point. The dormitory will be much quieter with most of the class gone off to the clans. I'm sure that will make her and the staff happier."

Gregory and Yukiko smiled and waved back at the eurtiks who greeted them. "Morning, Novices. Today is a big day for you," Ravol grinned.

"First day of the tournament," Gregory agreed.

"I believe you'll pass without trouble," Zenim said.

"He has a few bets going that you'll make it to the top eight," Steva chuckled. "We all do, actually."

"Oh? Did you get good odds?" Yukiko asked.

"Forty-to-one," Steva grinned. "We have all our free coin on you two."

Gregory frowned, "That's a lot of responsibility." His smile came back as he continued, "We'll manage it, though."

"We thank you," Velma told him, touching his medallion as she always did, then handing him his bagged snack. "Winning these bets will let us help our families."

"Quilet is betting on you, too," Steva said, motioning to the otter waving from the cleaning area.

"We plan to finish with the top spots," Yukiko said. "Once you have your winnings, use some of them, not all, to bet on us to manage that."

"I will," Velma as she touched Yukiko's medallion and gave her the bagged snack.

"We all will," Steva added. "No other novices have shown your level of dedication this year or any other I've been here."

"We'll do our best," Gregory told them as he went to get some tea.

"You won't be able to watch any of the bouts, will you?"

"No. We are here from second bell until twentieth bell," Velma replied to Yukiko. "We will be getting updates about the novices we like and dislike the most, though."

"We'll do our best not to disappoint," Yukiko said as she went to get her drink and join Gregory.

* * *

Rafiq greeted them when they entered the archive, "Morning to you both. The scrolls will be brought to your table. We weren't sure if you would be in today or not."

"That's fine, thank you," Gregory replied with a bow of his head.

"Are you both prepared for today?" Rafiq asked them.

"As much as we can be," Yukiko replied.

"I see. Let me not delay you further," Rafiq said. "I'll have it brought right over."

"Thank you," they said in unison, heading for the back.

Once they had taken their seats, Yukiko pulled out some paper and charcoal pencils, "Father gave me these last night before we left. Want to try one?"

"Magi Squares?" Gregory asked, seeing them. "Yes, I'd like to try one."

The two of them sat there working on the puzzles, not stopping when an archivist brought scrolls for them. Yukiko nodded a few minutes later as she set hers aside, wiping her hands on a cloth before she touched the scroll. Gregory finished a few minutes after that, frowning. He had guessed wrong three times during his and it bothered him. Wiping his hands off, he set aside the paper and picked up the scroll.

Sixth bell caused them both to stop reading. Gregory pinched the bridge of his nose, trying to relieve some of the tension building there. "This is harder to understand than anything else I've read in the archive. I know the words, but the meaning behind them is taking me longer to grasp."

"It isn't easy. The mind path will be hard," Yukiko agreed as she picked up her answers. "We can use wax tablets to erase these, then exchange them tomorrow."

"I'll need to get a wax tablet, then," Gregory said. "I never thought I would need one."

"I'll bring mine over tonight," Yukiko said as she gathered her things. "We can work on a few more then."

"Maybe I'll improve," Gregory said as he got his things put away. "Now, a stroll to the training hall to see what they have in store for us."

"Unless we're unlucky and have to face one of the better students right away, we should be fine for this round."

"True," Gregory smiled. "The fights don't start until the eighth bell, so we'll have some time before our bouts, even if we are in the first few."

"Mother and Father should be here just after seventh bell," Yukiko said. "We should greet them before the fights."

"Yes, and if we end up in different arenas, they should watch you."

"I'm sure they'll send Lin to watch your fights, at the very least," Yukiko said.

"Good day, Novices," Rafiq smiled at them as they were leaving the archive, "and good luck with your bouts today."

"Thank you," they replied, bowing to him.

Rafiq watched them go and wished he had been one of those chosen to watch the tournament. He stiffened when he felt a cold breeze behind him, "Chief, did you require something?"

"Yes," Sarinia replied. "I will be leaving shortly to sit with the others in the main arena. The archive is in your hands until I return. They are very studious, are they not?"

"Every day, without fail," Rafiq nodded. "They were working on Magi Squares when their scrolls were delivered."

"Yes, they have a thirst to learn," Sarinia smiled. "I have hopes for them, but first to see if they can reach the top eight. I heard a rumor that they are being trained by Armsmaster Gin Watashi. I thought he had stopped taking students, but it seems he has ties to Novice Warlin."

"That gives them a chance to make it, then," Rafiq nodded. "Not many armsmasters not in the employ of the empire or the clans."

"We shall see. Do make sure that any visitors are properly respectful to the archive. Throw them out if needed, and I shall deal with the repercussions."

"As you require, Chief."

* * *

While they walked to the training hall, they saw many other novices hurrying to the same place. "Need to hold your trump card until the final eight," Gregory mentioned during a moment when no one else was nearby.

"I intend to," Yukiko agreed. "Don't discount anyone, even if they've lost every other fight. They might have a chip on their shoulder, or they might have been bribed to injure you badly enough to keep you out of the final eight."

"I'll stay on my toes."

They arrived only a few minutes before the announcements would start and stayed toward the back of the crowd of novices. A large notice board had been set up outside the training hall, but nothing was hung on it. Gregory spotted Nick talking to Jason, Michelle, and his other associates. Hayworth and his friends were on the other side of the crowd, looking self-important.

"We took the long way," Yukiko murmured.

"Wanted to avoid any needless conflicts and didn't want to give Nick even more time to talk to us."

Gregory returned Nick's wave just as Magus Paul came out of the hall with four other cyan-robed magi behind him. Seventh bell chimed as the magi took up positions in front of the board.

"Novices, welcome to the mid-tournament. The next several days will set the ranking order of your class. Over the next three days, you will each face three of your peers in individual combat. The final eight will be chosen by the council if there are any ties in the standings. The match ups will be posted on a daily basis. On the fourth day, those who advanced to the final eight will be facing each other. The winners of those matches will go on to fight again the next day, with the two winners facing each other on the final day of the tournament. Outside of the bouts, your days are your own. If you fail to appear for your fight, you forfeit the match. The rules are simple: do your best not to kill your opponent, and no weapons are allowed. Any questions?"

"If we accidentally use too much aether or strike too hard and our classmate dies, what happens?" a random novice asked.

"They will be seen by the healer, and hopefully we can save them. We understand that when you are fighting, accidents sometimes happen. It is why each of you was told that not everyone graduates. You have two tournaments this year, plus any challenges you might face. The empire only wants the strongest of you. Make sure you are among that number."

When no one else had any questions, Paul nodded and turned to the board. He posted five sheets of paper, each headed with the name of one of the arenas and showing the matches scheduled there for that day. "There you are. Find your places, and may Aether guide you to victory."

Gregory and Yukiko hung back as the rest of the class pressed forward to see the board. Stepping back to give themselves room, Gregory spoke softly, "If it comes down to risking death or taking the loss—"

"The same goes for you," Yukiko cut him off. "Can't risk my heart now that I've found him."

Gregory smiled, nearly falling into her cyan gaze before quickly looking away to see if anyone had noticed. "Have to be careful around you or I'll give it away before the last day of the tournament."

Yukiko's lips turned up at the corners as she looked at the board, "Yes. It is difficult for me, too."

Gregory and Yukiko edged forward as the crowd abated. "Greg, Yukiko," Nick called to them, having been waiting for them. "Seems we won't be facing each other the first day, though Jason and Michelle have to face off. Do your best; the Eternal Flame has a reputation to maintain."

"We will win all our bouts today," Gregory said. "I just have to find out where and when I fight."

"See you later," Nick said, going to Michelle and speaking quietly to her.

"Main arena, both of us," Yukiko told him, studying the schedules. "The first fight in that arena at eighth bell is the two of us against each other."

Gregory shook his head, "The universe seems to be laughing at us."

"No holding back. We both need to fight to win," Yukiko said seriously.

Gregory nodded, "Our second set of matches?"

"I fight Fureno after ninth bell, and you fight Clement at tenth bell. He's one of Hayworth's friends, part of the group that accosted me on our first day here. I fight Clement at eleventh bell, and at four-teenth bell, you'll fight one of the undertrained novices who isn't in our other classes."

"Careful with Fureno. He's been hanging onto Nick's coattails, so he might have a trick or two up his sleeve."

"The same goes for Clement," Yukiko said as they headed toward the main arena.

"Meet your parents at the arena?" Gregory asked, changing the subject.

"That is what we agreed on. They should be there shortly, as the gates opened at seventh bell."

CHAPTER 45

Gregory tried to quell the unhappiness he felt as he gazed at Yukiko across the arena from him. Yukiko's parents had been shocked and disappointed that their first fight was against each other, but understood they had no recourse. Looking to the reserved box for the academy council, Gregory noted Master Damon, the black panther eurtik who worked at the archive, a number of other masters, and three grandmasters.

Magus Paul stood in the middle of the arena, motioning them both to him. Gregory steeled himself and moved to the Magus. "We will begin when the eighth bell chimes," he told them. "Follow my instructions and begin when I tell you to fight."

"Yes, sir," they answered together.

A moment later, the eighth bell chimed and Paul cleared his throat, holding up a gently glowing bronze circle. "Ladies and gentlemen, today we see what our novices have learned thus far. This is their first test of skill against their peers. This tournament shall determine which novices have grown strong, and which are lacking." Paul's voice carried easily to the audience seated around the arena, though it was not overbearing to Yukiko and Gregory. "We are joined by the heads of the academy," Paul bowed to the biggest box. "We hope our novices can show you something worth your time."

Paul stepped back a few paces and put the circle into his pouch. "Novices, face the boxes and bow." Once they had done as instructed, Paul spoke again, "Novices, face me and bow." When they had done that, he inclined his head to them. "Now face each other and bow." Once they had done so, Paul moved back a few more feet. "On my signal, begin. Do not stop unless your opponent is unconscious, surrenders, or I tell you to."

Gregory set himself into the defensive stance Yukiko had taught him, and she did the same. The two of them did their best to set aside their feelings, trying to concentrate on the bout. Taking a deep breath, Gregory felt calmness settle over him.

"Fight!" Paul shouted.

Yukiko was the first to move and she closed the distance quickly. A flurry of strikes forced Gregory to focus on defense, but he smiled when he realized she was following their normal sparring routine. As she slowed, he countered and began to drive her back.

The two of them flowed from attack to defense and back without slowing. To the crowd, it looked as if they were evenly matched. Both backed away at the same time, small smiles on their lips.

"Ready?" Yukiko asked now that they had warmed up.

Extending a hand, Gregory gestured her forward, his stance shifting to one Gin had taught him over the last few months. Yukiko smiled as she advanced, ready for the real fight to begin.

Yukiko held a real edge in speed and flexibility over him, allowing her to land far more strikes than he did. Gregory's counters, when they landed, made Yukiko back off before reengaging with him.

Neither wanted to significantly harm the other, but they both wanted to win, making the fight stretch longer than it should have. Gregory found his moment, managing to stagger Yukiko significantly enough that she dropped to a knee. Gregory tried to follow up and take advantage, but found himself abruptly off balance as his legs failed to move. A glance down showed the shadows pooled around his legs had deepened and were binding him. Jerking his head up, he was just in time to see Yukiko's foot coming at him.

Grunting as he went over backward, Gregory shook his head, trying to push himself back to his feet. He was slammed back to the ground by Yukiko landing on his hips, followed by a flurry of hand and elbow strikes to his face. Pulling his arms in, he covered his bleeding face.

Yukiko kept hammering at him, so Gregory was left with little other choice but to trade pain for survival. Jerking his upper body up, he uncovered his face and hugged Yukiko to him. His nose became a bright point of pain as Yukiko flattened it with an elbow, but he wrapped his arms around her and pulled her tightly to his chest. Yukiko squirmed against him, but Gregory held her tight, getting his feet flat to the ground and shoving. As they turned, Gregory went from clenching Yukiko to pushing her away, which forced them apart.

Getting back to his feet with blood dripping from his nose, Gregory met Yukiko's determined gaze and gave her a grudging nod, remembering that they had agreed to fight to win. Yukiko returned the nod and set her feet, ready to attack again.

Their next exchange of blows ended up being the last. Yukiko failed to block one of Gregory's strikes, and his open palm slammed into the spot directly under her ribs. She gasped as her legs buckled, unable to get the air she needed. Gregory caught her, slipping behind her as he did.

"Tap, Yuki," he whispered. "I don't want to go further."

Yukiko, feeling his arm go under her chin, slapped the ground three times.

"Hold! Warlin forfeits," Paul declared loudly.

Removing his arm, he stayed behind her, his leg holding her upright as she struggled to get her breath back. Standing slowly so as not to disturb her, Gregory bowed to Paul.

Yukiko managed to catch her breath. "You win," she wheezed.

"Face the box and bow," Paul told Gregory.

Gregory eased Yukiko to the side carefully so she would not fall, then turned to the boxes holding the important guests and bowed to them. When he stood back up, Yukiko was getting to her feet. Bowing to Yukiko, he gave her a worried smile.

Yukiko bowed her head, "Forgive me, but I don't wish to flex that far."

"Your match is over. Please leave the arena," Paul told them. "Be ready for your next bouts."

Gregory and Yukiko walked away from each other and headed for the doors, neither looking back as they left the arena floor. Gregory walked quickly, wanting to make sure she was okay. Yukiko walked more slowly, not wanting to face Gregory after battering his face so much.

When he got to the waiting area under the arena proper, Gregory's steps slowed. Hayworth was there, laughing at him. "Took that long to deal with that slip of a woman, and she broke your... nose?" The last word came after a noticeable delay.

Gregory felt the pain in his nose ebb as Hayworth faltered. Walking past Hayworth, Gregory gave him a cold smile, "I hope to see you tomorrow. And don't worry— your friend won't be faring any better."

Hayworth's lip curled up into a sneer, but someone calling his name distracted him. Gregory ignored him and the others who whispered after him as he exited the staging area on his side of the arena.

He found Yukiko a few minutes later. "Yuki?"

Yukiko met his gaze, her eyes searching his face, clearly worried. "Are you okay?"

"Worried about you," Gregory said. "The ring took care of the damage."

Yukiko dropped her gaze, "Good."

"Worried for me?" Gregory asked as he stopped a couple of feet from her.

"Worried you might hold it against me," Yukiko said softly.

Looking around and not seeing anyone, Gregory stepped forward, his hand going under her chin and gently tilting her gaze up to him. "No. We both had to fight to win, just like you said. I'd never hold that against you."

Blinking back tears, Yukiko gave him a tentative smile, "Partners?"

"For life," Gregory whispered.

Gregory stepped away from Yukiko at the sound of approaching footsteps. A moment later, a couple of people passed by them, heading for the stands.

Yukiko exhaled deeply, clearly pulling herself back together. "We shouldn't have to do that again until the last day," she said after a moment.

"Good," Gregory said. "Are you going to be ready for your next bout?"

"As ready as you will be."

Exchanging another smile, the two of them went up to the stands to watch the fights while they waited for their next matches. In her next fight, Yukiko dismantled Fureno quickly, leaving him unconscious on the sands in just a few minutes.

When Yukiko rejoined him in the stands, Gregory chuckled, "You didn't give him a chance."

"He upset me," Yukiko said primly. "I no longer consider him a friend."

Gregory frowned, "What happened?"

"Unkind words regarding my heritage," Yukiko said tightly.

Gregory's jaw clenched as he stared at the current fight without seeing it. "You're right. He's no longer a friend, and his friends are likely not ours, as well."

Yukiko placed her hand on one of his fists, "It doesn't bother me. Well, not as much as it used to."

Gregory gently took her hand between his, "I'm up against Clement soon. Don't know if I'll finish him as quickly as you did Fureno, but I'll make sure he isn't in the best shape for you."

"Focus on your fight. I'll handle mine," Yukiko said before lowering her voice to a barely heard murmur, "but thank you, dear one."

Gregory went up to face Clement when his name was called. They arrived in the center of the arena at the same time. Clement smirked disparagingly as he faced Gregory. His clothing was clean and fresh, as this was his first fight for the day.

"You were lucky in the first fight, fringer," Clement snickered. "You're about to eat your first loss."

"Quiet. Save the taunts for after the fight begins," Magus Paul told them. "Follow my directions when told." Paul had them bow to the boxes, him, and each other before instructing them to fight.

Gregory met Clement halfway; they had both gone on the attack. Clement was surprised when they clashed, not expecting Gregory to be as skilled as he was. Gregory capitalized on that shock and pressed the advantage. Clement did his best to stop the onslaught, but was flying through the air before he could even find his balance.

Gregory took a page from Yukiko, following his thrown opponent. Straddling Clement, Gregory rained blows down upon the prone man. Magus Paul shifted around them so he could see if Clement decided to forfeit or got knocked out. A minute went by and Gregory began to tire a little, but Clement stayed covered up as best he could.

As Gregory slowed, Clement tried to buck Gregory off while finally striking back. Gregory leaned back, causing the strike to miss, and was able to stay atop the downed man. Gregory's next strike came down like a thunderbolt, shattering Clement's nose and flattening it against the man's cheek.

Clement's eyes went glassy and he stopped trying to fight back, only feebly able to defend himself. Gregory hammered Clement three more times before Magus Paul called him off.

Gregory got to his feet and stepped back, bowing to Paul, then to the boxes, and finally bowing to his defeated opponent. Making his way back to the stands, he took the seat beside Yukiko again.

"Didn't give him a chance," Yukiko said with a hint of laughter in her voice.

"He upset me, and he was never a friend," Gregory replied with a snort. "What he said didn't bother me. Never had before, either."

Yukiko giggled softly, shaking her head, "Do you think he'll be ready in an hour?"

"I think he'll be ready, but he's likely to be more cautious."

Gregory was proved to be right an hour later. Clement had seen a healer and his nose was back in place, but was still slightly tilted to the side. When the fight started, Clement stayed entirely defensive, letting Yukiko lead the fight. It took her longer than it had Gregory, but Clement never managed to land a clean hit on her. The fight ended when Yukiko got a hold on Clement's arm and forced him to submit or have a broken elbow.

Gregory gave her a smile when she came back to their seats. "It's three hours until my next fight. Should we go find your—"

"Yu, your parents would like to find some food," Lin said, approaching them.

"—parents?" Gregory finished wryly.

"I find myself a little hungry," Yukiko said. "We have three hours."

"Your parents are aware."

"Very well," Gregory said as he got to his feet.

CHAPTER 46

They walked leisurely to the mess hall with Yukiko's parents. Hao commented on the streams, and especially the decorative fish in them, wondering if he could have a similar garden set up at their home. Yukiko informed him the fish needed a high aether content to survive, dashing his dream.

The line outside of the mess hall trailed down the path and across one of the bridges. "Goodness, do you normally have such a line?" Yoo-jin asked them.

"No. If you look, most of those in line aren't magi," Yukiko explained.

"Not enough of the kimonos denoting tier," Hao nodded. "I notice those of adept tier and above are on the second floor."

"You have to be at least adept tier or be invited by one of that status or higher to eat there," Gregory replied.

"Do you indeed?" Hao mused as he looked at the people eating on the balcony. "I'll make sure we don't have this problem tomorrow. I'm meeting with Magus Marcia Han at the fourteenth bell."

"You'll miss Greg's last bout," Yukiko said.

"I arranged the meeting before the tournament," Hao replied. "I can't change it now, Yu."

"I will be there to see it," Yoo-jin said patiently. "After that, you will be taking me to see where you sleep."

"Of course, Mother," Yukiko replied.

"And at nineteenth bell, we'll be taking you both back to Stabled Hunger for dinner again," Hao added. "You both said how good the food was."

"Their food is better than the novice food here," Yukiko said. "I was surprised that it was the owner's wife that cooks."

"A couple who can work together makes for a happy life," Yoo-jin smiled fondly at Hao.

"Indeed," Hao agreed.

"I'm surprised they don't get more business," Gregory commented. "The place was well run and had great food."

"Some people have unreasonable prejudices," Hao grumbled.

"Father always made sure to choose places that wouldn't cause problems if my... ancestry... came to light," Yukiko said softly.

"I still feel the pain of the first time you had to deal with that," Hao sighed sadly.

"That's in the past," Yukiko told him. "My betrothed knows my true worth, and that is all that matters. Comments can't cause the same hurt now, because my heart has been found."

Yoo-jin laughed softly, "Easy, Yu, easy. Your situation isn't known yet, not until the tournament ends. Oh, and the guards at the gate let us know that your curfew is suspended for this week, so we can return you after dark. There is no need to rush our time together, as it will be six months before we can visit again."

"We'll be here then, too," Hao agreed. "I've found the past few months difficult. My precious Yu wasn't beside me, helping raise my spirits every day. I was glad to see your letter when I arrived home."

"Is cousin Liang handling trade while you're here?" Yukiko asked.

"Yes," Hao chuckled. "You should have seen him when I presented the opportunity."

Yukiko laughed as she imagined it, "I can see it. He's always been hopeful that you'd give him a bigger role."

"Depending on how he does, I might give him part of the route," Hao said. "Been thinking I might want to spend more time at home."

Yoo-jin smiled at her husband, "Going to finally do as I've asked for the last six years?"

"Slowly, but yes, I'll start handing over the travel," Hao said, "if Liang can handle it. It'll be a couple of years, even if he is adept at it."

"A couple more years is soon enough," Yoo-jin smiled brightly. "We might have a grandchild by then."

Yukiko flushed red, "Mother?!"

"A mother can have dreams for her children," Yoo-jin giggled. "Calm yourself, dear child. After you finish learning, you're still under obligation to the empire via your clan for at least ten years."

Yukiko exhaled shakily, "Yes, of course."

Yukiko was saved from further discussion by the movement of the line. They had finally entered the mess hall building and were moving forward at a slow, but steady, pace.

"Not much to this place, is there?" Hao said disappointedly.

"Very austere, but that makes sense," Yoo-jin said. "Those training here might end up fighting in a war if the empire has another one."

Gregory and Yukiko exchanged a glance but did not comment on her mother's musing. Lin stayed quiet as well, but he felt comfortable in the mess hall; it reminded him of his time in the army.

When they got to eurtiks who were serving the food, the staff gave Yukiko and Gregory friendly smiles. "Novices, this will be your second meal of the day," Ravol told them.

"We'll be having dinner outside the academy today," Yukiko told him. "My parents wished to sample the food here."

"It looks like many parents do," Hao chuckled.

"We have food for non-magi," Ravol replied as he began to plate three meals for Hao, Yoo-jin, and Lin. "We apologize for the lack of diversity."

"I'm sure it will be fine as much as my daughter praises the food," Yoo-jin smiled.

"The same is true for you," Ravol told Gregory and Yukiko. "Since we have to create food for the non-magi, it reduced the options."

"It's fine," Gregory said. "Just serve us up."

"How were your fights?" Steva asked as they went down the line.

"Two and one," Yukiko sighed. "A true brute beat me in the first round."

"Heeey," Gregory frowned, which earned a giggle from Yukiko.

"You two had to fight?" Velma asked, looking concerned.

"Yeah. She almost had me, but I got lucky," Gregory said. "I'm two and oh. My last fight for today is in about two hours."

"A good start, then," Velma added. "People will start separating themselves from the rest tomorrow."

"We'll be doing our best," Yukiko said. "It was nerve-wracking to be the first fight in the central arena, though."

"Oh my," Velma said as she handed over their trays and touched their medallions, "that must have been terrifying."

"It was," Yukiko smiled. "Have a good day."

"Conversing with the animals as if they were worth speaking to?" someone a few places back in line scoffed openly.

Yukiko's back stiffened, and Gregory slowed as they had started toward the beverages. "Bigots, small-minded idiots," Gregory said loud enough to be heard by the person who had spoken as he stayed next to Yukiko.

"What was that, *Novice*?" the speaker boomed, getting the attention of everyone nearby.

Gregory looked back to see an apprentice glaring at him. Before he could reply, a magus appeared between them. "Apprentice, Novice, this is not the place for arguments. If you have a disagreement, take it to an arena after the matches for the day end."

"Sorry, Magus," Gregory said, bowing slightly, tray in hand. "I have no problem with the apprentice."

"I have a problem with *you*," the apprentice snapped. "I challenge you, Novice."

"Greg, not during the tournament," Yukiko cautioned him.

"No, I'm not going to stand for this. It bothers me as much as it bothers you, Yuki," Gregory replied. Looking back at the magus, Gregory spoke up, "Sir, would you be willing to adjudicate the challenge? I will accept if you do. The tournament bouts will be suspended in an hour for lunch. I would be willing to face him then; no aether and a single training weapon each."

The larger apprentice laughed, "Accepted."

"Foolish, but fine," the magus sighed. "Central arena in an hour."

Gregory bowed again before turning back to get some tea. Yukiko was frowning at him, but did not say anything as they followed her parents to a table.

"Was that wise?" Hao asked when they found seats.

"No," Yukiko replied grumpily.

"Probably not, but he upset Yuki," Gregory replied. "I'll get a naginata and end it quickly."

"Ill advised," Lin cut in. "You'd be better off fighting worse than you can. Hiding your talent until absolutely needed is better."

"That would make it even more dangerous," Yukiko argued.

"Yu, you must have faith in the one you love," Yoo-jin gently chided her.

Yukiko frowned, "I just don't want him to get injured because of some boor when we both need to be at our best."

"I promise, I won't get injured," Gregory said.

Yukiko sighed, "I feel as if it's my fault."

"No. That comment would have bothered me even if I hadn't met you. He's the same one who tried to trip me months ago, remember? He's obviously been waiting for a moment. As long as we don't challenge others, we control the variables, and if that's the case, we can win every time. Bishop taught us that."

Yukiko's lips twitched, "You're so confident in us."

"Of course," Gregory replied. "I know you're worth more than every other novice combined, including me."

"Just like you two," Lin snorted, his gaze going to Hao and Yoo-jin.

"Indeed," Hao nodded. "Yu is just like her mother, after all."

"I believe she found a man similar to her father, too," Yoo-jin replied serenely.

Yukiko shook her head, not rising to their bait. Instead, she focused on her meal and tried to ignore her worry for Gregory.

Gregory watched Yukiko as he ate his own food, wondering if he had made a mistake.

* * *

The hour went by quickly. Yukiko's parents enjoyed the meal, praising the cooks. Now they were in the stands of the arena, along with a few hundred others who had heard of the challenge and turned up for it.

Gregory picked up a wooden naginata from the waiting area under the arena, stepping onto the sands a few moments before the magus. The apprentice, Jenga, was already there, with a wooden odachi resting on his shoulder. The magus arrived exactly on time to adjudicate the challenge.

"Novice, Apprentice, this challenge is set for no aether and a single practice weapon each. What is at stake here for the challenge?"

"An apology," the apprentice sneered at Gregory. "I want him to bow before me and publicly declare that eurtik are nothing more than animals, and that he was wrong to question me."

"I would have him do the same, but to the cooks in the mess hall, apologizing for not seeing them as the people they are."

"Are you sure this dispute cannot be resolved peacefully?" the magus asked. When neither spoke, he nodded, "Very well. To the middle of the arena."

Standing a dozen feet apart, the magus had them bow to him and each other before he stepped back. "Fight."

Gregory did not move more than a foot as Jenga came forward, intent on ending it quickly. As the odachi came down in a brutal overhand strike, Gregory brought the naginata up in a beautiful parry, following it with thrusting the endcap into Jenga's gut. The apprentice wheezed, stepping back surprised and winded, feebly trying to deflect Gregory's follow ups. He was successful the first time, but in doing so, had pushed his own weapon out to the side. Gregory shook his head as he drew back on the haft of his weapon, then shot it forward. Jenga clutched his neck, the odachi falling from nerveless fingers as he tried to breathe.

"Stop!" the magus shouted. "Healer!"

The healer, who had been standing by, was already rushing toward them. Gregory stepped back, giving her room, and bowed to the prone apprentice and the magus.

"Are we done, Magus?" Gregory asked.

"Yes, this challenge is over," the magus replied, helping steady the apprentice while the healer forced a potion into the apprentice's mouth to heal his crushed larynx.

"Thank you, sir," Gregory said as he moved to the exit.

The magus watched Gregory go, "Who the hell is he?"

When he returned to Yukiko and her parents, Gregory lowered his head, "Sorry for having to do that."

"No worries, I made a tidy sum," Hao laughed. "So many who came were sure that you were going to lose."

"Father," Yukiko sighed, "I still can't believe you did that."

"Why? They were being disrespectful to your... partner," Hao replied, recalling just in time that announcements had not yet been made.

"Your skill might be doubted, but if you do that again, everyone will know," Lin said simply.

"We will need to be extra careful in the future," Yukiko said. "I have a feeling we'll have more challenges after the tournament ends."

CHAPTER 47

The last fight for Gregory was almost laughable— his opponent was one of the enchanters, who had already lost his previous two bouts. Gregory did his best to minimize the damage to the undertrained man while also trying to end the fight as quickly as possible. Afterward, Gregory bowed as required before leaving the sands.

Yukiko, Yoo-jin, and Lin were waiting for him when he emerged from the waiting area. "Well done," Lin said, "much better than some of the other fights. Too many others feel the need to brutalize their opponents if they have them so far outclassed."

"There's no reason to do that besides petty pride," Gregory replied.

"Now that the fight is over, we're off to see your sleeping arrangements," Yoo-jin said. "Please, Gregory, will you lead the way?"

"Of course," Gregory bowed and turned toward the dormitory.

When they arrived, the place was busy. Busier than Gregory had ever thought it would be. The staff of the dormitory were showing different groups around the exterior and interior. When Gregory, Yukiko, and her parents were changing to indoor slippers, Dia came out, speaking very respectfully to an older man that Gregory had seen before.

"He has been a very respectful novice," Dia said, bowing her head to the gentleman.

"As he knows he should be," Nick's grandfather sniffed, as if Dia were an idiot. "Since I've seen all I need to, I shall be on my way."

"I wish you a good day, Grandmaster Shun," Dia said, bowing low to him.

Shun caught sight of Gregory as he turned toward the door. "Pettit. I take it then that this is Novice Warlin and her mother?"

"Sir, you are correct," Gregory said, bowing respectfully to him.

"I've heard your clan has expressed an interest in having my daughter join," Yoo-jin said. "The Eternal Flame is well known, but surely you are aware that our family has ties to the Han Merchant Exchange."

"Yes, but your husband went to great lengths to leave them, so it seems unlikely your daughter would go back to them so quickly."

"That was years ago. Things can change in time," Yoo-jin smiled politely, giving nothing away.

"I see," Shun said evenly, but his eyes narrowed. "Well, we shall have to see what happens by the end of the tournament, yes? I do hope she can make it through it unscathed. She looks very fragile... like a bird."

Yoo-jin's nostrils flared, "She is made of sterner stuff than you think."

"I do hope that is the case. It is by fire that *impurities* are removed," Shun said as he came to a stop a few feet from them, replacing slippers with his shoes. "Of course, everyone who joins the Eternal Flame must prove they are strong enough to survive."

Yoo-jin did not reply, but did step aside so Shun could leave. Head held high and with a knowing smile on his lips, Shun walked past them as if they were merely servants waiting on him.

The moment he stepped out the door, Dia approached with a strained smile. "Greetings. I am Dia, the keeper of this dormitory."

Yoo-jin smiled warmly, "I've heard about you and your staff from my daughter. I'm most grateful for all you've done to assist her. I was hoping to see her room, and that maybe we could talk for a bit."

"It is a pleasure, Mrs. Warlin. Your daughter has been exemplary in her time here. She has garnered the attention of the five great clans and most of the minor clans, as well. Please, follow me, and I will personally show you around."

Dia took them on a tour of the dormitory, including areas that Gregory had never seen, like the staff areas, before leading them up to the third floor and Yukiko's room. "Here is where your daughter sleeps."

Yoo-jin walked into the room, looking it over with a critical eye. "Why is she on the third floor?"

"Rooms are assigned in the order of the novice's arrival. She was one of the last two to arrive. Once the novices begin to leave for the clans, those who remain can either keep the room they were placed in or move to an empty room. Currently, we have five apprentices still residing here, also."

"There is no status associated with each floor?"

"No. Novices are all equal before the tournament," Dia said, but one of her furred ears twitched.

"I'm sure you do the best you can, but some people have family that can exert pressure."

"We do the best we can," Dia replied with a tight smile.

"My daughter has only praise for you and your staff," Yoo-jin said as she took a seat at the table in the room. "Is there anything that would help this place run better that the academy doesn't provide?"

"We are given all necessary items," Dia replied formally.

"I'm sure you are. Now, let's set aside the professional language and speak plainly. I would like to show my gratitude to those taking care of my daughter by providing a gift. What would be appropriate?"

Dia stared at Yoo-jin for a long moment, "My staff would appreciate any luxury you would care to gift. I myself would be partial to some pascal leaf."

"I was wondering what you smoked in that pipe," Yoo-jin said, gesturing at Dia's obi, where the mouthpiece and small bowl could be seen peeking out of the folds. "Pascal leaf, hmm... yes, that I can accomplish. I shall have a package delivered for you and your staff."

Dia bowed formally, "You are most kind."

"Those who treat my daughter with kindness and respect are shown kindness in return. Those who upset her, well... my ire is given to them in turn, too. My husband will be here before too long, if you can have him guided up here when he arrives."

"Yes, madam," Dia bowed. "Would you like some tea while you wait?"

"Oh, yes, that would be lovely. Three cups, please."

When Dia left the room, Yoo-jin turned her gaze to Gregory. "Now, where is your room?"

Gregory pointed at the wall, "There."

"Does temptation make it difficult for you? Knowing that she sleeps but a few feet away?"

Yukiko went scarlet and Gregory flushed, neither of them looking at the other. "I've been respectful."

"Of that, I have no doubt," Yoo-jin replied. "Lin, why don't you wait downstairs for Hao?"

Lin hesitated before he bowed, "As you wish."

As Lin opened the door, a fox eurtik bowed to him, presenting a tray with three cups, "The tea."

"Bring it in," Yoo-jin told her. "Lin is just leaving."

"As you wish," the eurtik replied, stepping into the room and setting her tray on the table. "It is mugicha. I hope that's okay."

"That will be fine. Thank you."

Bowing low, the woman left the room. Gregory and Yukiko took seats at the table when Yoo-jin motioned them to it.

"Now that we have some time and no one is likely to get offended, we should speak plainly," Yoo-jin said as she sipped at the lightly steaming tea. "You will be proper during the waiting period, yes?" She directed the question at Gregory with a light tone.

"I would never do anything to dishonor Yuki."

"Good. My daughter can be a bit willful, though—"

"Mother—" Yukiko cut her off, only to be shushed by Yoo-jin.

"So make sure you resist her advances."

"Mother!" Yukiko snapped, her cheeks flaming.

"Dear, you take after me far too much," Yoo-jin smiled. "I had your father on the third day of our betrothal, even though we did not wed for a full year."

Gregory nearly choked on the tea he was sipping, and Yukiko looked mortified.

"Now, we won't make you wait nearly so long. The end of the first year is long enough and that's only a half year away. I won't forbid you from kissing and cuddling, but make sure it stays proper and clothed, yes?"

Gregory and Yukiko exchanged a glance, both of them beet-red. Each of them wondered if that would be okay with the other, while trying not to let on how much they would like that.

"Mother," Yukiko finally asked slowly, "why?"

"Because, dear child, as I've said, you take after me. It's best to give a little and hope than to forbid as my parents did. I recall all too well how that worked."

"I will make sure things stay proper, no matter how difficult it is," Gregory said. "Thank you for not forbidding us from showing each other affection."

"Of course. I'd rather my daughter be happy, but not at too high a cost. It'll be difficult enough over the next week for you two to not show your love for each other."

"Yes," Yukiko agreed. "I understand much of what you used to say now, Mother."

"I could see it when you found out he was injured. Ah, how protective you became," Yoo-jin smiled fondly at Yukiko. "Do your best to keep that fire burning, dear. And you, Gregory, stepping in to deal with that disrespectful churl at lunch. Though you should weigh your responses more in the future. If you let that always be what tips you, then your enemies will have an easy point to force you into conflicts."

"Yes, Mother," Gregory replied.

Yoo-jin smiled, "Not yet, but by the end of the year."

The conversation turned to lighter topics while they sipped tea and waited for Hao. Gregory excused himself to change clothing, and Yukiko took that chance to do so as well.

* * *

Hao arrived just after the sixteenth bell, a strained smile on his face. "Sorry for the wait."

"Pressed, did they?" Yoo-jin asked as she rose to her feet.

"We'll discuss it later," Hao replied. "It's a little early for dinner, but there are places I would like to stop on the way back to Stabled Hunger."

"Oh, they upset you," Yoo-jin nodded, seemingly reading more into his words and body language than either of the novices could. "Very well, let's be on our way."

"Father? Is it because of me?" Yukiko asked directly.

"No, or rather not just," Hao sighed. "I regret saying I'd always answer you truthfully as a child. We can discuss it after dinner."

Lin was chatting with Dia when they arrived downstairs to put their shoes back on. Dia bowed to them, "I hope you have enjoyed your visit."

"I did. I have no fear that my daughter is not being cared for. The package shall be along as soon as I can arrange it. Oh, I do need to know how many staff you have."

"It varies. Before the tournament, I have thirty staff. Once most of the novices head off to the clan manors, I'll have ten. The other twenty will get shifted to other duties."

"Very well, I shall make sure that all thirty have small packages, if you can arrange delivering them."

"I shall," Dia bowed formally.

"Thank you for caring for our daughter," Hao added.

"Sir, your carriage is being readied. Keeper Dia sent one of her staff to let them know."

"Ah, truly exemplary care," Hao chuckled. "Our thanks again. Come, let us not take up more of her time."

As they walked away, Dia pulled her pipe out of her obi and lit it while watching them. "I wonder what clan you will choose," she murmured as she blew the first smoke ring.

They chatted about the fights during the walk to the carriage. When they reached the stable, Lin nodded to the driver, who was one of the guards. "We will be stopping at a few places on the way back to the tavern. I have the destinations, as well as rough directions."

"Yes, sir," the driver saluted.

Lin opened the door, helping Yoo-jin and Yukiko into the carriage. Hao and Gregory got inside and Lin shut the door, climbing up to sit beside the driver. He leaned over, quietly giving the driver instructions.

"Father, are you trying to be secretive?" Yukiko asked with an amused smile.

"I doubt you know all my plans, Yu."

"Let me see..." Yukiko said slowly, placing a finger to her chin as she looked up. "An alchemist, an enchanter, and... possibly a clothier?"

Hao stared at her for a long moment, "Three of four, passable."

"Of four?" Yukiko frowned, her brow furrowing as she tried to think of the fourth.

"Oh, that is—" Yoo-jin began, but Hao put a hand on her knee, shaking his head at her.

Gregory spoke up, but slowly, "If you are planning to visit an enchanter and clothier, sir, we've had business with a couple of shops in that regard."

"Lagrand Clothiers and Hemet's Curiosities," Yukiko murmured, obviously still trying to figure out the fourth stop.

"Hmm. You back both of these choices, Yu?"

"Lagrand has done wonders for us," Yukiko said, motioning to Gregory's outfit. "Hemet at Hemet's Curiosities is shrewd. You'll like him, Father. I find myself at a loss for the last stop."

"Oh, good, I will get to surprise you," Hao smiled. "Luckily, the alchemist is our first stop. You can let Lin know where the other shops are when we're there."

CHAPTER 48

Entering Alvis Alchemy with the others, Gregory was surprised that the many scents filling the shop did not conflict with each other. Each herb's smell melded with the others, yet remained distinct enough that it could be singled out.

"Welcome," the middle-aged woman behind the counter greeted them with a professional smile. "How might I help you?"

"My daughter and her friend are novices," Hao said without greeting, "I'm looking for items to help them grow in power and skill."

The woman's smile grew wider, "Certainly, sir. Might I ask their ranking?"

"Why does that matter?" Yoo-jin asked.

"Powder that would boost a third circle ranked novice would not be as effective for someone in the seventh circle, but something meant for the seventh circle could hurt one of the third."

"Sixth, both of us," Yukiko answered.

"And during the first tournament? You must both have had good training," the woman said. "It never hurts to have more than what a clan might support you with."

"I'm looking to see them stocked from now until the next tournament," Hao said easily.

The shopkeeper just stared at him for a long moment, then her smile grew wider. "I'll be happy to assist. As sixth tier, they are likely to reach into the first circle of apprentice by then. Six months of powders, pills, and the like..." The woman looked into the middle distance for a moment. "What path do you each follow?" she asked after a moment.

"Why does that matter?" Yoo-jin asked again, but a little sharper this time.

"It doesn't, overall, but some of our items can give an extra boost to one on a specific path."

"I doubt it will matter enough," Hao said with a bored expression. "Can you do it, and if you can, how much will it cost?"

"We can manage your request, sir, but it would be best if we could have the supplies delivered each week. The fresher they are, the better it is for them. As for the cost—"

"Wait," Hao cut her off. "If you are willing to sign a contract, I will set up an account for the costs. This way, you are adequately compensated if prices fluctuate and I know that the vela is being spent as needed."

Gregory listened to them talk with raised eyebrows, shocked at what he imagined the cost would be. Yukiko took his hand briefly, smiling at him. Exhaling softly, Gregory tried to get over his shock, realizing this was what the rest of the shopping trip was likely going to be like.

"I would need the owner to approve of that deal," the woman said slowly. "Are you willing to wait a moment?"

"We have other stops to make," Hao said with a disappointed air.

"Please, sir, just give me one minute," she begged him.

"Very well."

A minute passed, and Hao motioned them toward the door. A few seconds later, the woman came bursting into the room, just as Lin opened the door.

"Wait, sir, please! He's coming," she gasped.

Hao paused before sighing, "Very well."

Lin shut the door again after giving the driver a wave.

A grumpy-looking man with squinty eyes came into the shop from behind the counter. "I'm Aldor Alvis. Who wished to see me?"

"I'm Hao Warlin," Hao replied, staring the man down.

"Warlin? The merchant?"

"My name is known, it seems," Hao chuckled without humor.

"Not many can break with a great clan," the man said, looking more respectful. "How might my humble shop help?"

Hao explained again what he wanted and Aldor nodded along with him, agreeing right away to an account to handle the transfer of vela as each order was delivered. Aldor quickly put together a package for each of them— leaves for bedtime and pills for the morning. Hao signed over a bond to Aldor for the items delivered now, and began penning a contract for the deal.

"Jin, please take them to the next shop, then send the carriage back for me. I'll be along once this is signed," Hao asked his wife.

"Yes, husband. Come now, let us see what else we can do for you," Yoo-jin smiled as she led them from the shop.

Lin had just gotten them into the carriage when a bracelet on his wrist glowed soft gold for a moment. "Good, they will be with him shortly," Lin sighed as he closed the door.

"What was that?" Gregory asked as the carriage began to roll.

"We have bracelets that let us summon our guards to us. Each one glows different colors depending on what sort of summons it is," Yoo-jin explained, showing Gregory a silver bracelet with six gems set into it. "Hao sent a minor summons. Five of our men should be with him shortly."

"It also helps guide them?" Gregory asked.

"Of course. It would be worthless, otherwise," Yoo-jin smiled.

Gregory fell silent as he again tried to imagine the amount of vela Yukiko's family had for them to speak so casually of enchanted jewelry that cost more than his village.

* * *

At Hemet's Curiosities, Gregory wondered what the old man would say and what Yoo-jin would do. Hemet came into the shop proper when the bell at the front rang, his pace slow and dignified, allowing him time to look over the group.

"It is good you see you again, miss. What can I do for you today?" Hemet said, directing his question to Yukiko.

"I would like to see the best items you have for them," Yoo-jin said, stepping forward. "I am Yoo-jin Warlin, wife to Hao Warlin, head of Warlin Mercantile."

Hemet bowed his head to her, "A pleasure. I'm glad this is a pleasant visit and not one where you try to get the bond back."

Yoo-jin laughed, "That would be amusing for you, I'm sure. The bank would balk at even the thought, since I'm sure my daughter sealed it properly."

"She did," Hemet smiled. "What kind of enchantments are they needing?"

Yoo-jin looked back at Yukiko, "You would know better than I."

"Anything that might negate the Eternal Flame," Yukiko said bluntly. "Besides that, it will depend on how much my parents are willing to spend. I know that there is a limit to how much we can use, as our aether would be pressed under the weight of your more advanced items."

"Yes. Not many novices consider that," Hemet nodded. "Very well, please give me a few moments. Would you care for some tea while I retrieve items of merit?"

"Yes," Yoo-jin said as she looked around the shop, "and three chairs."

Hemet bowed his head deeply, "As the customer wishes."

* * *

The three had finished their tea when the door opened and Hao entered the shop. "Looks busy," Hao chuckled.

As if summoned by Hao, Hemet returned with a display case. "Ah, this must be the master Warlin," Hemet said, bowing his head after seeing Hao with his hand on Yoo-jin's shoulder.

"Indeed," Hao replied. "What do you have to show us?"

"I have a few things," Hemet replied. "I have two rings of silver with ruby chips, which will reduce the heat of any flame within three feet of the wearer. They were made by enchanter Flem years ago when the Han Merchant Exchange almost went to war with the Eternal Flame."

"I'm fairly certain those rings were never sold," Hao said thoughtfully.

"The finished products haven't been," Hemet chuckled. "These are two of his early attempts. They won't stop the flame, but will reduce its effect. A novice is unlikely to have a flame of sufficient power to overcome these. The drawback is, of course, the need for the enchantment to replenish. These do so by drawing aether from bane cores that are touched to them."

"I see why he let them go; they are flawed twice over," Hao nodded.

"Yet priceless for a pair of novices who will face the chosen of the Eternal Flame in the coming days," Hemet replied easily.

"What else?" Hao asked.

"I have a pair of bracelets that will give the wearers a few seconds of shielding. They must have aether poured into them to recharge them. Not easy for a novice to do, and would take a month to replenish them entirely. With practice, they can be used a single second at a time or even less, I'm told."

"No time for them to get used to them during the tournament, then," Hao shrugged.

"What of these earrings? They will hold aether, allowing the magi to have some aether to spare beyond what they have cultivated their flames to handle." He pointed to two white metallic studs that were capped with sapphire chips.

"Mythrum," Hao said, looking at them, "expensive."

"But the only known metal that allows for aether to be stored," Hemet replied easily. "These can easily hold a lower apprentice's capacity."

"Extra expensive," Hao laughed.

Hemet cracked a smile and nodded, "I was asked for the best I have for them. This is the jewelry. If you give me a moment, I will have the last item brought out."

"By all means," Hao said.

Hemet was only gone a few seconds, returning with a pair of white leather gloves. "Glacial bear leather, infused with the powdered bane core from that same bear. These gloves will cause those touched by them to feel the arctic chill."

"An edge in hand to hand, to be sure," Hao mused.

"These are the best I can muster right now for novices."

"Yu, what do you think?" Hao asked.

"Depending on their prices, they could all be useful. The first two rings are potentially the most useful right now, as we are sure to run into at least one person favored by the Eternal Flame who will have their necklace."

"The rings are rare, very rare in fact, outside of the Han clan," Hemet replied.

"Them, the bracelets, and earrings. How much?" Hao asked.

"One hundred thousand vela," Hemet replied.

Hao chuckled, "Interesting. I'm assuming you're figuring each ring at ten, each bracelet at fifteen, and the earrings at fifty. Yes?" Hemet did his best to appear unflustered, but Hao chuckled. "Yes, I thought so. I'll give you seventy."

"Seventy?" Hemet asked evenly. "I might do ninety, but much less than that is nearly impossible."

"My daughter said I would like you," Hao smiled. "Seventy-five, because you have done right by her before."

"Eighty-five?"

"Eighty," Hao replied, pulling out a scroll and inkwell. "I'll sign the bond right now."

Hemet shook his head, "Who am I to tell a man no when his daughter is with him?"

"You wouldn't be a richer man," Hao replied as he began to fill out the bond. "Yu, come collect the items."

"Yes, Father," Yukiko said, getting to her feet.

Gregory swallowed hard, still trying to deal with how much money Hao was throwing down on their behalf tonight, and they had only stopped twice so far.

"Your ring and bracelet, Greg," Yukiko said, holding them out to him.

"Huh?" Gregory replied, blinking at her.

A soft smile came to her as she looked down at him. "Shocked?"

"Yes. I'm starting to realize just how much farther out of my reach you should have been."

"I'm glad I wasn't and that you accepted me."

Gregory matched her smile and took the offered items, slipping them on before standing up. "Accepted you? More like happy to be caught by you."

"Children, let's step outside," Yoo-jin said, ushering them away.

* * *

The next stop was Lagrand Clothiers, which did not take long, though again, Gregory had difficulty with the amount of vela being thrown around. Yukiko and he were both getting a wardrobe of clothing, including three more novice uniforms so they could be in perfectly clean uniforms no matter what might happen. The clothing would not be ready for a week, so Hao arranged to have it delivered to the academy for them.

The sun was setting when the carriage came to a halt outside their last stop. Hao stepped out and turned to face them with a broad smile. Yoo-jin shook her head at him as she stepped out. Yukiko paused halfway out before sighing, "Father, really?"

Gregory was hesitant to step out but did, his eyes climbing up the front of the building. "You aren't serious?"

"But I am," Hao replied, completely serious. "They might not have anything, but while the tournament is going on is when they hold the best auctions. I will be coming back every night to check. If you'd like to head to dinner instead, that is up to you."

"I would feel better if we stayed and made sure he behaved himself," Yoo-jin said.

"Yes, he does get a bit excited during auctions," Yukiko agreed.

Shaking his head, Gregory followed them up the stairs as Hao tried to protest their claims, but not strenuously enough to truly deny it. Entering together, they were immediately met by a young woman who wore a bright smile.

"Greetings, the auction is already underway. Did you wish to attend?"

"Is there a box open?" Hao asked, his tone aloof.

"We still have two open, sir, but they cost thirty thousand vela to use. That cost is deducted from your first purchase."

"You accept bonds, yes?"

"If they are properly backed," she replied, nodding.

"Show us to the box. If it is acceptable, I will take it for my family."

"Follow me, sir."

They were led up to the second floor and down a thickly-carpeted hall before she brought them to a door. Opening it, she stepped aside, "The paddle to bid is on the foremost chair."

Entering the room, Hao and Yoo-jin examined the box that looked down on the auction floor. Gregory took a deep breath, doing his best to accept what was happening tonight, as he looked at the thick velvet padded chairs and silver lanterns attached to the walls. Yukiko stayed beside him, not holding his hand, but as close as she could be. Lin stepped inside the door and to the side, staying against the wall.

"Yes, this will work," Hao said, returning to the woman. "Do you wish to have a bond now, or can we handle it after so I can just add in any purchases?"

"We will take three thousand vela as a deposit with the bond at the end," she replied.

"We'd like some refreshments, as well," Yoo-jin said with a sniff, pulling a small folding fan from her obi.

"Yes, madam. Did you have a preference?"

"Something light, a wine perhaps...? No, that won't do, magi and alcohol don't mix well. A berry tea."

"Right away," the woman bowed as she took the money from Hao.

Lin shut the door behind her as she left, and the others took their seats. Yoo-jin picked up the bidding paddle before Hao could take it. Hao frowned, but sighed when Yoo-jin met his eyes.

"Yes, I know. I still regret some of those purchases."

"Luckily for you, we were able to sell most of what you bought and so we didn't lose that much money," Yoo-jin replied with a fond smile. "I'm not going to give you the chance to make that near mistake again."

"What do we do?" Gregory whispered to Yukiko.

"If you see something you think is worthy, just let Mother know," Yukiko replied as she placed her hand on his. "She will do her best to get it," she added, looking at her father, "within reason, that is."

"Even my own daughter," Hao sighed theatrically.

"Sir, there is a reason we haven't gone near an auction house in the last five years," Lin added.

"Our next item up for bid is a relic from the Eurtik Empire," a deep voice announced from the stage. "It was held in a private collection until two months ago. A pair of handwraps, enchanted to turn the hands into shadow panther paws, with the four inch claws they are known for. We will start the bidding at fifty thousand vela."

CHAPTER 49

Gregory was still boggling over the sheer amount of vela that traded hands at the auction house when he woke the next morning. Yoo-jin had bid on an item or two, but never chased after them like the others seemed to.

Walking toward the archive, Yukiko finally asked a question that had weighed on her mind, "Greg, does it bother you?"

Gregory glanced at her as he was pulled from his thoughts. "It's going to take me a bit to get used to, and I kind of hope I don't get used to it. One of those items went for a million vela last night."

Yukiko looked down, "You didn't ask for anything."

"Everything cost more than my village by the time a winning bid was reached," Gregory replied. "I'm trying Yuki, but... I had thought Hemet's was bad enough."

"Maybe we shouldn't go with them tonight. We can go to the tavern and wait there."

"No. It's best if we go. Maybe we can make sure they don't buy anything we don't need."

"Mother knows better, but we'll go if that's what you want."

"Maybe by the end of the week, I'll be used to it," Gregory chuckled.

Yukiko gave him a knowing smile, "You won't be, but I find that charming. Too many others would be champing at the bit to spend as much as they could."

Gregory shook his head at the idea as they entered the archive. "Good morning, Rafiq."

"Morning to you both. It is still a surprise to see novices here so early during the tournament. I'll have the scrolls brought shortly."

"No need," Yukiko told him. "We're going to be doing Magi Squares for an hour only. We need to get our training in, such as we can. Between the tournament and family, we have even less time than normal."

"Ah, yes, that would be the case. Congratulations to you for your victories yesterday, and good luck today."

"Thank you," they said together as they bowed to him.

That jogged Gregory's memory, "We fought in the main arena yesterday, and one of the archivists was in the box. Is she the chief archivist?"

"Chief Archivist Sarinia," Rafiq replied.

"I hope she enjoyed her time yesterday."

"She normally dislikes the tournaments. They take her away from her duties here."

"Ah, I can understand that," Yukiko nodded. "Father used to get that way if he was away from the caravan for too long."

"Let me not delay you," Rafiq said, hoping to stop the conversation. "Training is important."

"We'll see you in an hour," Gregory said as they headed for their table.

Rafiq exhaled softly as he watched them go. His eyes flickered to the balcony that looked down onto the entryway where a patch of shadow winked at him and vanished. Shaking his head, Rafiq stopped one of the other archivists and made sure they knew to leave the two novices alone for the week unless they asked for help.

* * *

When they were packing up their things, Gregory was a little frustrated at how he was struggling with the Magi Squares. Yukiko was able to solve the ones he made easily. He absent-mindedly said goodbye to Rafiq as they left, trying to figure out how he could make his squares more difficult without them being impossible.

"Greg," Yukiko commented as they walked toward the training hall, "the last one was good."

"Huh?"

"The last puzzle you gave me to do. It was challenging."

"Oh. You seemed to breeze through them all pretty easily. I was worried I wasn't challenging you."

"Honestly, I was worried that I made yours too hard," Yukiko said. "I've been around them for years so I've had chances to work on them before. Father will be getting us his old ones, and Dia has agreed to have her staff prepare blank ones for us both."

"Is that what you stopped to ask her last night?"

"One of the things."

"What were the others?"

"Making sure she was aware that we would be receiving packages, valuable packages."

"Oh, that makes sense."

"Still earlier than anyone else," Gregory said a few minutes later when they reached the training hall.

"Good. Hopefully, we can train without interruption."

"That would be nice," Gregory agreed.

They went to one of the smaller rooms and put their bags to one side. Going to the middle of the room, they exchanged smiles and took the first position of their meditation stretches.

* * *

Gregory sighed, the chiming of the bell bringing him out of his aether cavern, where he had been doing the physical exercises to train both paths at once. Yukiko smiled when he looked at her.

"That was good," Yukiko commented. "Did your fire have green flashes appearing in it?"

"Yeah, I chalked it up to the powder and leaves from the alchemist."

"That was my thought as well, but I wondered if it was the same for you."

"Let's get going. They should be announcing the next set of matches," Gregory said as he snagged his bag.

"If we give them a few minutes, the initial crowd will clear out some and we might not have to deal with Nick and the others."

"Fair," Gregory admitted. "Wonder if we'll face any of them today?"

"If we do, the rings will come in handy," Yukiko said. "You have the core to replenish yours?"

"In my bag," Gregory replied. "I'm going to do my best to avoid using the bracelet, if I can. I'd like to have a surprise for the final eight, since I don't have a shadow teleport ring."

Yukiko shook her head, "It's been hard not to use it. I could end the fights so much more quickly if I used it at the start."

"Which is why you should save it for the final eight."

"Yes. If we both make it to the final eight, do you think we'll end up against each other before the final match?"

"It's pretty likely, honestly. But it'll depend on who's setting up the matches and if they're trying to rig it for anyone."

"Hmm, that is a good point."

"Wait and see," Gregory said, pausing by the door to the room.

"What is it?" Yukiko asked when he stopped.

"This," Gregory turned back to her and took her into his arms, kissing her softly.

Yukiko returned the kiss, her arms going around his waist as she snuggled close.

The moment drew out, but Gregory eventually stepped back. "Since we can't do that in public, I'm going to steal kisses when I can."

"Steal as many as you want," Yukiko murmured as she placed her hand over his heart. "My heart may have anything he wishes."

"Why do you call me that?"

"Because I found my heart with you," Yukiko replied. "It's hard to explain. My mother used to tell me a tale from her mother, who heard it from hers, and so on. We each have a heart in the world, the one who helps us live, truly live, instead of merely surviving. They were right. My world has become so much brighter and joyful since I met you. When I saw you the first time, my heart beat a little faster; when you caught me during the testing, I nearly fainted. Not from the strain, but because you cared enough to protect me."

Gregory stared into her cyan eyes, seeing the depth of her love.

"It gave me the courage to speak to you that night, even though I was sure you would spurn me, as so many who know my heritage have done." Yukiko's smile grew, "But you didn't. You welcomed me, even called me a friend, and suggested we help each other. My heart soared that you would be beside me, if only for a little while. I struggled to accept what I felt for you, trying to tell myself it was just a momentary thing, that I was betrothed. My heart wouldn't listen, though, for it beat inside of you."

Gregory felt awkward as he listened to her. His feelings for her now matched hers, but he knew they had not at the start.

"I didn't say anything to my mother when I wrote her because I wasn't sure what to do. I was torn between what my family would have of me and what I wished for myself. I was ashamed, yet happy, to live even for a little while longer with the dream that I could have you instead of my betrothed. I was going to tell her that first night... I was going to go and plead with her, beg her if needed, but..." Yukiko trailed off and her ears turned red. "I gave it all away when I reacted to you being injured. The anger I felt in that moment— I've never felt anything like it before. When Mother said we had to talk, I felt my world fall apart around me. I was so sure she was going to chastise me for being overly familiar with you."

Gregory recalled her face when she had left the room. His own heart had been nearly crushed.

"When we went next door, she asked me to tell her the truth. For a moment, I thought about lying, but I didn't. It was hard, but I told her, as I tell you now, that I had found my heart. She stared at me for what seemed like years, then her smile bloomed and she held me, kissing my head and telling me it was okay, that my heart was free to choose as it would. Then she told me that I had to find out if my heart was true, and we came back into the room."

Gregory smiled warmly as he recalled her awkwardness then, too.

"I tried to ask you, but I remembered you telling me your dream as a child of being a magi. It was wrong of me to ask like I did, but I wanted to know if I could be as dear to you as your dream." Her cheeks were flushed as she remembered that moment. "To be told that I was more important than the thing you had been wanting all your life... That was the moment I knew that you were deeply and truly my heart."

Gregory pulled her to him, gently, his arms around her waist as hers went around his neck. "I'm honored to be your heart, Yuki. I'll do my best to be the man you can always love." Leaning forward, he kissed her just as softly as before, but with infinitely more love.

Yukiko trembled in his arms when the kiss ended, resting her head against his chest. "My knees are weak. I know we can't, but I want to stay here like this forever."

"Tempting, isn't it?" Gregory sighed, kissing the top of her head. "We need to go see about our bouts, or we'll lose by default for not showing up."

"Yes, and we must show them that together, we are the best among them. They want to use me and they don't respect you, but by the end of it all, we'll stand atop them."

"I love your dual nature, Yuki," Gregory said when they separated. "Soft and loving, but fierce and aggressive when needed. I feel like I could take on the world with you beside me."

"If that is what my heart wishes, then I will make sure it is so," Yukiko replied with a trace of laughter.

Shaking his head, they left the room to find out who they were to fight today.

CHAPTER 50

The first two bouts of the day for both Gregory and Yukiko were unimpressive. They faced novices who had not trained as much, but had managed to get two wins each the day before. As the fourteenth bell chimed, Yukiko stepped onto the sands of the arena to face her third opponent of the day, Michelle.

Gregory sat beside Hao and Yoo-jin to watch the fight. Michelle had only lost a single fight against Jason, meaning this fight would likely keep one or the other from the final eight.

"Is she a good fighter?" Hao asked.

"She was Yuki's equal before we started training with Gin. Michelle hasn't kept pace since then. The problem is that she's favored by Nick Shun, and we know she has a necklace of flames. It's likely she'll have another trick, too."

"It's starting," Yoo-jin said to silence them.

Gregory felt his heart beat faster as he began to worry. Yukiko and Michelle bowed to each other last before Magus Paul began the fight. Michelle did not hesitate to use the necklace; a fist sized glob of fire formed in her hand and was thrown a second after the command to begin.

The audience was shocked into silence. This was the first display of serious magic any novice had used yet. Yukiko was caught off guard, not expecting Michelle to use the necklace so soon. She brought her hands up, and the globule of flame hit the light blue barrier that appeared. Her cry of pain carried to Gregory and his heart clenched hard. The barrier and globule both vanished, and Yukiko's left hand dangled at her side as if useless.

Michelle had no follow up ready, not expecting Yukiko to continue after the fire. Yukiko was gritting her teeth in pain, her left hand a mass of blisters. Thanks to the ring she wore, the damage inflicted had been greatly reduced, but it was still significant.

The two women exchanged some words, and Yukiko brought her left hand up so Michelle could see it clearly, clenching the injured hand. Michelle took a step back, unsettled by either the display or Yukiko's comments, but hesitated when Yukiko failed to follow up.

Yukiko settled into a defensive posture, extending her damaged left hand to beckon Michelle. Michelle did not advance, studying Yukiko carefully, clearly trying to understand her plan. Gregory just smiled as he realized what Yukiko had been doing the whole time.

"Why doesn't she attack?" Yoo-jin asked.

"Yuki is letting a ring heal some of the damage from the fire," Gregory replied softly. "Michelle sees a trap but doesn't know what it is, so she hesitates."

Michelle apparently decided that Yukiko was bluffing and came in to attack. A gust of wind blew sand up from the arena floor toward Yukiko, but they had seen Michelle fight earlier, so Yukiko was expecting the move. She closed her eyes as the sand flew up to not be blinded. She had only a split second to defend herself when she opened her eyes again, but she managed to slip the attack, using her right hand to push Michelle past and pivot with her.

The fight was soon similar to many of the other fights; strikes, kicks, and the occasional throw. Yukiko stayed on the defensive, taking some hits and returning very few, which seemed to embolden Michelle.

"Here it comes," Gregory said, having experienced the same trap Michelle was about to, falling for it at Gin's during their training.

Yukiko stepped back panting, looking spent, with her shoulders slumped. Michelle said something, her head held high as if she was already accepting the victory. Yukiko shook her head, saying something back before falling into a much sloppier version of her defensive stance.

Michelle laughed, but shrugged and rushed at Yukiko. Three steps short, Michelle suddenly pitched forward, her shadow tangled around her legs. Michelle rolled like they had been trained to do. Yukiko capitalized on the moment, meeting her with a vicious attack. Michelle's forward momentum was stopped cold and she fell backward, her eyes and mouth wide.

Yukiko did not stop; she followed Michelle down, climbing atop the other woman and hammering blow after blow into Michelle's face. Michelle was lost, feebly trying to defend herself as each strike connected with her face. A minute passed, then two, before Magus Paul finally stepped in and called the match.

Yukiko got off Michelle and bowed to the box, Paul, and Michelle before leaving the arena. The healer on standby rushed out to help Michelle— her face was covered with blood, her nose was shattered, her lips were split open in multiple places, and both eyes were swelling rapidly.

"I'll be going to get ready," Gregory said.

"Best of luck," Hao said.

"It's Fureno. Shouldn't be a problem."

He met Yukiko just as she was coming out of the waiting area. "How are you?"

"Fine now," Yukiko replied with a pained smile. "The ring helped. It doesn't stop all the heat, though. I bought enough time to continue, but it was far from pleasant."

"I'll keep it in mind," Gregory said, stopping a foot away from her. "You did good. You laid that trap beautifully."

"She was overconfident from the beginning. I should have expected the fire, but I thought she'd keep it as a trump card."

"I'm glad you managed to stop it," Gregory said, staring into her eyes. "I need to get ready. My fight is after this one."

"Nick," Yukiko nodded, "I feel sorry for his opponent. He's a fire magi like his grandfather, so he'll have more than just a single fire globe if you fight him."

"Hopefully that doesn't happen until the final eight."

"Be safe. Fureno is likely still fuming over his loss to me— it's been his only one."

"I'll be safe."

"The barrier used almost half of the aether the bracelet holds. We'll have to charge it as best we can tonight."

"Understood," Gregory said before he bowed his head. "I'll see you after the fight."

"I'll be waiting."

* * *

Passing Nick on his way to the arena floor, Gregory gave him a pleasant smile in passing, congratulating him on his quick victory. Nick smiled back, wishing him luck with his own fight. When Gregory stepped out onto the sands, Fureno was already there, sneering at him.

"You both know how this works," Paul said, not giving them time to exchange comments. "Face the box and bow."

Gregory did as he was told, not wanting to speak to Fureno anyway. He recalled Yukiko's judgement that he was no longer a friend and why. When he faced Fureno and was told to bow, he did, but not nearly as deeply as normal.

Paul arched an eyebrow, but instead of chastising him, he commanded them to fight.

Gregory feinted like he was going to rush Fureno, and the man did as Gregory expected, reaching for a necklace hidden under his clothing. A ball of fire appeared in Fureno's hand, but Gregory was already shifting. Fureno tried to guess where Gregory would be, but Gregory was able to dodge, rolling away from the globule of flame.

"What? No!" Fureno screamed as he watched the fire hit the sand and sit there, burning.

Gregory came out of his roll and rushed straight at the shocked novice. "This is for insulting Yuki," Gregory hissed as his fist crashed into Fureno's gut. Fureno completely failed to deflect the attack.

Fureno crumpled over Gregory's fist, wheezing. Gregory followed up with an edge strike to the back of his neck. Fureno's eyes crossed and he fell to the ground. Gregory glared down at him, kicking Fureno over so the novice was on his back. Placing his foot on Fureno's neck, Gregory looked at Paul. "I'll stomp down unless you stop me."

Paul just stared back at him and Gregory shrugged, raising his foot and slamming it down onto Fureno's weakly-protected throat. Eyes bulging, Fureno tried to breathe, but he could not and his eyes rolled back as he fell unconscious.

"Stop!" Paul commanded. "Healer!"

Gregory stepped back, turning to face the box and bow. He caught a glimpse of Sarinia watching him with an inscrutable gaze. Facing Paul, he bowed again before walking off the arena floor.

Nick met him in the waiting area beneath the arena. "That was more brutal than I expected from a friend."

"Fureno made a mistake and hopefully learned from it," Gregory replied bluntly.

"Did Michelle make a mistake as well?" Nick asked, keeping the same pleasant smile on his face.

"She did throw the fire first."

"Which brings up that I've not seen her necklace since I gifted it to Yukiko. Did she not like it?"

"You'd need to ask her."

"Greg, I thought we'd get along better. I am still willing to give you what you really want. I can manage that, if you and Yukiko join the clan. Her betrothal will be broken, and she'll be all yours."

"That is a tempting offer," Gregory said, feigning interest. "She's been resistant to the idea though. Something about the Eternal Flame subjugating those with eurtik blood in their veins."

"Ah, yes, I guess she would be, but that very reason is why you need to get her to. You'll be the one holding her leash. I can get you some powder that will make her more susceptible to suggestion. Just sprinkle it into her drink on the last night of the tournament. I'll have one of the magus nearby so she can make a servant's pledge to the clan. From there, she'll be all yours."

Gregory looked down, lips pursed as if contemplating the idea, fighting to keep the revulsion off his face. *I'll fucking make you pay for even suggesting that, you bastard,* he raged inside his own head. "Can you have it placed inside my room tonight?"

"Of course. It's the least I can do for a friend," Nick said, slapping him on the back. "Oh, one more thing if we face off in the final eight; you'll need to lose to me. Grandfather simply won't accept me not winning the tournament."

"Jason will throw over, too?" Gregory asked, not having to pretend to be shocked.

"He knows who will be leading the clan in another hundred years. Keep that in mind. In almost no time at all, I'll be the most powerful friend you'll ever need."

Gregory bowed his head, "You've shown me so much."

"That's what friends are for. Oh, if you end up against Hayworth in the final eight, do everything you can to maim him. It doesn't matter if you win, so long as he is publicly humiliated."

"I can do that," Gregory agreed. "Sorry I can't stay longer, but I need to go. Dinner."

"Do her parents resent you?" Nick asked as Gregory stepped away.

"No, they think I'm just a friend," Gregory lied, not looking back. "See you later."

Gregory was glad that Nick still had another fight, or he might have left with Gregory. Once he was out of sight, Gregory's teeth ground together and his hands clenched tight enough for his knuckles to pop.

Gregory had a smile on his face when he met up with Yukiko and her parents a few minutes later outside the arena.

"You did well," Yukiko praised him, restraining the urge to hug him.

Yoo-jin giggled lightly, "Oh, it is hard, isn't it, dear child? To be so close to your heart and unable to hold him? I remember those days. Truthfully, it is still hard today. Society doesn't like those who display such affection openly."

"Even my parents never did so," Gregory said slowly. "I never understood how hard that might be until recently."

"I will do my best to resist shaming the family," Yukiko sighed, "or, at least, bring as little shame as I can manage."

Hao shook his head, "She's still honest with us, at any rate."

"Come now, we have an auction to attend and then dinner," Yoo-jin laughed.

CHAPTER 51

Gregory stepped onto the sands of the arena with the afternoon sun sliding toward the horizon behind him. He was smiling because Yukiko had finished her fights with just the one loss to him. Her hardest fight had been against another of Nick's friends, Jamie. He had and used a fire necklace, but Yukiko dodged the flame entirely. Jamie was still a better fighter than Michelle had been, so the fight took longer. When she finally stood victorious, she had a black eye, a split lip, and a badly broken nose. That victory gave her a good shot to be in the final eight.

Clement and Hayworth's friend, Skippy, came out of the other tunnel onto the sands, a confident swagger to his walk. Gregory had seen Skippy's earlier fights and knew that he was going to be a challenge, since he had only lost a single fight.

It's curious that I've ended up in the main arena all three days, Gregory thought, but pushed the distraction aside.

"Novices, approach me," Magus Paul commanded.

"I'm going to give you a loss and maybe keep you from the final eight," Skippy sneered.

"Silence," Paul commanded. "Taunt each other once the fight starts. Now, face the box and bow."

The pair of novices bowed to the box, Paul, and then finally, each other. Neither of them charged the other, both settling into defensive postures.

"You rarely attack," Skippy said, grinning. "Hayworth noticed it and told me. That works for me, though."

Gregory frowned, wondering why Skippy seemed so relaxed, when a clump of hard-packed sand hit him in the back of the head. He staggered forward and glanced back to see another ball of sand shoot toward him. He jerked sideways, dodging the mass of sand, but he was now off-balance and had taken his eyes off Skippy.

A hard blow to his neck made Gregory's eyes water and he fell to his knees. Though his head was swimming, Gregory still had enough presence of mind to turn his head and tuck his chin as the arm wrapped around his neck.

Skippy laughed, not realizing his opponent had managed to shift enough to still breathe, although with difficulty. "Goodnight. Don't worry, I'll have fun with your bitch in the finals."

Anger flared and his aether responded, using the channels he had been building to infuse his body. His head cleared instantly as the aether helped steady him. With a grunt of effort, Gregory forced himself to his feet, dragging Skippy with him.

"What? No, you're supposed to—"

Gregory snapped his head back and felt Skippy's nose crunch at the impact. The arm around his neck loosened and Gregory used the moment, grabbing Skippy's arm and snapping himself forward. Skippy flew over his head, hitting the sand with an audible thump.

Skippy's watery eyes were wide and he made a flinging motion with his hand. Gregory jumped aside as another hard-packed dirt ball went whizzing by his face. That delay gave Skippy enough time to scramble to his feet.

"Fine. I wanted to save it for the finals, but fuck you," Skippy growled.

Gregory did not wait to find out what Skippy was planning, but rushed at him. The novice retreated with a sneer on his lips. Just as Gregory was about to reach him, he saw thin lines of blue energy going from Skippy's ring finger to a spot behind him. On instinct, he threw himself to the side in a roll. A ragged scream came from Skippy as he finished the roll and came back to his feet, turning to see what had made him scream.

"Healer!" Paul shouted, running toward the other novice.

Gregory stood there, stunned at what he saw. A shiver walked down his spine as he realized that it could have been him instead of Skippy if he had not followed his instinct.

A thick spine of hardened earth had come out of the ground, piercing through Skippy's body at chest height. The novice was slumped over it, unmoving. Blood coated the shaft and the ground around the dead man's feet.

Gregory turned to the box and bowed. Turning back to Paul and the healer, he could see them frowning as they inspected Skippy. He bowed to them and the dead man before heading to the exit.

Heading to the waiting area, Gregory stopped in the hall, breathing deeply as he imagined that same spike piercing him from behind. *Fucker tried to kill me.* The thought stuck in his mind. *Yukiko...* That thought got him moving again. He was jogging by the time he reached the waiting area.

When he exited the waiting area, Yukiko rushed to him. They stopped two feet from each other, aware of the others passing nearby.

"Are you okay?"

"I'm fine, Yuki. I—"

"Where is he!? Where is the person who killed my son!?" a booming voice echoed in the hallway. The crowd parted, revealing Yukiko and Gregory to a richly-dressed man, who was striding toward them with hatred etched on his face. "You!"

Gregory swept Yukiko behind him and faced the man, "I did nothing but dodge. Your son killed himself."

"Liar!" the man snarled as he drew a knife from his belt.

"There is no violence allowed outside of challenges," a calm voice said as an ancient man in a midnight blue kimono appeared before the enraged father, "and non-magi are almost never allowed to challenge. Your son used this ring," the old man held out a jeweled ring to the father, "which summoned the earth spike. That magic is beyond a novice, and is normally not seen until initiate or adept tiers. If you find the owner of this ring, you'll find the man who helped your son die."

The grieving father came to a stop, the calm air around the magi helping mollify his mind. "Grandmaster, are you certain?" the man asked as tears began to fall from his eyes.

"We have examined it. It is so. Please do not trouble the novice who only avoided death."

The nobleman took the ring, closed his eyes, and nodded at the magi. "I'm sorry. Forgive me, I need to take my leave."

"The academy is willing to assist, if you so wish," the magi replied. "May Mortum welcome his soul."

Turning on his heel, the noble sheathed his blade and walked away, head bowed. Everyone else nearby was staring at the Grandmaster. Gregory was shocked when the magi turned to him, and he bowed on reflex.

"Thank you, sir."

"Gregory Pettit, you are lucky to have survived that attack. You are one of only four undefeated novices. I shall look forward to seeing how you do in the finals."

Mouth dry, Gregory bowed again, the presence of the Grandmaster making it hard to breathe. "I will do my best, sir."

The magi smiled at him, then vanished. A light breeze fluttered down the hall. Everyone looked around, but the Grandmaster was gone as suddenly as he had appeared.

"Are you okay?" Hao asked, coming down the hall with Yoo-jin and Lin in tow.

"Yes?" Gregory said uncertainly.

"We can explain on the way, Father," Yukiko said, aware of all the eyes on them.

"Yes," Hao said, feeling the curiosity of everyone in the hall. "We have prior plans. Let us go."

Yoo-jin frowned as they walked through the academy toward the stables. "How do we find out if Yu made it to the final eight?"

"They told us that the keeper would be informed and notify us," Yukiko explained. "We can ask her to send one of the staff to Stabled Hunger with a yes or no."

"Probably for the best," Hao agreed. "Lin, take care of that, please."

"As you wish, sir," Lin said, breaking off from the group.

"How did you know to dodge when you did?" Hao asked as they continued their walk.

"Intuition," Gregory replied. "I knew he would have a trick up his sleeve and he wasn't afraid of me closing the distance to him. I had no idea it would be as lethal as it was."

"Listening to your instinct can always help," Hao nodded. "Most of my best deals have come from a gut feeling."

Yukiko's brow furrowed as they walked; she was thinking about Gregory's battle with Gin and how he had managed to strike the older man before the end. She stayed quiet the rest of the way to the stables, giving careful consideration to Gregory's intuition.

Lin rejoined them at the stables, "Keeper Dia will make sure we are informed once she knows."

"Good. Now to the auction house," Hao said. "My fingers are tingling, and a deal is waiting to be made."

* * *

The auction was almost over, and again, Yoo-jin had not won a single item. Gregory had become numb to the amount of vela being thrown around by the various clan representatives as well as the private buyers.

"Our last item of the night," the auctioneer boomed with enthusiasm, "comes from a ruin to the far north, said to predate even the eurtik kingdom."

Everyone leaned forward, eager to see what was going to be unveiled. Gregory's vision blurred and he knew it would be a black jade box carved to show various animals with ryuite gems for eyes.

"Buy it, please," Gregory said as the vision faded.

Yoo-jin raised an eyebrow at him, "Its price is likely to exceed yesterday's finale, and we don't even know what it is yet."

"Sadly, there is a drawback to this item. It is an ancestor-locked container, and we haven't been able to open it." With that, the auctioneer removed the indigo silk cloth that had covered the box. "The craftsmanship, age, and rarity of this item..."

"Mother, please," Yukiko said softly. "My heart has asked. Something I figured he would never do."

"It is hard to resist them, isn't it?" Yoo-jin gave her a fond smile.

"We shall start the bidding at—"

"A million vela," Yoo-jin said loudly, cutting him off as she held up her paddle.

The auctioneer blinked, head turning to find her, "A million vela it is, from Warlin Mercantile. Do I hear one and a half?" The auctioneer looked around the hall for the next bid.

Everyone looked from the box to Yoo-jin, curious why she bid before the auctioneer had even announced what the starting bid would be. A paddle went up from a box across the auction floor from them.

"Grandmaster Shun has bid one and a half," the auction smiled, "do I hear two million?"

"Why do you want this and nothing else we have seen?" Yoo-jin asked, not raising her paddle.

"It feels right," Gregory said, looking from her to Hao, suddenly worried that they would let the box be sold to someone else.

"Will no one bid against the Grandmaster?" the auctioneer asked.

Hao took the paddle from Yoo-jin, kissing her cheek. "This is mine, dear one."

"Very well," Yoo-jin said and settled back in her seat.

Hao stood up and all eyes went to him. "Grandmaster Shun, it is an honor to bid against you. Thank you for honoring my family by treating us as equals in this moment."

The watching audience turned their attention to the magi in the midnight blue kimono with the Eternal Flame emblem embroidered on its sleeves. Shun took a long moment to reply, "Warlin, this box interests me. I ask you to step out of this."

"Normally, I would thank the Grandmaster and do as requested. However, my family has asked this of me," Hao said inclining his head deeply. Turning to the auctioneer, he spoke calmly, "Three million vela."

The auction house was silent as all eyes went back to Shun, who was glaring at Hao as if he were some particularly odious insect. "You would stand against me for a prize I have declared that I want?"

Hao did not blink or turn from the pressure that rolled off Shun, though the audience between the men started to hunch up in fear. Gregory gripped the arms of his chair tightly, feeling the presence emanating from the Grandmaster. "For my family, I would bid against the emperor himself," Hao said simply. "The bid is yours."

"Four—" Shun began before he was cut off.

"Five million," Hao said.

Shun shot to his feet, grabbing the railing. The metal squealed in protest as it bent under the strain of his hands. "You would—"

"I would," Hao said, not flinching. "I faced down your contemporary in the Han clan to start my own trading house. I was sure you would know that."

"I'll make sure you regret this," Shun snarled. "Your daughter is barred from the Eternal Flame."

Hao shrugged as if the threat was little more than hot air. "Are you going to bid again, or can some of us go enjoy dinner?"

The railing snapped into pieces as Shun jerked backward, looking like he had been slapped. Without speaking, he left the box. Pieces of the broken railing fell into the crowd below.

Hao sighed, "It is so hard to find someone who can be civil during a lively auction bid. I believe the last bid was five million vela, auctioneer."

The auctioneer wiped his head with a silk handkerchief, "Yes, honorable Warlin. Yes, five million was the last contested bid. Does anyone else wish to bid? Going once... twice... sold."

The rap of the auctioneer's gavel broke the tension in the room.

People all over began to talk excitedly while others were quick to leave.

Hao turned back to his family and gave them a small bow before taking his seat. "There, it is done. I do hope it is worth the cost in both vela and trouble, Gregory."

"As do I, sir," Gregory murmured, staring at Hao with deep respect.

"Excuse me, sir," the receptionist said. "We need to settle the debt."

"Of course," Hao smiled as he pulled out a bond. "Five million vela, and you'll refund the deposit from earlier."

"Yes, honorable sir."

CHAPTER 52

G regory sat with the box on his lap all the way to Stabled Hunger, conflicted at having asked for it and the cost in vela and trouble. Yukiko sat beside him, her hand resting on his, her face troubled as she watched him. Yoo-jin was holding Hao's hand as the merchant did his best to keep a smile on his face, though his forehead was creased in discomfort.

Gregory carried the box in with them when they reached the tavern. It was lighter than he expected it to be, but seemed heavier due to the cost in acquiring it. The silk cloth cover had been included in the price, so at least it was not being shown off to everyone as they were led to the private dining area. Setting the box next to him on the table, Gregory tried to not pay it attention while their drinks were delivered.

"I'm curious what you intend to do with it now that you have it, Gregory," Yoo-jin said.

"I don't know," Gregory sighed. "I could try to open it, but I don't know how ancestor locks work."

"Like blood locks, though for ancestor locks you must come from the mother's line. Anyone who meets that criteria can open it. For a lock so old, the line might have died off, rendering it sealed for all time."

"A sage might be able to force the lock," Hao said tightly as he sipped his wine. "Not many sages in the empire. That's likely why Shun was after it. A sage would find a box like this interesting, and they would likely grant the person who gave it to them a boon."

Gregory was about to uncover the box when the staff brought their meal. Saved for the moment, Gregory did his best to focus on the food, but his eyes kept going to the silk-covered box.

Dinner ended with a wonderful berry tart and a pot of mint tea. Yukiko poured for everyone and, knowing they would not be interrupted again, Gregory removed the silk.

They all stared at the black jade, their eyes drawn to the engravings adorning the box. Every animal engraved on the box was life-like, and the ryuite chips caught the light in the room and reflected it back to make it look like they were blinking. Gregory traced the edges of the box, finding the nearly invisible line where the lid sealed along the top of the box. There was a slight indentation on the lid the size of a thumb print.

"Just nick a finger and press it to the lock?" Gregory asked, looking at Yukiko.

"Yes," she replied slowly.

Pulling his belt knife, Gregory stabbed his thumb. A bead of blood welled from the small wound and he pressed his thumb to the indention. Everyone held their breath, but there was no sound of a lock opening and they sighed in disappointment.

"Guess we should—" Gregory began, pulling his hand away. As he did, the lid shifted with him, sliding open a little.

"It's open," Hao whispered, his eyes alight with eagerness.

Swallowing, Gregory gently placed his hand on the lid and pushed it open. Inside the box was a pair of long, black, leather gloves. He picked one up and frowned at it, then brought it closer to his face. He squinted, seeing faint lines of some shimmering thread laced through the material. Yukiko took the other glove and examined it, seeing the same faint lines.

"Enchanted?" Gregory mumbled.

"We can find out," Yukiko said, slipping the glove on.

The glove shifted, contracting around her hand and arm, molding to her like a second skin. All of them were shocked when the color shifted, matching Yukiko's skin tone exactly in a few seconds. A moment after that, it seemed to have vanished entirely, melding seamlessly with Yukiko's skin.

"That is odd," Hao said, frowning as he stared at Yukiko's hand.

Gregory slid the other one onto his right hand and again, the glove appeared to vanish. "I wonder what they do? Besides being invisible while you wear them?" He flexed his hand and frowned. He could no longer feel the glove. He poked at his gloved hand with the other one and his frown deepened when he could not feel the glove with either hand.

Yukiko licked her lips, reaching for the place where the edge of the glove had been and tried to peel it off. She looked worried for a moment before the glove reappeared on her hand and she was able to take it off. "Okay, it isn't cursed," she sighed gratefully.

"We should have Hemet examine them," Hao said. "It would be prudent to ask Inda to take them, though, so we aren't connected to them. This is the kind of thing that should be kept a secret."

"There's nothing else in the box," Gregory said as he closed the lid. "Do you wish to have it?"

"Yes. We'll find a buyer for it," Yoo-jin said. "We may even recover today's expenses."

"I'll talk to Gin and see if we can use his apprentice for this," Hao said.

"Father, there isn't a need," Yukiko said. "I chose Hemet because he is known for keeping his clients' information secret. He has made his business based on that."

"Hmm... I still want a layer of deniability," Hao shook his head.

Gregory picked up the other glove and slipped it on, watching as it molded to him. "It's—" A knock on the door interrupted him, and he hastily covered the box with the silk.

"Come," Hao commanded.

A small woman in the livery of the dormitory, who had small, rounded bear ears, entered and bowed to them. Lin stood in the hall behind her. "Excuse me. Keeper Dia said I was to inform you about the final eight."

"Yes, thank you. Please continue," Yoo-jin said.

"The undefeated Novices Nick Shun, Jason Argon, Wallace Hayworth, and Gregory Pettit were selected. The other four spots are to be filled by Klein Armit, Yukiko Warlin, Franco Ichon, and Jenn Bean. The pairings will be announced tomorrow."

"Thank you," Yoo-jin smiled.

"Good evening," the woman bowed and left, closing the door behind her.

"Hopefully we don't fight each other in the first match again," Yukiko said wryly.

"Agreed."

"Lin," Hao said loudly.

Lin entered the room, "Yes, sir."

"Two tasks. Take the box and secure it. Send a message to Gin, asking him if we might engage Inda for a task that needs the utmost discretion."

"Yes, sir," Lin replied, bowing out of the room and closing the door.

"It is late, and I need to rest," Hao said, his brow still heavily furrowed. "Clashing with a Grandmaster is as tiring as I remember."

"The carriage will take you back," Yoo-jin said. "Gregory, will you leave the gloves with us?"

"Yes," Gregory said, taking them off and handing them to Yoo-jin.

"It seems your purchase might be worth well more than the cost. The box alone, if sold to the right person, should recoup most, if not all, of the initial vela."

"I'm glad," Gregory said as he rose to his feet, and bowed to them deeply. "Thank you for this, even though we don't know what the gloves do yet."

"Our daughter asked for it," Hao said. His smile was genuine, but visibly strained. "I'm sorry, today seems to have taxed me more than I realized. I need to rest. We will see you again tomorrow."

"Sleep well, Father," Yukiko said as she stood and bowed to her parents. "Thank you, Mother. Please take care of him."

"I always take care of my heart, just as you will," Yoo-jin replied. "Go, get your rest. You have a big day again tomorrow."

* * *

They approached the dormitory slowly, puzzled by the magi in cyan robes that were waiting near the entrance. One of Keeper Dia's staff came around the side of the building before Gregory and Yukiko were seen and motioned them to follow.

"What's going on?" Gregory asked as they followed her around the building, using a well-hidden footpath.

"The clans have sent representatives to officially invite the novices they are interested in. Keeper Dia had one of us waiting to show you the back way in."

"Thank her for us," Yukiko said.

"I will."

They were led through a back hall and up an unfamiliar staircase to the third floor, then left them with a bow. "Goodnight, and good luck."

"Thank you," they replied together.

They had just reached Gregory's room when voices could be heard coming up the stairs. Gregory pulled Yukiko into his room, wanting to avoid everyone. He closed his door gently, and the only light was the dim moonlight that filtered in through the single window.

The voices stopped approaching before they reached his room, then moved away. Gregory sighed in relief. "Maybe they'll leave us be."

"We can ignore them," Yukiko said softly. "We made it to the final eight; we'll get rewards from the academy depending on where we finish."

"Doubt it'll be as impressive as what your family is doing for us."

"Maybe not, but without clan backing, we'll need all the help we can get."

"Alone against the world," Gregory said, smiling at her. "I still like our chances."

"Greg, why did you ask for the box?" Yukiko asked.

Gregory felt the weight of the question. "It's hard to explain, but let's sit down and I'll do my best."

Gregory spent the next hour telling Yukiko about the odd flashes of insight he sometimes had, and how they always led him down the right path or helped him in combat. He finished by telling her about how he had known what the box would look like before it was revealed.

"I knew what it was and that it was right to acquire it, but that's all."

Yukiko nodded slowly, "I see. You kept this from me for good reason. Is there anything else you are keeping from me?" Her voice held no hint of anger or hurt, but sounded more like she was asking what he wanted for dinner.

"Your aether, when you first connected to it that first night. What was it like for you?"

Yukiko's brow furrowed for a moment, "A single blue flame in a dark space that gently licked out to touch my arm. It didn't hurt, and I knew it was my aether."

"My aether is different, at least when I truly connect with it," Gregory said, deciding to tell her everything.

More time passed, and Yukiko listened intently. When he finished, Yukiko looked thoughtful. "I see. Maybe you *are* truly touched by Aether. That might account for the flashes of insight."

"There's one more thing. I have an idea that maybe my magic is connected to raw aether," Gregory said. "I've been seeing lines of aether out of the corner of my eye since classes started. It was how I knew that Skippy was doing something I should dodge."

Yukiko shook her head, "My heart is truly blessed. I'm humbled to be told all of this. I will keep it secret even from my parents. There is reason to worry, though. If you are this blessed, others will hate you and try to stop you from growing in power."

"They won't be able to, not with you beside me," Gregory said, staring into her cyan eyes.

Yukiko's serious face lit up with a bright smile. "Well, then, I shall have to keep you close all the time."

"Please do," Gregory murmured as he leaned in to kiss her.

Their lips were an inch apart when a sharp rap sounded at the door. Gregory sighed, giving Yukiko a brief peck, then rose to his feet to see who was there. Opening the door, he saw Nick standing there. "What can I do for you, Nick?"

"I wanted to congratulate you on making the final eight. You, too, Yukiko," Nick said with a smile that felt off to Gregory. "Can I come in for a moment?"

Gregory stepped aside for him, shutting the door once he was in the room. "Something bothering you?"

"My grandfather told me that he had an altercation with your father," he answered, speaking to Yukiko. "He said that you had been barred from joining the clan. However," he said quickly holding up a hand to stop her from speaking, "I got him to reconsider. I don't know what happened at the auction house, but I have rarely seen him that angry. I couldn't get him to forego seeking repayment from your father, but he did agree to rescind his ban on you."

"If your grandfather has some issue with my father, then he has an issue with me," Yukiko said simply.

"I thought you might say that," Nick sighed. "If you join the clan, I'm sure he'll change his mind. I wanted you to consider it. It's only a couple more days until the clans can welcome new members into their fold."

Yukiko bowed her head and spoke truthfully, "I shall give it deep consideration."

"Same goes for you, Greg. The offer is still there, along with those considerations I told you about, if you wish to join. I'm sure our archivists can help find your magic."

Gregory nodded, "That would be nice. I doubt I'll be able to survive more than a single fight in the finals without magic."

Nick grinned, "Well, don't worry. I'm sure we won't meet in the first round."

"Speaking of," Yukiko said, rising to her feet with a yawn, "I need my sleep. Tomorrow comes early. Please excuse me," she bowed her head to Gregory and Nick.

Gregory opened the door for her, "Sleep well, Yuki."

"You as well, Greg."

"I should be going, too," Nick said once Yukiko left the room. Lowering his voice, he spoke in a whisper, "Even without her, you'll be welcome in the clan. I have word from those above me on that. Making it to the finals without using any aether, and undefeated? That has been noticed by many people. Though if you bring her, well, just imagine what you could be doing tonight instead of sleeping." With a wink, Nick left the room, leaving behind a small packet of powder.

Gregory's smile had frozen in place and, as he shut the door, it fell from his face. "I'm going to gut you, Nick," he growled, the words a bare whisper in the empty room.

Moving across the room, he began to undress. Thoughts of him and Yukiko in an intimate embrace filled his head, even as he tried to banish them. Exhaling deeply, he gave up on getting much sleep for the night as he slipped into his bedroll.

CHAPTER 53

Dia was sitting on the porch smoking her pipe when Gregory and Yukiko came out the next morning. They thanked her for having her staff help them the night before.

"You're welcome," Dia replied. "You have enough to deal with already. Have you chosen your clan yet?"

"No," Yukiko replied. "Neither of us has found a clan that seems right yet."

"Your rooms will be yours for as long as you need them," Dia smiled. "Or you can switch to different rooms after the tournament ends, if you prefer. I wish you both luck on your bouts today."

"Thank you, Keeper," Gregory said, bowing. "Good day. I hope it is calm."

"It should slow down now that the rush of parents and family has abated. In a couple of days, we'll see a mass exodus, and then the dormitory will be very quiet for a while until the new novices begin to arrive in a month or two."

With another bow, they left Dia and started toward the mess hall.

The mess hall was empty, except for the staff. When Gregory and Yukiko walked in, the five eurtiks on duty started clapping and cheering. The two of them smiled at the exuberant greeting, though they were rather embarrassed.

"That's a bit much isn't it?" Gregory laughed.

"No," Ravol grinned. "We won enough betting on you to pay off the servant debts for some of our family. We did as you said, though, and kept a little back to bet on you again."

"My wife and daughter are no longer indebted," Zenim added. "We can't break the rules, but we will do our very best for you both."

"My sons are all free," Steva added.

"My husband and parents," Velma was quick to chime in. "And Quilet has all of his children free of debt now, as well."

Yukiko waved to the otter who was in the cleaning area, getting a wide smile and wave in return. "We're glad it worked out the way it did."

"You have our gratitude, and if it's okay, our friendship," Ravol said as he loaded plates for them.

"Friends are good," Gregory said. "I come from the fringe; we view things differently there. If your family moved to Alturis, I'm sure they would find it friendlier than here."

"My sons might go," Steva said. "At least one of them will, just to see the birthplace of the man who helped him be free."

Gregory did not respond, unsure of what to say.

"Would he be willing to take a letter with him?" Yukiko asked. "Greg was going to write his family after the tournament."

"Yes, of course."

"Thank you," Gregory managed. "I'll pay the same it would cost me to send it via post."

"That isn't—"

"It is," Yukiko cut the eurtik off. "Accept it, please."

Bowing his head, Steva replied softly, "I will. I'll make sure he's ready after the tournament concludes."

"We'll be betting on both of you today," Velma said as she finished getting their plates organized. "And we hope to do so again tomorrow."

"That would be nice," Gregory said. "We'll do our best."

"Give your families our best wishes, as well," Yukiko smiled. "It's nice to know that we've helped others."

The four eurtik bowed deeply to them as they took their plates. "Our thanks," they said in near unison.

Gregory and Yukiko bowed back, then went to get tea.

"That was weird," Gregory whispered as they took seats.

"That they bet on us, or that they're thanking us?"

"Yes?"

"They explained why before," Yukiko reminded him. "I didn't mind the thanks. They're just grateful that their hope in us wasn't misplaced. The fact it will help their families is good."

"Hmm," Gregory muttered, considering her explanation while he ate.

* * *

They ate in silence, with Gregory thinking about the eurtik. He spoke up as they were walking to the archive. "I guess I don't mind, but I don't feel like I deserve it either."

Yukiko smiled warmly at him, "You're a good man, dear one. I've known others who would have asked for part of their winnings or other considerations for having been the key to their good fortune."

"Huh."

"Good morning, finalists," Rafiq greeted them as they entered the archive. "Best wishes for today."

"Thank you, Rafiq," they said together, giving him a shallow bow.

"Did your superior enjoy the matches?" Gregory asked.

"Most of them," Rafiq replied. "Here to study until it is time for your fights?"

"Here for an hour," Gregory said as fourth bell chimed. "We want to get other training in before they announce the matches."

"You could stay for two hours today," Rafiq told them. "They won't announce the matches at the main arena until the eleventh bell, and they won't start until the twelfth bell. The time before and after is filled with the apprentice matches."

"Two hours here, then two in meditation," Yukiko said. "We'll still have plenty of time to see my parents before our matches are announced."

"Sounds like a good plan," Gregory smiled at her.

"May your training be fruitful," Rafiq told them. "I wish to thank you. You weren't aware of it, but a number of us had wagers on you to make it this far."

"You, too?" Gregory asked with a raised eyebrow. "The cooks we knew about."

"Those of us who've seen your devotion to your training bet on you," Rafiq replied. "It is hard not to believe in those who strive to better themselves. None of the other novices come more than once a week. You two, though, you are here every day without fail."

"Who did you all bet against?" Yukiko asked.

"Certain magi who think less of us than they should," Rafiq said bluntly. "It was nice to see them upset in a way that didn't reflect badly on us or our superiors."

"Good," Gregory nodded. "Going to bet more today?"

"I've set aside a part of my winnings to do just that. It seems the losers are hoping to get some of it back," Rafiq's grin was wide. "We're just waiting to see who you're both matched up against and the odds."

"Have at it," Gregory chuckled.

"Can you place a bet for me?" Yukiko asked.

"Certainly," Rafiq agreed.

Yukiko pulled her coin purse from her bag and counted out two thousand vela in five hundred vela coins. "Half on me and half on Greg, provided we aren't fighting each other."

"I will make sure it is handled," Rafiq said as he took the vela.

"Come on, Yuki," Gregory said, shaking his head, "we need to get training. Have a good day."

"Good day," Rafiq replied to them both.

* * *

The ninth bell chimed and the two novices came out of their meditative trances. Both were covered in a light sheen of sweat from the physical side of the training. They shared a smile, pleased that they were growing faster and better than their peers.

"The fire seemed brighter for me today," Yukiko said as she wiped the sweat off her face.

"And the channels in the stone are larger," Gregory added.

"It's odd that we can manage this but others can't," Yukiko murmured as she started to gather her things.

"In a way. I was led to believe this takes complete belief that it is possible. I didn't doubt it."

"And I didn't doubt you," Yukiko smiled softly. "I should have, but I didn't. It's like the stars aligned when I met you. Everything has just gone right since that day."

"My life has been wonderful since that day, as well," Gregory said, wrapping his arms around her from behind as she stood up.

Yukiko leaned against him, sighing happily. "Dear one, you spoil me with your love."

"And you do me," he kissed the side of her neck, eliciting a shiver from her.

"Dear one..." Yukiko exhaled as she leaned into him a bit more, "we need to go."

"I know," Gregory sighed as he gently eased her away from him.

Taking a deep breath, Yukiko took a moment to make sure she was steady. She had not expected her legs to get so shaky when he kissed her neck. Once she was sure she was good, she moved toward the door where Gregory was waiting for her.

Gregory and Yukiko headed back to the dormitory, thinking that the most likely place to find Yukiko's parents or a message from them. They passed a number of visitors, overhearing snippets of conversation from them. Most seemed to center on the remaining eight novices and the merits of each. Both of them hid their smiles as they kept walking.

A hundred yards from the dormitory, one of the eurtik staff came out of a hidden path to meet them. "Greetings. Keeper Dia wished me to inform you that your mother is at the main arena, and that you might wish to remain scarce from the dormitory, unless necessary."

"Oh, why?" Gregory asked.

"Representatives of the smaller and mid-size clans are waiting to speak with you. The keeper is under the impression that you would rather not deal with them."

"Thank her for us," Yukiko said with gratitude, "she is correct. We'll return later tonight."

"Best of luck with your bouts," the eurtik bowed and disappeared back down the hidden path.

"Let's retreat," Gregory chuckled as they turned back toward the arenas.

They found Yoo-jin and Lin with the help of an usher. Yoo-jin was seated in a small private box. Lin stood guard, with his back to a wall.

"Where is Father?" Yukiko asked when they entered the box.

"Resting. He is still tired from dealing with Grandmaster Shun at the auction," Yoo-jin replied. "He'll join us for dinner. Once the fights are over for today, we will have ample free time since we won't be attending the auctions again."

"Did you have plans?" Yukiko asked her.

"I was thinking a visit to a tea house. It will help you unwind from the fights, and it's one of the things that has to be done before your betrothal is announced."

"That is lovely. Thank you, Mother."

"Of course, we've always done our best for you." She smiled at Yukiko, then turned to Gregory. "It seems the apprentices are having a tournament, as well. They are fighting in teams, apparently comprised of their clans."

"Interesting," Gregory said, looking on. He wondered why the tournament was different for the next tier of magi, and made a mental note to ask Rafiq about it.

CHAPTER 54

G regory did not realize how engrossed he had gotten in the fights until the last one ended just ahead of the eleventh bell. A magi walked to the middle of the arena and waited patiently for the crowd to quiet. He spoke with a deep commanding voice that filled the arena. "We pause now to announce the final eight in the novice tournament. Our fighters, like you, are present, and waiting to hear who they will be facing this day."

The speaker waited as a cheer rose from the crowd. Two large banners, which had been securely tied up on either side of the arena, unrolled so everyone could clearly see the brackets.

Gregory and Yukiko exchanged happy smiles. Their names were on opposite sides of the bracket, which meant they only had a chance to face off in the final match. Next, they looked for their first opponents.

"Franco Ichon," Yukiko frowned. "He has been the most brutal to his opponents."

"Yeah. You should use your ring and end him as quickly as you can," Gregory replied. "It'll tip your hand to Nick or Hayworth, but Franco wants to cripple those he fights."

"Yes, that is likely for the best," Yukiko nodded. "You have Jenn

Bean as your opponent; she's one of the best fighters in the class. She might only be five foot and weigh nearly nothing, but that hasn't stopped her at all."

"She'll be hard to beat," Gregory agreed. "Her physical enhancement magic easily makes up for her lack of physical presence."

"She's only had a single loss and that was to Jason."

"We'll manage," Gregory said. "We'll be meeting in the final, after all."

"I believe you'll both be fine," Yoo-jin smiled. "Gregory, you have your bout first. We'll be watching."

"I should get down there so I'm not late," Gregory said, getting to his feet. "I'll leave my things here."

"I'll keep it safe for you," Yukiko replied with a small smile.

* * *

Gregory was surprised to encounter Jenn in the waiting area under the arena. "Ah, sorry. I'll go to the other one."

"Unless you plan to attack me down here, it's fine," Jenn said as she stretched. "Everything I've seen from you indicates you aren't inclined to do that."

"I won't," Gregory admitted as he moved into the room. "Glad to see the healer was able to patch up the damage from the fire."

Jenn winced, "That was unpleasant. My magic does nothing to help with that. Slightly accelerated healing isn't any good when your skin and muscle have been melted. If that hadn't been my third fight that day, I don't know if I'd even be here, honestly."

"You're one of the top fighters in the class with your enhancement magic. It's going to be a damned hard fight. Without a trump card like that fire, how many can beat you?"

Jenn frowned and thought about his question, "Not sure if you are being honest or scheming something. As I've already told Nick Shun, I will not make a deal to lose a fight. I wish to win all of it."

"Wouldn't ask you to," Gregory said as he sat down, closing his eyes and starting to slow his breathing. "He needs to lose, regardless. If you beat me, make sure you're ready for his or Jason's fire."

"I thought you were friends with him?" Jenn asked curiously.

"Maybe when we first started talking, but then I saw beneath his mask."

"I see," Jenn murmured. "Which clan are you thinking of joining?" When Gregory did not reply, she turned around to find him in the lotus position, breathing slowly. "Spirit path? A pity," she sighed, going back to stretching, training her body path as much as she could.

* * *

When the call for them came, Gregory's eyes opened and he got to his feet. Jenn was already moving to the exit, well ahead of him. Taking a deep breath, he waited a few more seconds before he followed her.

When he stepped onto the sands, the crowd became even more animated. Magus Paul was not officiating. Instead, a grandmaster that Gregory had never seen before stood in his place. As he approached the magi, Gregory faced Jenn, seeing her resolve to win.

"Novices, making it this far is a great thing. The clans you join will gain honor from your presence. Even a loss here is still better than the majority of your peers managed. The rules are the same. Give us a good fight. Turn to face the box and bow."

They did as instructed, bowing to the boxes, the grandmaster, and then finally, each other. The moment they finished bowing, the grandmaster called for them to fight.

Jenn did not hesitate, already infusing her body with aether. She dashed forward, her leg snapping into a front kick. Gregory had seen enough of her fights to know that dodging at the start was the best way to survive the early part of the fight. Coming out of his roll, he was able to find her again before she closed the distance a second time.

Keep moving, make her use her aether, drain her of it, then, if I'm still able to move, I might be able to win, Gregory repeated his plan to himself as he dodged her next kick.

The crowd cheered, but the cheers died away as the fight continued. Gregory was not fighting back, but evading as much as he could. Each blow that did land made him grit his teeth, as it was as strong as or stronger than Gunnar could have managed.

Physical enhancement is impressive, Gregory thought as the small slip of a woman came at him again. *Got to keep moving*, he muttered in his own head as he waited for his ring to help heal the nasty bruises he felt forming.

A minute turned into two with Jenn chasing Gregory around the arena. "Why won't you fight?" she finally spat at him, coming to a stop.

"I am," Gregory panted as he faced her, his body an aching mess. "Can't face you head on while you have your aether." Spitting a bit of blood, he shook his head, "It's hard enough staying on my damned feet."

Realization dawned for Jenn, "I apologize. It was a good idea, but I'm not even close to being tired yet."

Gregory sighed. He felt his ring stop working as its energy was depleted, but he felt better than he had. "I'm not surprised," Gregory admitted. "It was my first gambit."

Jenn frowned, "Which means you have other plans."

The crowd had stopped cheering entirely, and a few even booed as the novices continued to stand there. Both of them glanced at the stands with exasperated looks.

"It matters not. I will win this tournament," Jenn said flatly.

Almost fully healed, Gregory shifted his stance and beckoned her. "Only if you defeat me."

Jenn scowled, "Fine with me."

She rushed forward and Gregory waited for her. Just as she planted her foot for the kick, Gregory lunged forward, slamming into her and taking them both to the ground. Jenn grunted at the impact — it felt like a wall had slammed into her. Shaking her head, she was surprised to find Gregory no longer above her. She saw him a few feet away, again set in a defensive stance.

"What was that?" Jenn grunted as she got to her feet.

"Good question," Gregory replied evenly.

The grandmaster watched impassively, glad that Gregory had finally taken an aggressive action, and the crowd settled back down for a moment.

"That won't stop me," Jenn said as she faced him.

Gregory beckoned her again, not replying to her words. With a growl, she shot forward, her speed enhanced to the maximum, a blur to most of the crowd. A scream of pain rose up from the arena and Jenn staggered back. One of her legs buckled under her as she tried to put weight on it.

"What?" Jenn hissed in pain, her leg nearly broken from her own attack. "What did you do?"

"Sorry," Gregory replied as he rushed forward, on the attack finally.

Jenn spun to keep up with him, but her injured leg nearly buckled on her, slowing her turn. Gregory kicked out, his foot slamming into her injured shin. Gregory kept his face blank as he attacked her injured leg repeatedly, always moving to her bad side, attacking her leg over and over again.

With the tables turned and the pain from her leg climbing, Jenn knew she had to act. When Gregory came in to attack her again, she lunged at him, intent on taking him to the ground. She miscalculated though, and Gregory had been waiting for her. When she lunged, he threw himself to the side. Jenn's fingers grazed his leg, but she missed grabbing him. Rolling back to his feet, Gregory rushed back at Jenn as she got to her knees. Slamming into her back, Gregory got his arms around her neck.

Jenn grunted, but she forced herself upright on her knees, then snapped her body forward. Gregory was surprised at how much leverage she was able to get as he went flying over her head. Jenn was not done. Her shin might be all but shattered, but her knees and hands were fine. Scrambling forward, she managed to grab Gregory's legs as he tried to get away.

"Now you're mine," she snarled, dragging him to her.

The crowd started cheering again as they sensed the end of the fight nearing. Gregory kicked at her as she pulled him ever closer, but she swatted his leg away. Jenn glared as she raised a hand, intent on making him pay. Seeing her target, Gregory grimaced, turning to the side enough that she hammered his hip instead of his groin. He smiled when her fist connected; the blow had been weaker than any other she had landed during the fight.

He sat up and grabbed her arms. She tried to yank them away, but failed. Eyes widening, she realized that her aether was all but gone.

"No," she spat, pushing herself forward and using her one free hand to hit him in the chin. Her hand was covered in blue flames as she used the last of her aether to strike him with her full enhanced strength.

His eyes rolled back in his head, but Gregory was able to stay conscious. He covered his face, waiting for Jenn to continue the attack while he blinked to clear his vision. When nothing happened, he moved one hand far enough to see Jenn sprawled atop him, unconscious.

"Winner, Pettit," the grandmaster announced when Gregory rolled Jenn off of him. "Healer, we need some help. She exhausted herself."

Gregory got to his feet slowly and bowed to the box. He straightened up and wobbled as darkness rushed up to swallow him.

CHAPTER 55

"He'll wake soon. There was only minor swelling and a broken jaw," a harsh voice said, sending waves of pain through Gregory. "See, he's waking up."

Gregory groaned and opened his eyes. He squeezed them shut as light stabbed into them like knives. "Pain," the word was whispered, but even that seemed too loud.

"It will pass on its own," the man said. "Give it a few minutes."

"You are sure?" Yukiko asked with concern.

"Yes. The last hit the other novice delivered should have made the match a draw, but this one has a harder head than anyone would expect."

"You may go, healer," Yoo-jin said politely, "thank you."

A soft hand touched his forehead a moment later, "Greg?"

"Head feels like a boulder hit it," Gregory whispered. "Who won?"

"You did," Yukiko replied softly. "Jenn used all her aether and passed out. You got to your feet after she hit you. The adjudicator declared you the winner."

The pain receded slowly. The soft, cool hand on his head brushed his hair, and his lips turned up at the corners.

"Now that you know he is fine, you need to get going, Yu. I will stay with him."

Yukiko's hand stilled on his head and was removed, only to be replaced by her lips. "I'm off for my fight. Wish me luck."

Gregory reached up blindly and caught her hand. "You don't need luck. You will win, and easier than I did." Pulling her hand down, he kissed it. "I'll still wish you luck, though."

"Go," Yoo-jin said gently. "He'll be waiting for you."

"Yes, Mother," Yukiko sighed as she gently pulled her hand away from Gregory.

"Your plan could have been better," Lin said after a few minutes of silence.

"If I had waited another minute, it would have worked fine," Gregory said with a grimace.

"If she had gotten ahold of you sooner, you would be in worse shape and would have lost."

"True."

"He did win, though," Yoo-jin said. "No one wins every fight without setbacks."

"That is also true," Lin admitted.

"I should have lost," Gregory muttered. "She had me outclassed in magic and skill. If she hadn't hurt her leg against the shield, I would have lost pretty quickly. It was only that which let me capitalize and win."

"It looked like you planned it," Yoo-jin commented.

"It was my worst plan, but she had a depth of aether I wasn't expecting, so I had to try it."

"Excuse me," a feminine voice said, "may I speak with him?"

"Of course," Yoo-jin replied. "We'll be staying in the room, though. I promised to watch after him until he is recovered."

"That's fine," the woman said. "You okay, Gregory?"

"Jenn?"

"Yes, they got me mobile again. Feels like a carriage hit me. I wanted to come apologize for hitting you like I did. I was just so upset that you had managed to stop me and I wanted to get a solid hit in on you at least once."

Gregory slowly opened his eyes, wincing. The pain was less, but not gone entirely. "You did that. If I hadn't delayed you as long as I had, you would have won."

"But I didn't," she sighed. "You better win the rest of the tournament. Then at least I only lost to the winner."

Gregory snorted, which caused his head to pound again. "I'll do my best."

"I wanted to ask how you made it feel like I hit a wall. Twice, once when you tackled me and when I broke my own leg."

"Enchanted barrier," Gregory mumbled.

"The healer said you're going to be okay, right?" Jenn asked, frowning down at him.

"Yes," Yoo-jin answered for him. "He just has a nasty headache that is supposed to fade shortly."

"Good," Jenn nodded. "I'll be watching tomorrow." A bell chimed, and Jenn looked over her shoulder. "The next fight is starting. I wanted to watch it, so I'll see you later."

Gregory frowned, his memory a little cloudy, but after a moment, he asked what was troubling him, "Didn't Yuki fight third?"

"Yes," Yoo-jin replied. "You've been out for a while. "Nick Shun won his match after yours. I believe that Hayworth is still being tended to by the head healer."

"Fire?" Gregory asked.

"A few of them, yes," Lin replied.

"Hmm," Gregory muttered as he wondered about how hard it would be for Yukiko to beat Nick tomorrow if she won her current fight. "Be safe, Yuki," he whispered as he waited for his headache to subside, closing his eyes again in the hope that it would help.

* * *

"Greg, are you feeling better?" Yukiko's voice pulled him from sleep.

Blinking, he saw Yukiko bending over him when his eyes would focus. "Hey. How did your fight go?"

"I won, but I won't be surprising anyone with the shadow leap anymore. Franco didn't stand a chance when he attacked me. I had backed myself against the wall, and he rushed me, expecting to pin me there. I vanished, he hit the wall hard, and then I broke one of his knees. He gave up pretty quickly when I started to grind it with my heel."

Gregory chuckled, "Well, turnaround is fair play."

"That means you both move on tomorrow," Yoo-jin said. "Lin is collecting my winnings and once he's back, we will be going."

"You bet on us?" Gregory asked when he sat up.

"Of course. Though you did give me a fright at the start of your fight. Yu didn't bat an eye, just kept telling me it was going to be okay."

"I'll end up facing Jason or Klein Armit, and you get Nick," Gregory frowned. "Are you going to be able to handle all the flames he threw during his fight?"

"I'll be fine. I have a couple of ideas on how to handle the fight. Will you be able to deal with Jason?"

"Nothing will stop me from reaching you," Gregory said seriously as he stared into her eyes.

Yukiko blushed a deep red at his words. "Oh. Then I will have to fight twice as hard."

"Now that you've both won and Gregory is feeling better, we can go. Tea, and then to meet your father for dinner."

A knock sounded at the door and Lin entered. "I have the vela."

"Good, let's go."

As they left the building, Gregory heard cheering behind him. "Did the last fight start already?"

"No, two adepts had a disagreement and asked to fight before the last match," Yukiko explained.

"I won't know who I face until later," Gregory said. "I'm thinking it'll be Jason, though. He's Nick's right hand and will likely be outfitted with quite a few tricks."

"That is likely, which means we will really earn the ire of the Eternal Flame."

Gregory and Yukiko shared a smile as they walked side by side, following Yoo-jin. Lin trailed them, shaking his head as he watched the two of them, comparing them to Yoo-jin and Hao from years before.

* * *

As they made their way to the tea house, Yukiko explained what Gregory should expect. She did her best to reassure him that it would be okay if he made minor mistakes, but as he would be following Yoo-jin and her, he should be fine.

"This is common for those who are about to experience a major life change?" Gregory asked.

"In the heart of the empire and major cities, yes. Even in most large towns," Yukiko replied.

"The custom has helped us avoid some bad deals, as well as helped assure us of good ones," Yoo-jin said. "The meditative nature of the ceremony helps focus the mind."

The carriage came to a stop, cutting off conversation. Getting out after the women, Gregory was surprised when Lin stayed behind.

"There is no place for him to wait without being involved," Yoo-jin explained when she saw Gregory hesitate.

Looking at the wall that surrounded their destination, Gregory felt a sense of peace begin to settle over him. The door opened, and a mature lady in an elaborate multicolored kimono bowed to them and motioned them inside. Gregory had to force himself to not thank her, as you were supposed to remain silent once in the garden.

The door closed softly behind them and the lady moved to the front, leading them down a path. Trees lined the path, screening the path so anyone on it could not see what might be beyond them. They moved at a slow, deliberate pace, and Gregory felt the peace of the area start to relax him.

Walking at the pace set by their guide helped Gregory find a light meditative state as the path wound around the interior of the walled area. They eventually came to a small square building near the center of the grounds. Pausing on the threshold, their guide removed her slippers and set them aside. The other three copied her, not putting on any other footwear as she opened the sliding door and entered.

The room was not large. In the center was a small fire pit where a covered pot sat. Gregory followed Yukiko, taking a seat beside her on one side of the room, with Yoo-jin to their left side and their hostess across from them. Once they were seated, the lady bowed again and presented each of them a small lacquered plate, upon which a single small confection sat.

Gregory accepted the plate with a bow of his own, setting it before him. Yukiko waited for the others to have their plates, then used the chopsticks provided to eat it. Bowing to their hostess, Yukiko set her chopsticks back on the plate. Gregory did as Yukiko did, though he almost dropped the morsel, being unskilled with chopsticks. The small treat melted almost instantly, spreading a warm feeling through his mouth, then down into his chest.

Their hostess laid out the tea service, wiping each item in a ritualized manner with a clean white cloth. Her total attention was on her task, cleaning each item in what was clearly a specific manner.

Once she had set aside the cleaned items, she picked up the kettle and poured a small amount of hot water into the ceremonial tea bowl. As she went about cleaning the whisk and the bowl, Gregory felt his mind start to drift.

The space to his right seemed to fall into shadow, which grew deeper with each breath. He kept his gaze straight ahead, knowing what the shadow represented.

"A tea ceremony? Well, that is one way to get my attention," a familiar silken voice said from the shadow. "Don't frown— they can't hear me. Only you can, since I'm not really here."

The hostess measured two scoops of powder into a tea bowl and added hot water from the pot, then used the whisk to combine them.

"She is a devoted woman. I should be jealous that she's getting all of your attention," the shadow pouted. "But how can I be when she brings you such joy? Yes, Yuki, not the hostess. You are supposed to get a sense of whether the path before you is a true one or a false one. What you get instead is me and my assurance that the path is true. Yuki shall be your most devoted and loving follower, and soon, your wife."

Gregory felt detached. He had questions he wanted to ask, but the moment just seemed to wash over him as Yukiko accepted the tea bowl from the hostess and drank. She handed it back to the hostess with her eyes closed, looking to be lost in a trance. Gregory watched the hostess rinse the bowl before making more tea.

"I know all of what you want to ask. I'll tell you one thing. Your path is going to be full of hardships, but also full of love. Yuki will help keep you on the right path; you two are perfectly matched for each other. It reminds me of... well, that's a topic for later. The tea is ready, drink up."

Gregory reached out, taking the bowl from the hostess. He bowed his head to her and drank. The thick green liquid felt like it opened the world wider to him. Handing the bowl back slowly, his eyes closed and the room vanished, leaving him in the opulent bedroom he had come to know when speaking with the darkness.

"There we are," the darkness giggled. "Now, we can have a little fun."

Yukiko appeared beside him. She appeared shocked when she looked around and saw him there in the room with her. "A dream again?"

"No dream, dear," the darkness said happily. "You and our heart are inside his meditative state. This is hard to do, so use these moments well."

"Greg?" Yukiko asked hesitantly.

"It seems we are both really here," Gregory said, reaching out to take her hand.

"This must mean we are on the right path, that we should be wed," Yukiko's smile could have blinded anyone who saw it.

"Yes," Gregory murmured as he reached up and brushed her hair back behind her ear.

"Something he wanted even more than me," the darkness sighed. "I was a little upset by that for a few days. I realized, though, that not only are you not trying to take him from me, Yuki, you are helping him grow even faster."

"Who are you?" Yukiko asked the darkness.

"He's spoken about me already. I am his aether, and he is my heart," the darkness replied with a laugh. "Your mother's tale is true in a way, but has lost some of its meaning over the long centuries since it was first spoken."

Yukiko's brow furrowed, "Your heart?"

"As well as yours, don't be jealous. You know that powerful men attract others. I have conquered my jealousy of you. Even though you get to be with him in the flesh, something I won't be able to do…"

"Greg?" Yukiko asked as she stared into the darkness. "I've seen this room before, in a dream."

"I know, I remember," Gregory admitted. "It was hard not to ask you if that was how you really felt."

Yukiko was blushing, but she shook her head, "It was. I hoped so much."

"Yuki, there is one thing I need to know," the darkness said, stopping them before they could follow that line of thought very far. "What would you do for him?"

"Anything," Yukiko replied without hesitation.

"Kill?"

"Yes."

"Support?"

"Yes."

"Share?"

"…"

"Come now, I shared him with you," the darkness said. "I could have whispered in his dreams and turned him away from you. Instead, I brought him closer to you."

"Share with you? Do I have a choice? You are his aether… he can't divorce himself from you."

"We'll leave it for now. But Yuki, if you ask nicely, I can let you share dreams together on occasion. That would let you get to *know* him before your wedding."

Yukiko went crimson and started to stammer, then she vanished.

"Sadly, our time is over until the end of the tournament. You are growing a following and that makes me happy. Next year will be even harder for you in some ways, but much easier in others. Until later, dear one."

Gregory blinked, coming back to his senses. The hostess was bowing to them and he bowed back by reflex. He got to his feet, following the hostess as she left the building. The moment was broken the second they crossed the threshold of the wall.

"Well?" Yoo-jin asked them.

Gregory and Yukiko shared a long look, each thinking about what had just occurred. Yukiko spoke slowly, "We are destined to be together. Our life is going to be complex, complicated, but full of love."

"Together," Gregory said softly as he took her hand in his, "forever."

"Then it was a success," Yoo-jin smiled. "Let's go eat."

Gregory frowned in surprise when he saw the sun was setting. "We were in there longer than I thought."

"Yes, that is normal," Yoo-jin said. "The mediation of the tea ceremony is a complicated thing. I'm sure the academy has books on it."

"I'll be looking into it," Yukiko said, her cheeks turning a light shade of pink.

Gregory corrected her gently, "We will."

CHAPTER 56

When they arrived at Stabled Hunger, Gregory smiled. He had enjoyed the food here and would be sad when they no longer came here to eat. The Warlin's guards took up the majority of the tables in the front room.

When Gregory and Yukiko entered, the guards all stood up and began to applaud them. They paused in the doorway, a little embarrassed at the showing. Lin chuckled behind them, patting them on the shoulder.

"Okay, that's enough. They still have to fight tomorrow to make it to the final round," Yoo-jin said. "We apologize for interrupting your meals," she added to the other tables. "Ramon, please give them a round of drinks on our tab."

The bartender bowed his head, "Yes, ma'am."

"Thank you," one of the patrons replied. "I take it they're both in the final four?"

"Yes. My daughter, Yukiko Warlin, and her friend, Gregory Pettit," Yoo-jin smiled. "They will be well-known by the end of the year."

The man she was speaking to nodded, "I'll have to keep my eyes open and see if either takes the top spot."

"One of them will take the top spot," Yoo-jin replied, sounding certain. "I would love to talk more, but we are keeping my husband waiting. Have a good meal."

Lin stopped to check in with his second in command while Yoo-jin, Gregory, and Yukiko continued down the hall to the private dining room. Entering the room, Yoo-jin smiled at her husband, "Dear one, how are you feeling?"

"Better, but still recovering," Hao replied. His smile widened upon seeing the two behind her, "I heard you both won, which is good."

Gregory was concerned about Hao's health. The merchant had deep circles under his eyes, his hands shook slightly, and it seemed like he had more traces of gray showing in his hair. "Yuki will be facing Nick Shun tomorrow. I'll be facing Jason Argon or Klein Armit, depending on who won the last fight."

"Jason will be your opponent. Word was brought to me while you were out," Hao replied. "I wanted to know before you arrived."

"You arranged that greeting?" Yoo-jin sighed with a fond smile.

"They need to get used to it, as they will become well known to many in the coming years."

"Father," Yukiko shook her head, "we have time."

"Not as much as you might think," Hao said seriously. "All the great clans are interested in you, and you have made it to the top four in the first novice tournament. I trust you to be able to handle those who will try to use you, but you need to guard him."

"I will," Yukiko said simply. "No one will harm my heart."

"The proctor who brought me in warned me," Gregory said. "I'm aware that not everyone who appears friendly will be. Nick has helped prove that point, as well."

"Good," Hao replied. "The drinks—"

A knock on the door cut him off. The owner's daughter came in, delivering drinks for them. Once they all had beverages, she bowed, "Your meals will be brought shortly."

"Thank you," Yoo-jin smiled. "Let your mother know that we are looking forward to it."

"Yes, ma'am."

Dinner was wonderful. The steaks were cooked to their individual preferences and served with a garlic honey glaze that had them all smiling. The vegetables were steamed so they were tender, but still firm. Dessert was cream puffs, served with honeyed fruit on the side.

Sipping the tea afterward, Gregory felt sated and a little sleepy.

"Oh, your gloves are being examined by Hemet," Hao said. "He sent word that he's having trouble with them. I left the box with him as well, so it will appear that we haven't opened it. He has already returned that. He offered to buy it until I told him the price. I've reached out to the Han clan to see if they would be interested and I should hear back from them tomorrow." Pausing, he looked down, "I'll likely be missing the fights tomorrow. I'm sorry, but it's taking me longer to recover than I had expected. I am discovering that I'm not as young as I used to be."

"Father, rest and recover. I know that you need time after moments like that. I'm not surprised that it's more extreme after facing down a grandmaster."

"We understand, sir," Gregory said, though he clearly did not.

"It's a family secret," Yoo-jin said to Gregory. "You'll learn once you officially join the family."

Thinking about his own secrets, Gregory could only bow his head to her, "I understand."

"In that vein," Hao said with a smile, "we will be holding your betrothal dinner at Gin's. We need to know by tomorrow night who you would like to attend."

Gregory and Yukiko exchanged a glance, wondering who they should invite. After a moment, they both had the same thought. "The eurtiks?" Yukiko asked first.

"Yes," Gregory smiled. "They've been our only real friends, though I'm not sure they would be able to attend. We'll have to ask them tomorrow."

"Do you have an approximate number?" Hao asked.

"At least ten?" Gregory asked Yukiko.

"At least, though depending on their families, maybe four or five times that. We'll ask and have them notify you here, Father."

"That will work," Hao nodded. "I had to invite Marcia Han. I apologize for that, but it is a concession to keep the Han clan, if not happy, at least neutral to us."

"I understand, Father," Yukiko replied. "Considering the Eternal Flame is going to be hostile, it will be good to have at least one of the other major clans not ranged against us."

"Hopefully the other great clans won't be as upset as the Eternal Flame is going to be," Gregory said worriedly. "Besides Grandmaster Shun being upset because of the auction, their two frontrunners are going to lose to us tomorrow."

"Yes, there is that," Hao agreed. "It would be good to find a clan you can both agree on, but with them against you, I can't think of any smaller clan that would take you in. If you would even want them to take you in," Hao finished.

"I'm fairly certain I've heard from all the clans that are represented inside the academy walls. I could check with Keeper Dia, she would know for certain," Yukiko said. "The clans not represented don't want to involve themselves in the politics of the academy, which is a point in their favor, but also makes it harder to know if we would fit in with them."

"If things stay the same, we will keep supporting you in place of a clan. Truthfully, we would anyway," Hao chuckled. "My beautiful daughter deserves everything I can give her."

"Dinner is done, and the two of you have a big day ahead of you. It would be best for you to get going," Yoo-jin said. "Get your sleep. I will be at the arena again tomorrow, waiting for you."

"Thank you, Mother, Father," Yukiko smiled as she rose to her feet. "We will do our best to make you proud."

"Thank you," Gregory bowed to them both. "I will do everything I can to protect and help Yuki."

The two of them left the older couple in the room. As they entered the main room, conversations stopped and all eyes turned to them. The tavern was busier than it had been and the room was now filled with people.

A man with wolf ears stood up and bowed to them, "My family thanks you."

"As does mine," another added, bowing as well.

As more of the customers in the inn spoke up, Gregory realized that the majority of them were eurtik, either full-blood or of mixed descent. Yukiko stood beside him, feeling just as awkward as Gregory was.

"We will be rooting for you tomorrow," another said.

"As you're facing two who will be joining the Eternal Flame, it's a bit poignant to us."

More comments of similar sentiment piled on and eventually, Gregory raised a hand to get them to quiet down. "We are honored that you are thanking us. We will do our best tomorrow, for both ourselves and all of you."

Gregory and Yukiko got into the carriage and were taken back to the academy. One of the staff from the dormitory met them short of the building and led them up the back stairs again.

"Is Keeper Dia free?" Yukiko asked their guide.

"I will let her know you wish to speak with her," the staff member said before slipping away.

"Your room?" Gregory asked.

"Since I asked for her, it's for the best," Yukiko agreed, opening the door.

They had just started to work on Magi Squares when a soft knock came on the door. Yukiko answered it, stepping aside for Keeper Dia.

"What may I help you with, Novice?"

"My family is holding an announcement party the night after tomorrow, and I was asked to find out how many would be attending," Yukiko explained. "It is family or friends for this event, but that is difficult for us. We don't have any real friends among the other novices, but you and your staff have been very helpful, so I would like to extend an invitation to all of you. It would be late, after the final match."

Dia's lips turned up at the corners, but she shook her head. "I must sadly decline. I'm to remain neutral in all things where those in training are concerned. I will ask my staff if any of them would like to go. Congratulations on making it to the final four, and best of luck on making it to the final."

"Very well. We had hoped, but we understand."

"I'll have an answer for you in the morning, if that is acceptable," Dia replied.

"Yes, Keeper, and thank you," Yukiko said, bowing her head to the older woman.

"Thank you, Keeper," Gregory added from his spot at the table.

"Of course. I shall look forward to hearing about the matches tomorrow," Dia replied, bowing her head before she left the room.

"Figures," Gregory sighed. "I had hoped, but I understand why the rule would be in place."

"Yes. We'll ask the cooks and archivists tomorrow when we see them," Yukiko sighed as she came back to her seat. "Let's finish these puzzles and then call it a night."

"That's probably best," Gregory agreed, stifling a yawn.

CHAPTER 57

Exiting the dormitory the next morning, Gregory and Yukiko were in good spirits. "Good morning, Keeper," they greeted Dia, who was exhaling a smoke ring.

"Good morning to you both. Good luck in your fights today. I have been informed that twenty of the staff, plus ten spouses, would like to attend your event. More would have accepted, but I need to keep some here to help run things. If you need it to be less—"

"That'll be fine," Yukiko said quickly. "The more friendly faces, the better."

"Very well. I told them to let me make sure it was okay for that many of them first. Are you going to return here before this evening?"

"No, we aren't planning on it."

"Very well. I will tell the clan representatives who show up to see you so they don't continue to take up a room," Dia said, drawing deeply from her pipe and blowing out a column of smoke rings.

They said their goodbyes and headed off to the mess hall.

"Do you think your parents are going to be okay with so many people showing up?" Gregory asked curiously.

"Yes. Gin's place can easily accommodate over a hundred, and Father will be able to make sure the food and drinks are ready."

"Is it usual for the betrothal party to be large?"

"This will be a small event compared to the last," Yukiko said, a little distant as she was thinking of her first betrothal.

"Huh. We didn't have betrothal parties. It's just the two interested parties telling their parents that they're courting."

"That would be nice," Yukiko smiled. "It would have been much simpler for us, too."

"True," Gregory admitted thoughtfully. "Not sure I would have admitted that I was so interested in you, though, especially since you were already promised to another. We might have ended up in the same place."

"No, it would have been easier for me to admit to you, my parents, and myself. Courting isn't quite the same as a betrothal, though. To most of society, a betrothal is a very serious thing, and breaking one is an insult. I'm sure Father will have made them sorry for doing so, which makes me happy. The one I was betrothed to was... like Nick and Hayworth."

"An arrogant ass?"

Yukiko giggled, "Roughly speaking and crudely said, but honest. It's one of the things I like about you. We might want to work on your tact a little to make it easier when we have to deal with people in powerful positions."

The eurtiks serving in the mess hall greeted them noisily. "There you are! We heard your match was very close," Ravol said to Gregory.

"Hers wasn't. We laughed for a long time over how you tricked your opponent into slamming into the wall," Zenim grinned at Yukiko.

"We are glad to hear you won't be facing each other until the final," Velma cut in.

"Having to face the two forerunners of the Eternal Flame today will be rough," Steva added.

"It'll be rough, but we'll do our best," Yukiko smiled. "The fights today are after high sun, so can we get snacks today as well, please?"

"Yes, I'll put them together while you eat breakfast," Velma said, quickly handing over Yukiko's plate and touching her medallion.

"Thanks. We'll need all the help we can get today," Gregory added as he took his plate, tucking his medallion back into his kimono.

"Before we go, my family is holding a party tomorrow night. I've been asked to invite my friends. Would you five," she glanced at Quilet in the washing area, "like to attend?"

"That would be difficult... we don't stop working until—"

"It'll be fine if you need to arrive late. Your wives and husbands are welcome to attend, as well," Yukiko cut off Velma. "It'll run late, as these things usually do. We're likely to miss breakfast the next morning, ourselves."

Gregory blinked, not having expected that, but accepted it. "We aren't friends with the other novices. You have all been welcoming and friendly to us, so we'd like you to come."

The four cooks exchanged a look and Ravol spoke up. "Are you sure? We're slaves, and—"

"That doesn't matter," Gregory cut in. "The only thing that matters is if you would like to come."

"Please," Velma said first, bowing low to them.

The others voiced their agreement and bowed. Yukiko looked over to see Quilet bowing to them from his station.

"I shall let my parents know that you five will be there a little late, and that your spouses will be there, too," Yukiko smiled. "We look forward to seeing you tomorrow morning for breakfast and for the party."

"We will look forward to it," Ravol said, echoed by the others.

"Oh, I need to get your snacks ready," Velma said, rushing off to do that.

* * *

"Good morning," Rafiq greeted them when they entered the archive.

"Good morning," Gregory and Yukiko said in unison.

"Working on Magi Squares again today?"

"Yes. We have a question to ask you. Would you like to attend a party my family is having tomorrow night?"

Rafiq leaned back a little, "An unusual request. Truthfully, I would like to accept, but I must decline. The rules of the archive forbid us socializing with those attending the academy."

"All archivists?" Gregory asked.

"Yes, everyone who works in these halls. I believe it was one of the reasons Master Damon left us to become the keeper of the blade."

"Oh, we apologize. We didn't know," Yukiko replied, bowing to him.

"No, it is fine. As I said, I would accept if not for the rules. I've never seen novices as studious as you. It makes me happy that at least some of the young are willing to accept our knowledge instead of just relying on the clans."

"We'll be in the back until just before the ninth bell," Gregory said. "Have a good day."

"You as well, and good luck to you both in your bouts today."

They smiled, bowing to him, before heading off to train the mind path.

* * *

Gregory and Yukiko shared a smile as they wiped off the sweat from training the body and spirit paths together. They knew they were making progress, even if it was not easily apparent from day to day. Afterward, they decided to use the bathrooms attached to the training hall. They split up to shower and refresh themselves before heading to the arena.

Gregory paused at the entrance of the bathing room, seeing that Magus Paul was currently using the facility. The plethora of scars that lined the older man's back and arms were disconcerting to Gregory. Shaking his head, he moved over to the bench and began to clean.

"Novice? Did you train this morning?" Paul asked when he noticed he was no longer alone.

"Every morning, sir," Gregory replied.

"Even though you're fighting in a couple of hours?"

"Because of that. It is only through training that we can improve.

I'll be replenishing the little bit of aether I lost and be ready for the fight."

Paul grunted, "Unusual. I believe the other novices are relaxing before they show up to the arena."

"No, sir. Yukiko is currently bathing, as well."

"She would be," Paul nodded. "The two of you are always together. It'll make it harder for you when the clans pull you apart."

"It would be, sir, if we were going to different clans."

"A single clan is getting both of you?" Paul asked with surprise. "It must be one of the five great clans, then. None of the others would be able to entice both of you. If it's the Eternal Flame, they will outstrip the other four great clans within a dozen years."

"It isn't the Eternal Flame, sir."

"I know it isn't my clan— you both visited it briefly months ago."

"The Iron Hand is a different sort of clan, sir. The fact it has completely dedicated itself to the empire made me seriously consider them."

"A pity. With your rapid improvement in fighting, you would have been welcomed," Paul shrugged as he stood up, moving to the tub. "Hopefully, whatever clan you choose is worthy of the martial talent you have." Sinking into the tub, Paul asked the next question with seeming indifference, "It isn't the Hardened Fist, is it?"

"No, sir. If I was going to join a strictly martial clan, it would have been yours."

Nodding, Paul leaned his head back against the edge of the tub, "Good. I would hate to have to face you across the battlefield before you could truly grow."

"Your clans clash, sir?"

"All the time. Other countries hire mercenaries from the Hardened Fist when they end up in conflict with the empire to help blunt our attacks. It's maddening, but the emperor allows it, so we only clash instead of wiping that clan from the empire."

"That is good to know. Thank you, sir, for teaching me on a day off."

"Every day is a day to learn, if one listens. Few novices seem to take the time to understand the words, though many apprentices quickly learn the folly of that."

"Why is that, sir?"

Paul cracked an eye open as Gregory got into the tub. "You don't know what next year brings?"

"No, sir. I come from Alturis. It's a village out on the fringe."

Paul grunted, "You don't fight like a fringer. Next year, you'll be learning how to fight in a group of your clan members. When you become an initiate, you will learn to fight commanding troops. As an adept, you will be given tasks to complete with those troops. If that all goes as it should, you will be deemed a magi and your clan will post you to a position that the empire has need of a magi at. That could be diplomatic, part of the border patrol, or even as a clerk, depending on your classes this year and what your clan deems you able to handle."

Gregory sat there, absorbing the new information. A minute later, he asked, "Are two magi of the same clan ever posted to the same place?"

Paul's lips twitched into a smile and he chuckled. "Thinking of your friend, are you? The answer is, it's almost as rare as hen's teeth."

"I hadn't thought to hear that saying here, sir."

"You're not the only magi from the fringe. We are not common, but we do happen."

"I never would have guessed, sir."

"I worked hard to make it that way. Fringers are given more shit than those who might be favored. I made it to the final eight in both my novice tournaments... never made it to the final. That year was hell, but it got me noticed by the Iron Hand. The next couple of years let me excel. You see, the common soldier respects a man who has done work in his life, more than they do some silk-clad dandy. Keep that in mind. The respect of your troops in the coming years can make all the difference."

"I have one other question, sir," Gregory asked slowly. "What if an initiate doesn't have a clan?"

"The academy will make sure they have troops, but it only

happens once every twenty years or so. They get the troublemakers and normally meet a bad end before they finish the adept tier."

"I see. I will remember, sir. Thank you."

"Now be quiet and let us enjoy the hot water until the bell chimes," Paul said, brushing off the thanks.

Gregory did not reply, but did as he was told. His mind kept turning over what he had learned, and how it might impact him and Yukiko.

CHAPTER 58

Gregory explained to Yukiko what Paul had told him on their way to the arena. Yukiko nodded, "We can always use my father's guards, if needed. I'll let him know. We'll need to find out how many troops we'll need."

"We can ask Dia or Rafiq. I'm sure one of them knows," Gregory suggested.

"Yes, they would likely know."

When they arrived at the arena, they were taken to a box where Yoo-jin was seated. They were surprised to see Hao sitting there with her.

"Father, you are feeling better?"

"Good enough to come watch my daughter put Shun's grandson in his place," Hao replied. "Also, these are for you, Gregory." Hao pulled the gloves from the belt pouch he wore. "Hemet gave up on them. All he could determine is that they have threads of Ryuite woven into them. He apologized and suggested getting a grandmaster, elder, or sage enchanter to look at them."

Gregory quickly slipped the gloves on, "Thank you for trying."

"He didn't charge since he wasn't able to learn about them," Hao replied. "On a good note, he said he knows someone who would pay the vela to purchase the box from me. He'll be in town the night after the tournament ends."

"Thank Aether," Gregory exhaled. "I'm glad, and hope they purchase it."

"We'll find out, but first, you have fights to focus on."

Gregory looked down at the arena, finally paying attention to the apprentices on the sands. Two groups were facing off, and Gregory began to understand what Paul had told him.

"Father," Yukiko said, reminded about the information Gregory had shared with her, "if we don't find a clan, we'll need some guards to act as troops for our third and fourth years, and possibly beyond."

"What?" Hao asked, leaning back.

Yukiko explained what they had been told. Hao nodded, but Lin looked a little grim.

"Sir, we don't have the numbers."

"Which is why she is telling me now," Hao said. "I'll need to know by the end of this year's study. Finding and training enough people in a year will be difficult." Looking at the apprentices below, his eyes unfocused, as he was clearly thinking about what was going to be needed.

Gregory watched the fight with growing trepidation, thinking of himself and Yukiko facing off against Nick and all of his friends. That was another reason to join a clan, above and beyond the other reasons.

Yukiko and Gregory watched the other fights while they waited for their matches. At high sun, they pulled out their snacks and ate them, knowing they would need every bit of aether they could get. Yukiko remembered to tell her father how many people to expect for the party the following night.

* * *

Gregory breathed deeply as he left the waiting area and stepped onto the sands of the arena floor. The same grandmaster from the day before stood in the center of the arena, waiting for him. The crowd was mixed in its reaction— almost equally cheers and boos. Some of those watching were clearly still unhappy with the way he had fought last. Once he reached the middle, Jason stepped out of the tunnel on the other side of the arena. The reaction of the crowd to Jason's appearance was far more favorable. Jason smiled and waved at the stands as he crossed the arena.

When Jason reached the middle, he gave Gregory a small shrug, as if apologizing for the spectators. The voice of the grandmaster that had intervened on his behalf with Skippy's father filled the arena.

"Ladies and gentlemen, guests and fellow magi, we have come to the final four of the novice tournament. Let us take a moment to celebrate the four finalists and cheer them on to do the best they can today. Novices, thank the crowd for coming out to see you fight."

The crowd erupted in cheers, whistles, and applause. Gregory was slower than Jason, who had immediately begun to wave to the crowd again. Instead of copying Jason, Gregory instead turned to the four cardinal directions and bowed to each.

"The winners of today's fights will face off tomorrow as our tournament week concludes," the voice continued once the cheering had died away. "The council thanks you for coming and sharing this time with us as we celebrate our novices and apprentices."

The crowd erupted again, and the grandmaster on the sands waited another minute before he spoke to the novices. "You know the rules," he stated bluntly. "Face the boxes and bow."

Jason's easy-going demeanor fell away, his face serious as he faced the boxes and bowed. Gregory noticed the shift, and knew he was going to face everything Jason had to throw at him.

Gregory felt a sense of peace as he bowed to the magi and finally, to Jason. This was his chance to prove that it did not matter if a great clan backed you; a fringer could still rise up and be the strongest novice.

"Fight!"

Jason did not hesitate, conjuring and throwing a ball of fire as soon as the word left the grandmaster's lips. Gregory was glad he had expected that as he came out of his roll, but when he turned back to face Jason, his eyes went wide at the next fireball already coming at him.

The shield came up, stopping the fire inches from him. His ring quenched the flames, but not as quickly as Gregory would have liked. The intense heat from the fire made his kimono smolder and his eyes dry out. He staggered back, glad when the fire winked out a moment later. Blinking, trying to get moisture back in his eyes, Gregory was shocked to see that neither of his hands were blistered. Jason was suddenly next to him, raining a flurry of punches and kicks down on Gregory with a fury he was unprepared for.

"Go down and it'll be over," Jason hissed at him. "Don't make this worse than it needs to be."

The strikes that Gregory managed to block with his hands and arms felt light, while every other strike hit with bruising force. The crowd was cheering and chanting Jason's name as he continued to bludgeon Gregory. Unable to get a moment's respite, Gregory knew this was not going to end well unless he could do something.

Gregory was able to get his balance back, but it took the last bit of charge in the barrier bracelet. Jason stepped back, shaking his fist after hitting the wall. Gregory spat blood and took a deep breath, meeting Jason's gaze.

"I knew I wasn't the only one with a trick or two," Jason said, flexing his hands to make sure he had not broken anything. "Surprised you survived the fire. Not sure how you managed to extinguish it. The barrier is surprising, but it can't have much left, can it?"

Gregory breathed deeply, aware that his other ring had been fully depleted so he would not be able to heal any further. "Care to find out?"

"Oh, I will," Jason chuckled darkly. "I hoped you would go down quickly, but since you didn't, well, don't blame me for what happens to you now."

Gregory did not like the sound of that, and he liked the sight of blue flames covering Jason's hands even less. "Physical enhancement? Didn't expect that," he admitted.

"You're the first one who's made me use it, so, hey, there's that," Jason smirked. "I'll end this quickly."

Gregory barely had a moment to prepare before Jason rushed him. Gregory fully expected his blocks to be overpowered by Jason's brute strength. They were both surprised when Gregory was able to deflect the four strikes.

Jason's eyes went wide, shocked that Gregory was able to stop him, and his attack faltered. Gregory was surprised as well, but instead of stopping, he countered. His fist connected with Jason's chin, staggering Jason back.

"What?" Jason asked in bewilderment. "You have physical enhancement? No, they know which gem lights up for that."

Gregory did not reply. His own mind raced as he tried to figure out what had happened. He knew he was not using aether like Jason was, but he had stopped the empowered attacks without strain or stress.

The grandmaster was able to conceal his amazement, keeping his face calm. The crowd was still cheering, expecting the fight to end soon. In the main box, the academy council and heads stared at the fight, at a loss to understand how Gregory had managed to stop the aether-fueled attacks. Yukiko's heart jumped into her throat when Jason's arms lit up with aether, but when Gregory blocked them, she beamed and her pride in him soared even higher.

"It doesn't matter... it must have been a trick," Jason spat. "Fine, I'll end it now. Accidents happen, after all."

The hair on Gregory's neck stood up and time seemed to slow as Jason reached for his left arm. Thick bands of aether formed around that arm, Jason glaring at Gregory. Gregory inhaled sharply as the next few seconds played out before his mind's eye.

Gregory threw himself to the right and rolled. He came up facing a different direction and threw himself to the left, then rolled twice more without slowing, coming back to his feet yards away from Jason, who was slack-jawed. Flames burned on the sand where Gregory had been.

The crowd was silent, in awe as large balls of fire formed and were thrown in the span of seconds. Novices could not wield the aether required to fuel those attacks, but Jason had thrown three of them in rapid succession. Gregory's erratic dodging had allowed him to avoid all three of them.

"Stop!" the grandmaster yelled. "Those were killing attempts, Novice."

Jason shook his head, "No, Grandmaster. The intensity of the flame was lower than normal and covered a bigger area." The blue flames on his arm winked out, "They would have burned him, but not been enough to kill."

The grandmaster considered, then nodded. "Very well. Since they missed him, I will let the match continue. Do not use them again."

"I couldn't if I wanted to," Jason muttered. "The stored aether is gone."

"Novice Pettit, do you wish to continue knowing the danger you face?" The grandmaster asked. "You can withdraw from the match."

Gregory shook his head, "I will not withdraw. I will win."

Those words enraged Jason, "Over my dead body!"

"No, just over your broken body," Gregory stated as he waited for the match to continue. He felt his aether working to help him heal. It was not as fast as the ring, but better than no healing at all. "Your loss to me will bring shame to the Eternal Flame."

"Fight," the grandmaster said an instant before Jason rushed at Gregory.

This time, Jason's whole body was covered in aether and he blurred as he came at Gregory. Gregory knew that waiting was going to be a bad idea, so he stepped forward to meet the attack.

When the two separated, Gregory was gritting his teeth in pain. He could feel the cracked ribs with each breath, and his left leg was barely holding him up. The aether covering Jason's body dimmed, then retreated to just his hands as he glared at Gregory.

"Why won't you just fall down?"

"Because I promised to meet someone in the next round," Gregory managed to hiss the words.

Jason laughed, "You think the half-blood will beat Nick? Are you a fool? He knows about her shadow leap trick. He'll never lose to that or her shadow trip thing."

"We'll see after we're done," Gregory gritted out. "You done talking yet? She's waiting for me."

Jason's aether-covered hands burned a little brighter. "Fine. I'll do what the last fighter should have done to you," he sneered

Gregory extended his left hand, silently beckoning Jason. *This is it. You have to find a way here, or it's over and Yuki will fight Nick and then Jason.*

Jason charged at him again, intent on crushing Gregory. His anger was easy to see, that the novice with no magic had forced him to use all of his trump cards and was still standing.

Jason's first punch was deflected to the right, forcing Gregory to put more weight on his injured leg. The pain surged, but he kept his balance as the follow up strike came. Gregory moved by instinct, his block forcing Jason's arm out and allowing his right hand to dart forward.

Jason staggered back a step, his left hand going to his throat, surprised that Gregory had managed to hurt him. The realization that his aether was all but spent flooded his mind; he had been so focused on the fight that he had not been paying it any attention.

The flames on Jason's hands dimmed and went out when he grabbed his neck. Gregory was glad to see that the other novice was out of aether. He stepped in to attack, his left leg supporting him just long enough to allow him to strike Jason under the sternum, driving out what little air Jason had left.

Both of them fell, Jason from the strike and Gregory as his leg finally buckled. The pain almost made him pass out, but Gregory gritted his teeth and climbed on top of Jason, intent on ending the fight. Jason was unable to defend himself.

Seconds ticked by as Gregory hammered the unresisting man, barely able to breathe himself, before the grandmaster finally called him off. Pushing off Jason, Gregory rolled to the side, hissing in pain as he tried to catch his breath. He looked up at the blue sky above him, which was slowly darkening as the pain in his chest grew.

"Healer!" the grandmaster commanded. "They both need your attention, now!"

CHAPTER 59

Gregory became aware of pain when he came back to consciousness. It was duller than he expected it to be, but still there. Peeling his eyes open, he found himself in the healing room again. An older man in healer's robes moved around, putting things away.

"What happened?" Gregory asked, his throat raw.

"You survived, though if there hadn't been healers on hand, you might not have. Your ribs were broken. One of them was splintered and pieces of it shredded your lung. A larger piece also hit your heart. You had a number of lesser injuries as well, including a severely fractured leg. You were injured worse than the other one, but since he stopped defending himself first, the grandmaster ruled in your favor."

"How lo—"

"Now that you're awake, I can get your friends," the healer said, cutting him off. "Don't move. We healed you, but your ribs will be tender for the rest of the day, and you should try to keep off that leg for at least another hour."

Gregory started to reply, but the healer left. With a sigh, he looked for some water, but no cup was to be seen. Yoo-jin glided into the room with a questioning look on her face.

"Water?" Gregory asked.

Yoo-jin stopped by the door and called into the hallway for assistance. Someone replied, and a moment later, Yoo-jin came over to the bed. "They will bring some. You've made a habit of barely winning, it appears."

"Yuki?"

"Fighting now," Yoo-jin replied. "She asked me to come and watch over you, but the healers kept me out until now."

"Your water, ma'am," a young woman with fox ears said, bringing in a small decanter and a cup.

"Thank you," Yoo-jin replied, taking the offered items. "He may have some, yes?"

"Yes. The healer just wants him to stay off his leg for an hour and not exert himself for the rest of the day."

"We shall wait here, then," Yoo-jin said as she poured a cup of water and handed it to Gregory.

The woman bowed and left them alone. Gregory took the cup and sipped, carefully, not wanting to take too big a drink and cough. "Did Jason survive?" he asked once he was sure he was not going to cough.

"They treated him on the field," Yoo-jin replied. "His throat was bruised and it hurt him to breathe. He had the air driven from him, but otherwise, he was fine. You did manage to black his eye and split his lip in the few seconds you beat on him before the grandmaster declared you the victor."

"Fighting the physically enhanced is more difficult than fighting a fire magi," Gregory sighed. "If she can get inside so he can't throw fire, she'll be fine. Nick isn't an enhancement magi."

"Let us hope you are right," Yoo-jin said, trying to hide her worries and failing.

"I have faith in her," Gregory murmured between sips of water.

"You do, don't you?" Yoo-jin said, looking a little better. "Tell me, when did you know you loved her?"

"It wasn't a knowing, it was a growing," Gregory replied. "I liked her from the first day. Truthfully, I probably lusted after her first. She is exquisite, easily eclipsing anyone I had thought beautiful before. Spending time side by side, I learned that she is smart, funny, and caring. The lust was tempered by friendship and the friendship grew. I was sad to learn she was betrothed, but not surprised. It would have been more shocking if she wasn't."

"You might be surprised on that score," Yoo-jin sighed. "We know she is beautiful, but people see the skin, hair, and eyes and they do not see her, they see her heritage. Sorry, I interrupted. Please, continue."

"Her heritage never mattered to me. Still doesn't," Gregory said, looking at the ceiling. "I'll never be able to pin down the moment when I knew exactly, but when you took her from the room to speak of betrothals, my heart died."

"Yes," Yoo-jin smiled gently. "You will be good for her, and she for you. Much like my dear one is for me."

"You and Hao, how did that happen?"

Yoo-jin looked into the distance, recalling memories years behind her. "We met during one of his business deals for the Han clan. He was working under a senior trader and I was a clerk for the shipping company they were making a deal with. Much like Yu and you, I knew on seeing him that he was my heart. It took some time to work out the details of the deal, and the two of us found time to get to know each other. Hao didn't know how smitten I was, but I could see that he was interested in me."

Gregory lay there listening to her, wondering if he and Yuki would be able to look back with the same fond remembrance. Time slipped by as she explained the difficulties they faced to become betrothed. Her father had been beside himself with anger about her choice, but her mother had been able to soothe him enough to agree to the betrothal.

"Prepare a room! We need the burn salve and the eye oils!" The deep commanding voice of the person in charge ordering people around interrupted Yoo-jin.

Gregory had been smiling, but on hearing the urgency of the words, his heart clenched. He tried to stand, but Yoo-jin pushed him flat, shaking her head at him. "Stay here. I will go. You don't want to break your leg again; she wouldn't forgive you."

Gregory was torn between agreement and pushing her away and going himself. Shaking his head, he tried to stand again. Yoo-jin sighed as she helped him up. "Lean on me, then."

Gregory did as she said, leaning on her and hobbling with his injured foot raised off the floor. Lin and Hao were in the hallway four doors down, both of them looking grim, and Gregory felt his heart tighten further.

"How is she?" he asked as they limped closer.

"She took a fireball to the side of her head at the end, but she didn't relent," Lin said without emotion. "She broke his arm when he burned her, then knelt on it and ground the joint down. He quit at that point; between the pain and her burnt visage glaring down at him while her fists slammed into his face, he couldn't handle any more."

"They're trying to save her eye," Hao said softly, clearly in shock. "Her hair was burned to the scalp. We were told to stay out of their way."

The family gathered around the door, waiting for the healers to come out. While they waited, Lin spoke into the silence, feeling a need to tell Gregory what happened.

"The fight started like yours; Shun used a series of fireballs and she used shadow leap to dodge them. He spun and launched more fireballs behind him, but Yu wasn't there. She had leapt behind the grandmaster. She was laughing at him as she came out from behind the grandmaster, using shadows to hold Shun. She went after him, but he used something that bathed the area in bright light, which banished the shadows and the bindings with them. By that time, she had closed the distance and they ended up in hand-to-hand."

Gregory listened, imagining the fight as it was described even as he stayed focused on the door waiting for word.

"She was fast, faster than he seemed prepared for. He managed to hit her several times, but they didn't make her back away. She was intent on sticking close to stop him from doing what he did. She was hurting him more than he was hurting her, but she slipped up and he was able to throw her and put some distance between them. Shun threw another couple of fireballs at her, but before they reached her, her shadow swallowed her and then she was behind him. He was able to stop her from getting his neck and the fight continued."

The sound of cursing in the room made them all go still and silent. Gregory's heart was hammering in his chest, and he strained to hear or see anything.

After a long moment, Lin continued, "Yu got the upper hand and got ahold of his arm. She was trying to make him submit," Lin's voice caught. "She should have just broken the fucking thing. Her moment of weakness is what let him hit her with the fire. The spectators went silent when she was bathed in the fire, though it only burned for a second. When she started hammering his face with his arm pinned under her knee, they went crazy. The magi called the fight, declaring her the winner, and the healers rushed in. They got her moving, with a healer beside her the whole way."

Once Lin was done telling about Yukiko's fight, they stood there in the hall, waiting. The seconds ticked by with glacial slowness. The woman who had brought them the water burst out of the room, running down the hall at full speed, not answering when they called after her. She was back a minute or two later with a small bag in her hand. She ignored them again, going right back into the room.

Time stretched, and after what seemed like hours, the fox-eared eurtik stepped out of the room. Seeing them all waiting, she bowed to them, "She is doing fine. The healers have her sleeping to let the medicine do its work. You might want to wait a few minutes before you go in, as... she is healing from a severe burn."

The older man from before stepped out of the room. "You may go, Mindie," he dismissed the woman, then focused on Hao. "She will have the full use of her eye again, but she will have trouble seeing for a day or two. I would urge you to have her forfeit the fight tomorrow so it can heal without further damage. She will be sleeping for an hour while the salves repair her skin. I recommend you wait so you don't have to see the damage yourselves; some find it difficult to handle."

"We can go in now?" Hao asked bluntly.

"Once the other healer steps out, you may go in," the healer replied. "She's lucky. The fire used by the Eternal Flame normally burns longer than it did on her. We would never have been able to save her eye if it had."

"We understand. Thank you, healer," Yoo-jin said, relieved that her daughter was going to be okay.

"I told you to stay off your leg and not exert yourself," the healer added pointedly, staring at Gregory.

"I'm not on my leg, and I'm resting," Gregory said flatly. "I'll gladly sit as soon as I can go in."

"Stubborn idiot," the healer muttered as he stalked away from them.

It was only another minute or two before the other healer left the room. "Don't try to wake her. She needs to sleep while the medicine works, but you can go in now."

The four of them entered the room and Gregory felt his blood go cold at the sight of Yukiko lying on the bed. One side of her face was covered in bandages. Her long flowing hair was mostly gone; only short white stubble remained on half of her head. A few long locks remained on the far side of her head. With Yoo-jin's help, Gregory got settled in the chair next to the bed. Resting his hand on Yukiko's arm, he closed his eyes and pushed down the rage he felt at Nick for what he had done. The four of them sat or stood in silence as time ticked away, waiting for Yukiko to wake up.

CHAPTER 60

Yukiko groaned softly, bringing everyone's attention to her. Her unbandaged eye opened slowly, "Greg?"

"Here," he said, giving her hand a squeeze. "Don't try moving your head— it's covered in bandages. They said you'll be fine, but your eye needs a day or two to heal."

"You need to forfeit the fight tomorrow, so as to not damage it further," Hao told her.

"I didn't think he'd throw one with me so close," Yukiko whispered.

"You should have broken his arm instead of trying to get him to submit," Lin said bluntly. "How often have I told you that it's better to be brutal and ask for forgiveness than to be merciful and regret it?"

"Too many," Yukiko sighed. "I was trying to mitigate the fallout of beating him and not joining the clan. I've paid for that mistake."

"Next time, break the arm, please," Gregory whispered.

"If that is what my heart wishes," Yukiko replied. "Is there water?"

Yoo-jin handed Gregory a glass of water. "Sip slowly," Gregory told her as he pressed the glass into her hand, afraid he might hurt her if he held it to her lips.

"I remember breaking his arm just as the fire came, but I don't remember anything after that," Yukiko said, after taking a sip.

"You ground the broken joint under your knee and hammered his face," Lin replied. "He wasn't resisting, and the adjudicator called the fight."

"We did it, Greg," Yukiko's lips bent up on the uninjured side, but the other side of her face could not move that far. "The two of us, above all the others."

"Yes," Gregory smiled with difficulty, seeing her struggle. "We'll have to defend that in six months. Everyone will be wanting to stop us during that tournament, and everyone should have their magic firmly under control..." He trailed off, wondering if he would.

"We'll find yours," Yukiko said, reaching out to squeeze his hand. "Mother, Father, I'm sorry for worrying you. Lin, I'm sorry I didn't heed your wise words."

"You'll be fine, so there is nothing to apologize for," Yoo-jin said, reaching out to touch Yukiko's foot.

"Just be more careful from now on please," Hao added.

"And no more mercy! They won't show you any— that has been proven," Lin added.

"No more mercy," Yukiko agreed.

"We have a couple of hours before dinner," Hao said. "Once you're ready to go, we will take our leave of the academy."

"We need to inform someone that she is forfeiting tomorrow's fight," Yoo-jin reminded him.

"Hmm, yes. There might be someone at the arena," Hao muttered.

A knock on the door made everyone but Yukiko look that way. Lin opened it to find out who it was. "Yes... Elder, how may we help you?" His voice went from demanding to polite as soon as he saw the lavender kimono the old woman wore.

"I came to check on our two finalists, and was informed they were both in here," the old woman's voice was strong and able, belying her gray hair and lined face.

Gregory reluctantly took his hand from Yukiko's, "We are, Elder."

Lin stepped aside and bowed to her, as did the others in the room.

"No need, Warlin. You are probably supposed to be still for a while, yes?" the elder said, stopping Yukiko from trying to sit up to bow.

"Thank you, Elder," Yukiko said, lying back down.

"From the look of things, you are unlikely to be able to compete tomorrow."

"The healer advised her to forfeit the round, elder," Hao said. "I have advised her similarly."

"Ah, yes. I was worried about that, considering what transpired. Very well, we would ask you both to attend the closing of the tournament so we can announce the standings. All of the final eight will be there to receive their rewards."

"I'm curious, Elder," Gregory said, "how do you determine who ended up in the other places after first and second?"

"The council decides based on how the fights went. For instance, Jason Argon finished in third, as his fight was a much closer thing than Nick Shun's. I wish you both a speedy recovery. You'll likely need to be back in full form shortly after the tournament ends."

"Thank you, Elder," they said together.

"Just one more question," the elder said, stopping halfway to the door and turning back to them. "Have you picked your clan? I know that every clan of note inside the walls of the academy has spoken to you or tried to speak with you already."

"No, Elder, we are undecided," Gregory replied.

"Curious. The top two novices and neither spoken for..." The elder seemed amused. "I do wish you the best going forward." She glided from the room, her kimono barely moving, so it looked like she was floating on the air.

"Well, that's done. We might as well get going," Hao said, dabbing at his forehead with a handkerchief.

"Yes," Yoo-jin agreed. "We will have all day tomorrow before the closing ceremony since there isn't going to be a fight. Maybe we should stay away until then, before we escort you both to Gin's."

"There's no curfew," Gregory said slowly. "Maybe we should stay outside the academy walls tonight?"

"A capital idea," Hao nodded. "Yes, we shall have the rooms next to ours prepared for you both tonight."

"Two days of sleeping in," Gregory murmured, oddly discomfited by the idea.

"We've earned it," Yukiko said. "Besides, we'll still be awake earlier than many others."

"True," Gregory said, helping her sit up.

"Lin, go see if they have a means to convey them to the carriage," Hao told the guard.

"Yes, sir."

Yukiko sat on the edge of the bed, looking at Gregory with her unbandaged eye. "Seems we gave each other a scare."

"Yes. We should make sure it doesn't happen again."

"As my heart wishes."

Lin returned with the fox-eared eurtik and a wheeled chair. "They have one for Gregory, sir."

"The lady should be fine to walk," the eurtik told them. "You'll need to carefully remove the bandage tomorrow morning, then lightly dab your face clean. Your vision in that eye might be fuzzy for a day or two, but it'll come back. If you experience vertigo, wear a patch until you can see again."

"Thank you," Yukiko said.

"You don't have a second chair?" Hao asked sternly.

"The second one is already in use, sir. I'm sorry."

"I can walk, Father. I'll lean on the chair," Yukiko said, getting to her feet. "I don't feel weak."

Gregory wanted to argue that she should take the chair, but if he did and injured himself more, Yukiko would be upset, so he stayed silent. Yoo-jin looked at the ceiling for a moment before shaking her head.

"I'll walk beside her to make sure she is okay," Yoo-jin said. "Lin can push the chair."

Hao grimaced but did not argue.

"If there isn't anything else?" the eurtik said nervously, backing toward the door.

"No, thank you," Yoo-jin gave her a smile. "We're just upset that our daughter was injured."

"I understand," the woman replied and left the room.

Lin moved the chair close to Gregory, who shifted into it, feeling bad he was the one in it instead of Yukiko. "I'm sorry," he said.

"It's fine, your leg was badly damaged," Hao sighed. "I just worry for her. We'll walk slowly, and if you feel faint at all, tell us and we'll find a different way," Hao told Yukiko.

"Yes, Father."

* * *

The trip to the tavern was slow, with the driver taking care to make it as smooth as possible. Gregory had difficulty getting into and out of the carriage without straining his leg, but managed without causing it to flare into a mass of pain.

The tavern was completely full— the main room was standing room only. Cheers, applause, and whistles filled the room as the people caught sight of Gregory and Yukiko.

Hao chuckled and had to shout to be heard over the noise. "It seems news of your victories has spread ahead of you." Taking another step forward, he raised his hands, and the room slowly quieted down. "The two are honored and flattered, but today came at a heavy cost. Please give them some space tonight as they are recovering, but enjoy the evening. Ramon, the next round of drinks is on me."

A path opened up, allowing the family to move through the room. Silence followed in their wake as those present got a look at Gregory limping and Yukiko's bandaged face. As they entered the hallway, quiet conversations sprang up behind them.

"Thank you, Father," Yukiko whispered, her hand lightly touching the bandage. "I don't think I could handle them staring."

Gregory took her hand in his, "It'll heal."

"Like your leg," Yukiko replied.

"Yes," Gregory agreed, still trying to keep his weight off it as much as possible.

Less than a minute after they had gotten seated, a knock on the door announced the owner's daughter. She bowed to them when she entered, carrying a tray with crystal glasses and two bottles.

"We have two wines," she told them as she poured. "One for the mistress and master; it is the favored vintage of the house. The other is for the novices. Its alcohol content is greatly reduced so that magi can enjoy the same flavor."

"Thank you, Nessa," Yoo-jin smiled. "We need the two rooms next to ours prepared, also. The novices will be staying here tonight."

Nessa's tail twitched, "Umm... we only have a single room left."

"I can—" Gregory began.

"Prepare it," Yukiko said, cutting him off. "We'll figure out who shall sleep where later."

Hao's lips pursed and he stared at his daughter.

Yoo-jin's lips trembled as she fought to keep the smile off her face. "Yes, that does make some sense," she managed to say with a straight face. "Please see to it, Nessa."

She bowed and left the room, glancing back at the two novices. Once she was gone, Gregory turned his attention to his wine. He sipped it, discovering that the flavor was predominantly blackberries. Hao and Yoo-jin looked thoughtful as they tasted the wine.

"This is good... the flavors blend well together," Hao nodded.

"Not as good as what we have at home, but yes," Yoo-jin agreed.

"Gregory and I will share the room tonight," Yukiko said without preamble.

"No, that is unacceptable," Hao said firmly.

"We are both injured, Father. Do you think we're going to ravage each other?" Yukiko said bluntly.

"Too much like your mother," Hao replied, grumbling.

"Dear," Yoo-jin said softly, taking his hand, "calm yourself." Turning to Gregory, she continued. "You will behave, yes? Even if my daughter does not?"

"I will not dishonor Yuki," Gregory said. "Besides, she's right. Neither of us is in any condition for anything improper." His cheeks were burning, but he managed to say the words without stammering.

"Just spending the night in the same room—" Hao began.

"A compromise, then," Yoo-jin sighed. "Yu and I will stay in our room, while you and Gregory stay in the new room. A little bonding time, so you two can get to know each other better."

Yukiko started to object, but instead sat back in her chair. "That is probably for the best," she admitted.

"I will agree to that," Hao nodded.

Gregory nodded, though he was a little sad that he would not get to spend the night with Yukiko. "Nothing to tarnish Yuki, it is a good idea."

A knock on the door interrupted them. Nessa and an older woman Gregory had not seen before were waiting with a cart loaded with covered dishes. Gregory felt momentarily bad about thinking the term horse-faced, but the horse ears, tail, and when she stepped into the room, hooves, made the thought seem a bit more fitting.

"I thought I would serve you myself tonight," the woman announced. "We thank you for your generosity during your stay with us. We almost never rent the rooms on the second floor, even during the tournament, so it's a novelty that we are sold out. With the inn just down the street, it's very rare for travelers to stay here."

"We prefer a calmer place," Yoo-jin smiled. "Though tonight, it seems to be quite busy."

"Yes, it's been packed all day," the woman replied. "Let's get to the food, hmm? We have pheasant for you and your husband, and bane fowl for the novices. Both have been cooked in a citrus sauce to enhance their flavor. The sides are wild rice with bits of fruit mixed in and lightly-buttered charid with herbs. The wine should complement the meal."

Nessa was busy serving them while her mother described the dishes. In the center of the table, she placed two extra dishes with more rice and charid. Once she was finished, she stepped back behind her mother.

"Thank you, Vana," Yoo-jin smiled. "We've enjoyed every meal you've prepared during our stay. If you weren't running a successful family business, we'd try to hire you as a cook and take you home with us."

Vana bowed low, "Thank you, that is high praise. I hope this meal also meets your expectations."

"Thank you," Gregory said, bowing his head to her, the smells making his stomach growl.

Vana and Nessa left them to their meals. Gregory looked down at his plate, his mouth watering. His eagerness dimmed a little at the charid; the long, green-stalked vegetables were not one of his favorites.

"Aether, this looks good," Hao said, cutting a slice off the pheasant.

Everyone agreed, and they all turned their attention to their meals. Gregory and Yukiko were glad to feel their aether being replenished as they ate. Near the end of the meal, Nessa came in again to check on them. Seeing that they were nearly done, she brought in a small cake and four small plates.

"Mother made this specifically for you," Nessa told them as she placed it before Hao. "Cheesecake— she hopes you'll enjoy it."

"Oh, it's been years since I had cheesecake last," Hao smiled as he deftly sliced the cake into four equal portions. "Thank her for us, please."

"Yes, sir. The room is ready for you, as well."

"We'll need two mats in there," Hao told her. "I'll be sharing it with Gregory, and my daughter will be staying with my wife."

Nessa nodded, "I will make sure both rooms are set up correctly, sir."

Gregory looked at the plain-looking white dessert with a questioning gaze. He picked up a tiny piece with his fork, wondering about the texture. His eyes widened slightly as the rich, creamy flavor permeated his mouth and he was quick to begin eating it in earnest.

"I guess you like it, dear one," Yukiko giggled.

Gregory froze, giving her a sheepish look, "I've never had anything like it." Slowing his pace, he made sure to savor what remained of his dessert.

CHAPTER 61

Hao was already awake and dressed when Gregory woke the next morning. Gregory yawned and stretched, "Morning, sir."

"Morning, Gregory. Did you sleep well?"

"I don't recall any dreams and I feel better, so, yes."

"Good. You should work on your card playing. I've heard magi tend to favor it over other games of chance. You should also spend some time on bones, if you are to command troops. It would be a good idea to have something in common with them."

"Yes, sir. I didn't expect to play cards with you and Lin last night after dinner."

"It is easier to pass the time and glean information from someone if they are focused on other things," Hao chuckled. "It seems my daughter chose well. Any lingering doubts have been put to rest now."

"I'm glad that your doubts are fading... *Father*," Gregory said with a smirk.

"Not yet, but in six months, that will be accurate," Hao nodded as he capped the ink he had been using. "You can work on this," he handed over a Magi Square. "I just finished mine," he added, putting a parchment away.

"Thank you. I'd like to go check on Yuki before I do anything else, sir." Gregory said, getting out of bed and putting his clothes on.

"I'll go see if they're awake," Hao said.

Hao returned as Gregory finished putting his boots on. "She's awake and asking for you."

Gregory followed him to the next room, where Yoo-jin and Yukiko were sitting and sipping tea. "Morning, Yuki."

"Greg, will you help remove the bandage?" Yukiko asked with a hesitant smile.

"Of course," Gregory knelt beside her. "I'll go slowly. Let me know if I need to stop."

Yukiko nodded, her hands clenched on her knees. "I will."

His hands trembled slightly as he found the edge of the bandage and began to gently and slowly peel it away from her forehead. The sound of breathing was the only sound in the room.

Gregory was glad to see unblemished skin as he worked. He went even slower as he pulled it away from her eye. A pad of clean cloth remained covering her eye as the bandage was removed. "Can you hold that while I finish the bandage?"

Yukiko reached up and lightly touched the cloth, clearly afraid of moving it.

When he was finished pulling the bandage away, the skin revealed was unmarred and healthy. "Done, Yuki. It's time."

Yukiko's hand trembled as she took the edge of the cloth in her fingers. With a shaky breath, she pulled the cloth away from her eye. A clear film coated her eyelid, still sealing the eye closed.

"Water, please," Gregory asked. "I'll clean it, Yuki. Just try to relax. They said everything would be fine."

"I'm trying, dear one," Yukiko whispered. "But if it isn't—"

"Then we'll find a way to fix it or we'll work around it. We'll be together the whole time," Gregory told her gently. Hao handed him a basin with a cloth in it.

"I'll believe in you," Yukiko said as her hands stilled.

Gregory swallowed hard, feeling the weight of her trust. Taking a deep breath, he wrung out the cloth. With infinite care, he began to clean the ointment from her eye. It melted away with hardly any effort.

"Okay, Yuki."

Her eye opened and she inhaled sharply. "I can see, but everything is a little blurry in that eye." She blinked rapidly and shook her head, "They did say it would improve. We'll have to wait and see."

Gregory's lips twitched at her inadvertent pun. "Better?"

Yukiko smiled at him, "Yes. Thank you." Leaning over, she kissed him lightly. "I just wanted you here, in case..."

"It's done now," Gregory said, not letting the other option linger. "We have all day before the ceremony and our dinner."

"Indeed, we do," Hao said. "You'll need to change into newer robes for the ceremony and change again into your best outfit for dinner. I sent Lin to speak with Keeper Dia about retrieving some of your clothing. He should be back soon."

"Thank you, Father," Yukiko said, still staring at Gregory. "Will you bring me some scissors, please?"

"We'll get them and give you some time," Yoo-jin said, rising to her feet. "Come, dear. They normally train for hours. We can let them have some time to meditate and talk. Yu, we'll be back at high sun."

"Thank you, Mother."

Hao looked like he wanted to object, but sighed and let himself be led from the room. Gregory watched them go before looking back at Yukiko, who was still staring at him.

"Yuki?"

She shook her head, placing a finger on his lips, "Wait, please, dear one."

His brow furrowed, but he kissed her finger and did as she asked. A minute later, there was a knock. Nessa was there with the requested scissors. Yukiko accepted them, thanked the young woman, then handed them to Gregory.

Once Nessa was gone, Yukiko turned her back to Gregory. "Please even my hair for me."

A little confused, Gregory gave the scissors an experimental snip, feeling them move easily. Looking at Yukiko's hair, he understood why she asked. More than half of her hair was little more than stubble from the fire. The rest was raggedly uneven.

Gregory took his time, starting with the stubble. Neither spoke as he worked. Time lost meaning for the two of them, both falling into an almost meditative state. The moment he set aside the scissors, Yukiko exhaled.

"Thank you, dear one. I didn't think you would be that shallow, but I worried that my hair being this short might be a problem," Yukiko said, not looking at him.

"I didn't fall in love with your hair," Gregory said softly, kissing the back of her neck.

Yukiko inhaled sharply, a shiver running down her spine at the kiss. "Dear one, please stop. I want it too much."

Resting his head against her, he put his arms around her and held her gently. "Sorry, Yuki. I'm not trying to tease you. I just want to kiss you and hold you."

Leaning back into him, Yukiko sighed, "I understand. I would love for that to be our entire day. The next six months will be difficult."

"Yes," Gregory agreed, his voice a little rough. "We'll manage, though, because we both want the same thing. To make your parents proud and to do the right thing."

"And your aether promised us dreams, so we can at least experiment there," Yukiko whispered with a shiver. "I would love that, if you are listening, Gregory's aether. Please make it happen occasionally, so we can be ready for when we do come together in the flesh. I'll share him with you. I have a feeling you are responsible for me being able to touch all three paths like him. I don't believe it's just because I believe it possible."

"You think so?" Gregory asked.

"If that was the only thing required, others would have done it before now, Greg. I know we've read scrolls where people touch two and then lose connection with one of them, but I don't believe it's just a matter of belief. We may be stubborn, but there are magi even more strong-willed, I'm sure."

"Maybe," Gregory admitted, considering her statement. "If that's true, though, what does that mean concerning my aether?"

"We'll have to ask her when we see her next. You mentioned speaking to her every time you grow in power. Just do your best to ask her when that happens again."

"Need to ask her for a name, too," Gregory admitted with chagrin.

"Yes," Yukiko agreed with humor. "Never asking her name is terrible, dear one."

Gregory sighed, "Yeah. I'll ask."

"Mother gave us time to train," Yukiko sighed. "We should do so."

"Yeah," Gregory agreed with a sigh of his own, but not letting go of her.

"Let me go, dear one."

Releasing his grip, Gregory started to move away, but Yukiko spun in place and grabbed his head. The kiss was unexpected and more aggressive than any they had exchanged to that point.

He pulled her closer as he returned the passionate kiss in kind. Yukiko shifted until she was in his lap, the kiss continuing as lips parted. Gregory groaned when she sat on him, his pressing need obvious to them both at that point.

Yukiko pulled back an inch, staring into Gregory's eyes. "That is how I felt when you kissed my neck." She shuddered and rested her forehead against his, "And when I kiss you like that, too. I think I'll feel like this whenever you touch me."

Gregory took a deep breath, trying to resist the urge to kiss her again. *Kiss her, lean her back, and then...* Shuddering, Gregory cut off the train of thought. "I'll do my best to stop teasing you, Yuki. Please, I need you to move." His hands tightened on her for a moment before loosening, "Or we'll have some explaining to do to your parents."

Yukiko giggled softly, "That would be awkward." With hesitation, she slid from his lap, "If you'll ask your aether for us..."

"I will, Aether, I will," Gregory agreed fervently.

"Magi Squares or meditation first?" Yukiko asked as she took a few deep breaths herself.

"Squares. I won't be able to clear my mind for meditation right now."

"You're right... I doubt I'd be able to, either."

* * *

They managed to complete a set of Magi Squares each before meditating for a couple of hours. Yoo-jin's knock brought them out of their meditation, neither having found the cavern.

"Are you ready for some food?" Yoo-jin asked them.

"That would be good, Mother," Yukiko smiled. "Thank you for our time to train."

"I was mildly concerned, but it's nice to know that you have better restraint than I did at your age," Yoo-jin replied.

"It was close, Mother," Yukiko admitted, rising to her feet. "Very close."

"Close is acceptable, as long as it goes no further," Yoo-jin smiled. "The private room is waiting. I should warn you— the front room is filled with eurtik. Your victories are being celebrated, more so because you faced the novices most favored by the Eternal Flame."

"Nick, Jason, and Grandmaster Shun are bound to be pissed," Gregory said.

"I'm sure they are," Yoo-jin agreed. "Be prepared to deal with them after today."

"We will," they said in unison.

"Come now, you won't have to deal with the crowd unless you want to. The stairs exit into the hallway near the dining room. Your clothes are here as well; we have them in the other room currently."

"We both need to train the physical path still," Yukiko said. "After we eat, we'll use the yard for an hour before we change."

"I'll make sure the guards are posted to keep you free," Yoo-jin nodded.

CHAPTER 62

They made it to the academy without having to deal with the crowded tavern. A squad of academy guards was waiting when they arrived. Hao told the rest of them to wait in the carriage while he inquired about their presence.

"Is there something I can help you with?" Hao asked the man with captain's insignia on his sleeves.

"We're here to escort the novices to the arena," the guard replied. "It is customary for the winner to have an honor guard."

"I see," Hao nodded, stepping aside from the door. "It is safe to come out," he told the people still in the carriage.

Gregory stepped out and the guards all snapped to attention. He moved aside so Hao could help Yoo-jin out of the carriage, then he copied Hao, offering his arm to Yukiko.

"Champion Pettit, if you and runner-up Warlin will follow me?" the Captain said. "We will escort you to the arena. Your family may follow," he added to Yukiko.

"We're in your care, Captain," Gregory said, stepping forward with Yukiko beside him.

The walk across the grounds was uneventful and Gregory

wondered why a guard was provided to the winner. *Something to ask Rafiq later, maybe,* he thought.

People were milling around the arena, but made way for the guards as they approached. Cheers and a few boos reached Gregory and Yukiko. The boos cut off abruptly and the sound of a scuffle broke out. Four guards broke off from the procession to break up the fight.

"Certainly is lively," Hao said.

"Those poor few should have known better than to jeer," Yoo-jin shrugged.

One of the guards turned to Hao, Yoo-jin, and Lin once they had entered the arena halls. "If you three will follow me, a box has been set aside for you to view the ceremony."

"Lead on," Hao said, then called out to Gregory and Yukiko, "We'll see you afterward."

Gregory raised a hand, but did not stop, "See you after."

Gregory was surprised that no other finalist was present in the waiting area. "Captain, where are the others?"

"Being taken up one by one to have their exploits celebrated. You'll be joining them shortly."

Minutes passed as they waited. The sound of boots brought his attention to the hallway. Another group of guards led a group of four apprentices into the room. The apprentices' yellow robes had the insignia of the Han Merchant clan on the sleeves.

"There they are," the tallest of the group said. "You both barely scraped through, then one of you withdrew from the final. Didn't care to fight each other again?" The question held the slightest edge of scorn.

"The healers told me to forfeit so my eye could heal," Yukiko replied with a shrug. "I'd rather keep it, and second place wasn't so hard to swallow."

One of the others laughed, "Point. Good thing the healers care for us during the tournament or we'd have had a few rough spots ourselves."

"Rumor had it otherwise," the leader of the group said, "apologies."

"Accepted," Yukiko bowed her head. "I'm sad we missed seeing your final fight."

"The Eternal Flame is less than amused today," another of the group smirked. "Their novices and apprentices both failed to take top spots."

"Will you be joining us?" the last of the four asked.

"We're still evaluating which clan is best for us," Gregory said. "Obviously, the Eternal Flame was snuffed off that list."

The four apprentices laughed at his joke and a few of the guards chuckled before the captain cleared his throat. "Prepare yourselves. We will be moving in a moment. We will lead, and the novices fall in behind us with the apprentices at the end. Move to stand before the council and do as instructed. When the ceremony is over, come back here so we may escort you away from the arena."

"Yes, sir," the apprentices said as a unit.

"Understood," Gregory and Yukiko added a moment later.

Seconds ticked by and the guards checked their uniforms. At some signal Gregory could not see or hear, the captain drew himself to attention. "In three... two... one... march."

Gregory was impressed at the perfect timing of the guards as they marched up the stairs and down the short hall to the arena floor. The sound of cheering started as a dim roar that grew steadily louder as they got closer to the exit. The guards marched out, splitting to the left and right to form a tunnel for the novices and apprentices. Each pair of guards came sharply to attention as Gregory and Yukiko passed.

Gregory kept moving at the same measured pace the guards had marched to, taking in the filled arena. The stands were jammed with people, all of them on their feet and cheering.

"Wave," one of the apprentices said just loud enough to be heard. Gregory and Yukiko both jumped a little, but started waving at the spectators.

The noise from the crowd grew even louder when the two novices acknowledged them. The ground shook just perceptibly when people began to stomp their feet as they cheered, clapped, and whistled their approval. Embarrassed and discomfited at the attention, Gregory looked away from the crowd to where he was going.

In the center of the arena, the other six finalists from the novices and the runners up from the apprentices stood. Two grandmasters and an elder faced them, waiting. Gregory recognized the elder as the same one who had seen them in the healer's hall. One of the grand-masters was the same man that officiated his last match, the other one was the that had stopped Skippy's father attacking him. All three of the greater magi stood with impassively regal bearing as they waited for the tournament winners to reach them.

Coming to a stop a few feet from the magi, Gregory stood straighter than he ever had in his life. Yukiko beside him mirrored his stance, and the four apprentices formed a line beside her. The council of the academy waited for a moment as the crowd grew quiet.

"Novice Warlin, your ability to fight even under extreme duress has been noted," the elder said. "Not many could continue to fight after their heads had been wreathed in flame. The healers have assured the council that you will recover. As the runner-up, you will be rewarded with gifts to help you increase your aether and your novice classes are considered successfully passed, allowing you to train as you see fit. We shall be looking forward to your performance in the next tournament."

The crowd grew raucous again, and the elder let them continue for a few moments before she raised a hand to quiet them.

"Honored council," Yukiko told them, "I was blessed to have instructors who helped bring the best out in me, and a partner in training that pushed me every step of the way. With that and the envi-ronment you foster inside the walls of the academy, I was able to rise as I have. I thank you." Yukiko made the deepest formal bow she had made in her life to them.

The council bowed their heads fractionally to her in return as the crowd cheered. Calling for silence again, the elder turned to face Gregory. "Champion Pettit, you faced challenging opponents and overcame them all. You faced trial by fire and pain, and even though the odds were stacked against you, you managed to find your way through to the top. The most frightening aspect for your peers is that you did it all without direct use of magic. The council has ordered the archive to do all they can to aid in finding your magic. We all look forward to the next tournament, especially if you are able to augment your abilities. Your rewards for being the champion are the greatest any novice could hope to attain. Besides the alchemical aides you will receive and your novice classes considered successfully passed, allowing you to train as you see fit, you will also be allowed to seek the counsel of the council once per member. Use those moments wisely. The strong rise to the top and grow stronger— that is the way of the magi. We look forward to the next tournament and what you might show us then."

The crowd exploded when the elder finished her speech, and she let them continue for a moment longer than normal. Gregory looked shocked, not expecting the nature of the final reward.

"Honored council, I never expected to stand here before you. As my training partner Novice Warlin said, it was because of her, the instructors, and the academy itself that I was able to achieve what I did. I dearly hope to learn of my magic, so I thank you in advance for the aid in discovering it." He bowed to them as deeply as Yukiko had, and the crowd went wild.

The elder waited a moment before she raised her hand for silence again. "Apprentices of the Han Merchant Clan, you have prevailed over your adversaries and claimed the top spot in this tournament. Your clan accrues honor for your achievement, and your rewards shall reflect that."

"Honored council," the leader of the group replied once silence had been restored, "we succeeded because our clan supported us to the best of their resources. Without the support of the greatest clan, we would not have prevailed as we did."

One of the grandmasters raised an eyebrow and his neutral expression dimmed at the apprentice's words, but he remained quiet.

"People of the empire and fellow magi, these are your champions.

Celebrate their success, and know it is magi like this striving for greatness that will keep the empire safe and strong," the elder announced as she stepped back from the groups, mirrored by the grandmasters. "Let the celebration begin and not end until tomorrow night!"

Once the elder was done speaking, the grandmaster who had frowned motioned with his hand and the council vanished from the floor of the arena.

"Back to the waiting area," the apprentice said as their group turned together and led the way.

Gregory and Yukiko exchanged a glance, sharing a smile and falling into step behind the apprentices.

Once they were all back in the waiting room, the apprentices let out whoops and started razzing each other. Gregory grinned at seeing the four celebrate as friends. The guards spread out into the room, waiting for them to be ready to leave.

"Top two spots? The clans will really be fighting over you now," one of the apprentices laughed. "Well, except the Eternal Flame. They're likely a bit upset with you both."

"A little," the leader snickered. "Did you see Novice Shun's face? Oh, he hates the both of you, and not just a little. If he could shoot flames from his eyes like some adepts can, you both might have died in front of the elder."

Gregory and Yukiko exchanged a glance. "We'll be prepared for him," Gregory said.

"At least you get out of classes," one of the others said. "I would have killed to get out of history and economics. So fucking boring."

"If Magus Han heard you say that," one of the others smirked. Her face scrunched up, and her voice shifted. "*Apprentice, if you dislike it so much, then you should join the caravan guards. Yes, that is what we shall do with you.*"

Gregory and Yukiko laughed along with the others, as the impersonation had been passable. The guards were all stone-faced, clearly not wanting to laugh.

"Speaking of, she'll be waiting for us. Let's go," the leader said.

"Hope you two decide to join the clan. Han always takes care of those who excel."

Saying goodbye, the apprentices left with half the guards. Gregory and Yukiko were left with the original guards who had brought them to the arena. They shared a long look, both of them smiling.

"Time for an important dinner," Gregory said softly.

"The dinner of a lifetime," Yukiko beamed.

"If you're both ready, then follow us," the captain said, before barking an order at his men. "Form up!"

CHAPTER 63

G regory tugged the sleeve of the white and green silk kimono he wore, not used to the way it felt. He had not expected the boots that went with the outfit, but Yukiko had contacted the cobbler at some point and got him a set that fit him perfectly. Glancing out of the corner of his eye at Yukiko, he smiled.

With her hair cut close to her head, she looked different than before, but no less beautiful to Gregory's eyes. Her kimono of green silk with white owls brought out her eyes and her skin. Her eyes shifted and she caught him watching her, making her smile brightly at him.

"What are your plans now that the classes have become moot?" Yoo-jin asked.

"We talked while changing," Yukiko replied. "We're going to continue with our schedule: waking early and having breakfast before heading to the archive to train the mind path. After a couple of hours, we'll go to Gin's to train spirit and body. Return to the academy for dinner, a little more mind training, then sleep. That will fill our days every day until the next tournament."

"While changing?" Hao asked with pursed lips, staring at Gregory.

"Our rooms are beside each other," Gregory reminded him. "We spoke through the wall."

"That better be the truth," Hao grumbled, glowering.

Yukiko rolled her eyes, "Father, please. If we were going to do something like that, we'd have done it already."

Yoo-jin giggled, "She is my daughter, after all."

Hao grumbled as he looked out the carriage window.

"That is if we can leave the academy during the week," Gregory said, bringing the topic back on point. "We don't know if it'll be allowed. We'll ask Dia tomorrow and find out, but that is our plan for now."

"Hmm," Hao grunted. "We'll be here tomorrow. We had planned on leaving the following morning. We should meet for lunch at Stabled Hunger and you can tell us then what your final plans are."

"That is fair, Father."

The carriage came to a stop in front of Gin's manor. Gregory caught scraps of laughter and music coming from the courtyard that was surrounded by the building.

Indara opened the door for them, "Please, honored guests, come in."

"That is a very good color for you," Yoo-jin told Indara. "It brings out your eyes wonderfully."

"Thank you," Indara bowed. "The guests are gathered in the courtyard and open ballroom, awaiting your appearance."

"There should be five more arriving late," Yukiko told her.

"I'm aware. The five who work in the mess hall of the academy. Their spouses are already here and asked if it was really okay for them to be late."

"Well, if everything is ready, let's proceed," Hao smiled. "Please, lead us to our guests."

Indara bowed to him, then led them into the house. She walked at a steady, sedate pace so everyone could stay in sync as they headed for the event. She paused just outside a closed set of double doors, looking back to make sure everyone was there before she opened them wide and proceeded into the room.

"Ladies and gentlemen, the stars of tonight's dinner and the parents of the eventual bride," Indara announced, her voice cutting over the music and bringing all eyes to the doorway.

The musicians stopped immediately, so the room was nearly silent as Hao escorted Yoo-jin into the room. The couple stopped a few feet in and bowed to the crowd, then moved aside so Gregory and Yukiko became the center of attention. Swallowing hard, Gregory escorted Yukiko into the room like Hao had and bowed to the room, Yukiko bowing with him.

"Now that the guests of honor have arrived," Gin's voice filled the silence, "let us pray to Aether and Vera that their life is full of love and prosperity."

All heads bowed, the room silent again as everyone prayed for the couple. After a few moments, Gin announced, "Now, let's greet the couple and wish them well ourselves."

The guests lined up to pay their respects to Gregory and Yukiko. Yukiko smiled, greeting each person warmly as they came forward. Gregory's smile was awkward, which made some of the guests feel more at ease, having been nervous themselves.

Yukiko placed her hand over her heart and spoke. "We thank our friends and family for coming to our betrothal dinner. We are honored and blessed to have you with us on this first step of combining our lives."

Gregory cleared his throat, feeling out of place as he mirrored Yukiko, "Thank you, all of you. Yukiko and I have never had a lot of friends, so we are honored and blessed that each of you considers us so. We hope to keep the bonds of friendship strong with you as we move forward with our lives together."

Applause and whistles were the enthusiastic response to the short speeches. Hao cleared his throat, turning all eyes to him.

"Honored guests, thank you for coming. We regret that Gregory's family could not be here in body, but we are sure they are here in spirit to witness this great day in his life. I was hesitant to accept my daughter's proposal that she marry him, but love will not be denied. After recent events, I know that Gregory loves Yukiko as deeply as I do my beloved wife. In six months, after the next tournament, Gregory will wed Yukiko. Then, we will celebrate two great events."

Yoo-jin waited for the cheers to die away again before she spoke, "This betrothal is unusual in our family. We never thought that our daughter would be a magi, nor that she would find her love during her first year. We have only asked that they do their best to grow, learn, and prosper together, while letting their love lead them. We hope that you will all be our guests again in six months."

Before the cheering could start again, Gin interrupted, "Hold a moment, I have something of import to say." Everyone stared at him, wondering why he had interrupted. "This home will not do for the wedding. I will find a suitable location, one that will honor both the bride and groom. My star pupils deserve to be shown to the world when they wed, and I will make sure the venue is perfect for them both."

Yukiko shook her head, "Gin, you are too kind."

"Nonsense! I have been waiting to see you married from the day of your birth," Gin replied. "Now let us drink, dance, and await the final guests. Once they arrive, dinner will be served."

* * *

The party lasted well into the night. The workers from the academy left one-by-one as the pressing need for sleep finally called them away. After the last guests were gone, Gin walked them to the door.

"You could stay the night here if you wish," he told Yukiko.

"We are returning to the academy for the night," Yukiko replied. "We need to find out if we will be allowed to train with you every day."

"Lunch tomorrow at Stabled Hunger," Hao reminded her. "I'll send the carriage to pick you up."

"Yes, Father," Yukiko replied.

"I thought you might want to return to the academy. I have another carriage waiting to take you back," Gin chuckled when he opened the door. "I will see you all at lunch, as well."

"I'll be happy to see you there," Yukiko smiled.

"Sleep well, dear," Yoo-jin said, giving her daughter a hug. "And you, Gregory."

"We'll do our best, but we've trained ourselves to wake before the sun, so it might be hard to sleep in," Gregory replied.

"We'll be fine, Mother," Yukiko said. "Take care of Father."

With the two couples separating into different carriages, the goodbyes took a little longer, but they were soon heading in opposite directions. Gregory yawned as the lateness of the hour finally caught up to him.

Yukiko yawned a second later, "Those are contagious."

"Sorry, Yuki. First one awake wakes the other?"

"Yes. We'll sleep later than normal, but I doubt it'll be later than the other novices."

"Do you think the clan recruiters are still waiting for us?"

"Doubtful, though I expect them to do their best to find us tomorrow," Yukiko replied, trying to stifle another yawn.

Gregory shifted to sit beside her instead of across from her. "You can rest against me if you want."

"Very kind," Yukiko replied as she rested her head on his shoulder.

Gregory put his arm around her shoulders and held her. "I'll wake you when we get there if you drop off."

"Dear one, thank you," Yukiko murmured sleepily.

* * *

The driver rapped on the front wall of the carriage, jolting Gregory and Yukiko awake. "We're here," the driver said loudly.

"Thank you," Gregory said, climbing out and helping Yukiko down.

The gates were shut and the guards on the walls watched as the two novices walked up to the postern door. The magi on duty there glared at them as she checked their medallions, then grudgingly let them through.

The path to the dormitory was silent and shrouded in shadows. "It's beautiful at night," Yukiko murmured as they walked beside each other.

"Peaceful," Gregory agreed.

As they got closer to the dormitory, they were surprised to see the front brightly illuminated and a dozen people sitting on the benches beside the door.

"So much for peaceful," Gregory sighed "Think we can slip around the back?"

"Yes, follow me," Yukiko whispered as she gathered her aether, thickening the shadows around them. "Just watch your step."

The people waiting were unaware that the pair they were there for had evaded them. Happy to find the back door unsecured, they slipped inside and went up the stairs to their rooms.

"Goodnight, dear one," Yukiko murmured, leaning over to kiss his cheek.

"Goodnight, Yuki," Gregory replied, returning the chaste kiss. "See you in a few hours."

CHAPTER 64

Darkness enveloped him and a soft hand gently stroked his hair. He blinked, frowning, and the darkness jerked away from him to fill the far side of the opulent bedroom. "You are growing so fast, dear one. Champion Novice and betrothed to Yuki. The rest of this year will certainly be exciting."

Gregory shook his head, wondering if he imagined the hand on his hair, extracting himself from the overly large bed. "I've been reminded by Yuki—"

"That you've never asked my name? That's true, but I wouldn't have given it to you before now, anyway. I'll answer to any name you wish to give me. It's easier that way."

"I'll call you Darkness, then, for you seem at home in it. Though I wonder why you hide yourself from me."

"Because you aren't ready yet, dear one. When you are ready, I shall reveal myself to you. I long for that day, for you to truly know me..." The voice trailed off with a heartfelt sigh of longing.

"You hear everything I do?" Gregory asked.

"I am part of you, so yes. I can perceive much more than you, though."

"And you knew what Yukiko had planned before, too," Gregory said slowly, thinking.

"I have my ways. All women do, dear one."

"I doubt there is another woman who has ways like you do."

Delighted laughter came from Darkness, "Flatterer, but you aren't wrong."

"You know the other questions I have for you," Gregory said as he looked around for a chair. One appeared behind him and he sat. "Will you answer them for me?"

"Yuki is correct— it's not just raw belief that makes it possible to tread three paths at once. The best magi in the world can touch two, and even fewer can walk them both. Of those, a fraction can truly combine them as you and she have. There have been less than a handful of people who touched all three, only one of which is still alive."

"The emperor."

"Toja," Darkness agreed.

"You say his name like you know him personally," Gregory said.

Darkness did not respond to his statement, instead shifting the topic, "As for Yuki's heartfelt plea to share this space with you, I have heard it and will do what I can, but it won't be often. It is very taxing for me, especially while you are still growing in power."

"We'll look forward to it," Gregory said, "thank you."

"And the last reason for your visit; I promised you answers about your magic."

Gregory's happy daydreams of having Yukiko with him in his dreams chopped off and his attention snapped to Darkness.

"Good to know I can still get your attention," Darkness chuckled. "Your magic is not like that of the others. Everyone else spins threads of aether tied to their very being. Yuki, for instance, so wanted to be ignored by the people who despised her for her heritage that her soul picked up a resonance for shadow. Shun's soul is tied to fire, as are the souls of most of his line."

"I just yearned to be a magi, not for any specific magic, though," Gregory murmured when she paused.

"Yes. Magic is also passed down through bloodlines. Bloodline magic can turn a small talent into potent magic. Shun, for instance, yearned for fire and his family has used fire magic for so long that it's tied to their blood. This is why, even as a novice, he is able to wield so much fire."

"So my magic is tied to my blood?"

"Indeed, dear one. Your mother's line carried a specific magic that the empire knows nothing about. This is why they haven't been able to discover anything about it. The few instances where it was recorded have been all but erased. On top of that, your soul has been tied to something even more primal than magic types. Gin was correct about his guess that your soul might be reborn."

Gregory's eyes widened as he considered the possibilities of what Darkness was telling him. "What do you mean more primal? Who was I before?"

"Both are very good questions," Darkness purred happily.

"Before we delve into those answers, let's focus on your mother's bloodline. She loved you so much, and it hurt her to know she wasn't going to be here for you. Your visions of possible futures came from her. You recently saw a memory, when meditating, of her seeing the future."

Gregory nodded slowly, recalling the memory that helped him so perfectly see her face. He had been so happy for that moment that he had not paid attention to what his mother had said, but now he did.

"That is why your father railed about your dreams and her dreams on your age day."

That memory came back to the fore of his brain and he nodded. "That's why he became so bitter. She told him about her dreams, of the futures she saw."

"Yes. He knew what would happen and tried to deny it, but in the end, it came to be just as she foresaw."

"Oh, Aether," Gregory said, understanding just how his father had become so bitter.

"Those moments can be brought about intentionally if you can walk far enough down the spirit path, which you are doing, but to force them will drain your aether."

"Okay. That's also how I was able to hit Gin, right?"

"That is a passive side effect. You will get occasional glimpses of what is about to transpire. I was referring more to knowing your friends will have three children, or what would happen to Yukiko if she followed a single path, or if you had denied her proposal of a partnership."

"I can force those moments, but it will drain me?"

"Yes, once you learn how."

Nodding, Gregory thought about the glimpses he had had. "How and why did they happen before then?"

"You had help," Darkness replied with a softer, more loving tone. "I'm always helping you as much as I can, dear one. Everything I've shown you has been to help you have a better life."

"I would have argued with Yuki about being partners if not for that glimpse of the future," Gregory said. "I can't be mad at you for helping me see what would come of that. But do those snippets always come true?"

"No. They are just the most likely outcomes. The future is not set in stone. If it was, why would anyone strive?"

Snorting, Gregory had to agree with her. "Why, indeed."

"It's almost time for you to go."

"You haven't answered the other two questions," Gregory said quickly.

"I haven't," Darkness said. "Your more primal side of magic, which triggered the ryuite, is to touch upon aether itself and is why you can see it being shaped. The few references of that magic have been all but erased from the empire. You'll be catching more glimpses of it and in time, be able to touch upon the threads yourself, altering, changing, or stopping the magic from working."

Gregory's jaw dropped and he shook his head at the idea of being able to manipulate aether directly. "I'd be able to stop the fire from being cast?"

"That is but one of the things you'll be able to do in time. It is also why Yuki can do what you can with the paths. You've wanted her with you, and because of that, your ability to touch upon all aether training has included her. She is right that it is because of you."

"Seems the women in my life are smarter than I am."

"That is as it should be, dear one," Darkness said warmly. "As for who you once were... I've waited a long time to say this to you. Welcome home, Aether... welcome home."

AUTHOR'S NOTE

Please consider leaving a review for the book, feedback is imperative for an indie author. If you don't want to review it then think about leaving a comment or even just a quick message. Remember, positive feedback is always welcome.

If you want to keep up on the latest updates, or the one stop shop for all the links, my website is the best place for that. Remember to subscribe to the mailing list to know when I publish a new book, and you get an exclusive short when you sign up.
http://schinhofenbooks.com/

Other places you can keep up to date on me and my works:
https://www.patreon.com/DJSchinhofen
https://twitter.com/DJSchinhofen
Fan group on Facebook for Daniel Schinhofen
https://schinhofenbooks.blogspot.com/

A big thank you to my editors, Jennifer York and Samantha Bishop. Also props to Geno Ferrarini, and Sean Hickinbotham for being my Alpha Readers. I'd be remiss if I didn't include my beta readers, in no particular order: Zee, Ian McAdams, Arthur Cuelho, Scott Brown, Dame, A.J. Bishop, Kevin Kollman, Jay Taylor, Justin Johanson, Kenneth Darlin, Christina Norton, Sawyer Aubrey, Aoife Grimm, Peter La Femina, hane Bird, Steve Robles, Tanner Lovelace, Tim?, Carl Gherardi, Brian O.

The cover for Aether's Blessing is brought to you by Anthony Bishop, a very talented artist. You can find him at https://grimmhelm. artstation.com/

A big thanks to my Patreon supporters who have gone above and beyond in their support:

Dragonkain, Mike Durie, Christopher B., Pamela Lunsford, Joshua Morris, Matthew, Joshua Graybill, Kenneth Darlin, Tristitan, Brett Hudson, Terry Wood-Davies, Andrew Dyes, J. Patrick Walker, Nathan Goforth, Kevin McKinney, Spencer Jefferson, Xiao, Robert Shofner, Grimmhelm, Sonicblackfox, John Curtis, Ryan Luttinger, Kyle Gravelle, Travis Btmb, Dedalus Inventor, Jack Ling, Roman Smith, Michael Erwin, Timithy Klesick, Nathaniel J Higgins, Crtl To, Chanh Pham, Winston Smith, IntheRaccon, Eli Page, Chace Corso, Dwayne Bullock, Susanne Lofböm, Alexander Rodriguez, Stephan Juba, Tara C. Mulkey, Jason Broderick, James Domec, Authur Cuelho, Eric Hontz, Charles Demarest, Ronald C Abitz, Michael Moneymaker, T3lain, Otis Coley, Jacob Tackett, Theodore Ursa, Caleb Bear, Jeffrey Buchanan, Masta Matna, Cody Carter, David Florish, William Merrick, Jeff Ford, Kevin Harris, Brian O., MrNyxt, Kevin Kollman, Tanner Lovelace, Jose Caudillo, Logan Cochrane, Korbin Wilson, Travis Hilliard, SpartanGER, Azrael 11197, Jack McCoy, Brandon Haag, J.G. Patton, Kori Prins, SubVersion, Damien Osborne, Adam Billingham, Paul Mallon, Michael Jackson, Chioke Nelson, Kenneth Steinagel, Pheonixblue.

The last big thanks goes out to Nick Kuhns, who helped get this book formatted for physical copies. You would literally not be holding this book if not for him.

Other Books written by Daniel Schinhofen:

Last Horizon: (Completed.)
Last Horizon Omnibus

Binding Words:
Morrigan's Bidding
Life Bonds
Hearthglen
Forged Bonds

Alpha World: (Completed.)
Gamer for Life
Forming the Company
Alpha Company
Playing for Keeps
Fractured Spirit
The Path to Peace
Darkhand
Gamer For Love

Apocalypse Gates Author's Cut:
Rapture
Valley of Death
Gearing Up
Elven Accord
Downtime and Death

NPC's Lives:
Tales from the Dead Man Inn

Resurrection Quest:
Greenways Goblins